THE
DOWNING
STREET WIFE

THE
DOWNING
STREET WIFE

**POWER. CORRUPTION. SCANDAL.
GLAMOUR. VIOLENCE. SEX.**

NOEL BOTHAM

JOHN BLAKE

Published by John Blake Publishing Ltd,
3, Bramber Court, 2 Bramber Road,
London W14 9PB, England

www.blake.co.uk

First published in paperback in 2006

ISBN 1 84454 083 9

British Library Cataloguing-in-Publication Data:

A catalogue record for this book is available from the British Library.

Design by www.envydesign.co.uk

Printed in Great Britain by Creative, Print & Design

1 3 5 7 9 10 8 6 4 2

Papers used by John Blake Publishing are natural, recyclable products made
from wood grown in sustainable forests. The manufacturing processes
conform to the environmental regulations of the country of origin.

Every attempt has been made to contact the relevant copyright-holders,
but some were unobtainable. We would be grateful if the appropriate
people could contact us.

With special thanks to my wonderful daughter, Tania, who devoted many hours to reading early draughts of this story, mixed tough criticism with approval and kept me abreast of current chat culture.
And, as always, to my wife, Lesley Lewis.

ONE

It was a union doomed from the outset. Two people from opposite ends of the social ladder brought together by lust in the one and greed in the other. It was as predictable as it was inevitable that one of them would pay dearly for the experience. It was equally certain it would not be the man.

Only mutual need decreed they should be there in the plush, secure penthouse apartment, high above La Zona Rosa, the squalid, nightlife district of Bogotá.

Physically, they were not an attractive pair. Angelinas Gonsález was tall and emaciated with faded red hair and tired brown eyes, although her heavy, dark-nippled breasts were still her greatest asset. There had been a time when men craved her body and her looks, but that was long ago when she still possessed the beauty and innocence of youth.

Now, at the age of 26, the once pretty face was ravaged by her constant companions and worst enemies – drugs, drink and despair – and the natural wear and tear of her demanding and uncompromising profession. She was no longer as sought after as she had been a decade before, and the unrelenting need to feed her habits and her seven-year-old daughter back in the hovel they called home kept her on the streets nearly all her waking hours.

Before, she told herself, *I would never have been with this pig. But, mother of God, I need his money… and I don't give a shit how bloodstained and dirty it is!*

Angelinas would never live up to her name again, for angelic she was not, but she was a far cry from the man who strained and sweated above her, whom she knew to be truly evil. She had heard too many chilling stories about him, recounted fearfully in whispers in the dark, to doubt their truth. Many had talked of this man, head of his country's dreaded secret police and the richest drugs baron in Colombia, and many had good reason to fear the hated 'Butcher of Granada', a title earned when a whole community of peasant folk had been slaughtered to cover up the rape and murder of an Indian child.

She had been afraid when his arrogant, sneering aide had announced the identity of her latest client. But by then she had been allowed a glimpse of the banknotes stuffed in a fat manila envelope produced from inside the man's half-open shirt, and her need overrode her fear.

Twenty minutes later, she had been transported from the reeking Bogotá slums to the luxurious penthouse, 30 storeys above the streets where she plied her trade. She had been ordered to take a bath before being hustled into a thick towelling robe, several sizes too large and, all too quickly for Angelinas, who had never before experienced the wonders of a marble bathroom, she was led into a vast bedroom.

There had been no conversation or foreplay, no offer of a drink before the act. Neither had she expected any of this. She had simply been ordered to strip – the action of a few seconds, as she was still naked beneath the robe – and then to kneel in front of where the General was sitting, large Havana cigar in one hand, a favourite French brandy in the other, in a deeply cushioned armchair.

The henchman left the bedroom without saying a word, but Angelinas knew what was required of her, and it was no more than she had expected. In fact, if she were honest with herself, with her faded looks, it was what most men wanted of her, rather than straight sex. She unzipped his trousers and, using both hands, eased his flaccid penis into her mouth. Angelinas' lips closed over the end of it, her tongue began flicking at its tip as her fingers slid down into the General's groin and started to gently squeeze and massage his balls.

For ten minutes she tried every trick in her considerable repertoire, but there was not the slightest sign that he was beginning to grow hard. Angelinas was becoming desperate, knowing from experience that men like this one would always see it as the whore's fault. And often the whore paid for her client's soft prick with a hard beating.

Suddenly the General roughly grabbed her shoulders and pushed her away.

Here it comes, she thought, and braced herself for the slap or punch that would certainly follow, but he surprised her by pointing to the kingsize bed, which had been placed against the wall furthest from the windows.

'Lie on the bed,' he growled through a cloud of cigar smoke. 'On your back.'

Angelinas lay back on the royal-blue, silk bed cover, closed her eyes and hastily recited a couple of silent Hail Marys. At least the pig wasn't going to beat her. Not yet, anyway, she reminded herself, as she shuddered and allowed her eyelids to open.

General Guillermo Aristos was just shedding the last of his clothes. He bent, wheezing, to pull off his socks. Naked, he was even more revolting than dressed, she thought. His short, fat body, with deep rolls of blubber around his waist, was almost alabaster white, and already wet with perspiration just from the exertion of undressing.

Only his heavily jowled face was red, due as much to his weakness for copious amounts of white rum and fine imported cigars as it was to the relentless equatorial sun. His mouth – a lipless, cruel slash beneath a hawk-like nose and deep-set, coal-black eyes – was like a lizard's. It was made all the more reptilian when he stood over her and licked his lips with a tiny, pointed tongue in anticipation of the act to come.

Angelinas could not believe this man was capable of passion, pleasure or love, and felt another involuntary shudder ripple down her spine.

Clumsily, he mounted the bed and, with grunts of exertion, positioned himself between her open legs, staring down at the thin tangle of pubic hair that she had taken to trimming herself, using a cheap, home-made version of a Brazilian wax, after having been told by a French sailor that this was considered 'très chic' in his home port of Marseilles. She neither knew where Marseilles was, nor what 'chic' meant, but the Frenchman had treated her well and had been generous... sufficiently so to make her feel less contempt for him than she did for the rest of her clientèle.

'Make yourself wet,' the General ordered gruffly, and took a last, long pull of his cigar before stubbing it out in an ashtray by the bedside.

His unblinking, cruel eyes never left her crotch as she slowly inserted her fingers into the soft, damp cleft between her legs, and began to stroke herself. Feeling herself back on home, and comparatively safe ground and, despite her revulsion for her latest client, Angelinas found the General's intense concentration on her intimate self-arousal beginning to turn her on.

Despite her earlier fear, she felt a tingle of excitement. She knew herself to be utterly vulnerable and exposed, but this was not an entirely unpleasant feeling. She allowed herself to believe she might get through this unscathed and, holding the lips of her vulva wide with the fingers of her left hand, she wet the tip of the middle finger of her other hand with her tongue and began stroking her clitoris in a slow, circular motion while thrusting her pelvis off the bed towards the General's face.

General Aristo continued to stare down at her, the sweat beading on his nose and chin, and dripping down onto her thighs, mingling with her own sweat and the juices from her vagina.

Soon it will be the moment, you little slut. Oh yes, soon it will be the moment!

Sensing some change in her client, Angelinas redoubled her efforts and felt her generous, rosebud nipples begin to harden. She raised her head from the bed, and now had the intense satisfaction of seeing the General's slug-white penis begin to grow hard.

With timing born of her years of experience, Angelinas abandoned her almost frantic self-arousal and reached forward with her cupped palms to embrace the throbbing firmness, gradually guiding his penis into her own wetness. As soon as he was deep between her thighs, he began plunging into her and his hairless chest flopped onto her, flattening her breasts and squeezing the air from her lungs.

She faked a soft scream of joy and began grinding her hips into his, meeting each of his thrusts with an equal one of her own. As she sensed the pig on top of her mounting to a climax, Angelinas tried to rearrange her features into a smile of encouragement.

'Come on, General, finish it,' she rasped between laboured breaths. Mother of God, if he didn't finish soon, this old bastard was going to squash the life out of her. He must have weighed 150 kilos at least.

'Finish it, *querida*... I know you're nearly there... finish it now,' she urged and, with a massive effort, wrapped her legs around his buttocks, and joined in his frantic rhythm. She then reached down to squeeze his balls in one hand while inserting a finger from the other into his anus, made slippery by dipping it into her own juices.

General Aristo looked down with utter disgust at the grotesque and wasted face beneath him. Drops of his sweat had caused her mascara to run in spidery, black rivulets, down the over-rouged cheeks onto her scrawny neck. He couldn't believe he had lowered himself so far to be with such lowlife scum. *I am Aristo, I can have anyone I want*, he reminded himself. But the urgent spasms in his groin where she still worked on him with her fingers, triggered the real reason for this whore being here. She was an anonymous piece of filth from the great, open sewer which formed the slums of Bogotá. She was unimportant, unwanted and, above all, would not be missed. Not by anyone who mattered, at least.

When she disappeared, no one would come looking, just as no one had come looking for the pretty peasant child, whose wretched death he had covered up by slaughtering the inhabitants of a whole village, or the hooker who had been picked up casually off the streets for him, just like this one, during a recent trip to Miami.

All women were worthless, that's why he had to make them pay. None of the bitches could make him climax the way he used to. And it was entirely their fault, a female plot to prevent him from feeling any joy or release. But now he knew the way to beat them.

He had discovered it by accident when the teenage girl began to scream. As his hands closed around her smooth, slim neck to cut off her terrified cries. Her petrified eyes staring up at his, he had experienced the greatest climax of his life. As the last spasms shook her young body, he had emptied himself inside her in a shattering orgasm that had seemed to last an eternity.

Now it was time all over again to enjoy his power over women

'Finish it, General, finish it,' Angelinas gasped again, almost pleadingly, it seemed, to the bucking animal above her. He remembered the teenage girl's terrified pleas, so much more erotic to him than the fake passion from this bitch.

'That's just what I'm about to do, you stinking whore,' he snarled and, heaving his upper torso off her, he put his hands around her skinny neck and began to squeeze.

Angelinas knew instantly this was no perverted sex game, and that her worst nightmare had suddenly become terrifying reality. As quickly as his hands closed on her neck, hers had abandoned their urgent ministrations around his genitals and reached for his wrists. But they were thick and hard – the only fat-free area of his body – and she could not release them. The whole of the General's weight had now been transferred to his lower torso and she was pinned to the bed, unable to move.

Incredibly, though her head was beginning to feel light and dizzy, Angelinas could still feel him moving inside her, filling her utterly with his hardness.

So intensely involved were the two in their life-or-death struggle that neither of them had noticed the door to the bedroom open or the two, darkly-clad figures move swiftly across the thickly carpeted room to the bedside.

The first voice was low-pitched but, even so, easily audible above Aristo's harsh breathing and the rasping gurgles from Angelinas' failing efforts to hold onto life. She attempted to reach around his broad shoulders to gouge his eyes, but was several inches too short. Now her arms were beginning to flail limply, as she lapsed into unconsciousness.

'I think that's a good place to stop, right there, General, if you please.'

As Angelinas slipped further away from consciousness, the voice seemed like a hallucination, and she succumbed slowly to the intense pressure around her throat. But for General Aristo, there was another reason to be convinced that the voice was not an imaginary one. It was the unmistakable cold steel of a handgun pressing against his right temple.

'I said "Stop", and that was an order, General!' The voice had developed a harder edge to it which was confirmed – if confirmation was needed – by added pressure to the gun muzzle against his head.

Glancing to his right, the General had no trouble identifying the silenced Smith and Wesson .35 revolver that could, at any moment, blow his brains out. But the man holding the weapon was a complete stranger. Dressed all in black and over 6 feet tall, he had a thick mop of blond hair and penetrating, pale blue eyes, a Roman nose and a wide, generous mouth most women would find irresistible. It was a strong, expressive face and not one in which adversaries might expect to find much sympathy.

He looked down at Guillermo Aristo with a mixture of revulsion and unquestionable superiority. He tapped the General on the forehead with the silencer and gestured towards Angelinas, whose neck was still held in a vice-like grip, and whose movements had all but ceased.

'Time to let go of the lady's throat,' he said, as before, in fluent Castilian. But Aristo was certain he was neither Colombian nor even South American.

'Who are you? What do you want?' the General spat out. 'Whatever you're being paid, I'll double it.' Even with a gun to his head, he still showed no fear. His incredible arrogance seemed impervious to other emotions... except perhaps, anger. 'Don't tell me you give a fuck what happens to this whore. She's just a piece of shit!'

The intruder shook his head and eased the gun away from Aristo's head. 'Wrong reaction, fuckhead... ' With incredible speed and devastating force, he raked the sharp edge of the gun barrel down the side of the General's right cheek, stripping it open to the bone and creating an inch-long jagged tear below the corner of his mouth.

The force of the blow wrenched Aristo's gleaming new set of upper teeth from his mouth and sent the denture spinning to the carpet. He screamed, animal-like with pain, and released his hands from Angelinas' throat, covering his bleeding face as he cowered away from the man in black. 'José... Matias... ' he yelled from behind his hands. 'Get the fuck in here!'

A new voice answered him. 'They've both gone away... permanently... along with a few of your other chums outside.'

Aristo's head snapped round and he stared in disbelief. This was also uttered in fluent Spanish, but this time it was clearly the voice of a woman. Even in his slightly bemused state, and with his head starting to throb with the pain in his face and mouth, when he saw her he couldn't help but appreciate the beauty of this second stranger. She was extraordinarily attractive, with tumbling red hair, a full, sensuous mouth and stunningly vivid, violet eyes. She was also dressed in black, but her sweatshirt top and jeans still revealed a truly voluptuous figure.

The General had always thought of his Bogotá penthouse as an impregnable fortress. On the thirtieth floor of a block he owned himself and let out to his own people, whose lives he owned as surely as the homes they lived in, it was the ultimate safe house.

His enemies regarded life as cheaply as he did himself, and he had too many ever to take risks. He never travelled without a dozen bodyguards and in an armoured limousine, and his personal protection squad occupied the whole of the twenty-ninth floor where the main lifts terminated. Only one guarded lift had access to the General's living quarters; no other buildings overlooked it, or offered a nearby vantage point.

General Guillermo Aristo experienced his first stirrings of fear in more than half a century. Who in God's name were these fucking people? 'How did you get in?' he growled.

'Easily,' said the man with a slight grin. 'But we'll leave it to your friends we met outside to explain the details.'

Fear now lurked in the General's piggish, black eyes as the meaning behind the stranger's mocking words sank in. He began to gabble, 'Who sent you? The President? I'm richer than him… I can give you anything you want… just name your price.'

'Not your president, but someone who dislikes you just as much,' the intruder said calmly. 'But then again, you're not very likeable, are you?' Raising the pistol slightly, he fired two shots into the General's brain just inches from his temple.

9

Aristo did not cry out or even have time to look startled. In a split-second, the butcher had become the butchered. The bullets slamming into his skull threw the top half of his body onto its side, though his lower torso remained lodged between Angelinas' thighs, where her legs stayed locked in a near-death grip around his waist. Blood, brain matter and fragments of bone were splattered in an obscene pattern on the wall behind.

'OK, let's get out of here,' said the man calmly, turning from the carnage in front of him, and unhooked a miniature two-way radio from his belt. He pressed transmit. 'Two to go,' he said cheerfully. 'Call in the chopper.' He had switched from Castilian to flawless public school English. He was already halfway across the room, but the woman hadn't moved.

'Oh shit!' she said, also in English. 'What bloody rotten timing. Why couldn't she have stayed under just a few more seconds?'

In a few strides her companion had retraced his steps and joined her, looking down at the bed, where Angelinas, still partly trapped under Aristo's corpse, was staring up at them, her brown eyes wide in terror. She was frantically sucking in air but seemed too traumatised to speak.

'She saw everything,' said the woman, sadly. 'Poor cow.'

Angelinas didn't understand a word they said, but before she even had time to guess what was about to happen, the woman raised the silenced pistol, which had been hanging loosely at her side, and fired three shots quickly, one after the other, so there barely seemed an interval between them, bullets puncturing the prostitute's breast in a tight group just below her left nipple.

Angelinas' body scarcely moved; she just went limp as death overcame her.

The man tapped his companion on the shoulder. 'Come on, we don't have time to mourn. She was going to get it anyway if we hadn't arrived when we did – at least this way was faster.'

The woman's eyes flashed a warning and she wrenched her shoulder from beneath his hand. 'Do you have to be quite such a bastard all the time?' she hissed. 'I know she had to go. She saw us, didn't she? That's why I did it, but I don't have to enjoy it.'

'Let's talk about that later,' said the man. 'But right now I think we'd better get our arses out of here. Any minute now we're going to have more company.'

Shouts could be heard elsewhere in the building, and the sound of heavy hammering on the lift doors they had jammed earlier on the floor below.

At the door the man paused briefly to slip a small visiting card from his breast pocket and flicked it onto the bed where it lay, face up, its only marking being the one-dimensional, black image of a salamander.

Seconds later, they were racing up the emergency staircase to the roof, where another man, also dressed in black, held open the trap door.

The sounds below were now drowned out by the steady throb of a small, unmarked Bell helicopter, which had descended to a few feet above the flat roof. As they ran the 20 metres separating them from the chopper, its underbelly searchlight – which the pilot had used for the last few seconds to guide him in – was turned off.

Quickly, the three of them scrambled aboard and within moments, the engine sound increased and the small craft, now all but invisible against the night sky, was slipping away towards the nearby mountains and safety.

TWO

Robert 'Bobby' Temple, Britain's first Labour prime minister after nearly 20 years of Tory rule, studied the small group of men he had summoned to the Cabinet room with unconcealed satisfaction. The five key members of his inner Cabinet had seated themselves randomly at the long, oval table, large enough to take a couple of dozen ministers, and all of them wore the same satisfied look as their leader.

The unprecedented scale of their election victory had taken even the most optimistic member of the new Modern Labour Party totally by surprise. Now, 30 days after Bobby Temple had been summoned to Buckingham Palace for the formal kissing of hands, when he had been asked to form a new Government, many could still not believe the miracle that had seen the Tory members' ranks decimated at Westminster.

Bobby smiled as he remembered the conversation with his Minister for the Arts, just half an hour before calling this emergency meeting.

'My God, Bobby, I still keep having to pinch meself to make sure I'm awake and not dreaming,' Sam Copthwaite had chortled in his broad Yorkshire accent. 'There was a bloody Lady Bullshit in me office this morning, who I'd still have been doffing me bloody cap to a month ago. You know the type… face like a bulldog lickin' piss off nettles. But she was all over me…"Yes, Minister, this" and "Yes, Minister, that". I think if I'd put me boots on't top of me desk she'd have bent over an' licked them to a shine!'

There had been dozens of similar conversations in the past four weeks, the Prime Minister content to let his followers enjoy their historic moment of triumph. At a meeting of the faithful one week after the General Election he had promised them there would not be another Tory Government in power again for at least 15 years. Had he revealed to them his secret agenda for Modern Labour, though, he might just as easily have promised them no change of Government in his lifetime.

Now the time for celebration must come to an end. It was the moment to let these key members of his Cabinet know just how he intended to bring Modern Labour, and the country, into line with his own vision of the future, and explain how the momentous events in Russia in the past month, which had completely overshadowed Modern Labour's victory on the world stage, would be capitalised on, to help bring about this glittering new dawn for Britain, the party… and, of course, Bobby Temple.

The rapidity with which the changes in Russia had been brought about had left most Western powers reeling, their leaders scrambling like headless chickens to assemble new strategies and policies to cope with a situation none had dreamed could ever recur in their lifetimes.

In his now historic television broadcast to his people, the ailing Russian president had tearfully and emotionally announced his irrevocable decision to step down and that his final decree, already signed, called for immediate presidential and general elections.

Even after less than a decade of democratic rule, the Western powers should have been able to predict the outcome without the need for high-powered political analysts or crystal balls. But they had become so conditioned to believing their so-called Soviet experts, who all confidently predicted the Russians would never reverse their breakneck plunge into capitalism, that none of them had seen it coming.

Capitalism in Russia had indeed worked for a comparative handful of unscrupulous entrepreneurs, corrupt government officials and the Soviet criminal fraternity, whose callous viciousness, horrific violence and sneering indifference to their countrymen's plight had created the most rampant underworld regime in history.

Most of Russia's capitalised industry was bankrupt, its workers unpaid for months and its armed forces and the Police existing on IOUs, indebted to those few shopkeepers and landlords who were still able to advance credit. The mass of the people were starving, while seeing foreign investors and home-grown gangsters siphoning out of the country whatever money was being made. Most were terrified to open their doors, even during daylight hours, for fear of being mugged or murdered in their own homes.

When Ivan Brekov, a junior minister in the previous government and a steadfast Communist supporter throughout the ensuing years of change, threw his hat into the presidential ring, and called on his fellow Communist supporters across the country to campaign for a return to the old standards, the Russian people rallied to his banner in their tens of millions. Brekov promised an end to corruption and lawlessness, huge investment in state industry and farming projects, regular pay for the Police and armed forces, and a more promising future for the young in the shape of better, free state education for all, right up to university level. He also promised a proper welfare system and to revitalise the country's hospitals and clinics and ensure free healthcare for the masses.

The opposition parties had attacked his promises as lies and unrealistic daydreams, demanding to know where the money would come from to finance this Utopian society. Brekov's answers stunned his opponents – and several Western Governments and multi-nationals – and brought further millions of supporters flocking to add their voices to his campaign. He would confiscate the funds of any individual or company shown to have exploited the people. All proceeds derived from criminal activities would be seized by the State and vigorous legal proceedings would begin to recover all such funds already transferred to overseas banks. Lastly, he pledged continuing encouragement of foreign investment in Russia. But the profits these investors made, he warned, would be kept at a reasonable level by special taxes. No longer would foreign cowboys be allowed to rape the mother country's mineral wealth and other natural resources without paying handsomely for the privilege, he vowed.

Three days after Bobby Temple's landslide election triumph in Britain, Ivan Brekov was sworn in as Russia s new and freely elected President, with a Communist Government majority that all but eradicated the opposition.

Once more the hammer and sickle flew boldly over the Kremlin... and the Western world waited with collective bated breath for Brekov's next move.

Temple had been the first world leader to personally congratulate Brekov on his overwhelming victory. As soon as he had received the news from the British Embassy in Moscow, he picked up the telephone on his desk and placed a call to the Kremlin. It was received with genuine pleasure by the new master of all the Russias, who himself had telephoned Downing Street just three days earlier within an hour of Temple's return from the Palace. This was hardly surprising, the Prime Minister now reflected, as he and Ivan had shared rooms together at Oxford for one year when Brekov had been sent on an exchange scholarship in Politics more than two decades earlier.

'Big day for you, Ivan.'

'Big days for us both, Bobby. Do you keep thinking you're still dreaming? I know I do.'

'Too true,' Bobby replied, laughing openly down the phone. 'But we finally made it, my friend. Just as we always said we would. Do you still remember all the wonderful schemes we used to come up with when we were half sloshed on cheap booze?'

'Too fucking true, Bobby! And those toffee-nosed girls with pursed lips and wide open legs. I remember those, too.'

'That doesn't sound very statesmanlike, Mr President,' he laughed out loud again. 'I think you and I need to talk, don't you?'

Brekov's voice was serious. 'I think so, too, Bobby. And I also think I'm going to need your help. It's time we stopped being bossed around by the fucking Americans and some of your so-called European partners. Those bastards can't wait to shit on you at every opportunity they get. We made the big mistake of not giving in to the Nazis 50 years ago, eventually whacking their arses. Neither they nor the other whingeing arseholes in Europe have ever forgiven us.'

Bobby couldn't help grinning at Brekov's colourful language. At Oxford he had developed a love of expletives and devoted almost as much effort studying them as to his lessons in Politics, Economics and Philosophy.

'You don't have to remind me, Ivan,' he replied. 'Some of them have been on to me already, all with tricky new schemes designed to dip their hands deeper into British pockets. Well, they are in for a few surprises. If we set our minds to it, Ivan, we can bugger the bastards. So let's keep in regular contact and see what we can come up with to get their sphincter muscles twitching.'

It was Bobby who had taken the Russian under his wing when he arrived in Oxford. He had provided application forms for the Labour Club and the Oxford Union and proposed his new roommate to both. Brekov, who spoke perfect English, had quickly agreed with Bobby that the brand of Socialism being advocated and debated in the university Labour Club was far too weak for his own taste, and conversely, the two young men had found their own firebrand political views far too strong for the stomachs of the Wilsonian-style Socialists of the Oxford Labour Club.

Eventually, they stopped going to the meetings and instead would sit in their rooms, long into the night, discussing how they would change the world once they were in positions of power. They found they agreed on most issues, and on one they were absolutely certain. Both were going to make it to the top.

In that year, the two men had grown very close, had double-dated some of the most attractive and eligible female undergraduates and had found themselves in some very questionable situations while trying to puncture the pomposity and snobbishness which they both believed existed all around them at Oxford.

Though of very different physique, the pair of them had two other things in common. Charismatic charm and devastating good looks. People swore shaking hands with either of them was like receiving an electric shock. Whatever 'it' was, they both possessed it in abundance... and then some.

Bobby Temple was a fraction under 6 feet tall, slenderly built, with a body that visibly benefited from the 20-minute workout he enjoyed every morning. He had a boyish handsomeness that would stay with him into middle age, a wide engaging smile and inviting, ice-blue eyes. Women were excited and seduced by his charming, effortless sexuality; men enjoyed his very masculine camaraderie, his directness and honesty... and trusted him. Neither judgement could have been wider of the mark. Temple was a devious, self-centred, self-serving opportunist with a hidden bullying streak, which had already begun to manifest itself as he grew older. His unfailing good humour and effortless charm were no more than skin deep, painstakingly cultivated to cover up the ruthless ambition smouldering beneath.

Women would always play second fiddle in Temple's world, that of politics and international intrigue, which he believed always was, and should remain a bastion of male domination. An unadventurous lover, if he had to admit it, he wasn't stimulated by overt female flirtation. Temple liked to date girls, but only as image-boosting accessories, not because he wanted to get laid. He certainly wasn't gay, but he was much too interested in his own priorities to devote any time or energy to someone else's needs, emotional or sexual. Temple had coined a word to describe men like himself, men who indulged in the sexual act with women, but far preferred the company of men in all other circumstances. He was, he said, 'homosensible'.

Ivan Brekov was the complete antithesis of this. He just couldn't get enough of women, and women felt the same about him. Brekov possessed a special kind of wildness, a charged, animal-like quality the opposite sex found irresisitible. He was stocky, with deep-set, smouldering black eyes, an uncontrollable mop of jet-black hair and a slightly lop-sided smile, which could light up the world. To Ivan, sex was a religion, its altar the naked female body. He was its high priest and chief recruitment officer and, within a few months of arriving in Oxford, his sexual prowess had already become legendary. His politics, while as deeply radical as Temple's appeared to be, were more forthright and openly expressed. He didn't like the way the world was going, and believed his own true Socialist policy to be the only curative. Just as a Christian would have looked directly to the teachings of Christ for guidance, so Brekov considered Lenin's original doctrine a yardstick for government.

Temple had gone on to marry a brilliant and politically active television journalist, tipped to become one of the youngest anchorpersons on record. With her naturally blonde hair, long legs, blue eyes and full lips, she looked more like a film or pop star than an incisive, broadcasting phenomenon with a burning sense of justice. In her habitual black designer outfits, colleagues, opponents and government officials alike unanimously declared June Temple more sexually alluring than any naked Page 3 girl. Before her engagement to Bobby was announced, two senior governors of the BBC, old enough to be her grandfather had seriously propositioned her for a date. One had even gone so far as to admit to his penchant for severe black uniforms and thigh-length, black riding boots. When she had shared this with Bobby, he smiled and then made a note of the names for possible future use.

June's father was a self-made millionaire industrialist and a socialist of the old school. She had inherited not only his brains, but his political views as well, and that's how she had met Bobby. He was 26 and had finally been given his reward for three years of envelope licking, door-to-door canvassing and acting the willing gofer for all and sundry among the older colleagues in his local Labour Party constituency committee. He had then been selected as Labour candidate for the Earl's Court constituency. Not much of a reward, some claimed, because his chances of ousting the incumbent Tory candidate were little better than nil. Jim Callaghan's government had fallen after a vote of 'no confidence', and Margaret Thatcher was leading the Tories into this 1979 general election as though her policies were God's words written in stone. Her confidence had gone stratospheric, and no one with any sense at all doubted she would win, and with a handsome majority.

Bobby's opponent – a fat, balding, 50-year-old ex-army major, with a handlebar moustache and a voice like a strangled toad – was seeking a third term in Parliament and was equally as confident as his leader. With more than a 4,000 majority at the last election, and with the opinion polls heavily favouring his party, he felt more than usually complacent about keeping his seat. This also meant retaining the half-dozen, well paid directorships his MP status had brought him.

In the last two elections Bobby's predecessor had been of a similar age to the Major, and his energetically fought, but unimaginative campaigns had been rewarded with a safe seat to fight in the East End, where the incumbent Labour MP decided not to stand for re-election. Major Percival Fitzwilliam's first comment, on learning Bobby had been selected to oppose him, was, 'Why have they put up a boy to do a man's job?'

Fitzwilliam had failed to understand, or to take into account Bobby's single-minded determination, which was a tactical mistake, and his utter ruthlessness, which would prove his downfall. He could hardly be blamed for the second omission, though, given how carefully concealed it was from everyone.

Neither had Fitzwilliam, nor his workers, taken sufficient notice of an unprecedented influx of non-voting immigrants into the Earl's Court area in the past four years, mainly from the Antipodes. This new population displaced many of the original, middle-class, mainly Tory-voting residents, who had found their new, raucous, nightlife-loving neighbours – and the significantly expanding gay and lesbian community, as well as a proliferation of ethnic-oriented high street shops – both alien and repugnant to their essentially middle-class British tastes.

Bobby was an excellent speaker, with boundless energy and utter commitment. He mapped out a gruelling schedule taking him to more than thirty organised meetings a week, as well as many hours of door-to-door canvassing, which took him to every key street, as identified by his PR team, in the London constituency.

His apparently natural good humour and boyish charm won over many of the undecided voters, pre-eminently among the female electorate, but he was deeply cognisant that his efforts alone, even with the assistance of a score of helpers – including an enthusiastic, attractive and vivacious young television presenter named June Prestwick – were in themselves insufficient to swing the vote successfully in his favour. Throughout his campaign, focusing exclusively on beating the incumbent Tory candidate, he took care to be scrupulously fair to his pompous, patronising opponent. Bobby had already discounted the Liberal and other fringe party candidates as little more than minor distractions.

He stuck to the issues, attacking what he honestly believed to be the miserable record of the Tory party, extolling his own party's policies. Even when attacked on a personal level by Major Percival Fitzwilliam, who scathingly denounced his youth, his inexperience and his lack of military leadership training, Bobby, though urged to retaliate by many of his supporters, refused to be drawn into personal mud-slinging.

Bobby could afford to play the perfect gentleman in public; that was a part of his overall strategy. Unbeknown to supporters and opponents alike, he had another, secret schedule, shared only by himself and Jack Benson, a fanatical socialist of his own age, cautiously cultivated, then gradually installed as his *éminence grise*, a loyal and trusted adviser. Bobby identified Benson as a prime recruit during his early political career, and spent many painstaking hours probing the extent and depth of Benson's political commitment, while skilfully wooing him over to his personal cause.

Benson, a trained accountant with an exceptional, analytical brain, was a cold, intense young man who had always found it difficult to forge even the most casual relationships. Until meeting Bobby, he had very few acquaintances and no friends. That someone as charismatic as Bobby, who could take his pick of those with whom he wanted to spend time, should derive so much apparent pleasure from his company, had a profound effect on the young accountant. Bobby gave Benson his unreserved comradeship and made him a trusted confidant. In return, Benson offered his devotion and unstinting loyalty, and had pledged his unconditional and everlasting support. Bobby quickly understood that his faithful lieutenant was as amoral as himself. There were no lengths to which he would not go to promote the party's – and Bobby's – best interests.

One day Jack Benson would be recognised in his own right. In politics as an MP and in the media. He would become known and both feared and respected as the chief architect of the general election campaign which would sweep Bobby and his party to victory and land him in Number 10 Downing Street.

Through discreet questioning and several evenings spent following the impeccable Major Fitzwilliam after dark, Benson was able to report back to his delighted lord and master that the MP for Earl's Court had a potential chink in his otherwise impenetrable moral armour. The long-time husband and father of three occasionally enjoyed a sortie to a highly dubious basement club – the Pink Flamingo, off Soho's Brewer Street. There, he liked to sit and drink with one or other of the club's young, topless hostesses. He was essentially a voyeur, reported Benson; the Major didn't indulge in groping the near-naked girls, but was simply content to look. 'Stupid bastard,' Bobby said, rubbing his hands together gleefully. 'He's kindly provided us with the rope, now let's hang him.'

Completely ignorant of her client's identity, in return for a £20 note, willingly and with much giggling, the topless hostess Fitzwilliam particularly favoured confided to Benson when the Major planned his next clandestine visit. To Peter Basham, the *News of the World*'s crop-haired, elderly news editor, the tip-off from a freelance journalist, one of Benson's few casual acquaintances, was manna from heaven during an otherwise sleaze-free, lacklustre general election campaign. £100 slipped to the club's manager, and the assurance of valuable free publicity, was enough to get a *News of the World* photographer and a female reporter secreted in a dimly-lit booth, ready to pounce. A further £50 to the hostess was sufficient to make sure that, at a suitable moment, she would thrust her ample breasts under the astonished Major's double chin and plant a smacking kiss on his bald pate.

Almost blinded by the rapid-fire flashes from the snapper's motor-driven camera, the panicking Major suddenly found his companion's place taken by the girl reporter, whose first question, asked with an innocent smile, was, 'Does Mrs Fitzwilliam approve of your little trips down here, Major?'

The headline on the front page of the *News of the World* that Sunday, just three days before the election, screamed:

MP MAJOR'S SECRET EXERCISES WITH TOPLESS CLUB HOSTESS

Merry romps with naked girls
Tory MP Major Percival Fitzwilliam, dubbed 'the merry Major' by the topless birds of pleasure at Soho's Pink Flamingo Club, will find himself on a serious charge before commanding officer Maggie Thatcher this morning.

The 50-year-old member for Earl's Court, pictured here in a clinch with his secret girlfriend, 19-year-old club hostess Delila Sweetjoy, claimed their relationship was perfectly innocent.

'It's not at all what it appears,' said the Major, who is standing to retain his Earl's Court seat in the coming General Election. He refused to make any further comment and left the nightclub with his head covered by a red napkin.

Miss Sweetjoy, who is training to be an actress, later broke down in tears, but admitted between sobs, 'We have been meeting like this, in secret, for months. He told me he loved me and wanted me to be with him always.'

Bobby threw down the newspaper and grabbed Jack Benson in a bearhug.

'What a wizard you are, Jack, an absolutely, 100 per cent, bloody spell master! Let's just see the blustering old buzzard talk his way out of this one. Maggie will have his balls for earrings by noon for this.'

He released the beaming fledgling political assassin and began pacing around the living room of the Earl's Court flat he had rented for the duration of the election campaign. 'It's far too late to withdraw him now and bring in a replacement. They can only try and brazen it out and claim the girl is lying – which, of course, we know she is. But who else is going to believe him after seeing that picture? Guilty is hardly the word for how he looks. No, you've stuck it where it really hurts, Jack, and the Tories are stuck with dear old, merry Major Fitzwilliam and the charming Miss Sweetjoy!' He paused for a moment. 'And what about the girl? Talk about recognising your 15 minutes of fame and milking it for all you're worth. From what you told me, the poor old bugger never even kissed her. Now she's telling the world at large all about their affair. Women take some beating in the treachery department, God bless 'em.'

'Well… that, and perhaps the £10,000 the *News of the World* are paying her for her exclusive story,' said Jack, still smiling.

'Then God bless Rupert Murdoch, too,' said Bobby. 'Anyway, this calls for a celebration drink.' He reached for a bottle of Famous Grouse whisky and two tumblers and placed them on the low table between two faded armchairs that had seen much better days. 'Christ only knows how I'm going to keep a straight face when I have to tell the press how unfortunate all this is. And, of course, what a clean campaign I've fought, and how I believe the electorate will still make their decisions based on the issues as they've been presented, and not be influenced by sensational stories in the tabloid press. Like fuck they won't!' he roared, and flopped into an armchair, raising his brimming glass to his faithful henchman. 'Here's to us, Jack. This is only the beginning… you and I are going to go a long way together.'

Jack Benson preened like a pet which had been thrown a particularly juicy titbit by its master. 'I'm so glad you're pleased, Bobby,' he said. 'You deserve to win. The means are unimportant.'

'Too true,' smirked Bobby, 'and let it always remain so.'

Three days later, in the packed town hall, the Returning Officer, who could scarcely be heard above the din of celebrating Labour supporters to whom the result had already been leaked, announced voting figures for the various candidates. He ended with the words, 'I therefore declare that the above mentioned person, Robert James Temple, has been duly elected to serve as the Member of Parliament for Earl's Court.'

Bobby had won with a majority of nearly two thousand votes. His overjoyed parents were the first to congratulate him, followed by Jack Benson. But Bobby's third well-wisher was all long legs, blonde hair and sparkling blue eyes spilling tears of joy. To cheers from the floor of the hall, she gave him a lingering kiss, full on the lips. Courtesy of the television and press cameras, it was seen around the country the next day. Most of the national newspapers carried the picture, including the *Sun*, which used it on the front page with a small, cutaway shot of Major Fitzwilliam, under the headline: 'YOUNG ROMEO OUSTS DISGRACED TOPLESS MAJOR'.

Without making a single move, Bobby woke the next morning to discover that he and Miss June Prestwick – the blonde bombshell cheerleader at last night's victory celebration – had become an item. With growing interest, he read the hastily cobbled together potted biographies of his 'girlfriend' contained in the newspapers. Stunningly beautiful, witty and highly intelligent, she was the daughter of a millionaire socialist industrialist, who had already proved herself to be successful as a television journalist at the comparatively young age of 27. 'A fitting Juliet for Labour's latest, and youngest MP Romeo, Bobby Temple...' declared the *Sun*.

Bobby nodded his head approvingly. That's two lots of thanks to Rupert Murdoch this week, he grinned to himself. This girl, June Prestwick, had all the looks and the right qualifications. Bobby's passion was politics and he had studied it from every possible angle. He knew that at constituency level, and in most cases way beyond it, the old adage about a good woman being behind every good man could not have been truer, and that became ever more accurate as you rose to the higher echelons of the political establishment. From the start he knew just how high he was going, and that he would need an exceptional and beautiful partner to help him along the way.

'My God, I think I'm in love already,' he sneered to himself cynically and reached for the telephone, punching in the number of the local Labour Party headquarters, where some of his supporters were still celebrating. 'It's Bobby Temple here,' he said, and felt a surge of pleasure on hearing the quick gasp of awed surprise at the other end. 'We have a girl... no, a woman... working on the team named June Prestwick. Can you give me her home number please?'

Three months later, Bobby and June were married in the chapel of the Palace of Westminster, which contained the Houses of Commons and the Lords. Her father, Gordon Prestwick, gave the bride away, the Best Man being the recently deposed Prime Minister, now leader of the Opposition, Jim Callaghan. Jack Benson, who had hoped to be asked to fulfil this role, was disappointed but understood why Bobby had chosen his party's leader. And hadn't Bobby, who had become instantly popular among his colleagues at Westminster, promised him a decent seat to contest in the first suitable by-election that came along?

The reception was held in a huge marquee on the Commons Terrace overlooking the Thames and, in his most characteristic role as everyone's favourite uncle, Jim Callaghan soon had everyone roaring with laughter as he upheld the Best Man's traditional responsibility of ridiculing and praising the groom. He ended on a serious note. 'After this terrible winter of discontent, which has seen the Labour Party's fortunes much diminished, Bobby Temple has succeeded in reversing a national trend and has soundly beaten a

Tory incumbent, and with a whopping majority. His is the modern face of Labour and he, and those like him, will ensure the Labour Party does not remain long out of government. From one ex-Prime Minister and a new friend, I would like to propose the toast to the groom… and next Labour Prime Minister, Bobby Temple.'

Everyone cheered, Bobby managed to look suitably modest, and no one believed Callaghan's prediction to be anything more than political flattery tailored to the occasion. Except, that is, the groom himself, Jack Benson, and the bride.

The new Mrs Temple was in a state of total bliss. She was no impressionable young teenager coping with her first crush and had experienced her fair share of romantic flings, including a couple of fairly involved relationships. But this was the first time she had ever been completely in love. Her hair seemed to shine more luxuriously, her skin glowed with health and vitality and her eyes sparkled more brightly than the gleaming diamond engagement ring Bobby had presented to her just a week after his election triumph.

'I love you, June,' he had said, his voice gentle and husky with emotion. *I should have been a fucking actor*, he told himself as he watched her expressive blue eyes start to well up with happiness. *I deserve a fucking Oscar for this.* 'I would be honoured, and count myself the luckiest man in the world, if you would agree to become my wife. Will you marry me, please?'

Her answer had been to throw her arms around him and kiss him so passionately, her tongue probing deep into his mouth, that he was left gasping for air.

'Does that mean yes?' he finally managed to say.

'You bet your life it does, Mr Bobby Temple,' she laughed. 'I love you more than anybody or anything else in the world. This is the happiest moment of my life.'

They had made love that night, and several other times since, and Bobby had made a huge effort to get it right. What he lacked in finesse, he more than made up for with energy and enthusiasm and he made quite sure June climaxed each time – at least once. Between the sheets, June turned out to be an untamed tigress. What she was capable of with her large, soft lips and muscular tongue pushed even Bobby, who had always been fairly ambivalent about sex, to new levels of excitement. He still loathed, though, all the kissing and cuddling women claimed to need after the physical act itself was over. But Bobby had programmed himself not to blow this relationship before it culminated at the altar, and he provided the requisite number of cuddles and kisses after climax and even forced himself, on a few occasions, to lower his face between her thighs and lick and suck her clitoris after he had come.

June claimed to love the taste of his sperm and happily swallowed it down when he climaxed. He found it required steely determination to kiss her after she had taken him in her mouth and brought him to a delicious orgasm, but even more so to return the favour and use his tongue on her: the combined taste of her juices and his recently ejaculated semen made him feel quite sick. And June, he discovered, was a woman who, when roused to climax, produced a copious amount of warm, slippery liquid from the dark cleft between her legs. He damn near choked to death through gagging on a couple of occasions. *Christ*, he told himself, *if June and Ivan had ever met and landed up in bed, they would probably have drowned. How the fuck can people actually enjoy doing this night after night?*

Their honeymoon was spent in a split-level suite in the Hyatt Hotel on Grand Cayman, the largest of the British tax havens in the region, off the south-west coast of Cuba. It was there they read about the tragic suicide of Major Percival Fitzwilliam. Faced with continuous public ridicule, the loss of prestige and office, his future uncertain – his directorships had been withdrawn the day after the first *News of the World* exposé – the Major had fallen victim to extreme depression. The decision by his wife and children to leave him proved the last straw, and, in full view of passers-by, Fitzwilliam hanged himseld from the balcony of his third-floor apartment.

According to press reports, he had left a letter claiming that he had been set up, that he had never had a relationship of any kind with Miss Sweetjoy and that unknown scoundrels had deliberately plotted to ruin him. Delila Sweetjoy, who was to open shortly in her first professional part in a newly-written fringe theatre production, *The Mistress Factor*, gave her reaction in the words of an even more infamous lady of pleasure, from a decade earlier, 'Well, he would say that, wouldn't he?'

June refused to allow herself to be upset by the news. 'After all,' she told Bobby, 'He had only himself to blame. If he hadn't been having a sordid affair with that girl behind his wife's back, he would never have been exposed. Who could possibly have benefited from his public disgrace? I suppose the only one who could have really gained from it is you, my darling. But you had him beat before all that nonsense came out. The best man won, that's probably what he couldn't take.' Bobby uttered a murmur of agreement and pretended to be engrossed in his newspaper. *I couldn't have put it better myself*, he chortled inwardly, *so I'm not even going to try.*

Eighteen years later, Bobby looked across the wide Cabinet table at Jack Benson, his Chancellor of the Exchequer and Deputy Prime Minister, seated directly opposite in the time-honoured place for those in his office, and winked conspiratorially. Now recognised as Bobby's personal – and also his party's – spin doctor, Jack lowered a lazy eyelid in reply and offered as close to a grin as he could muster.

This is the moment. Bobby was surprised to feel a tremor of excitement ripple through him as he stood. *Even after all these years in the game. I can still get stagefright.*

He pushed his chair, the only one at the table with arms, away behind him and leaned forward slightly to rest both palms flat on the table. The others fell silent and he glanced up and down the table, bathed in glorious spring sunshine that streamed in through the tall windows running the full length and across one end of the Cabinet room.

'Today is going to go down in history as the day the British Government stopped following someone else's lead and went in a direction completely of its own choosing,' he began, knowing he had caught everyone's complete attention. 'I know you all agree that we – and that means Britain as well as Modern Labour – must regain our independent voice in the world.'

A chorus of approval came from around the table.

'Thank you,' he smiled. 'Ever since the war, we have been under America's thumb. However benevolent the control, they have been the masters and we have done their bidding. We have supported them in their bullying, military adventures around the world, however unjust some of us have believed them to be.

'All this talk about a special arrangement is bullshit, and we all know it. What that really means is that if the American President snaps his fingers, then the British Prime Minister rushes over to Washington and licks his arse.

'They have used Britain as a garden shed to store their nuclear weapons and they've turned our whole country into their front line of defence. Their multi-nationals manipulate our economy and have taken away some of our oldest customers by means of bribery, blackmail or under-the-counter political deals. Fair competition is just a myth with the Americans. The President smiles and offers friendship, knowing his agents are out there stealing our traditional markets and turning our real friends against us by any dirty means possible.'

There were further nods of approval around the table, though Bobby noted that the Foreign Secretary, Alex Turner, was beginning to look a little apprehensive.

Fuck him! thought Bobby, *he'll soon toe the party line if I threaten to take away his nice new job and his lovely new homes, not to mention the nice new salary and all the perks that go with the title.*

'The same goes for our partners in the European Union. They talk about the value of community spirit. Well, the only community spirit I know of comes out of a bottle... and I'm talking about a decent glass of whisky, not the terrible filth they brew up across the Channel.

'I'm fed up with watching the French mobs smash and burn our lorries and destroy their cargo before they leave the docks. They do the same to Italian goods coming in from the East and Spanish goods from the West, and we all know that not a single one of these criminals has ever appeared in a French court to answer for his actions. Now we're told it's the lorry drivers' turn to block the ports and hold their Government to ransom once again. The man in the Elysée Palace may be easily intimidated, but this time, if they act, they'll be in for one hell of a surprise when they see our reaction.

'The snivelling French and the Germans have turned Europe into their own private club. They believe they can make the rules and break them at will while the rest of us are made to play fair. The continental farmers are the most corrupt in the world and every rotten, contemptible governing body, right down to local council level, is taking advantage of inbuilt loopholes to rip off millions in grants from Brussels every day. And that means from the British taxpayers.

'Now the Germans are discovering the real cost of reunifying their country and the French economy has gone down the pan, I can see the day coming very shortly when Britain is going to be the only net contributor. We have supported Europe morally, financially and with our people's life blood for almost a century. Very soon, we will be paying all their bills as well.' He paused for a moment. 'And that is no longer all right with me,' he said.

Everyone looked at him, but only the Foreign Secretary spoke. 'What exactly are you saying, Bobby? That you don't want us to get more involved with Europe? We've promised the public a referendum on that already, and we're also due to make a policy statement on the single currency issue. None of what you're saying now was mentioned before the election.'

'Of course it fucking wasn't, you idiot! Do you think they'd have voted us in if we'd told them the whole damned truth in advance? No party is stupid enough to confide their real plans to the people before election day. Not even *after* that, if they can avoid it. The rules are very simple – you tell them one thing, and then, when you're in power, you do another: 'the economic climate has changed'; 'circumstances have changed'; 'the fucking moon has changed its orbit…' It doesn't matter. You give them an excuse and then get on with it. As long as you can pull the odd rabbit out of the hat, and know when to smile, they'll go on loving you.

'To be a successful prime minister, you have to be a conjurer. It's all smoke and mirrors. Churchill was drunk every day, but he is still acclaimed as our greatest wartime leader ever. The fact is that he was a wicked old war-monger, who loved sending men off to fight and die. But he was also a great orator and made a few memorable speeches. So he got away with it.

'Wilson loved Havana cigars but he would stub them out inside the front door of Number 10, and pick up his pipe before he went out because he believed, rightly, that it gave him a 'man of the people' image. Maggie promised to look after small businesses and protect the middle classes. Instead, she almost annihilated them. If you're looking for sincerity in politics, Alex, then you're in the wrong business.'

His voice grew cold as he stared at his Foreign Secretary. 'I don't want anyone to have any illusions about this, Alex. And that goes for everyone here. If you're not coming along for the whole ride, then I'll expect your resignation this morning. I would prefer everything to be nice and unanimous, but this is fucking going to happen one way or another, whether some of you like it or not. I want that to be very clear.'

No one at the table said a word, and Bobby noticed, with amusement, that Jack Benson's cynical smile was back in place and he was gently nodding. Jack had assured him before the meeting that no one would have the guts to oppose him.

Alex Turner was looking slightly embarrassed and wouldn't meet Bobby's glare, but after only 30 ministerial days of flexing his political muscles and enjoying the considerable power he now controlled, he wasn't ready to chuck it all away on a point of principle. The rest carried on staring at Bobby, wide-eyed, waiting for him to get to the punchline.

'I believe it's time for us to stop acting as Europe's stooge,' he told them, 'and it's way beyond time for us to stop being America's obsequious lackey. There is another, far more important market and ally available to us, and one to which we are ideologically more suited than all the rest – that is Russia.'

He paused again to allow the new information to sink in. 'I have already spoken to President Brekov and, together, we have agreed the outline of a remarkable new treaty between our two countries.'

Now, even Jack Benson began to pay more careful attention. This part had certainly not been on the agenda when they had discussed the Cabinet meeting privately in advance.

Bobby Temple's eyes burned with an inner zeal. 'Sit back and relax, my friends, while I explain to you my plans for our future.'

Jack Benson did not relax. Instead, he sat a little more rigidly in his seat. Everything he had heard earlier had come from a familiar script. Now, Bobby had just indicated, they were about to venture into new territory, with which even the Chancellor was unfamiliar. In some deep part of his brain, Benson was aware of a faint disquiet. It was some moments before he recognised the rarely heard sound of distant alarm bells ringing.

THREE

Bobby would probably have reacted angrily had he overheard the conversation in Downing Street, later that day, between his wife and Jack Benson. In the past, neither of them had ever sought to engage the other in private conversation. Both believed – and, until now, rightly – that their only common interest had been loyalty to Bobby Temple. In every other way, they were completely unalike.

June had always felt a deep discomfort, verging on revulsion, in the presence of her husband's most trusted and supportive lieutenant. She found his unctuous, servile manner both unnatural and unhealthy. His dependence upon, and utter dedication towards Bobby were the stuff of legend in modern politics and, if Benson had ambition, apart from this sycophantic role, it had never manifested itself. He was cold, efficient, ruthless and devoid of compassion, fully justifying his nickname 'The Ice Pick', and it seemed to June that his near-worship of Bobby had meant subjugating his own personality entirely. She had never seen him with a partner of either sex, and secretly categorised him as a self-emasculated eunuch. The mere thought of him touching her made her skin crawl.

So she was hardly expecting his visit, and was certainly not overjoyed when he came to her small, private sitting room seeking, he said, a 'private chat'. This room had doubled as an office since the election, when Bobby suggested she take a temporary sabbatical from her key job in the Current Affairs department at the BBC; it had now become her sanctum.

The heated argument this had provoked was still unresolved, and June, who had worked hard to establish her influential role in the fiercely competitive arena of current affairs and politics, was determined to bring a speedy end to her enforced retirement. Hers was an important voice in public debate, independent of her husband, and she deeply resented his arrogant assumption that, as prime minister, he now had the right to demand that she put her career on hold.

As in all things, she took for granted that Benson would support Bobby in this private battle as he did in everything else. So when he came, so unexpectedly, knocking on her door, she was instantly suspicious, and on her guard.

His opening remark lacked Benson's usual peremptory style. 'Could you spare a few moments for a private chat? I think it's important we talk.'

June, seated at her desk, leaned back in her chair. 'That depends on what it is you want to chat about, Jack. It isn't a habit you and I have exactly worked on developing over the years.'

Benson, who was acutely aware of June's feelings towards him, acknowledged her remark with a wry, but humourless grin, and came straight to the point. 'I'm not happy at the way Bobby is steam rollering us all into a partnership with Comrade Brekov – and I thought that maybe you might not be either.'

This brought June upright in her chair, a sudden spark appearing briefly in the sapphire-blue eyes, which now observed him more carefully across the desk. Benson knew he had her full attention. It was the first time in more than twenty years that she had ever heard him utter a word of criticism against her husband.

Benson drew up a second chair and sat at the desk facing her.

'He no longer discusses his plans with anyone… even with me. He just tells people what to do and stifles any objections by demanding their absolute loyalty.

'I know you and I have never really seen eye to eye over things, and I don't expect you to suddenly change your view and confide in me, but we are the two people closest to Bobby and I don't believe you can be any more comfortable than me with the decisions he is now taking.

'I can support a public confrontation with France, and even a cooling-off strategy towards the Americans, but his ideas involving Brekov are far more than radical. These are policies coming from some secret agenda I personally knew nothing about until today and I believe that they oppose our country's entire historical and political ethos.'

June stared at him, amazed, not so much by his words, as by the fact that he should be saying these things to her. She would not have been more surprised had she heard the chief Beefeater had run off with the Crown Jewels.

Benson seemed to take her silence as criticism. 'He is planning things which neither I nor the rest of the party know anything about. These appear to be policies which were worked out with Brekov when they were still undergraduates. They take no account of world changes in the past twenty-odd years. I happen to believe that some of these policies could be extremely costly to us as a nation, and possibly highly dangerous to boot.

'Despite what you might think, I can usually get him to recognise the logic in not pursuing certain goals but, on the subject of Brekov, he refuses even to listen.

'He tells me I must trust him, as I always have, to do the right thing. But I can't do that. Not this time. There are fundamental freedoms at stake. You know how powerful he has become and I'm not certain that I can get support from the other Labour members to rein him in.

'That's why I needed to talk to you. You're the only other person close enough to Bobby to be able to influence him at all.'

June finally nodded. Every instinct in her body screamed at her not to trust this man, to order him out of her study immediately. But the cold, logical part of her brain said to wait... and listen to what Benson had to say.

'He and Brekov have never lost touch,' she said. 'Bobby has always believed them to be ideological twins, that the destinies of Russia and England are somehow linked. The fact that they have both been chosen to lead their countries at almost the same moment and with massive support from the ordinary people makes them believe it even more... that history has chosen them to make major changes in the way we all live.'

Now it was Benson's turn to nod in agreement. 'On May Day, they plan to announce a new, joint strategy. A special peace treaty. And that, I believe, is just the start of it.'

'I know,' said June, anxiety flooding her expressive eyes. 'That's his dream, but it goes a great deal further than that. Though, surely, the Labour Party will never let him do it. At least that's what I keep thinking to reassure myself. I can't imagine there are more than half-a-dozen people in the whole country who would want this merger to go ahead. The Cabinet must still have some authority.'

'Far less than you might want to believe,' said Benson. 'They are all terrified of him. None of them want to risk losing their new perks and power.'

'It can't be like that for all 430 of you. What the hell are you, and all those bloody MPs, going to do about it? Surely you have the numbers to keep him under control?'

'To be frank, those who are not scared shitless think he's the Messiah, and I can't see them doing a bloody thing. The ordinary MPs don't really know what's going on anyway. At the moment, most think he is God... he can do no wrong. They owe their seats in Parliament, and whatever power they imagine that now gives them, to him. By the time they wake up, he'll have done the deal with Brekov and there'll be Russians flying into all parts of Britain.'

June shuddered. The vision Benson's words conjured up, she realised, was all too real. She had known about Bobby's wild proposals for days now, but had dismissed them as little more than improbable fantasies, a throwback to his student days. But Benson's obvious concern now made her accept, however reluctantly, that there was a great deal more substance to Bobby's plans than mere daydreams, and Benson appeared to know far less than she did herself. That realisation in itself was frightening – but more so because she found herself looking at the man in front of her, a man she had always mistrusted and found personally to be repulsive, as a potential ally.

'What do you suggest we do?' she said, at last.

'Well, first, I don't think it would be advisable, at this stage, if he knew you and I were on speaking terms. Certainly not that we have been discussing his policy decisions. I'll try to raise support in the Cabinet. If I can get them to believe everyone's acting together, then they might just have the courage to do something. But we shouldn't hold our breath.'

June's face softened slightly. 'You've always been his political conscience… and reminded him of true Socialist ideals. It took a century to forge them and now he's in danger of abandoning them completely.'

Benson met her gaze and said gravely, 'I'm not asking you to do it to help me because I'm fully aware of your feelings about me. But I do believe you have a real love and loyalty towards the country, and the party, and that for these reasons alone you'll do what you can. The alternative is too awful to contemplate.'

FOUR

Belmont Place, built in 1730 by the first Duke of Surrey, sat on a flattened mound surrounded by some of the finest and most coveted real estate in Britain. There were 2,500 acres, including a 50-acre wood and a 40-acre lake which had a small, man-made island at its centre.

The present owner, Peter Flint, had built a large gazebo on the island and liked to go there for picnic lunches on hot, dry summer days, ferried out from the shore by one of his boatmen.

He tried to convince himself that it helped him to remember his childhood and appreciate just how far he had come. Then he would inwardly chuckle, *Admit it, you fucking old fraud, you only want to go out there when there's some ripe young woman around and you feel randy. It's the one place no one can see what you're up to.*

True, the gazebo was as large as the shack in Pennsylvania where Flint had been born. It was from there he had watched his father, of whom the family saw little, trudge off to work at the privately-owned pit three miles away, and 12 hours later watched him trudge home, blackened and exhausted by hours of back-breaking toil at the coalface.

When Flint was seven, his father had been killed in a tunnel collapse half a mile underground, for which the wealthy owners accepted no responsibility and refused even the most meagre compensation. His mother had been forced to accept menial cleaning jobs and to take in washing to keep her family together, just so that he and his two older sisters could continue to share one tiny room, where Flint was never able to call anything his own.

She had also performed other services on the tattered couch in the room which served as kitchen, living room and her bedroom. But Flint had been too young to understand why some of the local tradesmen and husbands, in the households where she cleaned, would come calling after dark. Or why he and his sisters had to be locked in their room when these friendly neighbours wanted to see their mother.

His sisters, who were both older than him, and already taking more than just an academic interest in boys, would sit exchanging knowing looks on these occasions, and sometimes when the men would cry out – as though in pain, it seemed to Flint – the girls would giggle and clutch one another and laugh at him when he showed his concern.

He left home to seek his fortune when he was 15 and had vowed then rather to die than ever experience again such desperate, soul-destroying poverty.

The Flint family had rarely enjoyed the luxury of meat but, today, several herds of deer and cattle roamed his huge estate, though ironically, with such an abundance of red meat available to him, Flint had virtually become a vegetarian.

Being forced to share a room with others for the first 15 years of his life had made one major, lasting impression on him. He had become obsessed by a need for privacy and, with unlimited funds at his disposal, he was able to indulge this obsession to excessive lengths.

At Belmont Place, the wild and domestic animals were kept in and, more importantly, unwanted visitors kept out, by a 10-foot stone and brick wall, running a little over 8 miles around the whole estate. Jagged shards of broken glass were cemented atop its entire length and a continuous, high-voltage cable provided further dissuasion to any would-be intruders. In addition, the whole perimeter was surveyed by vibration sensors and closed-circuit television, monitored from inside a special security centre within the main house.

There were only two breaks in the wall. One was to the south of the property and sealed by two stout, oak gates kept almost permanently locked. The other, a massive, twin-towered lodge – once occupied by the head gamekeeper, but now used by the owner's private security guards – was a tribute to the latest, high-tech systems now available on the international security market.

Heavy steel barriers, electrically operated from within the gatehouse – a 10-foot square cube of bullet-proof glass – were only raised to let known, or carefully screened, individuals in or out, and provided the main, overt defence against intruders. This was backed up by razor-edged, tyre-shredding steel blades which could be projected upwards from below ground level, 10 feet either side of the barrier, at the flick of a switch.

From dusk until dawn, powerful halogen floodlights turned the approach roads and surroundings within a 50-yard radius of the entrance into simulated daylight conditions, and the turn-off from the busy, main Reigate–Dorking dual carriageway, 100 yards away, was clearly marked, with large signposts, illuminated at night, to the effect that this was a private road leading to private property.

In time, Peter Flint had succeeded in turning his English estate into a virtual fortress, and today he rarely set foot outside its boundaries.

A stronghold it may have become, but it was far from being a prison. Once through its formidable entrance, those visitors fortunate enough to be invited within were faced with a three-quarter-mile drive along a two-lane road, which lazily traced a winding route through the rolling acres of park and woodland, to end at a vast, 100-yard square, gravelled forecourt, set in the great U-shaped splendour of the house itself. At its centre, a magnificent fountain sent great plumes of water high into the air to tumble and splash into the circular basin that surrounded it.

All night, this fountain was brightly illuminated from below, as were the whole house and the trees, gardens and lawns close by. There was a wide choice of different coloured lights, which could be selected by pressing a few keys on the master computer or on one of its many mobile extensions. Flint always carried one in his pocket and liked to amuse guests by 'making things happen'.

In one of the cellars, which resembled the control room at NASA headquarters, a set of powerful computers operated one of the most advanced lighting and electronics systems in the world. Music, climate control, television and sound and lighting – inside and outside the house – were controlled from this nerve centre. In some parts of the house even some of Flint's rare paintings were automatically rotated on command from this basement control room.

At the centre of the north side of the forecourt, a dozen semi-circular stone steps, in gradually diminishing concentric rings, led up to a marble terrace and the massive, colonnaded portico entrance to the three-storey, former stately home.

Inside, the hall and main reception rooms were on a gargantuan scale, and furnished in palatial style, with treasures from five continents lavishly distributed throughout.

The main staircase, directly across the granite-tiled hall from the front door, was fully 5 metres wide and carved from the finest Italian marble. It led, in a single, impressive flight directly to the first floor, where it divided into two staircases running up the side walls of the atrium-like entrance hall, a vast space capped by the second-floor ceiling, from where a truly colossal chandelier hung to below first-floor level.

In the basement, adjoining the gymnasium, sauna, steam baths and an icy plunge pool, was a 30-metre swimming pool based on an ancient Roman design. The wine cellar, with space for 10,000 bottles and kept almost fully stocked, was thermostatically controlled to a constant temperature of 10°C.

In all, there were more than forty bedrooms and bathrooms and staff quarters on the top floor. Half a mile from the house, a new block accommodated 60 of the groundsmen, security guards, grooms, stablehands and domestics who were permanent employees.

To the sides of the house were additional outbuildings, garages and a small, tiered, covered grandstand, complete with bar, adjoining a well-appointed show ring. Stables for a dozen thoroughbred horses ran behind the stand.

At the back of the house, a broad terrace running the length of the building overlooked formal gardens, designed by the renowned Capability Brown, and a second ornamental lake which contained hundreds of rare Koi carp. At the front, the only man-made addition to nature was the main roadway, sweeping up through the lush green meadows from the distant main entrance.

Along this road, in the 20 years since the present incumbent of Belmont Place had taken occupancy, had come some of the richest and most powerful men and women on earth. All had come at the behest of, or as supplicants to, this remarkable man, whose wealth and power far outstripped that of the majority of his visitors.

Peter Flint was a charismatic entrepreneur of the old school. He counted royalty and heads of state – even the American President – among his intimate circle, and they were pleased to call him a friend. As his Wall Street admirers put it, 'He did it his fucking way, and God help his opponents!'

If he had any fault, it was his passion for women and his need to possess them completely. It had led him into some extremely messy love affairs – over which the international tabloid press had had a field day – and into four marriages, which the gossip columnists revelled in dissecting for a scandal-hungry readership and which they had, without exception, scornfully pronounced inadvisable and foolhardy in the extreme.

That someone who could be so brilliantly astute in his business dealings, and in his choice of underlings, could be so inept in selecting his brides, was a source of much amusement and discussion among both his legions of enemies and the public as a whole, who loved to read the lurid, gutter press accounts of the misfortunes of someone whose riches went far beyond their wildest dreams.

Most tabloid readers on both sides of the Atlantic knew more about the intimate details of Peter Flint's marriages – as told through the divorce courts, and by one of his wives in a provocatively vivid, kiss-and-tell autobiography, which had become an instant global bestseller – than about any of their neighbours.

'If I'd fucked her as often and in as many different positions and places as she claims,' Flint loved to tell friends, 'then why the hell would I have wanted to get rid of her? The trouble was, I wasn't getting any. She'd found a way of keeping the staff happier than anything I could put in their pay packets. When I finally chucked her out, I had to send two-thirds of the male staff packing at the same time. And losing some of them hurt a lot more than losing a whole bordello full of Shirleys,' he would add wistfully.

Shirley had been the first Mrs Peter Flint. Divorce from her had taught him a great deal more about protecting his fortune than it had about choosing his wives, and the carefully worded pre-nuptial agreements – worked out by teams of the finest and costliest brains in the legal profession – had become an obligatory prelude to marriage.

Two more Mrs Flints had come and gone, and each had attempted to improve on the generous, multi-million-dollar settlements, so eagerly agreed to and signed before their trips to the altar. But despite brilliant and impassioned speeches by their lawyers, the original architects of the pre-nuptial contracts proved to have been worthy of their fees.

Yet no such agreements with the media were possible, and each time the tabloid gossip columnists played the stories for all they were worth, and left Flint marvelling at the way in which pictures of himself, with assorted bimbos and unknown actresses, managed to surface at just the right moment. This, more than anything else, had driven him into secluded isolation.

His main legal adviser, Rupert Jackson, who had known him since their Harvard days together, often told him, 'If you gave as much thought to where you put your dick as you do to where you put your money, then you'd be a happier man. Give it a break from time to time and it just might last a bit longer.'

Jackson, a life-long bachelor, was well known for his pet homilies, which he freely offered to all and sundry. His favourite was: 'If it flies, floats or fucks, rent it by the hour.'

'Trouble is with you, Peter, you just want to own everything – including women,' he would say sternly. And Flint would reply, laughing, 'You keep paying the rent, Rupert, and I'll be happy staying the landlord.'

It was true that he did own vast blocks of real estate in some of the world's major cities and was one of the biggest industrialists in the free world, including a little-known interest in a major arms manufacturing group, but his real wealth had originally come and was still derived from oil. Black gold. Liquid affluence. This had made Peter Flint the largest individual oil producer in the world.

Small of stature, a legacy of his miner forebears in Pennsylvania, and now in his seventy-first year, Flint could have easily passed for a man in his mid-fifties. At seven every morning, he worked out in his private gymnasium under the guidance of a personal instructor for half an hour. This would be followed by a further half-hour in the pool – the unheated, Olympic-sized, outdoor one, unless it was exceptionally cold.

He still had a thick mop of hair, albeit now liberally streaked with grey, and his stamina and enthusiasm for business – and women – remained those of a man half his age.

He had a mouth which could, and usually did, offer a pleasant, boyish smile to the world, but his most telling features were his penetrating, deep-blue eyes, which at times danced with laughter... and could, on other occasions, be as cold and unfathomable as the grave.

Most amazingly, he had lost none of his appetite for sex and took pride in never having experienced the embarrassment of failing to rise to the occasion, though he knew of men twenty years his junior for whom this was frequently the case.

In fact, the only slight discomfort he experienced was when he woke, as he generally did, with an erection, having kicked off the bed covers in the night. The maid, who habitually brought his morning orange juice and tea at 6am – for Flint had fully embraced the English upper-class habit of sleeping in a separate bedroom to his wives – had, at first, reacted with pink-cheeked confusion to this very physical expression of her employer's undiminished libido. But she had eventually learned not to be flustered by this early morning evidence of his flourishing sex drive, though secretly the sight filled her with frustration and longing, and anger that her husband was never this rampant, having become an early victim of his nightly beer-swilling sessions, and the accompanying persistent brewer's droop.

Four o'clock in the afternoon, on this particular day, found Flint sitting, as usual, in his study, with its magnificent, panoramic view of his own landscaped idyll and the distant South Downs. It was his favourite time of day and he liked to sit at his desk, a prized antique that had once belonged to the famous French philosopher, writer and sceptic Voltaire. He sat facing the floor-to-ceiling French windows, which stretched the length of the room. Two of the remaining walls were entirely covered with bookshelves containing his priceless private collection of rare manuscripts and books, and the fourth wall featured a superb Adam fireplace, in which, offset by air-conditioning in the summer months, a cheery log fire burned all year round. Above it hung a single painting of cornflowers by Van Gogh for which Flint had paid £10 million, and which he valued above all his other possessions.

Flint loved the English ritual of afternoon tea and liked to take it alone, in his study, every day at this time. At precisely 4pm, his butler entered the study with a tray containing a silver tea service, a single china cup and saucer and a small plate of ginger cream biscuits – an irresistible favourite and the only deviation from an otherwise rigidly controlled diet. 'Thank you, Frank,' he murmured as the butler poured a cup of the English breakfast tea he favoured, and silently withdrew.

As Flint was about to take his first sip, his reverie was interrupted by the soft buzzing of the grey telephone on his desk. He frowned in irritation and replaced the cup on its saucer untouched.

This telephone had an ultra-private number known only to half a dozen people. All other calls were answered by the operator, and the majority would be handled by Jennifer, his long-time secretary and private assistant, in the main office.

Flint hated to have his ritual interrupted. *This had better be damned important*, he thought, and reached for the receiver.

'Hello, Peter. How are things there with you?'

The voice belonged to one of the very few men for whom Flint had total respect and with whom he had forged an intimate and lasting friendship. Their conversations had become regrettably few of late, as his friend had had much to occupy his time in recent years.

'Fine, thank you, Gordon,' he replied warmly. 'Though I doubt you troubled to call me just to ask after my wellbeing. What can I do for you?'

The voice at the other end chuckled. 'Straight to the point as usual, my old friend,' he said. 'But you're right. I need your help.'

The remark caused Flint to sit a little more upright in his chair. It was very unusual for this man ever to need to ask for help of any kind.

'Just name it, Gordon,' he said, his voice becoming immediately serious. 'If it's something that can be done, then you know I'll do it.'

'Thank you, old friend,' said the caller, his voice equally serious. 'I expected no less, and I rather think you *can* help. I want you to organise a very special dinner party at Belmont Place.'

'A dinner party?' Flint allowed his surprise to be heard. 'What the hell's so difficult or special about that?'

'Hear me out, please,' interrupted the caller. 'This one has to take place exactly when I say and you won't be able to change anyone on the guest list. That is most important. You have only five weeks, until the 27th of next month, so the invitations will have to go out straight away. I have already had checks made and I know that, as of now, all the guests are free to attend.

'I'm really sorry, old friend, but some of them you will have to invite in person. I know how much you dislike that kind of intimate involvement, but when I give you the list, you will understand why it has to be done this way.'

'But, Gordon,' Flint said, 'I'm not quite sure what you're driving at... Maybe I'm growing old and senile, or just plain fucking loopy, but why is throwing a bash here so darned important?'

'I'm sorry to do this to you, Peter, I really am, but this could be the biggest favour you have ever done for me, or for anyone else for that matter. I can't impress on you just how important I consider this to be. When it's over, I'll let you know the whole story. But for now, all I can ask is that you trust me.'

Flint considered for a moment. 'OK, Gordon, if you want to play it that close to your chest, it's all right by me. But I don't need to tell you that I wouldn't do this, completely in the dark, for anybody else. Even though it is only a dinner.'

'Thank you, my friend, I knew I could count on you. Now I'd better tell you who your guests are going to be. And it is essential that they are invited in this order and that each is told that the others have accepted. That way there'll be no drop-outs. Is that clear?'

'Sure… it's as clear as mud at the moment, but no doubt it'll become clearer when you tell me who my guests are.'

'Well, I wouldn't count on that, but thank you for being so understanding. Again, I can't overstress the importance of what I'm asking you to do. Now if you have pen and paper ready, I'll read you the guest list.'

Flint drew a writing pad towards him and selected a pen from the silver stand at the front of his desk.

'OK, I'm ready.'

As the list grew, Flint's frown deepened, and his eyebrows rose involuntarily at the mention of some of the names. By the end, he looked totally bewildered.

'That's just about the strangest mishmash of dinner party guests I would think it's possible to come up with,' he said once the caller had finished. 'I doubt if some of these folk have ever been in the same room with each other before now, never mind sat down at the same table. This is not some kind of joke, is it?'

'I only wish I could say it was, Peter, but I'm rather afraid it's not. It's just about as serious as one can get,' said the caller. 'I'm going to leave it to you to come up with a suitable reason for asking them. Perhaps some cause close to your heart, like setting up a new art foundation, or something on those lines. Whatever it takes to get them there. Please… I'm asking you not to let me down on this one.'

'OK, Gordon, you've got my word on that. I'll give it my very best shot.'

The caller allowed himself another chuckle. 'By the way, I don't want you to be out of pocket over this.' He was fully aware of

Flint's almost legendary meanness when it came to private hospitality, even though the oil tycoon had given away tens of millions to art galleries and charities worldwide. 'You can send me the bill for this bash. And that means being as lavish as you like.

'Thank you for being so understanding, old friend. And keep me in touch... me personally, that is. No one else must have an inkling of my involvement, at my end as well as at yours. I'll be waiting to hear from you.'

As the line went dead, Flint stared at the telephone receiver in his hand for several long seconds before gently replacing it on its stand.

That's got to be the oddest fucking conversation I've ever had. What the hell is he up to? It doesn't make sense.

His tea sat cooling and untasted in front of him, and his bewilderment grew as his eyes ran up and down the list of names, over and over again. *What the hell is so damned important about a dinner party?*

At last, he shook himself slightly and reached for the green telephone. Jennifer was on the line in moments.

'Yes, Sir?'

'Could you come through straight away, please, Jennifer? I've decided we're going to hold a rather special dinner party, and I'm going to need certain telephone numbers and addresses.'

FIVE

Brilliant morning sunshine streamed through the leaded windows of the third-floor Kensington Palace window, adding an almost ethereal incandescence to the glistening, naked body of Princess Katherine, Duchess of Worcester, and ex-wife of Prince Henry, third in line to the throne.

She was kneeling astride her latest riding instructor and Olympic equestrian gold medallist John Basset-Smith, who lay spread-eagled beneath her, and was working herself up to a wild and noisy climax.

With her knees tightly gripping his hips and her balled fists pressed into his heaving chest, the princess bounced her gloriously rounded backside faster and faster on his thighs and began to shout as she neared an ecstatic orgasm.

'Oh, Jesus... fucking fantastic!' she yelled, and her words turned into a scream of pure animal pleasure as she rose and sank slowly one last time, her whole, taut body shuddering, her eyes tightly closed.

John Basset-Smith, his own climax still eluding him, tried to move up and down inside her.

'Nearly there,' he cried, his own eyes now tightly closed with the effort.

'Of course you are, darling,' drawled the Princess, gracefully dismounting her gasping partner and sitting on the edge of the emperor-sized bed. She took his right hand in hers and guided it to his now redundant but still tumescent penis. 'Be a good boy and finish that off by yourself, will you? I'm feeling quite overcome.'

She laughed, flicking her trademark blonde fringe off her forehead with one hand while scattering his midriff with tissues from a box by the bedside with the other. And without another glance at the supine, groaning figure on her bed, she rose and walked towards the half-open door of her bathroom.

'Let yourself out, darling, there's a good boy. I'll call you again when I need you,' she said as she closed the door behind her. As she waited for her bath to fill, Princess Katherine – known to press and friends alike as Kate – examined herself in one of several full-length mirrors, and smoothed her hands over her firm, rounded breasts, moaning gently as she brushed across the dark, prominent nipples, still deliciously sensitive after such a satisfying orgasm.

She twisted sideways to get a better view of her virtually flat stomach and perfect breasts. At 32 and after giving birth to two children, a boy and a girl, now aged eight and six, Kate was justifiably proud of her figure, which would not have disgraced an athletic teenager.

'Pretty damned good,' she murmured to herself. 'You, my darling, are one sensational piece of fucking arse.' Her full, sensual lips, parted in an involuntary grin, revealed perfect, sparkling white teeth. Her radiant, cobalt-blue eyes twinkled mischievously and she poked out her tongue at herself in the mirror. 'You can have anyone you want, my darling. Anyone at all you damn well please,' she crooned to her reflection. 'Including a few royal in-laws if it takes your fancy.'

Her words triggered an eerie metamorphosis, wiping the famous, generous smile from her lips and replacing it with a sneering, wolf-like grin. 'Princess Heartbreaker' the press had named her. They hadn't seen anything yet.

Kate giggled and stepped into the enormous, sunken marble bath which stretched the full width of the bathroom and was surrounded on three sides by mirrors. She settled down into the hot, soapy water and reached for the telephone on the nearby table. Kate loved nothing more than long gossipy phone calls with her friends while soaking in her bath.

She pushed '9' and her private secretary was instantly on the line. 'Yes, Ma'am?'

'Hi, Audrey. I'm ready to take calls now if anyone comes through. And if the galloping Major isn't out of the playpen in ten minutes, use the crop across his withers will you… and turn him loose?'

She replaced the phone, giggling, and reached for the soap. Kate knew from long experience that Audrey was unshockable, but she couldn't resist trying on occasions.

The Princess trusted her secretary implicitly. The rangy, country-bred spinster had been a trainee teacher at Kate's last school, and had discovered, all too quickly, that she was not cut out for a career in education. She was too easily intimidated by some of the older, more rebellious girls and an easy target for a good hard-luck story.

Kate, who had herself been both bullied and taken advantage of at school, had empathised with her unhappy apprentice tutor, and they had become, if not friends, at least mutual commiserators in Kate's final year at Bexley Ladies College.

Kate's only qualification on leaving was a report commending her for her 'enthusiastic' membership of the school dramatic society – she had played the cat in *Dick Whittington*. The Head believed, and probably rightly, that as the only daughter of a senior British Duke, Lady Kate was in little need of impressive academic achievement. She had validated the Head's opinion by becoming engaged – at the age of 19 – to

Prince Henry, Duke of Worcester, second son of the Queen and a Captain in the Cavalry.

One of Kate's first actions after the engagement was to summon Audrey Pilkington to Buckingham Palace and offer her the job of private secretary. Through 13 years of non-stop controversy, a disastrous marriage, an even messier divorce and almost permanent scandal, Audrey had been the one, steadfast figure in Princess Katherine's life. Dependable, loyal and utterly truthful – to the Princess – she would willingly have laid down her life for her mistress. Kate had no secrets from Audrey. She knew that no matter what she did, she would never incur a breath of criticism or protest from her faithful servant.

Kate was convinced that if she ever chose to dive headfirst into the flames of Lucifer's eternal furnace, then Audrey would probably plunge after her without a moment's hesitation.

It was Audrey who had hugged Kate's head to her breast, stroked her soft blonde hair and calmed her with meaningless comforting clichés when the Princess caught her husband adulterating the marital bed. Not with one of his many ex-bimbos, but a mutual American business friend – a young Bostonian ex-college football star.

Kate had been devastated, and was scarcely able to comprehend what she was seeing. Not that it was that complicated, she was able eventually to explain jokingly to others. Henry had his prick firmly up Richard's arse and seemed to be humping for England.

'I ought to have known,' she sobbed to Audrey later. 'All those fucking pretty cavalry officers. Jesus Christ. Now I know what they mean by "secret manoeuvres". The British royals have to be the most decadent and fucking perverted family in history.'

And much later, when she was fully recovered, and her confidence restored by a scalding affair with her youngest Royal Protection Squad officer – still love-sick, but long since reassigned to other duties – she had tried to explain things more fully to Audrey.

'The present lots' problems all began with little Prince Albert,' she told her secretary. 'When he came over to marry Victoria, he brought his boyfriend, a German baron, with him. In between siring a disgusting number of children, he and the Baron were at it like rattlesnakes every opportunity they got. Which probably accounted for Queen Victoria's po face.

'And when Albert was older, and wanted to live out his days with his true love, he asked Victoria for a divorce. Her answer was pretty unequivocal. They were staying at Windsor Castle at the time, and some in the family believe she got the gillie, Brown, to come down and bump him off... and that's how Brown came to have so much influence over her for years.

'But the end result was that Albert came out of Windsor in a coffin and the official verdict on his death certificate simply said "Windsor drains". Victoria's private diaries were completely destroyed by her daughter, probably to hide the truth of that and other episodes. So we'll never know the full version.

'But little Albert's homosexual genes have inflicted a lot of damage on the family in the past 100 years. Edward the Eighth turned out to be a queer... He only married Mrs Simpson because she was delighted to let him fuck her up the arse. Can you imagine? He gave up the throne of England just so he could indulge in his favoured bit of nookie. The present batch are all as queer as £3 notes. The public have no inkling of what they're really like.

'That is why it's so damned infuriating that everyone thinks Henry is such a dashing, macho man and a kind of modern-day Casanova. They ought to have seen the pathetic little runt trying to hide his boyfriend's arse behind his hands and whimpering on about being in love. I told him he had brought a new meaning to the phrase about serving his Queen, and I trusted that this particular queen had been impressed. For I, as sure as hell, was not.

'I ask you, what on earth is so romantic about wiggling your dick around in someone else's shit?'

Kate had found one great consolation. The press – who could not understand what had gone so suddenly and terminally wrong with the royal marriage – had inevitably blamed the mutually agreed divorce on Kate and her rumoured 'affairs' with bodyguards and aides. But more importantly, it had cost Henry dearly where it hurt him the most – in his wallet.

Kate got to keep her huge grace-and-favour apartment in Kensington Palace and their miniature stately home, Sweetwater, near Cranbrook in Kent. She was also entitled to £5 million in cash and half a million a year until the children came of age.

Oh, how I loved squeezing his pips 'til they squeaked, Kate reminded herself, as she luxuriated in the steaming marble bath. Few outside the actual family were aware of Prince Henry's inherent meanness. Agreeing to part with each pound had been like having it, Shylock-like, sliced from his living flesh.

Kate's reverie was interrupted by the soft buzz of the telephone. She dried her left hand on a small towel and picked up the receiver.

'This should improve your morning,' said Audrey. 'Peter Flint.'

Kate waited until she heard the click of Audrey putting the call through and then said, 'Good morning, Peter. How's my favourite American this morning?'

The smile was obvious in his voice. 'Always better for hearing you, Ma'am,' he said.

'The name's Kate, Peter, to my friends. And I hope you're still my friend.' She added coquettishly.

'Indeed I am,' he replied. 'But if people were to find out you were friends with an old profligate like me, it would do serious harm to your reputation.'

'What reputation?' giggled Kate. 'The press have me fooling around with half the palace staff as it is. Perhaps it's time they learned about the real beau in my life.'

Peter, who had, from their very first meeting, recognised in Kate a common love of flirting, found himself laughing in turn. 'Even though he's old enough to be your grandfather?' he said.

'I just happen to be looking for a grandfather figure,' said Kate. 'But from the look of you, I really don't think you're old enough.'

'It must be the Irish in me that loves flattery,' said Flint, 'but I just can't resist it. Especially from you. Now, to be serious for a moment. I hope I haven't interrupted anything important.'

'Not at all,' said Kate. 'I was doing an evaluation on someone earlier but that's come to an end.'

'Was the person satisfactory?'

Kate grinned: 'He came through the try-out all right. But I'll need to explore further before I'm completely satisfied. Now what can I do for you?'

'I would dearly like you to come down to Belmont Place for dinner. I'm inviting a small group of people I want to sound out about a new idea I have for an Arts foundation. It'll be big and a bit different and I'd love your input... if it's not too much trouble.

'I want to make it April 27th, if that's all right with you. And, of course, I would be delighted if you would like to stay overnight. With your chauffeur and a maid – and, of course, your bodyguard.'

'What a delightful idea!' said Kate immediately and with genuine pleasure, for her flirtations with the infamous rake were not, she had to admit, entirely without foundation. 'A definite "yes" to both invitations. It'll give me a chance to pursue my predilection for good-looking older men.'

'I look forward to it,' said Flint with a chuckle.

After turning off the telephone on his antique desk, Flint smiled broadly, partly in anticipation of seeing the beautiful young princess again, and partly because, with her instant acceptance, Kate had made his job of rounding up the other people on his list that much easier. Who the hell in their right mind was going to turn down an invitation to sit at a table with

HRH Princess Katherine, Duchess of Worcester, the world press's favourite cover girl and the most talked about woman of the century?

He gazed through the French windows towards the distant South Downs. If only he knew what in God's name this was all about, he might even be able to relax and start to enjoy it.

SIX

Careb Sinclair, the man who was Salamander, took a long swallow of chilled Krug champagne from a tall-stemmed, fluted Venetian glass and watched with unconcealed admiration as his house guest emerged from the large, oval swimming pool set in an immaculate, English-style lawn.

She gracefully mounted the wide, marble steps at the end nearest the main patio which ran the length of the villa's south side and waved. 'You can pour me a glass of Voss,' she called in a slightly husky voice.

Careb waved an acknowledgement. She looked, he thought, exactly like the medieval descriptions of sea nymphs. So stunningly beautiful as to tempt bewitched sailors from the safety of their boats into the boiling seas.

Her red hair, sleek and wet, cascaded down her back almost to her waist and her matching triangle of pubic hair glistened with water droplets. She was completely naked – and just as completely at her ease. A slight smile played around her full, seductive lips and triggered sparks in the depths of her almond-shaped, violet eyes. Her lithe, willowy figure carried an even, golden tan, unspoiled by bikini marks, and her full, natural breasts completed the picture of supreme sensuality, her large, brown nipples swollen and erect from the effect of the cold water.

Emma Vale was the most beautiful and erotically charged woman Careb had ever known and he had generously sampled the world's leading competitors in the field. Yet he also knew there could never be a chance of unleashing the raw sexual energy that remained confined within that exquisite body. Any attempt to release it was doomed, in advance, to absolute failure. For this heartbreakingly beautiful angel was, Careb knew, a tragically flawed creature. In truth, an angel of death.

To most people, Emma was a vibrant and captivating young woman, at her physical peak and full of sexual promise. In reality, she was in a state of permanent frigidity, totally devoid of all sexual feelings, immune to all attempts at arousal.

As he watched the perfect body, in classic catwalk style, glide seductively towards him across the freshly mown grass, Gabriel wondered, perhaps for the thousandth time, at the strange hand that fate had dealt this striking and almost awesomely beautiful woman.

Blessed with such a flawlessly perfect body and finely chiselled features, she became the natural focal point at any gathering and was so tantalisingly desirable it seemed immeasurably cruel to him that she was impervious to any physical or mental sexual stimulus. With this part of her psychophysical mechanism frozen in her own perpetual hell, she could neither feel nor react.

Her story was not unique. In an age when criminal gangs, savage rebel forces and ruthless terrorists proliferated and held half the countries of the world in the grip of lawlessness, it had become almost commonplace. But it was no less tragic because of that.

For more than a decade, Emma's father and mother had been aid workers in the Middle East, based in southern Lebanon. It was, for them, a tough but rewarding life, and for their only daughter, who had known little else but the inside of refugee camps from birth, it was, at worst, tolerable.

That is, until the morning their village was attacked by a marauding, leaderless and undisciplined band of fundamentalist rebels. They killed all the adults in the village, including Emma's parents, whom they casually beheaded. Only Emma and two other teenage girls were spared, along with the Catholic priest, Father Benjamin, who represented a Christian charity and doubled as the local schoolmaster. More worldly wise than his charges, he knew their reprieve was, at best, only temporary, and that they had been spared only so they could be the providers of better entertainment later. He began to beg for mercy... not for the girls, but for himself.

On his knees, hands clasped together in supplication, Father Benjamin confessed his willingness to sacrifice any number of other lives in exchange for his own. He would become their slave, their plaything, suffer any degradation rather than die.

But his captors, possessed of even less compassion than his own Church's ancient Inquisition, soon wearied of his whining and, cuffing him into silence, kicked him into a corner of the school room.

Emma, at 14, was by far the prettiest of the three girls, and was already maturing, her body showing an early promise of the woman to come. One of the rebels ripped her thin cotton dress and pants from her and spread-eagled her like a sacrificial offering across a school desk.

But the planned entertainment, featuring Emma as the star attraction, was suddenly interrupted by the unscheduled arrival of an Israeli special services squad, operating deep inside the Lebanon. In the fierce but brief firefight that ensued, the eight-man Israeli team disposed of four of the rebels. Three others managed to escape during the fighting.

Already badly traumatised by the brutal murder of her parents and the noisy slaughter of the Arabs, Emma had climbed down from the desk and was slumped on her hands and knees, sobbing and clutching her torn dress across her breasts. The blood of the

Arab who had stripped her was splattered across her body and she was shaking uncontrollably with terror and revulsion.

But she was utterly unprepared for what came next. The men she had assumed to be her saviours hauled her roughly to her feet and forced her again onto the desktop. Meanwhile, accompanied by much screaming, the two other girls were forcibly stripped and laid out on neighbouring desks. The three of them were then systematically and savagely raped by the eight soldiers.

The pain and the horror on top of what they had already gone through was almost more than Emma could bear. She prayed for death as a release but concluded that God, like his representative in the corner, had forsaken her.

Finally, it appeared to be over. But for Emma there was to be no respite. For her, far worse was still to come. The Sergeant, a burly, balding man in his mid-thirties, made an obscene remark to his men which she didn't understand but which set them all off laughing. They all gathered around her and helped him manhandle Emma over onto her hands and knees on the desktop. They then held her down as the Sergeant anally raped her.

The searing agony of this vicious assault caused Emma to scream repeatedly at the top of her lungs until the soldier grabbed a handful of her hair and slammed her forehead against the desktop, at which point she mercifully lapsed into unconsciousness.

Her last sight was of the priest, cowering in the corner, terrified for his own safety but unable to tear his eyes away from the dreadful acts being performed on the three schoolgirls. And to her mind, it was almost as if he was enjoying the spectacle.

Finally, they were done. Quieter, now their lust had been satisfied and with their consciences starting to refocus, with downcast eyes, unwilling or unable to look now at the pathetic, ravaged bodies of the teenagers, the soldiers hauled up their trousers and gathered up their weapons, and with a couple of very forced, ribald remarks and a few animal-like grunts of mutual congratulation, they went on their way.

When Emma recovered consciousness she felt as though a fire was burning inside the lower half of her body and when she looked down she saw that her legs were streaked with blood.

She was just aware of the priest crawling towards her. Later, she would remember naively thinking that this man and his God – who had done nothing to provide for them when they needed it most – was finally coming to her aid.

Nothing could have prepared her for the horror of what took place next. When he reached her, he pulled himself to his feet, and seizing hold of her blood-stained legs, forced them wide apart. Hauling up his cassock, he lunged inside her and with loud groans of pleasure completed the violation she had suffered from the soldiers. This final, and by far the most brutal act of betrayal destroyed the few tattered remains of trust in the Church – in all types of authority, in fact – within her. It was too much for her to cope with, so her brain protected her the only way it could. She sank into an anaesthesia of oblivion with the symbol of this consummate deceit and hypocrisy in her mouth threatening to choke her: a gold cross suspended from a chain around the priest's neck.

It was much later, towards dusk, when Emma awoke and found the other girls either unconscious or asleep. She knew that all three of them needed urgent medical treatment. But first there was a score to be settled. The need for revenge was like a pounding and all-consuming demon, a burning crusade which had completely possessed her and she knew that, until she satisfied her desire, she would be unable to perform any other act.

She found the priest in his room, asleep in a rocking chair, with an ugly smirk playing at the corners of his fleshy lips. Emma searched until she found a large hammer, and she did not stop raining blows to his skull until the whole of his bloated, self-satisfied face was obliterated, the head just a bloody and unidentifiable pulp.

When her rage was spent, Emma removed his cross and chain, used his cassock to wipe off the blood, and placed it around her own neck. Only then did she go in search of help.

A week later, when she felt physically recovered, Emma discharged herself from hospital in Beirut and, after telling her story to various sympathetic Palestinians, was guided to a PLO cell where she was trained in the art of terrorism.

She was a diligent student and, in the ten years that followed, she became a celebrated leader of the organisation and a dreadful scourge of the Israelis, both military and civilian.

Being acclaimed a heroine meant nothing to her. It was only her very personal vendetta that mattered. That, and a determination to expose the corruption and sickness within the Catholic Church.

Careb had met her during the final stage of a violent skirmish near Jerusalem where he became pitted against a team of Mossad agents from Israeli intelligence and found an unexpected ally in the shape of a PLO group led by Emma. He had rescued her from a hazardous situation which would probably have led to her capture or death and, during the night which followed their escape, they spent many hours talking. Soon afterwards, he had recruited her to Salamander.

Now she was one of his most trusted lieutenants and, he rapidly discovered, she was becoming an indispensable part of his everyday life.

As she joined him on the patio, he handed her a frosted glass of Voss mineral water. He raised his own glass of vintage champagne, and clinked it gently against hers, his pale-blue eyes meeting her gaze.

'Here's to mayhem… and damnation to our enemies,' he proposed.

Her husky chuckle was approving. 'And may the rewards for the victors be generous,' she added.

'As we are about to discover very shortly,' said Careb, with a conspiratorial wink. 'I've just had a call, which means that if we accept the challenge, we will very soon be facing our biggest assignment to date.'

'What do you mean, "If we accept the challenge?" Is there any doubt?' Emma rubbed the cold glass absent-mindedly against the gold cross dangling between her breasts and flashed a mischievous grin. 'We've done nothing at all since Bogotá. I'm starting to get stale.'

Careb's grin widened. Any suggestion that Emma, who ran ten miles every morning before breakfast and worked out with him in a 'no holds barred' two-hour session in the gym every afternoon, was becoming stale, was on a par with the notion that there were still fairies living at the bottom of the garden.

'You're *stale*? Where did my bruises come from then?' he laughed. 'Let's talk to Davey and the three of us will decide after that.'

She laughed and followed him to the back of the orchid-and-vine-covered patio, where large, mahogany-framed armchairs were clustered around a low table. Her glass was still in one hand and the half-empty bottle of mineral water, plucked from its ice bucket, was in the other. She had made no move to cover her nudity.

Even knowing that her sexual feelings and responses were set at absolute zero did not immunise Careb from their potent effect, and he was acutely aware that the psychological demons which prevented her from indulging her sexual magnetism did not mean it was completely wasted.

Emma had learned to use her seductive charms to devastating effect in disarming her intended victims. More than once, with incredible daring and when no other solution presented itself, she had stripped and walked naked into a room, where the men inside had died before they could gasp in wonder.

As she topped up her glass with the mineral water, Careb took a white towelling robe from the back of one of the chairs and wrapped it around her shoulders.

'You'll excite the staff,' he told her. 'Though I fear it's far too late for the master,' he added ruefully, his voice carrying a hint of mock despair. 'But I'm resigned to only wrestling with you on the exercise mat when you're beating the shit out of me. Now cover up, Emma, and give a man a chance.'

She shrugged her arms into the sleeves, folded the gown around her and sat in the chair opposite, tucking her heels under her buttocks like a cat settling into its most comfortable position prior to a nap.

'Sorry,' she said, head bowed, and peered at him through the fluttering upper lashes of her big violet eyes. Careb laughed out loud. This pure angelic spirit before him seemed possessed of all the fragile innocence of a young novice with not the slightest hint of the cold-blooded killer lurking just beneath that soft, golden skin. What a truly amazing woman.

He reached for a mobile telephone on the table and dialled a preset number. It rang only twice before being answered by a male voice, strong and pleasant, with the pronounced, musical lilt of the Irish.

'This better be important,' the voice said. 'Because you'll be getting a piece of the wrong side of my mind if you're just after passing the time of day.'

Careb laughed. 'And what is it you're doing that can't be put off to talk with an old friend?' he asked.

'Well, if it's yourself, Careb, there's no need to worry,' said Davey. 'But I was just finishing off a bit of daubing, which needed my whole attention.'

Davey had begun painting years before as an antidote to the darker side of his life and he now enjoyed a considerable reputation in the art world. Two of his works were prominently featured among Careb's own collection, including a stunning portrait of Emma.

'Though now you're on, I suppose even that can wait for a while.

Let me put down this palate and get the young lady to cover up, and I'm all yours.'

Careb had little difficulty imagining the scene. The craggy-jawed, tousle-haired Irishman had not just kissed the Blarney Stone… Careb always maintained he had swallowed it whole.

Despite his vocation, Davey was a confirmed romantic who fell in love with dizzying frequency. Women found him equally irresistible.

'So how is my favourite American?' Davey asked after a few moment's pause. Careb was speaking in his natural Boston accent, which he almost always used when with his real friends.

'Just perfect,' he replied. 'Emma's with me and sends her love. She's looking forward to seeing you.'

'Ah, that one. If only it were true,' mused the Irishman. 'A million tons of sexual dynamite and a fuse nowhere to be found. But tell her I'll keep hoping… What's this about seeing me?'

'We'd like you to come over. There's a very big job on offer with an eight-figure price tag for each of us.'

Even Emma, who was listening carefully to the conversation, widened her eyes and pursed her lips in a silent whistle. Careb paused a moment for Davey to absorb this information and continued, 'We'll be competing against the English on their home ground,' he added.

Further silence. 'It just became a very attractive proposition indeed,' said Davey. 'I'll be with you both in the morning. Might even join you for your run. Until then, blow a kiss to the fair Emma for me.'

Davey gently replaced the telephone on its stand and slowly rose to his feet. 'A chance to have another go at the English,' he breathed. 'Now there's a fine thing.' He stared out through the large picture window which ran the length of his living room to where the dark-blue waves were lashing themselves to billowing white foam on the jagged rocks below the cliffs. His dark, emerald-green eyes were wide open but he was visualising a very different scene to that of the tropical landscape outside.

As his memory tumbled backwards down the years, he could see, as though it was that very morning, the ancient shepherd's cottage of hand-hewn stone and slate, which had stood all those years ago, as it probably still did today, on a wooded hillside, midway between the villages of Cootehill and Rockorry in County Monoghan, and ten miles from the border with Northern Ireland. Far enough away to be safe from the hated British soldiers and isolated enough to escape the attention of those misguided Garda who did not espouse the cause of Sinn Fein.

The early evening sunshine sent long, dancing shadows stretching across the lush green, ragged lawn at the back of the cottage, where two men kicked a worn leather football between them. They were dressed almost identically in blue jeans and trainers and the white skin of their exposed torsos was evidence of how little time had been spent that year in the sun.

Two women were stretched out on sun-loungers. One, her eyes closed, wore a skimpy bikini and her skin shone darkly golden against the bright yellow cotton. Long auburn hair had been blown partly across her face by the light breeze and caressed the edges of full, open lips. The other woman, in a loose-fitting, flowery gingham dress lay with her hands clasped on her swollen belly. Her generous mouth was spread in a smile and lively, dark-green eyes followed the antics of the men.

God knows, they had little enough time for such innocent fun, she told herself. Like thousands of schoolboys before them, they had bundled their shirts and jackets, and set them on the ground – 10 feet apart – to make a temporary goal mouth.

The taller of the two, with a narrow face and eyes the colour of Whitby jet, set deep above a slightly crooked nose, was in goal. His cousin – smaller, squatter, with blond-streaked hair receding from a wide, furrowed forehead – lined up for a mock penalty kick.

'This is it, Liam,' he called. 'You don't stand a bloody chance, man.'

'Is that right, you little bastard?' replied Liam. 'In that case, I suppose you wouldn't mind having a small wager on it.'

'Always after me bloody money. But I think I've got the beating of you this time,' said Brendan Gallagher. 'One punt says it's a goal. Are you on?'

'You can consider it already lost,' grinned Liam, preparing himself on the goal line with arms and legs spread wide.

At the bottom of the garden and stretching its full width was a small orchard of a dozen or so fruit trees which cast their shade almost to where the two women were lying. On the main branch of an apple tree, almost obscured by the leaves and clusters of dark, red apples, a boy in his early teens, with an untidy mop of black hair, lay along the bough on his stomach. This was Liam's brother, Davey, 20 years younger than the lads below him, the product of a drunken night when his parents became a little too carried away in celebrating their silver wedding anniversary. It was 'the good Lord's way of playing his little joke on us', as his mother put it. His father, Tom Carey, saw it as an irresponsible bit of tomfoolery gone wrong, and one which he ought to have been old enough and wise enough to avoid. But they both loved the boy, and lavished much affection on this unexpected, late addition to their family.

It was a love shared by Tom's five older children, especially Liam, who never complained at being asked to look after his kid brother... whenever he was at home, that was, which, for the past two years, had been rarely.

For his part, Davey hero-worshipped his eldest brother. He didn't know all the finer details but, like most of the kids in the area, he knew that Liam Carey was a big noise in the IRA, with at least, so it was reputed, half-a-dozen kills to his name. His pride in Liam was sometimes almost too much to keep to himself. He would have loved to shout his brother's terrorist exploits to the whole world, but was only too well aware of the dangers of a loose tongue.

Davey knew exactly what he wanted to be when he grew up: a trusted gunman for the IRA. One like his brother, who would help drive the English scum from God's own country.

But, for the moment, his mind was fixed on other, less noble thoughts. For, in truth, for the past ten minutes, his gaze had been fixed on the nether regions of Liam's girlfriend, Siobhan. She was lying on her back with her legs spread suggestively apart, and some of the thin material of her bikini briefs had slipped to one side, revealing a tuft of fine, red hair and a tantalising glimpse of a scarcely identifiable, darker area beyond.

Almost as though she was aware of the transfixed pair of eyes above her, Siobhan, her own eyes still closed, spread her legs even wider apart and eased the thin triangle of her pants further aside with one long, red-nailed, teasing finger.

Davey held his breath and became increasingly aware of the throbbing hardness between his own legs thrusting urgently against the branch to which he was clinging. The previous night, he had listened to the moans and screams of pleasure issuing from Siobhan's lips as his brother drove into her in the next room, the thin cottage walls scarcely muffling even the lowest sounds.

He had timed his own scalding climax to hers as she shouted, 'Now, Liam… Jesus… Please… Fill me now… '

Today, almost all of that wonderful, yearned for, forbidden cleft was revealed, though it was still too obscured by shadow to be easily identifiable.

Davey's excitement was becoming difficult to contain, but he had also been aware of the banter between his brother and Brendan and the wager that had just been struck. His attention switched from between Siobhan's legs to the laughing men, whose enjoyment of the moment was clear to any observer.

Brendan took a weaving, lumbering run up to the ball and slammed it towards the goal. Liam dived to his right, fingers outstretched, reaching for the arching leather ball.

But they failed to make contact.

At the very moment they should have touched and diverted the ball beyond the makeshift goalpost, Liam was thrown violently backwards, a good couple of metres, towards the cottage wall.

His grin became a look of shocked, disbelieving horror, and half his forehead exploded in a spray of red and grey mist as great gouts of blood fountained from his chest. Without enough air left in his ruptured lungs, his scream dissolved into an obscene gurgle in his blood-filled throat. His eyes seemed to start from their sockets but by the time his mutilated body slammed into the grass they had become dull and lifeless.

Brendan was the first to realise what was happening… that they were under attack. He screamed, 'Liam… Oh fuckin' hell, no!' as he launched himself in a dive towards one of the goalpost jackets.

But just as Liam's fingers had failed to make contact with the ball, Brendan's were just inches away from the 9mm Uzi submachine pistol that lay hidden beneath his jacket, when a spray of automatic fire raked across his back and sent his whole body twisting into a somersault. It ended with him sprawled, motionless, across his cousin's blood-soaked chest.

The troops, in camouflage gear and with their faces blackened, had first opened fire from the edge of the wood but were now halfway across the garden, almost beneath the apple tree where Davey was clinging, terror-stricken, to the bough. Since the initial burst of fire he hadn't moved or made a sound. He felt paralysed with a fear not even his worst nightmares had prepared him for.

One of the soldiers had stopped just a few feet below Davey's hide-out. His M16 rifle was pointing at the pregnant woman, whose body he now straddled, its muzzle pressed against her tightly-stretched stomach. She was sobbing and pleading with him not to harm her baby and was trying to force her fingers beneath the rifle barrel, as though she could protect the life within her with her bare hands.

The soldier, his mouth open wide in a fiendish grin, pulled the trigger and sent half a magazine of nickel-plated bullets through her body.

'That's one less fucking Irish kid joining the IRA,' he snarled and then laughed out loud. It was the most chilling sound Davey had ever heard.

Siobhan had meanwhile tumbled off the sun-lounger onto her hands and knees and was crawling towards Liam's body, which lay motionless after the opening burst of gunfire.

One of the other soldiers quickly stepped behind her and brought down a heavy army boot into the small of her back, causing her to collapse. She looked up, over her shoulder, straight into the small black snout of her assailant's rifle and screamed – just once. It was a scream so full of horror that, 20 years later, in the dead of night its echoes still brought Davey shuddering awake and drenched in sweat, wrenching himself away from the dreadful moment when the soldier opened fire and Siobhan's beautiful face exploded into fragments of bone and gristle, and blood and flesh.

The eight-man unit of 22 SAS Regiment quickly produced body bags and, in seconds, had efficiently bundled the four corpses inside, zipped them closed and dragged them into the woods, destined to be buried miles away in an unmarked grave. These were the tactics used by the Special Forces – the men fondly referred to by Prime Minister Margaret Thatcher as 'my boys' – during her premiership. They struck without warning, and usually from ambush, their victims simply disappearing without trace.

Since witnessing the massacre of Liam and the others that day, Davey's loathing of the British had been all-consuming, and he turned the white heat of his hatred on the organisation responsible for the destruction of his family, and his country: the British SAS.

In time, he fulfilled his wish to become an IRA gunman, and had avenged their deaths many times over... until the ceasefire, that is. Davey cursed the movement's leaders for becoming soft and willing to swap the gun for a say in the political future of Northern Ireland.

It was in the aftermath of the ceasefire that Davey had been approached by Careb Sinclair. The American had offered an attractive proposition to the young IRA killer. A promise of great riches and, occasionally, the chance to strike a major blow to the detested British.

The offer had followed a bizarre interview and initiative test Careb had conducted with Davey, and seven other possible recruits, on a bleak and isolated stretch of moorland in Devon.

Davey smiled as he remembered the occasion. At one point, Careb had divided the seven men and one woman into two teams. Two makeshift goals using rocks had been set up and, as Careb lined up the teams against each other, he told them, 'There is only one rule in this game, and that's that there are no rules at all.'

First to react was Davey, who stooped and snatched up the ball in both hands and ran to the opposing goal, throwing it between the posts. His reaction had simply confirmed to Careb that Davey was far and away the best of these possible recruits. One other candidate, Simon Wojak, had also been invited to join Salamander.

It was the opportunity to pit himself against the British and create mayhem in England which was being discussed on the patio of Careb's villa, on an undeveloped stretch of Thailand's coastline to the north of Phuket, on the morning after his telephone call to Davey. It was this that had led to the Irishman flying in early from his home in Vietnam.

Davey had become Careb's other most trusted lieutenant, and he had taken to discussing all proposals for their services with Davey and Emma before accepting or rejecting them. He believed it was their traumatic childhoods and similarly flawed natures that made the pair such perfect sounding boards.

The current request had come, as usual, through Careb's trusted broker in Hong Kong. This prominent Chinese businessman was a former client of Salamander, who had rescued his small son and daughter from Malaysian pirates. The kidnappers had seized them in a raid just off the coast in the notoriously dangerous South China Seas, where the client and his family were enjoying a leisurely cruise, having ignored all warnings.

When the man and his children had been reunited following a successful storming of the pirate stronghold, the businessman had sworn his life to Careb in gratitude.

He was impervious to all other financial inducements or threats, and it was only through him that a select and trusted number of other agents around the world could lodge a request for Salamander's help.

The latest request would be a truly perilous undertaking involving a siege and the need to defend against all-comers for up to a week. The risks were enormous and the chances of the whole team coming out alive were slender indeed. The job, Careb told them, would require a 15-man unit.

For this, the broker advised him, the client was willing to pay $150 million. There was a further $50 million budget for specialist equipment. It meant that each member of their squad would receive $10 million.

The usual rules would apply, Careb reminded them. If any member of the team should be killed, then his or her share would be divided equally between the others.

The target was in England, the deadline just one month away. As Careb spelled out the details, Davey and Emma began to exchange excited glances. To succeed in this mission would mean pulling off the most daring and hazardous operation in modern history. But in compensation and direct proportion to the risks, the rewards were the highest ever offered.

'There is one other important piece of information you need to know,' said Careb finally. 'It not only suggests an escape route when things reach a climax. It will also explain why I have selected the team that I have. They are not the first choice and they are not the most endearing characters. But there is a reason for that, too.'

And he told them.

To the three people gathered on the patio of Careb's villa, there was only one thing, above all others, that really mattered: the challenge. When Careb finally finished briefing them and answering their questions, he put it to the vote. There was a unanimous decision to go ahead.

Careb's first move was to telephone his Hong Kong go-between. His instructions were simple – half the fee and all of the equipment budget to be paid in advance. Five million dollars of the equipment money would be retained by the Chinese businessman as his fee.

Once Careb had ended his call to Hong Kong, he told Davey, 'You'd better move in here. None of us is going to get much sleep in the next month and there's zero room for mistakes. On this one, if we get it wrong at this stage, then eventually somebody will have to pay for each of our mistakes with his life.'

The Irishman nodded his agreement, then cocked his head, quizzically, on one side. 'Not that it makes a real dram of difference,' he said, 'but I'm not quite certain if we are the good guys or the bad guys this time.'

Careb grinned, and shrugged his shoulders. 'I suppose that really depends on which side you're looking from… wouldn't you say?'

SEVEN

Georgie Brown, the nation's darling, scratched his varicosed, bare buttock and broke wind loudly. He pulled a face, the kind he usually reserved for a contestant on his show who had made a stupid mistake, and fanned the foul-smelling gas away with the duvet. All Georgie's expressions were deliberate, endlessly rehearsed in front of a large mirror. Not the slightest slant of an eyebrow or the twitch of an ear happened naturally.

Georgie was a one-man industry, and his expressions and catchphrases were his chief marketing assets. Nothing spontaneous happened in his life, and there were few situations for which he did not have a well thought out and thoroughly rehearsed contingency plan. Relentless, never-ending groundwork – it was to that, he told interviewers, that he owed his phenomenal success. It had won him, he boasted, more than 20 million fans, and earned him a pound in the bank for each and every one of them. As Georgie might have put it himself, 'I mean that, ladies and gentlemen, from the bottom of my heart.'

At the age of 52, Georgie was hosting his sixth and most successful television show, *Take It From Me* – now in its tenth series – and it was still number one in the ratings by a long margin.

'You can't take it with you... but you can take it from me,' had become the catchphrase on everyone's lips and, to his adoring fans, Georgie was the yardstick against which all other TV show hosts were measured, and found wanting. He was the Chairman of Cheer, the Maestro of Mirth, the Host with the Most... Mr Television himself.

They worshipped him and he, unashamedly, basked in their adoration. Today, he would drive his Bentley Continental – 'Brown always buys British' was another of his slogans – down to Teddington in Surrey, where the studios sprawled alongside a peaceful stretch of the Thames. There he would record the third show in the current series, which would be aired at peak viewing time on the following Friday.

The company had given him a new director this season, a highly professional northerner with a string of hit shows to his name, including a long-running, successful Sunday variety show from Blackpool. Notwithstanding the man's excellent track record, Georgie had, as always, greeted this proposal with tantrums and objections – none of them logical, and all of them sparked by a barely controllable, utterly irrational fear of failure.

Georgie liked routine. This meant keeping the same set every week, the same gags, the same hostesses, the same cameramen, the same team in the same studio. A new director meant change; someone who would want to stamp his own personality on the show. This usually meant an attempt to alter the set or the pace of the show, and Georgie wouldn't allow it. Never. It was his stardom at risk, his popularity at stake – and the director had better fucking appreciate it.

But to everyone's relief, and surprise, the new director – Jeff Morgan – had shown a genuine understanding of Georgie's paranoia. The beefy, cigar-chewing Yorkshireman had grasped Georgie's two, almost dainty, hands in his great shovel-sized mitts and thrust his walrus moustache just inches from his superstar's ear and growled, 'If it's not bloody broke, then why bloody fix it? I'd like to keep t' bloody show just t'bloody way it is. All reet?'

Georgie nodded vigorously, the special nod he kept for the achievers on his show. He froze, though, when Morgan added, 'Except for one thing... I've got an idea about those two lovely hostesses of yours.'

Georgie prepared to do battle. It had all seemed just too good to be true.

But three weeks later, he was still sniggering at the simple but beautifully lewd idea the Yorkshireman had dreamed up for their mutual entertainment. He started to laugh out loud as he heaved his way off his enormous bed and headed for the bathroom. Georgie's investigations into Morgan's reputedly shining reputation had failed to reveal the hidden depths of depravity to which he would be prepared to stoop. The director had suggested putting the show's pair of sexy hostesses in bright orange wigs for the new series.

'That way,' he had explained to an intrigued Georgie, 'when we're tired of screwing them, we can swap them for new ones and the public will hardly be aware of it. On top of that,' he added cunningly, 'it means neither of them is going to become too popular with the viewers, and stop them from paying attention to the real star of the show, which is you.' In this, he revealed far more knowledge about his new star's secret fears than his predecessor, who had gradually been increasing the girls' participation in the show.

Too fucking right, thought Georgie. One of the girls, Jeannie, a raven-haired beauty with a stunningly enhanced chest and a smile to match, was already receiving a bulging weekly postbag that was beginning to attract attention from the company bosses. This brilliant idea would focus all the attention back where it should rightfully be – on Georgie, as the only recognisable star of the show.

Jeannie was already starting to bitch about the orange wig, but fuck her. No one would dare defy the star's wishes. If they wanted to keep the top-rating show, they would have to bow to the brightest, most dynamic star in the firmament, which at the moment was Georgie Brown. For him to switch to another channel would be a disaster for the company.

Georgie's ego, like his mean spirit, was legendary in the business. Behind his back he was the most hated man in television. His ruthless disposal of other performers whose reputations had, at times, threatened to eclipse his own, had become widely known in the world of entertainment. 'Never do anyone a good turn if you could do them a bad one' was Georgie's motto. He didn't need a hired gun to waste the opposition. Georgie did his own dirty work, and enjoyed every moment of it. But his reputation among his own kind was at dramatic odds with the way he was perceived by his adoring public. To them, Georgie was the ultimate Mr Nice Guy, an icon, the person most welcome in the nation's sitting rooms.

His trademark look – a leering, lopsided, impish grin – had the public enraptured, and his admonishing catchphrase, 'Well, you're a mean one,' coupled with another knowing smirk, was the best known on television, and a must for any up-and-coming impressionist.

To his millions of fans he was Sweet Georgie Brown, the nation's darling. To his fellow performers and studio workers, he was an obnoxious tyrant, notorious for his meanness. Even his handful of friends were hard pressed to come up with a single, admirable quality. 'He's a pro' was usually the best anyone could offer.

Colleagues visited him at home, only because they dared not refuse what was tantamount to a royal command, and those who chose to entertain him did so only because they needed his patronage.

He was a true misogynist, a confirmed bachelor, who considered women useful for only one purpose. 'Any woman standing is not in her natural plane,' he would say, with a disarming twinkle. But the women who had experienced him first hand knew that no joke was intended, other than the one on them.

Georgie would never direct a serious comment at a woman. After flashing his famous grin, and offering a quick peck on the cheek, he would thereafter ignore them. Women who came on to him were categorised and rated, and if they were thought sufficiently worthy, would receive an impersonal call from an aide, naming a time and place. If they were unable to adapt to Georgie's schedule, then they were not contacted a second time.

There were plenty of others, all dying to take their place. Not that Georgie was particularly good-looking. His nose was too long, his eyes too close together and his hair was receding. Add to that a middle-aged paunch which he kept tightly corseted while shooting the show, and breath permanently reeking of brandy and cigars, and he didn't really seem to have an awful lot going for him.

Apart from one thing… a single attribute.

What Georgie Brown did have, in spades, was that most potent, tantalising and seductive quality of all – star appeal. He had 'it'. Georgie Brown was a megastar, a household name, spanning the generation gap and transmitting his magic appeal to mothers and daughters alike.

There had been hundreds, possibly thousands of one-night stands over the years, but only one woman, Alison Best, a 45-year-old alcoholic, had come close to sharing Georgie's life, and only intermittently at that. Her successful singing career crashed when the number of drinks she needed to enable her to face an audience started to affect the key and the lyrics. Much of the time she lived alone in a tiny flat in West London. Once there had been a penthouse in Mayfair with a hot tub on the open patio, surrounded by servants and hangers-on. But that was long gone, along with the mink coats, the jewellery and even her platinum albums, which had been sold off to subsidise the dwindling royalty cheques in order to pay the rent and the unrelenting booze bill.

Having a place of her own, however cell-like, helped her to preserve her fragile independence. But now there was nothing left to sell. All she had left of any value were a few fading photographs and memories.

She had even considered offering herself for money. She laughed inwardly at the preposterous notion while recognising, deep down, that this ridiculous scenario might soon have to become sordid reality. Surely there must be some old fan who would still pay handsomely for the pleasure of sleeping with his idol from the past. But that step, she knew, would take her into another world, one of depravity, humiliation and utter hopelessness.

Desperation was pushing her towards that final indignity but, so far, she had managed to hold back. An easier alternative, she knew, was to sell her story. Newspaper reporters were forever pestering her and offering huge sums to tell all about her downfall and her relationship with Georgie. Yet to Alison, going down that road was just as great a betrayal of her beliefs and integrity as selling her body. It was simply another route to the same, ultimate humiliation, exposing her soul and her shame to a sensation-seeking public. *But fucking hell*, she told herself, angrily, that morning, *what could be more disgusting and degrading than living and sleeping with Georgie Brown?*

Her on-off relationship with Georgie had lasted now for 20 years, although she had to admit it was not a relationship which showed a great deal of promise. Any dreams she may once have had about a future filled with happiness, and leading to an old age of mutual contentment, had long since turned to nightmares. She lived with Georgie when it suited him, and until the rows became so painful and humiliating that she would scurry off to her kennel, as she called her home, to recover emotionally.

Their liaison, she often told him, would have provided a lifetime's study for a psychologist. It survived on a hellish maelstrom of love and hate, dependency and contempt, abuse and ridicule.

'I wish to fuck she would just top herself,' Georgie would whine to his cronies.

'He treats me worse than a whore,' Alison would sob in drunken self-pity to her few remaining close confidantes. 'All he wants me for is dirty sex and something to wipe his feet on. I would love to watch him rot in hell.'

But their tragic, emotional roller-coaster showed no real sign of easing off, and in her heart she knew that eventually it was destined to engulf them both. They had become an emotionally unstable and destructive habit, one to which they were both still irresistibly drawn like moths to a flame.

As with most bad habits, theirs was overwhelmingly addictive. Thus they hurtled onwards towards disaster, neither of them wanting openly to recognise either the course they were on or having the desire or will to break free.

Currently, Alison was staying in Georgie's luxurious bachelor apartment in Marylebone High Street. She had managed to stagger the few steps from the bedroom to the kitchen, and was coughing her way through her second cigarette of the day while she waited for the kettle to boil. There was a faint hope that the tea might ease some of the pounding in her head.

A quilted dressing gown, open at the front, exposed sagging flesh and the onset of fat and cellulite, a legacy of a lifetime's boozing and unhealthy eating. Some days she would forget to eat entirely but, by some weird quirk of nature, the deterioration of her body was evident only from the neck down. Her face had, miraculously, survived. Two decades of totally unrestrained self-abuse had left not a single wrinkle or blemish on her darkly, exotically beautiful face. Her brown eyes still harboured a mischievous twinkle, a wanton promise, and her full, sensual mouth offered the possibility of deep, soft kisses. She wore no make-up and had allowed her dirty blonde hair to grow in its natural, wildly curling style.

Alison had dropped her personal trainer along with her singing career and believed this was the real cause of the 40-odd pounds she had accumulated in all the wrong places. She also blamed gravity, which she claimed pulled her arse, tits and gut towards her feet. Her drunken logic invariably drove Georgie wild with exasperation and he would inevitably end up screaming that she should therefore remedy the situation by walking on her fucking hands.

That morning she was doing something else which infuriated him: opening his mail. Her drink-affected reasoning had an answer for that, too. If she permitted him to have access to the secret places of her body and endured his foul perversions, then he should allow her to share the secrets of his morning mail.

This morning, disappointingly, there were only two letters, one a bill from a local restaurant where Georgie had an account, and a large cream envelope with an impressive logo of an oil rig on the reverse side.

First making a mental note to interrogate Georgie as to whom he had been entertaining so regularly and lavishly at the restaurant – his inherent meanness made this a significant departure from the norm – Alison turned her attention to the more intriguing of the two letters.

Moments later, emitting girlish squeals of delight, she scuttled back to the bedroom, where Georgie, still naked, was in the ensuite bathroom having a pee.

Seemingly unaware of what he was doing, Alison grabbed him by the arm and tried to spin him round. The resultant arc of yellow urine sprayed up and across the wall and onto her dressing gown.

She stared down at the foul-smelling wetness beginning to soak through her robe, temporarily silenced, but still clinging to his arm. Georgie switched hands and redirected himself back towards the toilet bowl. 'For fuck's sake, you stupid cow! Can't you see I'm in the middle of taking a piss? What the hell's got into you?'

Then, with a suspicious frown – the one he usually used on contestants temporarily flummoxed by one of his embarrassingly personal questions – he said, 'You're not on the fucking scotch already, are you?'

'Don't be stupid, Georgie,' Alison admonished him. 'And try and control that thing of yours… I swear, if it comes near me again, I'll cut the bugger off.'

Then she remembered why she was there and began to dance excitedly around the bathroom. 'Guess what… we've been invited to dinner at Belmont Place by Peter Flint the billionaire. Princess Kate is going to be there… and what's her name, the Prime Minister's wife.'

'June Temple,' murmured Georgie, whose fascination with politics was secondary only to his primary obsession – himself.

'That's right!' nodded Alison. 'Her. But think about it… Princess Kate. We might even be seated next to her. Ooh, it's going to be fantastic.'

Georgie snatched the letter away from her. 'What makes you think I'd take you with me even if I did decide to go?' he snarled. 'I'd be much better off asking a real lady to join me… someone sober.'

Alison grabbed the top of the letter with both chubby hands and waved it in front of his face. 'The hell you will,' she spat, twisting her features in rage. 'It has my fucking name on the invitation as well. So what do you say about that, Sweet Georgie fucking Brown? Read it and weep, you bastard! Before you dare to think about taking another bitch with you, then just you be warned that I'm going to be there as well. So think how you're going to fucking explain that one to the Prime Minister's wife and the other stuck-up twats.'

Georgie stared at the two names printed on the invitation and saw immediately that Alison was right. How it had happened was anybody's guess. 'Then I won't go,' he said. 'How about that?'

'Do as you like,' sneered Alison. 'But I'm going, and if you don't escort me then I shall spend the whole of dinner telling them about the real Georgie Brown, the sick, fucking pervert I share a bed with.'

One thing Georgie had developed in his early career was the ability to perform complete about-turns when tricky situations called for them. It was just one of those occasions right now, he recognised, and he reached, mentally, for the right contingency plan.

Flashing his 1,000-volt grin, the one he normally reserved for winning contestants or the company's programme controller, Georgie let go of the invitation, pulled Alison towards him and wrapped her in his naked arms. 'Of course we'll go together,' he said, in what he believed was his most seductive voice, 'and you'll be the belle of the ball.' *And the next time I get your fat arse out of here, you are never, ever going to move back in, you fucking slapper*, he promised himself.

'It's going to be just like old times,' cooed Alison in his ear. 'We'll knock 'em dead.' But as she looked over his shoulder, her face had become contorted with hatred. *And after that, I'll call my old friend at the* News of the World *and agree to do the kiss-and-tell story of the century,* she promised herself. *But first, I'll get the pig to pay for a couple of Botox sessions and maybe a touch of collagen. And while he's at it, he can get me a really amazing gown to cover up the rest. That way, I'll look absolutely stunning for the tabloids… 'tragically beautiful', they'll say …* and Alison began to smile.

EIGHT

Bobby Temple sprawled back casually in his old leather armchair in the Downing Street office. He was jacketless and the top two buttons of his white shirt were undone. One leg was hooked over the chair's padded arm and in his right hand he held a heavy, cut-glass tumbler half filled with Famous Grouse whisky. A swathe of spring sunshine streaming through the tall, south-facing windows caught him in its spotlight glare and set golden highlights glinting in his light-brown hair.

Portraits and busts of some of his predecessors looked impassively down from the walls and pedestals. *Like judges from history*, thought Bobby. *With not very much to impress them*, he concluded, eyeing the quartet who had hurried here after receiving his summons.

Lined up in front of him, in plain wooden carvers, four members of his Cabinet sat for all the world like students arraigned before their professor. The most relaxed of these was Jack Benson, who, following Bobby's lead, had shed his jacket and hung it on the back of his chair, showing off wide gold-and-silver braces depicting medieval knights. His glass contained iced Welsh spring water.

Foreign Secretary Alex Turner and Home Secretary John Potter wore dark suits — neither of which, Benson noted with amusement, were bespoke. Both had refused a drink and both sat awkwardly, almost on the edges of their seats, waiting to learn why their master had summoned them. Both were clearly nervous.

Defence Secretary Peter Westcroft, a dinosaur from the Callaghan Government of the 1980s and self-appointed baton-carrier for what remained of the extreme left wing of the party, sat next to them, looking more at ease. *Too close to complete senility to be apprehensive*, thought Bobby, who had briefed him ahead of the others. A necessary precaution, he had decided, because Westcroft often had difficulty in grasping hold of complex scenarios at the first time of telling.

Bobby had plucked him from backbench obscurity and given him ministerial and Cabinet rank. It was in recognition of his talents, Westcroft told his friends and constituents. 'In gratitude for his servility and unquestioning obedience,' the Prime Minister told Jack Benson.

His role, a cameo part in today's Commons drama, would see him promoted to leading man tomorrow, when Bobby had chosen to raise the curtain on a portentous new era in Britain's history. The Defence Minister would be guaranteed a widespread, if not completely enthusiastic press, after his ministerial maiden speech, predicted Bobby.

After his briefing, Peter Westcroft had, as foreseen by the Prime Minister, produced neither comment nor objection, but in a memorable display of toadying had pledged his absolute support.

The four men, each in his own way, were already aware that the Bobby Temple stretched out in front of them was no longer the same party leader who had led them to election victory just five weeks earlier. The boyish charm and reassuring smile had been replaced, at least in private, by a ruthless, uncompromising determination and an unsettling, patronising sneer, which he no longer made any attempt to hide. The promise of gentle Socialist reform had became a strident demand for radical change.

Almost everyone in the Parliamentary Labour Party knew that events in Russia had caused Bobby to rethink and reschedule his agenda – to speed up certain changes, and to scrap some of his softer reforms in favour of more Draconian measures. Most of his ministers could not even imagine the end game towards which their leader was now hauling the party, and the majority of them weren't particularly concerned. They recognised that it was no longer a party agenda based on conference resolutions or manifesto pledges, but had become a personal and secret agenda in which the party faithful had never been involved and which would never be open to debate by his ministers or anyone else. But, again, this was not cause, they believed, for any great concern. After all, Bobby had led them to an unprecedented victory and they were prepared, at the moment, to trust him with the future.

Nevertheless, Bobby's opening bombshell, concerning the latest blockade of Channel ports by French farmers and lorry drivers, was enough to make these key members of his Cabinet suddenly pay much closer attention. It was the first such blockade to take place since the new Government had come to office, and press and TV pundits had been speculating all morning as to how Bobby would deal with the situation. The consensus was that, like all previous British Prime Ministers, he would send a strong protest to the French Government and remind them of their obligation to keep roads open, leaving British drivers to continue on their way as best they could.

The Prime Minister's actual response left two of his Ministers sitting, literally, open-mouthed. Jack Benson sipped his water and seemed content just to observe the others' reactions. Peter Westcroft simply grinned obsequiously and nodded vigorously.

John Potter was the first to recover. 'But the French will never stand for it,' he warned, his panic driving his voice up half an octave, the thin, breathy tone contrasting oddly with his sheer size. He was broad-shouldered with thick thighs, forearms and wrists. Even his fingers were wide, though stubby and calloused, a memento of his days as a steelworker. His broad boxer's nose, deeply cleft chin and wild, bushy eyebrows somehow combined to give him a solid, dependable look. A shock of unruly, greying hair around a Franciscan-style bald patch added an almost benevolent touch.

The Prime Minister, however, was in far from benevolent mood. 'Then it will cost them dearly. I told you the other day that the time for sweet-talking the French is over. No more "Mr Nice Guy"... now we use the big stick.'

'But how the hell do you intend to make it work?'

'If you had been paying proper attention, you would know,' said Bobby sharply. 'If all of you do exactly as you're told and play your parts in the right way, then I expect a satisfactory result. Leave it to me to deal with *les grenouilles*.' His stare was implacable.

Westcroft shifted uncomfortably, nodded sagely, then looked baffled, shooting a quizzical look at Jack Benson.

'Frogs... ' Benson said helpfully, smirking patronisingly at his colleague.

'Ah... yes, of course... ' Westcroft muttered, still clearly struggling to take in the significance of the Prime Minister's words.

Bobby turned to Alex Turner, who had remained silent throughout. 'I intend to make this announcement in an hour's time, during PMQs.'

Prime Minister's Question Time, the weekly half-hour sessions in which the Prime Minister could be quizzed on any subject by his fellow MPs, made him the most accountable politician in the world. Bobby was determined that these public and often embarrassing inquisitions would be curtailed in the very near future. But that moment would have to wait.

'While I'm answering questions in the Chamber, I want you to get the French Ambassador over to the Foreign Office, and leave him in no doubt about my intentions. I've printed out exactly what I want you to say, and I don't want you to deviate from that by a word. Is that clear?'

'But... '

'No "buts", Alex. The time for "buts" is long gone. You will do this for me without fucking up... or would you rather I found someone else to handle it?'

To Turner, the pale-blue eyes seemed to bore deep into his skull and he found himself physically trembling. He looked at his watch. It was 11am. Five minutes to walk back to the Foreign Office, then less than an hour to summon the French Ambassador and get him to his office. It would be unthinkable to let Monsieur Lecomte hear the news before he arrived at the Foreign Office.

He stood and extended his hand towards his boss. 'It'll be done just as you want it, Bobby,' he said, struggling, and failing, to keep the tremor out of his voice. He managed to look the Prime Minister in the eye as he took the prepared statement and even attempted a weak grin. 'Make *les grenouilles* hopping mad, eh?'

'Good boy,' said Bobby, in his most patronising tone. 'You'd better run along and get things started,' and he shooed Turner from the room with his free hand while taking a sip of scotch from his glass in the other.

'Now, John... ' He turned to face the still seated Home Secretary. 'You don't have any problems with this, do you?' John Potter shook his head violently from side to side, not quite able to trust himself to speak without stammering. He hated himself – and Temple – for the effect the Prime Minister was having on him, but was far too terrified to stand up to him.

'You know exactly what you have to say after Jack has given the broad details. Just keep it short and sweet.' He delivered his orders in a tone of supreme authority.

'What about questions?' Potter's eyes darted about the room, unwilling to be snared by those of his master, but he eventually succumbed. The pale-blue orbs bore into him, as Temple smiled. There wasn't a trace of the smile in his eyes, however.

'You know the form, John.' He paused. 'Long overdue... numbers left to dwindle to disgraceful danger levels by uncaring Tories... pay allowed to fall below a reasonable amount in real terms... the thin blue line stretched almost to breaking point after scandalous years of Tory neglect and apathy. All the usual crap.'

He stood up abruptly, signalling that the audience was over. 'Get the picture? I'm sure I don't have to spell it out for you. Promise them the fine detail tomorrow. All right?'

Potter nodded. 'Ay, Bobby,' he sighed. 'But I hope to Christ you know what you're at,' he said flatly.

'I do, John.' Bobby took a few paces forward until he was standing over the Home Secretary, who cowered even more pathetically in his chair.

Bobby's downward gaze softened and took on the familiar boyish grin. 'We're about to have some fun, John. So lighten up and enjoy it. That's what being in power is all about. Exercising that power and enjoying all the resulting fun and games. It's time we reminded everyone – our green, warty neighbours included – who gives the orders round here,' he said cheerfully. 'And let's not forget that it's time for the Yankees to doodle their last dandy. They'll know soon enough that their bucks stop with me now. The honeymoon's over, John. No more time for trivia. Today we start to govern, and I promise you that everyone is going to sit up and take notice.

'The Tories kindly left us with a huge war chest full of surplus cash. It could, of course, be used to buy us the next election by augmenting pensions and allowances and lowering taxes. But spent my way, it will keep us in power for the next century and beyond.'

Quickly fastening the top button of his shirt, and sliding the knot of his tie into position, Bobby slipped into the jacket Jack Benson was already holding out for him and strode towards the door, his blue eyes blazing with an almost evangelistic fervour.

'Let's go and raise some blood pressure,' he laughed, and led the way along the winding corridor towards the front door and Downing Street, where a black, chauffeur-driven Daimler limousine with tinted windows was waiting.

In their long and extremely eventful relationship, Benson had rarely thought to question Temple's judgement or motives, but now he found himself, for the second time in a week, looking at his friend and mentor with a strangely unfamiliar feeling of unease. That June Temple shared his forebodings had considerably escalated his own concerns, but that didn't mean he was ready to jump ship immediately.

He shook his head in annoyance. He had followed Bobby Temple this far and the rewards had been beyond his wildest dreams. He pushed the momentary doubts out of his mind and immersed himself in pleasant anticipation of the drama about to unfold in the Commons.

Virtually every seat in the historic chamber was occupied, and the public and press galleries were packed. Rumours emanating from the Downing Street spin factory had let it be known that momentous events were about to unfold. In the offices at Westminster, a thousand civil servants crowded around Ministry television sets and national newspaper editors reclined in executive armchairs immersed in the preamble to the live feed on their flat-screen TVs, surrounded by excited minions.

The word was that something big was about to go down, and no one wanted to miss the moment.

A few seconds after midday, the newly appointed and inexperienced Leader of the Opposition, Michael Rushton, rose to enquire what the Prime Minister proposed to do, if anything, about the disgraceful conduct of the French farmers and lorry drivers who had completely barricaded all exits and entrances to the Channel ports in protest at rising fuel prices.

'The Prime Minister has talked tough in the past when he was not in a position to take action,' Rushton said mockingly. He was a big man with a strong West Country burr, and he now thumped the Dispatch Box in front of him and waved his order paper at Bobby Temple who was 10 feet away on the Government front bench. 'Now that it's up to him, I wonder if we can expect to see him put his money where his mouth is and turn tough talking into tough action?'

As the Tories brayed derision from the Opposition benches, Temple took his time stepping up to the Dispatch Box.

An Opposition voice called out, 'Cat got your tongue?' and another yelled, 'No... he's got a frog in his throat,' which raised a gale of laughter from the benches opposite, and even caused the Prime Minister to smile darkly.

'I want to make my position absolutely clear on this present situation,' he began quietly. 'The French Government's attitude is politically and morally indefensible. This crisis, like similar ones in the past, is not of our making.' His voice had begun to rise.

'It is – and there is no doubt in my mind about this – the deliberate policy of the French Government to turn a blind eye to the iniquitous activities of these habitually selfish miscreants – the thugs and trouble-makers – which positively encourages them to defy the right of passage through their ports of Her Majesty's subjects.

'Those who make laws should not break laws,' he roared. 'Not to respect the wisdom in this old adage is a perilous mistake which could easily lead to anarchistic minds imagining they had the support of such a Government. I want the French Government to understand that we have the will and, I trust, the full backing of this Parliament to protect the rights of our people.

'Democracies are naturally peace-loving, but that does not mean we will tolerate being pushed around. It is time for us to defend our way of life as a nation and ensure international law should prevail over the use of force.'

Bobby paused to sip from a glass of water. He was speaking, as usual, without notes. There was absolute silence in the Chamber.

'At this precise moment, my Right Honourable Friend, the Foreign Secretary is delivering an ultimatum to the French Ambassador.'

At this there was the sound of sudden, muffled gasps and a low whispering rippled around the Chamber. Words like 'ultimatum', coupled with 'Ambassador', were sufficient to send a chill down the spines of many of the assembled Members of Parliament.

'Three successive Conservative Prime Ministers over 13 years have stood impotently by, while the French have repeatedly broken international laws and disrupted the legal passage through their ports of British citizens and our goods. Disruptions that have cost this nation and its citizens hundreds of millions of pounds; disruptions caused by the deliberate and lawless destruction of British property by French rioters, aided and abetted by the French Government.'

This blunt accusation brought gasps of astonishment from some MPs and cheers and foot stamping from the more militant element on both sides of the House. Bobby looked around the Chamber and continued: 'Not one French rioter has ever been arrested, charged or taken to court for any of these illegal activities. The French Government, who signed the Treaty of Rome and agreed to keep open its country's roads for the free passage of vehicles of all nationalities, has not once attempted to act under this law, or in any way fulfil its legal obligations to the international community.'

This brought cries of 'Shame' from the backbenchers.

'The French have flouted international law and neighbourly decency for far too long. We are therefore, today, informing the French Government that we consider them responsible for all losses and delays experienced by our citizens during this dispute, and until such losses and compensation for delays are reimbursed by them, in full, I have instructed the British authorities to seize all French vehicles in this country and hold them here indefinitely.'

Some MPs on both sides of the House cheered loudly and stamped their feet. Others offered muted calls of 'Hear, hear'. But many sat in their places in stunned silence.

'The liberty of the individual throughout the Continent, as well as from Britain, to travel unheeded is paramount. It is in defence of this liberty that I have taken this action today.'

As the Prime Minister sat down pandemonium broke out in the Chamber. Order papers were brandished, along with shouts of congratulation, admonishment, disbelief and sheer astonishment from both sides of the House. Michael Rushton rose amid calls for 'Order... ' from the Speaker. It was several minutes before the hubbub died down completely.

'Am I to understand,' he asked, 'that the Right Honourable Gentleman has already told the French to either pay up or have their transport in this country seized? Are there to be no diplomatic attempts to resolve this matter before resorting to threats?'

Bobby waved him down and returned to the Dispatch Box. 'As usual, the Right Honourable Gentleman, the Leader of the Opposition, has failed to understand a statement in plain English.'

Much laughter and jeers from the Labour benches.

'I have not told the French to pay up or have their transport in this country seized. I have told them unequivocally that their transport here *will* be seized and will only be released when they have repaid in full all our losses and compensation. They have repeatedly ignored normal diplomatic efforts to get them to intervene in these disruptive and costly demonstrations. A strongly worded message to the Elysée Palace sent more than 18 hours ago has, as yet, not even received an acknowledgement.

'Our predecessors were far too weak and appeasing, and because of it, the French have become used to our accepting their failure to discipline the bullyboy farmers and lorry drivers, whose unchecked tantrums against their own government have become a European disgrace. I believe the stick and not the carrot is the right way to get results in this case, and have acted accordingly.'

Twenty minutes later, Bobby Temple left the Chamber to the cheers of his supporters, the full backing of the Opposition and qualified blessing of the Liberal Democrats.

As editors across the country cleared the front pages of evening and daily newspapers, the Commons still had one further surprise in store for its members. After Prime Minister's Question Time, the Speaker announced there would be a special statement from the Chancellor of the Exchequer.

Noisy speculation over the possible French reaction to the Prime Minister's pre-emptive ultimatum gave way to expectant silence as Jack Benson casually propped himself on one elbow at the Dispatch Box and gazed around the Chamber. Those nearby saw that, like the Prime Minister, he had no leather-bound folder or notes of any kind in front of him. He also began quietly.

'The Prime Minister has today declared a stand, by this Government, in defence of law and order. We want it to be known that this theme is one of the most important of all our policies, and will include a very positive assault on the criminal element in our own society.

'In the coming days, the Home Secretary will be declaring a whole series of tough new laws and more appropriate – by which I mean more severe – punishment for criminals. Let there be no misunderstanding – we are determined to reduce the awful incidence of crime in our streets and in our homes – a figure which has increased annually under our predecessors, but which we are committed to cut drastically.

'In order to help us win the battle against crime, I propose to increase the wages of the police, the armed forces and the prison service – of all ranks – by 25 per cent across the board effective from midnight tonight.

'This will assist the Home Secretary and the Minister of Defence in recruiting 50,000 new policemen and women and 50,000 new members of the armed forces over the next 12 months. My Right Honourable Friends will be giving more detailed information on these recruitment plans later today.'

As the hubbub started up again, even louder than before, Jack Benson slipped out of the rear of the Chamber and headed back towards Downing Street.

Well, Bobby, he mused, *you've bought yourself the loyalty of the Police and the Army. Now we'll wait and see how far they choose to follow you.*

He found Temple already back in his office, his jacket and tie removed, sprawled in the same armchair and with his glass recharged. He motioned to the side table which contained a well-stocked bar. 'Help yourself to a drink... a real one this time. You've earned it. So far, the TV people seem to be in favour. I suppose that's because nobody likes the French. Trouble is, they just won't play the game unless you give them a whack. Agincourt and Waterloo taught us that. The moment you threaten their creature comforts, they roll over and stick out their tummies to be tickled. Hitler recognised it and kept them performing tricks and fetching sticks for six years.

'Sky News is using words like "daring" and "decisive". Nobody seems to have got a reaction from the French yet, though Alex said poor Monsieur Lecomte almost fainted with shock when he gave him the bad news. It took Alex ten minutes to convince him he was being serious. He thought the President might even want to withdraw him, so Alex said to make sure he wasn't travelling home in a French car.'

Bobby grinned broadly: 'I guess this means that Alex is on board for the whole ride.'

'Whatever the whole ride entails,' added Jack softly. 'I still don't know all the details and I've been part of the team for years.'

'I promise you'll be the first to know everything,' said Bobby, chinking glasses with his deputy. 'We are going to have a Britain to be proud of. Today it was time to stick it to the Frogs. Tomorrow we deal with the Yanks. They are going to holler and scream and tell us how we've broken their hearts. But they're going to get what's coming to them. And it's about fucking time!'

NINE

June Temple's sapphire-blue eyes darted around the drawing room of the Downing Street apartment, finally fixing on her husband. Now in her early forties, She was still stunningly beautiful and her long legs, bare beneath the short grey skirt, were smooth and unblemished.

His wife's powerful sexual allure failed, as usual, to register with Bobby Temple, whose own libido, never a match for hers, had sunk without trace. But he did note the challenge in her look and the slight flaring of her nostrils, the unmistakable signal that she was more than just a little pissed off. She rested her hands on a tall-backed leather Chesterfield, facing him on the opposite side of the room. It was a position Bobby had seen her adopt during television debates, usually standing behind a lectern, when about to take on a difficult or hostile interviewer and he prepared to defend himself.

'I'm never going to be able to think of this place as home,' she opened flatly. 'I wish to God we had never given up the house. I felt comfortable there... I belonged.'

Bobby took advantage of her pause and spoke up, his face arranged in a sympathetic-cum-conciliatory smile. 'I'm sure we'll all get used to it in time,' he offered sweetly.

'You don't get it, do you?' his wife interrupted, her eyes beginning to flash with anger. 'I know you're in your element here. This is the nerve centre, where the commands will go out that will create history, change the world.

'But that's not the way that I or our son see it. This is not home it's like living in a bloody museum. The pictures are on loan from art galleries. I know they are all masterpieces and probably priceless, but I didn't get to choose them and they're not to my taste. Neither is the furniture. It belongs in the V and A. And the plumbing was probably put in by Gladstone.'

'You can change anything… everything,' said Bobby quickly. 'Call in the designers today. Redo all the bathrooms. And there are 10,000 paintings in the National Gallery alone which… '

She cut him short. 'Christ, that's your answer to everything, isn't it? The instant fix. The Bobby Temple magic make-over. Well, there's more to making a home than putting up new pictures.

'There's the fact that you and I are becoming strangers to one another. God knows we saw little of one another before the Election, but at least I had my friends living nearby. And David could cycle round the corner to see his friends as well, whenever he fancied it. You don't get many 15-year-old boys and girls cycling down Downing Street to drop in for a game or a chat in the evening. And the few friends of mine who have ventured here and gone through the rigmarole of getting past the security gates and the police and the bodyguards and the bloody doorman are not very keen to repeat the whole bloody ridiculous exercise.

'I could even cope with you not making love to me for months on end… ' She paused. 'No, that's a lie… I can tell you right now that I'm not very happy about that situation, not happy at all.'

She had even begun to suspect there was another woman in Bobby's life. One of the dozens of gorgeous-looking, dynamic political groupies, who had found semi-bogus jobs as part-time researchers or public relations consultants in and around the Commons. But after months of cloak-and-dagger-style investigations and endless questioning, she had been forced to the equally depressing conclusion that Bobby and she were hopelessly sexually mismatched. He just didn't share the same needs. In fact, his lovemaking had tailed off dramatically within weeks of their return from honeymoon, before she even knew she had become pregnant.

Somehow, she still managed to partly satisfy her own undiminished and fundamental need for sex by using a vibrator. But it wasn't enough. She craved the deep abandonment, the affection and the closeness that the sharing of sexual intimacy brought.

Yet whenever she had tried to tackle him about the absence of lovemaking in their marriage, he fobbed her off with excuses about his tiredness and his preoccupation with the party, and switched subjects.

She had actually toyed with the idea of dissolving powdered Viagra into his bedtime drink last thing at night when the usual gambits of parading in skimpy, sexy underwear, wearing exotic perfumes, or confronting him totally naked had failed.

'But it's not just our dormant sex life that's the problem,' she hurried on, to avoid Bobby visibly shutting off, as he did whenever she plucked up the courage to confront this issue. 'I barely see you at all now and, when we do meet, we don't really speak to one another any more. You just mumble things you think fit into a domestic context – that's not sharing a life.

'I don't know what you're thinking any more, what your plans are for the future. And I'm not just talking about the bloody country now... I'm talking about us. There was a time when you wouldn't mention a new policy idea to anyone until we'd talked it out together first. Now, I have only a vague notion of what's going on. You're becoming a stranger and I don't like it. We went into this marriage as equal partners. Now I'm not sure if we're even on the same team. I can't remember the last time you said you loved me. You used to say it all the time at the beginning. And you used to want to make love to me as well.

'What's happened? Don't you love me any more? What have I done? Is there someone else?'

Bobby reached out his arms, palms towards her, as though trying to calm a petulant child. He had seriously underestimated how unhappy she had become and mentally upbraided himself for letting things go this far. Tonight he would fuck her stupid, he decided, no matter how revolting he now found it.

'Darling, I know it's been tough for you... ' He smiled wryly and moved towards her, wrapping his arms around her. 'But it's early days and there have been a thousand and one things to take care of. I haven't been able to discuss all of them with you because, if I did, there would be no time left to run the country.'

Bobby lowered his voice to a soothing, hypnotic tone, as he had often used in his early days to pacify the more volatile members of his campaign team.

'I promise you that as soon as we're settled in and everything is running smoothly, I'll be able to spend a lot more time with you. And if you or David are still homesick in three months, then we'll move back into the house in Pimlico and I'll use this place just as an office.'

He stroked her hair gently with one hand, tucking a stray blonde wisp behind her ear, then lifted her face up to look at him, cupping her chin.

Bobby was still a charismatically attractive man and, when he turned on the boyish charm, June still found him very hard to resist. She found herself smiling, despite the inner hostility she still felt towards him, and Bobby started to relax.

'This business with the French... ' she said, abruptly changing the subject. 'I know it's just a storm in a teacup, but are you sure you haven't over-reacted?'

Bobby laughed, feeling on safer ground. 'Didn't you see the news this morning? They've already sent the *gendarmes* in and the barricades are coming down. The batons were in action and some of those bullyboys are going to wake up in a cell with pretty sore heads. What's more, the Spanish and the Italians are loving it. They've both suffered in the past at the hands of the French farmers, having grape and olive trucks overturned at the borders and set on fire.

'Neither felt strong enough to take on the French alone, but now that I've made a stand, they have come in 100 per cent behind me.'

June still looked troubled. 'It seems so unlike you to take such a right-wing stance,' she said. 'And this business with the Americans... have you thought it through from all the angles?'

Bobby's gentle features hardened in an instant. His eyes narrowed and his jaw momentarily clenched. 'The people in this country have been starved of strong leadership for far too long,' he said sharply. 'I need to demonstrate that, in electing me, they have chosen the right man. To the French, I'm a bloody pain in the arse. But this morning, to the people of this country, I'm a bloody hero. The *Sun's* headline today was "TEMPLE ORDERS FROGS TO HOP IT"... Everyone knows now that I'm not going to stand for their bullshit any longer. Or anyone else's, for that matter.'

The smile returned to his face. 'We don't intend to go any further into Europe. You know that's the official party policy and I thought you agreed with me on that.'

June placed a hand on his arm. 'I do Bobby. That's exactly what I think. But it's your plans for the Americans I'm not so sure about. Of course we want to be free of outside pressures, but I'm also aware that America's commercial interests are linked inextricably to our financial, industrial and political strategies. But is this the right way to go about things? We risk losing all of their support and friendship over this. Mightn't we be using a sledgehammer to crack a very small nut when other, more discreet methods might achieve the same result?'

Bobby took her hand in his and, summoning up the energy to produce his most sincere tone, looked her directly in the eyes.

'June, my darling, being too closely linked with the Americans will cost us a great deal more than publicly pissing them off. More than half the countries of the world are passionately anti-American and can offer us a great deal if we are seen to sever the so-called "special relationship" between us. Just wait and see...' he purred, trying to boost her confidence. 'Ivan Brekov, for one, is going to be right behind us on this one.'

June's uneasiness increased visibly at the mention of the Russian leader's name. 'He's going to have his hands far too full with domestic problems to spare any thought for the outside world,' she reminded him. 'He wants us at his May Day parade for the kudos we can give to him. Please be careful, Bobby. Ivan has no scruples and no loyalty to anyone outside Russia. Don't let him use us, will you?'

Bobby's thoughts were racing as he reviewed his conversations with Ivan Brekov. They had been in virtual shorthand, referring to ideas drafted two decades ago at university. He doubted there was any way June could have overheard and worked out what was being planned. He dismissed it as being her uncanny political sixth sense at play.

'There's no question of that happening,' he replied lightly. 'I'll handle Ivan the way I always have. But don't forget, when they start to develop their oil and mineral reserves, Russia will become a staggeringly wealthy nation.' His eyes sparkled with conviction. 'I intend to see that British business gets the cream of the orders to help them achieve their goals and gets most of the rewards and credit for dragging the Soviets into the twenty-first century.

'After May Day, we will have a favoured trading agreement with Russia which will be the envy of the whole world, particularly the Americans.'

June removed her hand from his. There was something about his zeal which had triggered a primitive instinct in her, suddenly making the hairs on the back of her neck tingle with discomfort.

'Don't plan to change this country so much it becomes unrecognisable,' she said quietly. 'Remember, our son has to grow up here.'

Then she abruptly reached behind him for a large, gold-embossed card, which she had placed on the mantelpiece earlier. 'There's an invitation here from Peter Flint for me to attend a dinner at Belmont Place on the 27th. It's to discuss a new Arts Trust he is setting up. It doesn't mention you, you'll be pleased to hear, so you won't have to sit there and make trivial small-talk. But I will be accepting the invitation.'

'Not my cup of tea,' Bobby agreed readily, pleased to change the subject. 'Though I know you'll have a good time. I'm sure that randy old sod fancies you something rotten, so don't let him corner you alone.'

If he did, I don't think I'd remember what to do, June thought, and shocked herself by a sudden, overwhelming urge to be swept up in someone's arms and become the focus once again of a man's passion.

TEN

Wayne Bryan was short, bald, overweight and the biggest-earning singer in the world. Royalties from his records, a six-country tour and merchandising had added over £25 million to his bank balance in the past year alone, and his lifetime earnings topped £400 million.

Wayne was a superstar. He was also arrogant, rude, cruel and gay and he probably didn't have a single genuine friend in the world. Not that he gave a fuck, as he was happy to tell anyone paid to listen. Even his partner of five years, Lynsey St John Beauchamp – a fashion designer of limited talent – with whom Wayne claimed he had the most amazing sex life, loathed him.

With a full champagne glass in his hand, Wayne was standing in the huge bay window in the first-floor snooker room of his mansion, overlooking Hampstead Heath. He was wearing a rich, burgundy Versace shirt, crimped white jeans and crimson sneakers. The shirt was open at the front to show off the large, diamond-studded platinum ring which pierced the rock star's navel.

The photographer from *Hi There!* magazine was nearly finished, and silently thanking any gods within hearing distance that it was almost time to go. Steve Walls had had it with Mr Wayne fucking Bryan.

They had worked their way from the bedroom, where the singer – through lascivious sucking noises and the crazed fluttering of his heavily mascara'ed eyelashes – tried to lure him onto his emperor-sized, gold pedestal bed. They had then progressed through the drawing room, study, library, dining room, music room and garden, ending up here, in the gentlemen's games room.

Steve's rejection of Wayne's advances in the bedroom had meant that the remainder of the photographic shoot had turned into a nightmare, with Wayne becoming increasingly vulgar.

The photographer pushed a nervous hand through his hair, debating whether to take the picture using the pose Wayne had adopted, or to suggest he move to another part of the room, bending over a shot at the snooker table with the massive and beautiful Adam fireplace in the background.

Professionalism won out. 'I think it would be a terrific shot with you actually at the table, playing... at the end by the fireplace.'

Wayne's small, piggy eyes glinted behind his designer glasses. 'You're becoming really fucking boring, Miss Pushy,' he spat out through flabby, glistening lips. 'What perverted ulterior motive do you have this time? You want to show off my bald head and make me look like a fucking billiard ball, or you want me bending over so you can take me up the arse?'

He sniggered obscenely and then tossed back the whole glass of champagne in a gulp. 'Shoot me here or not at all. And I can tell you now that as soon as you're gone I'm going to be on the phone to Muriel Deeds. If you haven't forgotten, dearie, your publisher and I go back a long way. I'm going to tell her just how fucking amateurish you are. Just another little fairy who begged to suck my cock. She's spending £500,000 for you to do this shoot and she's not going to be happy when I explain how you've fucked it up. Is that all right with you, you little wanker?'

Steve took a slow, deep breath and continued to keep the motorised camera whirring away. 'That's up to you, Mr Bryan. If you are not prepared to pose for the other shot then I think that about wraps it up. I'll get my things together and get out of here.'

Wayne strode over to the open double doors and screamed, 'Leroy, get your fucking black arse up here now!'

Seconds later, the tall, broad-shouldered Jamaican, who had earlier greeted Steve Walls at the front door, bounded up the wide main staircase and paused in the doorway. He wasn't at all out of breath. Wayne Bryan glared at the photographer and told Leroy peevishly, 'Miss Pushy here is about to fucking leave. Make sure she goes without pinching any of the silver.' And he flounced out of the room.

It took Steve ten minutes to collect all his camera and lighting equipment and store it in the boot of his Megane coupé. As he left through the front door for the final time, Leroy pressed a concealed switch, which opened the 10-foot wrought-iron gates, and told Steve, in a deep, velvety voice, 'Don't worry too much about the boss, he can't help being like a bitch on heat... or just a bitch. It's that time of the month, you know... ' and, as he slowly winked his right eye, his mouth broke into a dazzling smile.

Wayne Bryan, meanwhile, had sought out his partner in the study. As always, his flirting with the photographer, followed by the abuse, had made him highly sexually aroused. He found Lynsey going through the morning mail.

'Come on, luv, I feel as horny as hell,' he said, beckoning the younger man with his forefinger. 'Come and do what Daddy likes best.'

'Perhaps Daddy would rather take a look at this first,' said Lynsey, pushing a shock of golden hair off his forehead as he waved a gold-embossed invitation in his free hand. 'Peter Flint wants us to go to dinner.'

Wayne's erection, however, was pressing painfully against his unyielding jeans, and it urged him to action as a higher priority than a dinner invitation – no matter who it was from. The finger still beckoned, but more urgently. 'Fuck that!' he snarled. 'Get your little arse upstairs right now… this won't wait.' And he started marching towards the doorway.

Lynsey continued to wave the invitation. 'According to Flint's accompanying note, two of your favourite girlfriends are going to be there,' he purred.

Wayne turned back. 'Who?'

'Princess Kate and June Temple,' said Lynsey. 'Peter Flint would appreciate your reply as soon as possible. So… d'you want us to go?'

Wayne's cock began to soften, and he suddenly became all businesslike. 'Well, what the hell are you waiting for? Send off an acceptance straight away, and telephone his secretary as well to say we'll be there. Then I'd better phone Kate and see what she's planning to wear… I don't want to clash.'

ELEVEN

When Glen Grant walked into The Ivy restaurant, all conversation ceased. In the Ivy, London's premier eaterie, where celebrities were two a penny and stars all part of the daily menu, this was quite a feat.

But Glen Grant was no ordinary celebrity – he was a megastar, the hottest property in Hollywood for over a decade. And he had become the number-one earner at the box-office.

He stood 6 feet 2 inches from his shaggy blond hair to his cowboy-booted toes. His eyes were slate grey, with flecks of green, and he had a powerful, well-exercised body, his deep golden tan attesting to a life of outdoor activity.

He was the most adored movie star on earth and his big, slightly lop-sided grin, which he almost habitually wore, showed that he knew it and loved every second of it. At 40, he had the world at his feet, and was sufficiently decent not to let that affect him.

Glen nodded to a couple of acquaintances as he and his companion were shown to their half-booth table. The woman with him was a generously proportioned brunette with an ultra-modern, urchin-style haircut which didn't suit her unfashionable, round face. She believed her designer suit and blouse made her look chic, but they were both a size too small and the overall effect emphasised her curves, making her look slightly comic. Today she need not have worried – all eyes were on Glen Grant.

But Helen didn't care. It was she who was sitting with him, and at the best table in The Ivy. They were completely booked up for a fortnight, she had been told when she telephoned for a reservation. But when she had mentioned the name of the man she was entertaining, a table had materialised in an instant. And not just any table, either.

As long as the photographer was outside to take their picture together as they left, this would go down as a 'heaven' day in Helen's diary.

Helen Shakespeare was the chief feature writer for *Hi There!* magazine and Glen had agreed to the rare interview to publicise his new picture, a multi-million-dollar action movie called *No Mission Impossible* in which he played a Special Forces hero.

Glen had taken a classic road to stardom. Spotted by an ad agency talent scout, while working in a Santa Monica bar, he had quickly been signed up by FCUK for a major national hoarding and magazine campaign. This had led to small parts in a couple of daytime soaps and a larger speaking role in a big Hollywood movie. Eventually he had been nominated for an Oscar for Best Supporting Actor. He had been given the leading role in his next three films and they were all smash hits. An Oscar for Best Actor in the film which followed put him right up there with the Hollywood greats.

He had a beach house, a mansion in Laurel Canyon, a ranch house in Palm Springs, drove a red Aston Martin and enjoyed a constant succession of beautiful girlfriends. In fact, he was every inch a movie star.

But this Romeo lifestyle was history, he was telling Helen

over cocktails. For the first time in his life, he was going steady with a girl.

'She's Rachel Friedman,' he told her proudly. 'Though why a beautiful English rose from the Royal Shakespeare Company should chose to hang out with an old-time prairie dog like me I just don't know. But from now on, I intend to be a one-woman man. I'd be a complete idiot if I risked losing her.'

Glen crossed his fingers tightly under the table. Only that morning, before Rachel arrived at the Ritz from Paris, where she had been filming *St Joan*, he had rewarded a young fan, who had managed to sneak up to his suite past all the security people, by letting her give him a blow-job. *But that doesn't count*, he told himself. *It's been proven by a president in a court of law… I never actually had sex with that woman!*

Ironically, at that exact moment, Rachel Friedman, stark naked and with her back arched, was rocking her hips furiously back and forth beneath the pounding cock of the young chauffeur who had just driven her from the airport.

She had watched him eyeing her in the driving mirror all the way from the airport, and had undone two more buttons on her blouse to let more of her cleavage spill into view and *really* give him something to fantasise over.

When they arrived at the hotel and he stepped out to open her door, she saw, as she had expected, that he had a huge hard-on pressing against his black uniform trousers.

'Park this thing, and then bring up this briefcase yourself, in person, to suite 346,' she told him. 'And don't forget to bring this as well,' she added, patting his groin affectionately.

She had hardly let him into the suite before unzipping him and easing his cock into the open. She clutched it in both hands for a moment and then told him, 'Come with me and get your clothes off, fast.'

The chauffer, barely out of his teens, was too stunned to do anything other than obey. It seemed to him that within seconds, he was astride Rachel Friedman – the instantly recognisable actress Rachel Friedman – and thrusting deeply inside her. No foreplay had been necessary as she had been soaking wet with anticipation from the moment he mounted her and she had guided his cock inside.

Now she locked her legs around his waist and almost lifted herself from the bed as she pushed herself more furiously to meet his bucking hips, biting his shoulder savagely so that he screamed along with her as she came with a massive shudder, triggering his own, scalding climax inside her.

Just two minutes later, she was hustling him out of the suite and closing the door in his face without another word being spoken. *Though no doubt he'll have plenty to say to his mates in the pub tonight*, she thought.

Then she hurried over to her briefcase, opened it and removed a tortoiseshell powder compact. Looking around the room, she spotted a large, gold-embossed invitation card that had been slipped into the edge of the mirror above the fireplace.

She placed it on the table and spilled some of the powder from the compact onto the polished surface. Then, with a visiting card from her briefcase, she separated the cocaine into two lines, unscrewed the ink cartridge from a ballpoint pen and used the barrel to sniff a line of the white powder up into each nostril.

As she wiped up the last few grains on her finger and rubbed them absent-mindedly into her gums, she noticed that the invitation was to a dinner being given by Peter Flint at Belmont Place. It was addressed, 'To Glen Grant and partner... '

There was no question in Rachel's mind as to who that would be.

Mmmm, she thought, *is there a current Mrs Flint, or not? Not that it really matters. A billionaire husband would do very nicely, thank you.* Once he was in range, her sexual magnetism and charm would be impossible for him to resist. And Mrs Flint sounded so much better to her than Mrs Grant.

TWELVE

As the Speaker called for order in the House, Bobby Temple strolled unhurriedly to the Dispatch Box, brushed the hair back from his forehead with the fingers of his right hand and waited for the noise to subside.

Once again, the Commons was packed, word having gone around that the Prime Minister was to drop another political bombshell, as he opened this special debate on Defence. Only that morning it had appeared, unannounced, on members' order sheets.

No one professed to know exactly what was going on, but there were a dozen or more different rumours sweeping round Parliament. Though none, Bobby had wagered with his deputy, would have been as wild as the truth that he was about to reveal. It would be, he knew, as much of a shock to his own side as to the Opposition. Only Jack Benson and Peter Westcroft knew the full details, and the secret was safe with them; with Jack because of his loyalty, and with Peter because he was terrified of Bobby's reaction if he so much as breathed a word.

The rest of his party were far too unreliable to be trusted with something this important. Modern Labour resembled nothing so much as a giant sieve, leaking a constant torrent of information to the media. Some, a tiny minority, spilled the beans to reporters because they believed it was for the good of the party. Most did it because they loved to see themselves in print or, preferably, appear on television. Nothing protected the votes back in the constituency more than being on the box, talking knowledgeably about something topical, which is why they were so rarely consulted or informed before a major change in policy.

Bobby held up his hand for silence, and leaned into the Dispatch Box. 'I will preface my main remarks by covering the outcome of the events during the past two days. As I expected and, as some of my honourable friends are by now aware, the French reacted as predicted and, on immediate receipt of our ultimatum, sent in the riot police and had every Channel port open again within two hours. Their apologies, and their assurances that all claims would be settled immediately, persuaded us that on this occasion we need not detain any of their citizens' motor vehicles on this side of the Channel. But they received a strong reminder that this plan would be put into action immediately if similar scenes were to occur, or the penalties remain unpaid.'

This brought a chorus of 'Hear, hear' from both sides of the House.

Bobby waited until there was silence once more. 'The liberty of the individual is paramount and we are convinced that the layer upon layer of unnecessary and restrictive bureaucracy emanating from Brussels is stifling our basic right of freedom. It may be that the idea of the granny state is attractive to many of our neighbours, but we are determined that Britain will remain a free spirit under Modern Labour.

'The moves towards federalism do not find favour with us as a nation. I say now, unequivocally, that we cannot and will not endorse any system that threatens to diminish Britain's sovereignty and its ability to influence events in its own, unique way.

'We feel we are being held back, dragged down, by some of the traditional and emotional ties we have, both with our near neighbours, and with those much further afield, who, while purporting to be our friends, continue to undermine our markets and attempt to influence our economic and political status in ways that always support *their* best interests and not our own.'

His voice had slowly been rising until now he was almost shouting: 'I believe the time has come to say "enough is enough".'

Dramatically, he lowered and deepened his voice. 'We believe that we can perform better on the international stage if we dance to our own tune and no one else's, free of all foreign interference in our national affairs.

'Our soldiers, sailors and airmen perform many valuable duties around the globe against terrorism and in the pursuit of democracy, humanity and fair play, and the protection of our unfortunate and weaker fellow human beings.

'No British member of our armed forces should ever risk his or her life in a situation that has not completely originated or been genuinely supported by our Government and people. For half a century, we have allowed certain foreign Governments to exercise or base their armed forces and, in some cases, weapons of mass destruction, in our home waters, in our air space or on British soil. We believe that this is no longer acceptable if we are to exercise a truly independent role in world affairs.

'We will therefore inform those Governments who have enjoyed the use of our facilities in the past that it will no longer be permitted. There will be no exceptions. This includes the armed forces of the United States, who will be asked to vacate all their British bases forthwith.'

Cheers from the left-wingers of his own party, who had long campaigned to send the Americans packing, were drowned out by shouts of 'Shame', 'Disgusting' and even some of 'Traitor' from the Opposition benches, who had almost all risen to their feet and were giving full vent to their anger.

It took the Speaker more than five minutes to bring a semblance of order to the Chamber. Finally, he was able to ask the Prime Minister to continue.

'I have given the Government's decision on this subject and will now throw it open to debate before a vote. My Right Honourable Friend, the Minister for Defence, will open for the Government, but before that, I must advise you that I intend this Bill to go through successfully and that, by the end of this week, all foreign military personnel will have been given their marching orders.'

Uproar broke out again as Bobby sat down, but he waited only until Peter Westcroft took his place at the Dispatch Box before slipping out through the rear of the Chamber. He didn't need to sit through the ensuing debate. He knew what every man and woman in the House knew just as well. With a clear, overall majority of 70 seats, and an utterly subservient and adoring parliamentary group of members behind him, his wishes would be rubber-stamped before the day was out. To them, Bobby Temple was a god.

He turned to Jack Benson who was matching him stride for stride along the dimly-lit Commons corridor. 'When they think they have God by the toe, they really have the Devil by the fist.'

Benson gave him a puzzled glance.

'It's an old English proverb,' said Bobby, grinning wickedly. 'It means they haven't quite worked out yet who they're really fucking with. But I intend to show them… very soon. The fun has only just started.'

But from Benson's face, it didn't look as though he was yet experiencing much of the PM's promised fun and gaiety.

THIRTEEN

Ashley Luther Bodin MP handed Beverly Gladstone a large gin and tonic the way she liked it, lots of ice and no lemon, and with his free hand reached over the beautifully sculpted curve of her left buttock and picked up the white dice from the backgammon board.

Beverly took the drink and watched the two dice roll to a halt.

'Jesus, Ashley,' she said with a giggle, 'you don't give me a second to catch my breath. You're so bleeding eager to beat the crap out of me!'

The broad Cockney accent was at unexpected variance with her low, husky voice, classically etched profile and milk chocolate-coloured skin. Beverly Gladstone was a devastatingly beautiful, black model, tall and slim, with exquisitely full breasts. Her straight, ebony hair was cut sharply and expensively along her neck line by Big John, London's most sought-after hair stylist, and her jet-black eyes, flecked with dancing, diamond sparkles, were set wide above a straight, aristocratic nose. She was blessed with a sensational face, made all the more beguiling by what had been described by one besotted critic as 'the widest smile in London'.

She was not wearing a bra – she had never felt the need – and her generously rounded breasts threatened to burst out of her lime-coloured, Lagerfeld sleeveless top with every breath.

Outside, the Thames gently lapped the bank beneath Ashley's Chelsea Harbour apartment, the evening was damp and cold, but in the luxuriously appointed living room a splendid log fire flickered warmly in the grate of a massive, carved fireplace.

Somewhere in the background, a Diane Cilento album played softly. Ashley laughed out loud. Beverly was wearing a navy, micro miniskirt and sleek, dark stockings, and, he hoped, the scarlet suspenders that had featured in her latest, raunchiest and most talked-about TV commercial.

'Don't think that by flashing a little more flesh you are going to distract me,' he said. 'I'm impervious to all your charms.' He reached for, and turned over the doubling dice. 'You're in trouble, girl, and you know it.'

Ashley was a dead ringer for Will Smith, with a ready smile to rival that of his Hollywood lookalike. But there the similarity ended. Ashley had made a lucrative living out of racism and, if truth were known, promoting, rather than helping to eradicate it from British society.

He was the founder and head of ARMIES – Anti-Racism Movement in European States – and the £20-a-year subscription from its many thousands of supporters provided him with a privileged and enviable lifestyle, as well as a powerful platform, a voice that could not be ignored, and real influence over a restless, simmering and resentful section of the huge black community.

A move into politics was a natural progression, and Ashley played it dirty right from the very start. He chose a constituency in South London which had a large black majority, where unemployment was high and crime at record levels. Relations between public and police, particularly the black public, were, in contrast, at an all-time low. He used bribery, blackmail, intimidation, threats and brutal beatings to influence the Labour Party selection committee and, unsurprisingly, was duly selected as their candidate in the forthcoming General Election, which was expected to produce a landslide Labour victory.

They lost, largely thanks to Neil Kinnock's ill-advised and premature victory celebrations at a pre-election jamboree. Ashley Luther Bodin was, however, elected as a Member of Parliament, and with a substantially bigger majority than his predecessor. Large numbers of black youths roaming the streets on the day of the election were enough to keep many potential Tory voters safely locked up in their homes.

The subject of racism had dominated his campaign and coloured every speech he made in the House. He was loathed and distrusted by almost all of his colleagues – with the exception, that is, of one.

Bobby Temple recognised a fellow traveller when he saw one. Here was someone as amoral as himself, who was willing to play it dirty and take risks to get what he wanted. 'He doesn't need to campaign in his own constituency in future elections, he's already got it sewn up,' he told Jack Benson. 'We can wheel him in to every big immigrant area in the country and in ten minutes he'll have the ethnic minority convinced the Tories and the local police are tied up in a racial conspiracy to suppress and victimise them. In those areas, he'll be the equivalent of a 10 per cent swing in our favour.'

So Ashley found himself courted by his Party's new leader and, when the General Election came round, he was only too willing and happy to oblige his new friend and support those candidates where the 'local brothers' might have a possible influence on the outcome.

With success came further recognition and, despite the many warnings to Bobby of highly disreputable connections between Ashley Bodin and the criminal underworld, he summoned the black militant to Downing Street and told him he was to become a junior minister for the arts.

Already, in the five weeks since his appointment, Ashley had made two cultural visits abroad: one to New York for talks with the city's black mayor, and a group of affluent, black wheelers and dealers in Harlem; the other to Colombia, ostensibly to explore the possibilities of a folk music exchange between the two countries.

The visits – both, naturally, at the public's expense and with an entourage which included several rather exotic and glamorous advisers – were mildly criticised by the press until Bobby Temple let it be known that Ashley had the full support of his new boss. The sniping stopped immediately.

'He's invited me to join him on the Moscow visit,' Ashley told Beverly, as they sipped their drinks.

'Sweet,' she replied.

'Oh, he probably thinks that being seen with a black stud like me gives him some kind of street cred. But what the fuck! Let's just ride with the good times. The man thinks he knows what he's doing, so why not let him run with the ball?

'I've got my own agenda, anyway. I'm planning to inject a big Colombian production into London's West End before the summer,' Ashley chuckled to his beautiful companion. 'And I expect it to run and run and run.'

'Yeah… whatever,' grinned Beverly. 'And I bet this particular production stars rather a seductive white' she paused, and looked at Ashley over the rim of her glass. 'Powder, that is. Your buddy, Temple, couldn't have been more helpful if he'd been your business partner. Are you sure he isn't looking to cut himself in?'

'Don't you worry your lovely head with notions like that. His only interest in me is selling his ideas to the black folk. He's so into his new deal with Russia he can't see a thing, even when it's shoved right up his nose.

'Whacking the French and the Yanks is all part of it. He's softening people up for the really big one. They just happen to be on his agenda, but only as stepping stones to the major one. He's obsessed with this guy Brekov, so don't be a bit surprised if he has all the schoolkids learning Russian soon.'

Ashley leaned back in his chair and steepled his fingers beneath his chin. 'Bobby Temple has just about everybody conned when it comes to where his real ambitions lie. This guy is the Houdini of political sleight of hand. Nothing he ever does is for the reason people think.

'Everyone is convinced that Modern Labour has taken the Party to the centre right, or even to the right of centre. The press have analysed it to death and convinced themselves and everybody else that this was his great strategy to win the Election, that people are sick to death of trades union domination. They're convinced this is the final farewell to the bad old militant left, the closed shop, the Greenham Common crusading lesbians, the swingeing taxes on the rich, and all that clap-trap. They think Labour has grown up.' He slowly shook his head. 'Bullshit!'

Beverly eyed him expectantly, her curiosity aroused. 'So who's he outwitted, and why?'

'Everybody – the press, the public, the fools on TV and his own backbenchers. Mister Bobby Temple is not a wolf in sheep's clothing, he's the Devil masquerading as a saint. You should always be wary of a man with a vision. Well, believe me, cup cake, this guy's vision should have everyone running for the hills!

'When he talks about running the country, he means running every last detail of everybody's lives. Get used to the maxim – Bobby knows best – because that's what's going to be rammed down your throat until you want to throw up. You won't be able to go for a shit without asking him which kind of toilet paper to use, and which hand you should wipe your arse with.

'The press say he hoodwinked the left-wingers to gain power – and they are absolutely correct. But they are about to find out it was only a very temporary thing, a transitory phase in the party's development. They'll find it was the right-wingers and the public who were just as badly fooled. He's going to double-cross the whole fucking lot of them, every last self-satisfied, self-serving bastard. The Party leaders welcomed him in with open arms. And now the wolf is in the pen, he's about to eat them for breakfast.

'When he tells the faithful that the party will be in power for 100 years, they cheer him exactly the same way the Germans cheered Hitler in the early days when he talked about a 1,000-year Reich. But do you think ordinary people would have cheered if they'd been given a glimpse of what the man's true vision was? They didn't have a clue what Mr Hitler was up to, and neither does anyone here have a clue what Mister Temple's intentions are. They're not honourable, you can bet your sweet arse on that.

'Temple is twice as dangerous just because he seems so harmless. By the time people wake up and realise he's not the nice bloke from next door they think he is, but a complete nutter, it's going to be too late.

'No more ballot boxes, no more freedom of choice, no more democracy... It will be the Gospel according to Saint Bobby. Bobby knows best, remember?' He grinned wolfishly. 'Hail to the Chief.'

Beverly's look had turned to one of bewilderment. 'But can't you do anything? The people who know... can't you stop him?'

'Only a handful know where he's going and they're either too shit scared or greedy to say anything, or they're being carried along by the dream.'

'What about you?'

'Do I look like a complete idiot? Christ, I'm the last person who wants to stop him!' said Ashley, 'It'll suit my own plans perfectly. Nothing like a bit of social and political turmoil to distract the authorities. It's like the old magic man says – if everyone is looking one way, then you can deal yourself a fortune right under their noses. Then it's "Hit the Road, Jack" for you and me, baby, and a lifetime of pure, unadulterated luxury from there on in.'

Beverly brightened considerably. 'Now that's what I like to hear,' she said, flashing her famous smile. 'I'll drink to future luxury any time.' And she clinked her glass against his. 'Meanwhile,' she pointed to the backgammon board, where she had thrown a double six, 'here's an opponent who's not planning to let you get away with anything. Time to up the stakes again, my darling,' and she reached for the doubling dice.

Ashley clicked his fingers. 'Talking of luxury and fortunes reminds me... We have an invite to dine with ol' Mister Moneybags himself, Peter Flint. It'll be a good introduction to the kind of life we can look forward to living in the very near future.'

FOURTEEN

Saul Goldman was a very angry man – that much was obvious. His entire face, including his bulbous nose, had turned a mottled purple colour. He was too angry, in fact, to sit. Instead, the American Ambassador to the Court of St James's paced the royal-blue carpet of his luxurious office that overlooked the manicured lawns of Grosvenor Square.

Many of the trees were sprouting early leaves and a few ornamental cherries, in full blossom, painted bright splashes of colour in the weak spring sunshine. It was nearing evening and the trees were filling with birds already returned from their north African winter migration.

But Saul Goldman, who usually found great pleasure in watching the seasonal changes in the pretty London square, was oblivious to its charms today.

'The man's nuts!' he roared. 'He can't just turn his back on Europe and the US of A and remain a world player. He talks about friendship in one breath and then treats us worse than some of our fucking enemies!'

'Is it that really what troubles you, Mr Ambassador... or is it that you're going to have a problem parking your aeroplanes in somebody else's backyard?' asked his visitor mischievously.

Sir James Waddington was one of the Tory grandees who had organised the downfall of Margaret Thatcher in 1991. He had resigned his seat before the recent election to concentrate on his vast business interests. His pro-European stand was at odds with current party policy, but he was still a powerful influence at Tory headquarters.

'The Germans aren't happy with the size of your military presence there now,' he continued. 'They and the French are both promoting the idea of a European defence force, and I'll hazard a wager they won't be taking orders from anyone with an American accent.'

Saul finally stopped his pacing and slumped into the worn and comfortable leather armchair, which he had had shipped over from his home in Vermont. He had felt the need for some creature comforts after reluctantly agreeing to accept the ambassadorship from the President, who also happened to be a long-time friend.

'Bobby Temple must have a couple of aces up his sleeve to pull this stunt,' said Saul. Then a new idea struck him. 'Unless he wants something from us, and he's just opened negotiations without bothering to warn us in advance.'

Sir James pondered this for a moment. 'Well, whatever game he's playing, he's certainly got his cards held well and truly close to his chest. I swear only a handful among his Cabinet have the vaguest notion of what's really going on. He has the whole party too mesmerised to realise how little any of them are participating in, or even know about his plans. He's led them through the most amazing election victory in their history and has most of them still believing he can walk on water.

'At the moment, the man can do no wrong, and that's dangerous for everybody... for the Labour Party and for the country. He's taking decisions now that will have momentous repercussions and the really scary part is, I'm convinced this is only just the beginning.'

For a long time, the two men faced one another across the Ambassador's emperor-sized antique desk, contemplating this latest twist in the chequered history of their two nations.

'What are the chances that it's all a bluff to use as a lever to get what he wants in Europe?' Saul finally suggested, developing his earlier idea.

Sir James laughed drily. 'If that's the case, then it would be a reversal of everything he's said publicly throughout the election campaign. His manifesto is openly anti-European. Which is exactly the right way to play it. It goes entirely against my own beliefs but that is what the vast majority of ordinary people want. They've been forced to say a very reluctant goodbye to pints, pounds and miles, but they'll be damned if they're going to give up pounds sterling. The euro is on the skids and nearly everyone in Britain seems delighted.

'No, I think he's up to something a damned sight more devious and potentially harmful than that, and I also believe it involves the Russians. I get the impression that things are building up prior to his visit to Moscow and his May Day appearance with Brekov. It probably means they're planning to announce some favoured trade deal between us. Except that Russia is in no fit state to become a valued economic partner with anyone.'

'That's what bothers me,' said Saul quickly. 'We must be missing something very obvious, my friend. But I, for one, can't imagine what it is. The President is refusing to let himself get worked up about this. He's all for waiting and seeing what develops, he says. I thought he'd be really pissed and I'd have to tell him to ease up. But it's just the opposite: I'm the one with the hornets' nest up my *tochas*, and he's trying to reduce the swelling!

'The one thing we do have in common is that neither of us has got the measure of Mr Temple. He's so full of contradictions, he's a very hard one to read.'

Sir James nodded. 'If he had any real values, family or otherwise,

I would feel a lot happier and a lot safer. But he hasn't. There are even suggestions doing the rounds that his marriage may be in trouble.'

Saul raised an eyebrow: 'Is that rumour really true?'

'As far as I can tell, yes. There's nobody else involved, nothing like that. But I'm told she feels pretty neglected. "All politics and no play make Bobby a dull boy" sort of thing. And Mrs Temple, I'm sure, doesn't approve of some of his more extreme policies. She is a very traditional Labour supporter... just like her father.

'But whatever influence she might have had when they were in Opposition, I imagine it will have evaporated the moment he got the keys to Number 10. There's nobody there to steer him in the right direction. Or, more importantly, to stop him going in the wrong direction. That's what makes him so dangerous.'

The two lapsed into silence again, their speculation about the Prime Minister's goals or motives exhausted.

Sir James broke it by standing and moving towards the door. He had a meeting with the current Tory leader, Michael Rushton, which he imagined would be something of a repeat of the one he was just leaving. But he also reckoned he still had time to pop in on his mistress beforehand. She would be in her apartment in Shepherd's Market, just a two-minute stroll from the Embassy. He had mentioned going there during the afternoon, which meant, almost certainly, that she had been waiting for him for hours. She would probably want to chastise him for his tardiness, Sir James thought, and shivered in anticipation over what form that particular punishment would take.

'Let's keep in close touch,' he murmured to Saul Goldman, as they shook hands. 'There are bound to be more surprises, and not, I feel certain, very pleasant for either one of us.'

As soon as Sir James had left the office, Saul paged his secretary on the desk intercom. 'I'll take calls again now, Martin,' he said.

The reedy voice of his secretary squawked through the speaker, 'Certainly, Sir. There was one personal call while you were in conference with Sir James. It was from Peter Flint. He wanted you to call him at Belmont Place when you were able. Shall I get him for you now, Sir?'

Saul smiled in anticipation of talking to his fellow countryman and faithful confidant.

'Do that, Martin. I could sure use a friendly voice this morning.'

FIFTEEN

In every generation, a Catholic priest emerges in Britain with free entrée into all levels of government, big business and even royal circles. Father Luke Large was the current such representative, a beaming, bustling, cherub-faced Franciscan friar with, as befitted his name, an enormous love of his fellow men and an impressive girth to match. The latter, together with his calling, had earned him the nickname 'Tuck' among his fellow Franciscans and the public at large.

For more than a decade, he had been employed by the late and saintly Cardinal Hume as his somewhat unorthodox special adviser and as his eyes and ears in the Palace of Westminster. When Hume died, Luke was kept on by his successor.

In his time at Westminster, Father Luke had become an essential fixture at any political bash, particularly those thrown by the Tories. His presence at gatherings of all types was soon taken up by the Labour ranks after he received Bobby Temple's wife, June, into the Roman fold. She was just the latest in a wide spectrum of politicians and their partners who had turned to Rome when the Church of England voted to ordain women priests in the early 1990s.

But Father Luke's influence also extended far beyond

Westminster and deep into the City of London, where some of the top decision-makers in the Square Mile cited him as a 'close friend'. These often stone-hearted capitalists almost fought one another to win his favour and bask in the warmth and goodness which he seemed to carry with him like a benevolent aura.

His faith was absolute, profound and unshakeable. And his life was mostly lived in Franciscan simplicity. He dined as a guest at some of the richest tables in the land, but his prevailing passion was to help the homeless and the destitute through the Passage, an organisation founded by Cardinal Hume.

'I'm more of a Robin Hood than a Friar Tuck,' he would cheerfully inform his wealthy contributors as they forked out large donations to his favoured charity. 'I take from the rich and give to the poor.' And, usually, they would laugh more deeply and press another cheque into his hand.

The new Cardinal, David Bower, had taken an immediate shine to Luke and confirmed him in his position, which had angered many of the traditionalists at the Cathedral, who were jealous of the friar's social standing and his popularity with journalists. They resented the way his simple combination of kindness, coupled with an utter belief in the beauty of God, brought a much more favourable response from the people than the Church's standard and more stylised dogma.

Like Cardinal Bower – a stooped, softly-spoken Highlander with a devotion to his native distillation – Luke enjoyed a glass of fine malt whisky. At times, he would blush with schoolboy confusion when he became, as he put it, rather too spiritual for his own good.

But on these occasions, as when he was perfectly sober, Luke emanated goodwill to all men – or at least almost all – as it was his basic nature to look on the bright side of things, and attribute to his fellow men the best of intentions.

But at this moment, as he carried out God's work, even Luke's naturally sunny disposition and his faith in the love and wisdom of his Boss, had been shaken to their very roots. He had believed until now – after 20 years of listening to people's darkest and, all too often, repellant revelations – that nothing he might hear in the confessional could surprise or shock him.

Now he found his mind reeling with the horror of what he had just been told. And his fear was all the more intense because these secrets had been divulged in absolute confidence and were therefore sacrosanct. They could not be repeated to another living soul.

It was warm in the cathedral but Luke shivered beneath his Franciscan robes as he listened to the chilling words whispered through the screen from the adjoining booth. The well-spoken woman's voice seemed vaguely familiar, but Luke was more concerned with warning. The Church in Britain was in terrible danger, she told him. The nation about to join with the forces of darkness, to merge with the ungodly. The Catholic Church, which had survived the bloody scourge of Elizabethan and Cromwellian Protestant enforcers, was now facing a far more powerful threat. The Communists, soon to be flooding into Britain, were declared enemies of religion. Only with the use of violence, the woman confided to her confessor, could their takeover now be prevented.

His mind was still reeling as he grappled with the dreadful implications of what he had been told, when the voice, clearly strained with desperation, whispered again, 'Father, forgive me, for I have sinned.'

Luke's eyes darted wildly around the confessional, as though searching for some divine message that might inform his response. But when nothing appeared, he found himself relying on the standard response to a thousand or more confessions.

SIXTEEN

Uniquely, in Britain, Peter Flint employed a frogman as a special cleaner on his Belmont Place estate, for one of his most sensational additions to the original building had been a vast, underground dining room featuring a glass ceiling, which was also the bottom of a small, artificial lake with a large collection of giant Koi carp.

On the morning of Flint's mysterious dinner party, the frogman was at work below the lake's surface, cleaning the glass bottom with a large mop. The inside had already been polished to a sparkle to offer the guests a stunning, rippling view of the sky above.

At dusk, the submerged floodlights would automatically cut in and transform the dining room into a fairytale, underwater haven. Yet the decor of the room itself, with its handmade, deep-pile, aquamarine carpet and exquisite eighteenth-century furniture, prevented it being either vulgar or garish. It was, simply, the most spectacular and breathtaking dining room in the world, and had cost over £3 million to create.

At one end, a large, natural rock waterfall occupied the whole width of the room and the curtain of water, cascading from above, appeared to come from the lake itself. It tumbled into a deep pool before disappearing, unseen, through a subterranean tunnel. In fact, powerful electric pumps sent the water back up to the surface, emerging from a small mound of rocks at one end of the lake, cleverly disguised as a natural spring.

The side walls of the dining room stretched a full 60 feet in length and were of aquamarine-veined marble, which was partly obscured by dozens of randomly hung paintings, many by very accomplished artists and forming an extremely eclectic and valuable collection.

The wall opposite the waterfall was dominated by massive double doors opening inwards from a circular, pillared reception room, which was constructed throughout in white marble. The floor, inside the ring of Greek pillars, was covered by a vast, circular white carpet and the room was lit by a single, spectacular, six-ringed chandelier. Opposite the doors to the dining room, a wide, carpeted staircase rose 10 feet to a square landing, before turning back on itself, left and right, up to the ground-floor level of the mansion.

A white Bechstein grand piano, which would be used that evening to entertain Flint's guests as they sipped his vintage champagne before dinner, was being tuned. It rarely needed tuning, but with so many discerning guests invited, he wanted to be certain that everything was perfect.

He had already inspected the table layout and the flower arrangements throughout the ground-floor rooms, and in the bedrooms to be occupied by Princess Kate and June Temple, and was as certain as he could be that everything was up to his exacting standards.

Now he made his way to his study where his Chief of Security, Jim Weston, was already waiting. 'Do sit down,' Flint told the craggy-faced, 6-foot 4-inch Texan, as he made his way to his own favourite chair behind his desk. Jim dropped his heavily muscled 18-stone frame into a large, leather settee, smiled lazily at his employer, as he always did, and stretched his legs out in front of him.

Jim had been with the billionaire oil tycoon for 40 years, having saved his life during a violent union clash in one of Flint's oil field disputes in the 1960s. Then a rookie cop, he had flattened three union heavies who were using Flint as a human punchbag, tossed his unconscious form onto the back of a pick-up truck and somehow managed to drive him to safety and away from the attention of the angry mob.

Flint's thanks had come in the shape of a hefty cheque and the offer of a job as his personal bodyguard and security adviser. Jim had already been an admirer of the slightly built, tough-talking oil man, and turned in his badge to hitch his star to Flint's. It was a decision he had never had to regret in the four decades since. As Flint's corporations had grown, so had Jim's bank balance and responsibilities. Shares given him by his boss years before had long ago made him a millionaire, but far more important to Jim was his relationship with the man who now faced him across the wide desk.

Over the decades and through a series of hair-raising, shared adventures around the world, the two men had become genuine friends. And even though Jim would never act in a familiar manner towards his boss in public, the bond of deep respect, loyalty and trust between them was unmistakable.

This final briefing, before any event, was a familiar though unnecessary ritual, and simply a final reassurance, for both men, that every possible eventuality had been foreseen and catered for, and that nothing was likely to interrupt the smooth flow of the occasion.

'I doubt we'll have any problems other than, perhaps, a couple of our guests overindulging and becoming a bit vocal, so just let the security team blend into the background as usual,' said Flint, opening the cigar humidor on his desk, tossing one of the hand-rolled Cuban cigars to Jim, and selecting another for himself. 'I imagine you've thought about everything else, as you always do.'

Jim Weston held a match to his cigar and sucked it into life, then blew a stream of pale-blue smoke towards the ceiling, closing his eyes in contentment. 'Everything's in order,' he said. 'Princess Katherine will have a Royal Protection Squad policeman with her and there's a Special Branch guy with Mrs Powell. Those two will stay in the house on the top floor and will eat with the staff downstairs. We won't need them again until morning. The rest will all be sent back to the main gate after dropping off their passengers, and those who are waiting will be given tea and sandwiches there, and will have television to watch.

'I've got the usual two-man team on the main gate, who will be relieved at midnight. Three others will be patrolling the grounds and watching the house. And, as always, there'll be two others on the monitors in the security centre here.

'I've double checked with the local Reigate Police and they'll have a car here to take over from the escorts from London when the Princess and the Prime Minister's wife arrive. They'll be keeping an eye on the place, as they put it, until the two ladies are off the premises in the morning.

'Apart from that,' he added, and allowed his grin to stretch wider, while his bright, blue eyes twinkled, 'the only security problem I can foresee is you having to fight off some female admirers tonight.'

Flint chuckled, 'I must admit, there are one or two coming I might have had serious thoughts about when I was a bit younger. But they'd have to be looking for a grandfather figure to find me attractive now.'

'Jesus! What bullshit,' drawled the Texan, stabbing his cigar at Flint. 'Given half a chance, you'd whip one of them over to that sex grotto you have on your island while the other guests are still sipping champagne. And probably a second one while they're having brandy.' The two men laughed in easy companionship.

'The day you stop chasing pretty young gals is the day we bury you, and you know it.'

Jim and Peter Flint exchanged smiles. Flint's notorious appetite for sex was a constant subject of banter between them.

The huge Texan rose to his feet in one fluid movement and nodded to his boss. 'I'm just going to drive around the grounds one last time and visit the gatehouse, then I'll come back here for when the first guests arrive.'

'Take care,' said Flint, and wondered immediately why he should choose to offer a word of warning before such a commonplace social function as tonight's dinner party. But for some reason that he couldn't fathom, he felt unsettled. *Perhaps I've got a sixth sense about something*, he thought, and tried to shake off his vague unease. He knew it was probably because he did not know the real reason why he was throwing this party – *the truth is*, he reasoned, *I hate being kept in the dark.*

As he followed Jim Weston from his study and turned towards the stairs, he wondered if his friend would ever disclose the real reason for tonight's gathering. *Whatever the reason for their being here, he mused, I may as well just buckle myself in, hold on tight and enjoy the ride.*

SEVENTEEN

At Pagward Hill, the former Second World War fighter station near Godstone, two ex-army, 6-ton trucks were parked outside the one remaining, dilapidated hangar. It was a concrete and corrugated iron monstrosity that had never been expected to last much beyond the war, and had briefly been home to a flying school in the 1970s, before finally being abandoned in 1984. Two armed men, wearing balaclavas and carrying tiny two-way radios, were stationed, under cover, near the entrance to the airfield.

Pagward Hill had been hurriedly thrown together during the national panic early in 1940 just in time for the 'few', as Winston Churchill was later to immortalise them, to be called on to save their country, at an appalling cost to young lives.

Now, apart from the occasional tramp, who sought shelter in the hangar, no one ever went there. Exceptionally, the previous day had seen a great deal of activity, involving the coming and going of an ex-US military Chinook helicopter, which had deposited a large quantity of arms and a dozen men and women, who had spent the night in self-inflating tents, concealed within the decaying walls of the hangar.

The arms shipment had included the most sophisticated military equipment available on the world market, and also some items classified 'Top Secret' and still believed by the governments who had developed them to be securely under wraps.

The bulk of this shipment had been transferred to the two trucks, which, until minutes earlier, had also been concealed in the hangar. Now their drivers were in their cabs and waiting for the final order to move out. The remaining weaponry had been placed in a third truck, which, for the time being, would remain hidden, and in the Chinook military helicopter, which still bore the camouflage finish and insignia of the United States Air Force. For now, the giant twin-rotor transport aircraft was positioned out of sight behind the massive hangar doors, until its call to arms later that same day.

Careb Sinclair and Emma Vale stood talking outside the hangar door. There was little warmth in the thin, late afternoon April sunshine and a chill north-easterly wind buffeted the aerodrome. Emma was wearing a one-piece, burgundy ski outfit that hugged the contours of her body.

'A body,' said David Carey, to no one in particular, as he joined them, 'which only God or the Devil could have made. That's the kind of body most women could only achieve in their dreams.'

Emma's violet eyes shimmered and her lips split in a wide grin as she turned to hug the Irishman. 'Careb's absolutely right,' she told him. 'You should give the Blarney Stone back, Davey Carey,' she laughed, 'let someone else use it for a while.'

'Ah, sure, you're a tough one, Emma. This isn't just flattery, you know. I'm deadly serious,' Davey told her amicably in his broadest County Monoghan accent.

Emma laughed aloud and hugged him even tighter. 'Well, if I decide to start a relationship with an Irish pixie in the near future, I'll bear you in mind.'

'Oh, you're just teasing me, now. What's a beautiful young thing like you want with an old dinosaur like me? Unless it's pity or charity you'd be offering… ' he added hopefully.

Their banter was cut short by a squawk from the two-way radio attached to Careb's lapel.

'Go ahead.'

'We've got company… a police patrol car. One man – the driver – and a woman… both in uniform. They've just let themselves in through the main gate and are on their way up to see you. Any instructions?'

'No, Gordon… stay where you are. Thanks for the warning.'

Careb Sinclair unhooked the radio from his lapel and slid it into the right-hand pocket of his black jacket and said to the others, 'Probably locals. You both know the cover story, so if we can keep this friendly and simple, let's do it. Here they come now.'

A small four-door, white saloon car with police markings and emergency lights on the roof approached smoothly across the tarmac and stopped about 10 feet from the trio. As the engine cut out, the only sound was the swirling of the stiffening breeze, now strong enough to send some leaves and bits of debris bowling across the airfield. *Like tumbleweed through an old Wild West ghost town*, thought Careb momentarily. Then the car's front doors opened and the two occupants got out. The driver looked young enough still to have been at school. Tall and good-looking, he had already spotted Emma, who was standing half-turned to the sun, so that her flawless features were etched in sharp contrast, one side glowing visibly and the other tantalisingly in deep shadow. He took in the vision, straightened his cap and walked towards the waiting trio.

The WPC was in regulation dark-blue serge, though with a skirt that appeared at least a couple of inches higher than the norm. *Sign, perhaps, of a hidden rebellious streak*, speculated David Carey. Strands of dark curls spilled from her peaked cap, with most of the cascade gathered in a loose knot at the base of her neck. At 5' 6" she appeared to weigh no more than 45 kilos. Her trim figure was probably the result of regular workouts, thought Davey, preparing himself for the worst. She might have been a couple of years older than her colleague, but there was very little in it. The pair seemed ridiculously young to be representing the local forces of law and order.

Careb stepped towards them. 'Can I help you, officers?' he asked. 'My name is James Arthur.'

'Good afternoon, Mr Arthur. I'm PC George Thompson and this is WPC Jones. We're from Godstone. There have been several reports of helicopter activity and heavy lorries in and out of here in the past 24 hours, and we have had no notification about the airfield being reopened. Perhaps you could tell me what's happening?'

Careb put one hand, nonchalantly, into the trouser pocket of his black jumpsuit and waved his free hand casually towards the waiting vans. He smiled at the two police officers. 'I'm sorry you've been kept in the dark, constable. I'm sure it was a Ministry oversight. They should have informed the local police headquarters. If you like, I'll pop down and see your boss as soon as I'm through here and fill him in.'

'That would be the Chief Superintendent, Sir. But perhaps it could save you a visit if you would like to explain to me what's going on.'

Not as naïve as he seems, thought Careb, continuing to smile reassuringly. 'Certainly. We are using this and other small, abandoned airstrips in a special defence exercise. Some of our European neighbours and the Americans are involved. It began yesterday and will be all over in another 24 hours. Then you won't see us for dust. There are no weapons being discharged or fixed-wing aircraft flying in to scare the local residents. It's all rather low-key actually, probably a bit of a waste of time. But you know how the pen-pushers back in Whitehall love to think up new war games.'

The policeman stared hard at Careb for a few moments, then visibly relaxed and grinned. 'Our lot are just as bad,' he said. 'I'll let the Chief Super know you'll be popping in later this evening. The station's in the high street, just off the green – you can't miss it.'

His remarks were made to Careb but his eyes had been irresistibly drawn back to Emma, who rewarded him with one of her warmest smiles. With obvious reluctance, he tore his eyes from her and turned towards the car, but the WPC stayed put. 'While we're here, George, we might just as well have a look around.'

Her companion looked uncertain. 'What's the point?' he said.

'The Serge's bound to ask for details so we may as well spend a couple more minutes here – and at least have something to show that we've actually been here.'

She moved towards the nearest truck and PC Thompson, with a resigned shrug, reluctantly trudged after her.

Careb exchanged glances with Emma and Davey, who had raised his eyebrows in mute comment and, still smiling, followed the two police officers over to the truck.

'Why is everyone in civvies?' asked the WPC. 'You don't usually have non-military types driving army trucks like these. If you can just switch off the ignition,' she added to the driver without waiting for an answer, 'I would like to take a peep in the back.'

'I'm afraid that's impossible,' said Careb. 'It's classified material, you see. I'm not at liberty to let you look.'

The young policewoman's eyes widened with growing suspicion. 'Well, failing that, I'll just have to ask the Chief Super to come up here and talk to you himself.'

The young constable took her arm. 'I don't think it's worth making a fuss over, Jen. Let's leave them to their games and we'll get back to the station.'

She shook her arm free and rounded on him, her mouth set in a stubborn line and her eyes now betraying traces of annoyance. 'We're not leaving yet… I just think there's something funny going on,' she said, 'and I want to check these vehicles.'

Davey Carey lit a cigarette and gently exhaled the smoke. 'If you'd like to come into the hangar I'll show you everything, missie. I can see you won't take no for an answer.'

He nodded the way and fell into step alongside her as she walked towards the partly-open hangar door. Careb, Emma and the constable ambled along a few steps behind. When they reached the hangar, Davey dropped back a pace and gestured to the WPC to go ahead.

'I'm sorry to have to do this, sweetheart,' he murmured, and, raising his right arm, swept the side of his rigid palm in a fast chopping action across the back of her neck. She collapsed to the ground without a murmur.

Before George Thompson even had time to react, Careb doubled him over with a short, powerful elbow jab to the stomach, then cut off his sudden, agonised gasp for breath with an even shorter, but equally powerful fist to the side of his jaw. The young constable dropped heavily to the ground.

Carey took another pull on his cigarette and called to the two men who were stowing gear aboard the Chinook helicopter. 'If you gentlemen will assist for the moment, we'll truss these two turkeys nice and tight so they won't do any squawking until we're safely on our way. And, Emma, dear, perhaps you could drive their little squad car in here so it's nicely out of sight.'

He looked down at the unconscious policewoman. 'Quite plucky for an English girl. Maybe in other circumstances… ' His voice tailed off and he grinned across at Careb. 'I know, I'm just an incurable romantic… I would have liked her to have stayed awake on our first date, though. It's very poor form, don't you think?'

Careb returned his grin and looked at his watch. 'I think as soon as we've gift-wrapped this pair, we can be on our way. We don't want to be late for the party – it just wouldn't be the same without us.'

EIGHTEEN

Princess Katherine was the first of Peter Flint's guests to arrive, and the American billionaire, alerted by the entrance gate security guards, was waiting on the terrace at the top of the front steps of Belmont House when her cream, chauffeur-driven Jaguar purred to a halt on the paved driveway below. Before the limousine had fully stopped, Kate's personal protection officer had leapt from the front passenger seat and was opening the Princess's door.

Kate spotted Peter Flint as soon as she stepped from the car, and gave him a cheerful wave. She was wearing a black Versace trouser suit with calf-high Russian cossack boots, her blonde tresses spilling from beneath an angled, peaked, black leather cap.

'I swear you're more handsome every time I see you, Peter,' she called, bounding effortlessly up the dozen wide steps towards him. *And it's true,* she thought. *He's got a body like tempered steel and looks most men would die for. He does this to me every time... perhaps it's time I did something about it.* 'It's really nice to see you again.'

'Likewise, Your Royal Highness,' said Flint, leaning forward to kiss her proffered cheek. But at the last moment, Kate turned her head and kissed him firmly on the mouth. She grinned at his momentary confusion and shook her finger at him. 'I keep telling you, Peter, that my name is Kate to my friends. And I need friends like you... badly!'

She gave him a brief hug and turned to the woman who had followed her up the steps.

'This is Margaret Clayton, who looks after me.'

Flint offered his hand.

'And you know my detective, Tim Mortimer.'

Flint smiled a welcome. 'Yes, he was down here last week, checking things over with Jim.' He shook hands with the plain-clothes policeman. 'It's good to see you again. Jim is in the house waiting for you. My butler, Gordon, will see that your cases are taken to the right rooms, so if you, Kate, and Miss Clayton would like a drink before you change for dinner, we'll go inside.'

The Princess linked her arm through Flint's and they led the way into the house. In the vast entrance hall, Margaret Clayton paused. 'I think I'd rather go straight up and make sure your things are unpacked and don't need any last minute pressing,' she said. 'There'll be time for a drink with Tim later.'

'Fine, if you run me a bath I'll be up in 20 minutes.'

Still arm in arm with Flint, she lowered her voice. 'Now you can tell me all the latest gossip. It's said that if you haven't heard about something then it isn't worth knowing. And I also want your promise that you'll take me out to your secret island before I go. I'm told that some very naughty goings-on take place out there.'

Despite reminding himself that he was old enough to be this beautiful young woman's grandfather, Peter Flint felt the almost irresistible quickening of the pulse and stirring in the loins that had preceded hundreds of amorous encounters in the past.

'If that's your command, Ma'am, then how could an old roué like me possibly refuse you?'

They entered the guest drawing room grinning inanely and Flint guided her over to a Texas-style long bar which stretched almost the length of one wall.

'What's your fancy?'

Kate opted for a Campari and tonic and, as the barman was

fixing it, Flint's butler, Gordon Payne, entered the room and announced June Temple's car was approaching the house.

Flint was again in position at the top of the marble steps when June, also accompanied by a protection officer, stepped from her car.

'I'd forgotten how utterly lovely your home is, Peter,' she called. 'Especially on a sunny spring day like today. There were several baby deer back there playing on the grass in front of a bank of daffodils. It made me believe that London was a thousand miles away.' She paused and looked back across the fountain glimmering in the strong afternoon sunshine. 'It seems difficult to believe there are awful things going on in the world when you're surrounded by all this, Peter,' she said wistfully. 'It's just so beautiful.'

As she reached the top of the steps, Flint opened his arms and gently hugged her, kissing her tenderly on both cheeks.

'Nothing ever happens down here,' he said softly. 'And no matter what else happens, my day is made already. It's lovely to see you here again. Let's go straight inside because Kate Worcester is already here and we were just about to have a drink. She's stopping the night, like you, so the three of us will have a bit of time together before the others arrive.'

He led the way into the huge drawing room where Kate was perched on a bar stool swirling her drink.

'I don't think you two need any introduction.'

Kate rose as they walked over to the bar and the two women touched cheeks.

'Hello, June. He really does have something special to be able to attract the most beautiful woman in the country to his table.'

'I was about to say the same thing,' laughed June, who then asked the barman for a glass of mineral water.

Two of the most talked about women in Britain – both blessed with the looks and figures of catwalk models – leaned casually against the bar, side by side, eyeing Peter Flint through two pairs of the most striking blue eyes he had ever seen.

He would not have been normal, he thought, if he hadn't felt a wave of arrogant satisfaction at the outrageous flirting of which he was the focus. 'Why two such beautiful ladies should be so kind to an old man is beyond me,' he said with a broad grin. 'But if my maker chose to call me in right at this moment, then I don't believe he would ever get me in happier mood. So let's drink to each other and to the future and that many more good times lie ahead.'

'To us, and to the future,' the three said in unison, and their glasses met with the clink of fine crystal. Just at that moment, Flint thought, he noticed something dark, fearful perhaps, in the depths of June Temple's flawless cobalt eyes before she joined in the toast. Perhaps he was mistaken, for Kate had clearly not noticed anything, and happily continued the banter.

'Perhaps your husband suspects that something is going on between you and Peter,' she teased, 'and that is why he has embarked on this America bashing... in order to get his own back.'

The smile disappeared immediately from June's face and she looked suddenly serious. Kate could have kicked herself for spoiling such a happy mood.

'I don't think he actually cares a damn who I happen to fancy,' June said sadly. 'I'm afraid his political moves have nothing to do with such run-of-the-mill emotions as jealousy.' She suddenly checked, as though realising she had said more than she intended. 'Oh, do forgive me, let's not spoil tonight by going into an analysis of Bobby's policies.' Her face abruptly became drawn and miserable. 'Everything is a crusade with him at the moment. Ordinary feelings are the first casualties... Perhaps, though, if you did sweep me off my feet, Peter...' a grin transformed her face, 'it might get his attention.'

'Great,' bubbled Kate, glad of the chance to gloss over the uncomfortable disclosure of genuine sadness. 'But I'll have you know I might give you a run for your money. Or perhaps...' she added mischievously, 'he'll settle for the two of us together.'

Flint, also happy to see the turnaround in June's mood, laughed out loud. 'That's one hell of an invitation. All I can say is that the spirit is willing, but I'd better take a rain check until I've had my latest MOT and a full service. But right now, I think it's time we all headed upstairs to get changed for dinner.'

He pressed a button under the bar counter and, moments later, Gordon Payne entered the room.

'Gordon, could you please show Princess Katherine and Mrs Temple to their suites. If you could both be down by seven o'clock, that's when the other guests are arriving.'

Kate set down her empty glass. 'You've certainly picked a strange bunch of advisers for your new project, Peter. Eclectic is hardly the word to describe them... I can understand Glen Grant and Rachel Friedman, and even Wayne Bryan and Father Luke. But I'd love to know why you've invited that awful little man, Georgie Brown. And as for Ashley Bodin...' she grinned.

I couldn't agree with you more, thought Flint, *especially when it comes to Georgie Brown.* 'I really am seeking an across-the-board opinion on this one, Kate. So I've spread a pretty wide net. It should make for a lively evening... particularly if they all live up to their reputations.'

NINETEEN

By seven o'clock, all 13 guests and their host had assembled in Belmont Place, and Georgie Brown had so far, indeed, fully justified his reputation.

The eight men, with the exception of Father Luke, who wore his traditional black suit and dog collar, were wearing tuxedos. The six women were all wearing evening dresses. Kate wore a silk, knee-length creation in cobalt blue to match her eyes. It was sleeveless, backless and accentuated her fabulous breasts, while showing every curve of her sensational figure.

June had opted for a simple midnight-blue, sleeveless silk dress which stopped just below the knee, showing off her beautiful, shapely legs.

Alison Best and Rebecca Goldman had settled for rather more traditional outfits. Rebecca's austere black dress, with beautifully-worked embroidery detail on the sleeves and hem, was mid-calf length, while Alison had gone for more of an evening gown feel, with puffed sleeves, plenty of gathered material and a generous, plunging neckline.

Rachel Friedman wore perhaps the most daring little number – a figure-hugging, chocolate-coloured sheath, which was almost see-through, with apparently very little underwear. Her large, dark nipples were just visible beneath the delicate, net-like material, and when Georgie Brown saw her he nearly had apoplexy. Alison had to kick him hard on the ankle to stop him staring. Georgie, unable to resist closer inspection, edged ever nearer to Rachel, until he found himself within touching distance, should the opportunity arise.

At first, the actress was oblivious to Georgie's attentions. From her arrival with Glen Grant she had stuck, limpet-like, to Peter Flint, making it clear that, to her, no one else in the room mattered. She was finally alerted to Georgie's proximity by the reek of stale cigar and brandy-sodden breath. Finding him ogling her only inches away, his eyes transfixed by her breasts, she took a quick step backwards, her face twisted in revulsion.

The TV star's famous leer – the one he usually reserved for his show's hostesses – creased his face. 'Well, you're not shy in coming forward, are you?' he chortled. 'And you can certainly take that from me.' He adopted his most characteristic, impish grin and rolled his eyes, expecting the laughter and applause which usually followed his famous catchphrase

But Flint, Glen Grant and Beverly Gladstone, who were the only ones close enough to have heard him, did not even smile. Rachel looked at him as though he were something she had just found under her shoe.

'Who are you?' she demanded imperiously in her best Lady Macbeth voice. 'And before you even answer, kindly stop breathing on me.'

Georgie's leer disappeared abruptly, and his eyes narrowed. 'Who am I?' he growled.

'Don't you know either?' Rachel purred innocently. 'How sad. Perhaps someone could remind you.'

The grins on the others' faces signalled to Georgie that he had definitely lost the upper hand, but before he could snap out a suitably witty riposte, Peter Flint smoothly intervened. 'This is the famous television show host, Georgie Brown,' he explained. 'One of the best known faces on British television.'

Georgie relaxed, and treated them to his most modest grin. 'It's nice to meet you,' he smirked. 'And I mean that, ladies and gentlemen, from the bottom of my heart.'

Again, one of his most famous catchphrases failed to draw the customary delighted smiles from his audience. It was, for Georgie, a unique situation. He was Sweet Georgie Brown, the nation's darling, and everyone was supposed to love him.

'Well, Mr Brown, I'm afraid I don't watch pop or children's television,' said Rachel, turning her back on the stunned star. 'Though I'm sure the viewers who do are lucky not to have to suffer your breathing on them from the screen. It would play havoc with the ratings.' And she returned her full attention to Peter Flint.

Before Georgie could make an even bigger fool of himself, Alison pulled him away by his sleeve. 'Don't waste your time on that stuck-up bitch,' she hissed, years of experience telling her that only a generous dollop of flattery could divert a calamity. 'You're ten times more famous than she is, and you've got more than a pair of tits to offer the public. Real talent.'

Georgie, recognising the truth of what she was saying, smiled broadly and tapped Alison affectionately on the bottom. 'Too right. She's only a fucking clothes horse when all's said and done,' he whispered back. 'She probably owes her career to the casting couch, the stupid bitch… '

Alison stiffened, but bit her tongue. Time enough, after tonight, to have her revenge, she thought. But tonight was not going to be spoiled by one of Georgie's tantrums. She steered him towards one of the other small groups, made up of the American Ambassador and his wife, Luke Large and June Temple.

In another group, Princess Kate was inwardly squirming as a fawning Wayne Bryan regaled her with details of his latest concert triumph in New York. His boyfriend, Lynsey St John

Beauchamp, and an amused-looking Ashley Bodin were with them, but until now it was Wayne who was doing all the talking and all of it about himself.

The pop star's deep burgundy, silk tuxedo enclosed a ruffled, pink silk shirt that was barely visible beneath a huge and floppy purple bow-tie. A large lavender silk handkerchief drooped from the pocket of his jacket to complete the effect. He stood, one hand on hip, the other in his side jacket pocket.

He's a bigger queen than my ex-mother-in-law... and my ex-husband, thought Kate, and could not help smiling inwardly.

Wayne, believing she was smiling with pleasure over the news of his recent success in America, could barely contain his air of triumph. To have lured Princess Kate into his small entourage from the party's start was a real coup, a cause for celebration. And he was delighted that all the guests had been carefully chosen from the 'A' list; they were worthy of his company. Even the sleazy buffoon Brown was a megastar.

'I haven't seen the seating plan for dinner yet,' he told Kate, with a simper, 'but I do hope I'll be close to you.'

'That would be lovely, Wayne,' she smiled, knowing, that at her own, earlier request, Peter Flint had placed her between himself and Saul Goldman, and opposite Glen Grant, whom she had lusted after since she was a teenager. Wayne Bryan would find himself at the other end of the table.

As one of the white-coated waiters passed by with a silver tray, she exchanged her still half-filled champagne flute for a glass of fizzy water, and turned to Ashley Bodin, flashing him a friendly smile. 'Well, Mr Bodin,' she said, 'what new cultural delights are you planning to bring in from the Caribbean to give us pleasure? What hidden gems have you got up your sleeve?'

Ashley grinned in reply. This party was all about power and glamour, he had decided, and they didn't come much more powerful or glamorous than HRH Princess Kate.

'I doubt there aren't many delights you haven't already experienced, Ma'am,' he replied, looking her straight in the eye. 'Of a cultural kind I mean.'

Kate almost laughed aloud at his daring innuendo. 'Oh, I'm sure you have all sorts of *objets d'arts* which would surprise me,' she answered teasingly, joining in the game, 'but I might just have some little gems of my own that you might be interested in.'

Christ, she's actually coming on to me, he thought, surprised and slightly incredulous that he found the experience so welcome. 'I'd love to discuss some of your ideas with you... in more detail,' he replied.

'The pleasure would be all mine,' she said, smiling sweetly. 'I'll have my secretary call you to arrange something.'

'Bloody hell, he's a fast worker,' Lynsey whispered to Wayne Bryan, waving his champagne flute in Ashley's direction. 'He's just been invited to shag your mate, if I'm not mistaken.'

The tubby singer, who had been more interested in tossing back a second glass of champagne than following the exchange between his special friend and the Labour minister, stiffened. 'You've got a dirty mind,' he snarled at his boyfriend, gripping his free hand tightly in his own and squeezing hard. 'Why on earth would she be interested in him?'

Lynsey tried unsuccessfully to free his hand. 'I'm sorry, Wayne,' he murmured, 'I must have got it wrong, as usual. Kate's above that sort of thing.'

'And don't call her Kate,' hissed Wayne. 'She's Her Royal Highness to shits like you, and don't you ever forget it.'

If only you knew just how much of a shit you are, thought Lynsey, putting down his glass and rubbing his freed fingers with his other hand. But he said apologetically, 'No, sorry... I won't forget, Wayne.'

Kate, who had caught the angry exchange between the rocker and his lover, saw that Glen Grant had abandoned Rachel Friedman, who was flirting outrageously with her host. The tall actor had strolled, with his trademark cowboy gait, to the far end of the room, where a blazing fire leapt and crackled in a vast Adam fireplace, surmounted by a giant Venetian mirror.

She sidestepped her group and quickly covered the 30 feet of expensive Persian carpet to where the tousled-haired actor was staring over his glass into the dancing flames.

'I just love fires. There's no experience quite like curling up on a thick rug in front of a good blaze especially after a hot bath.'

Grant turned and grinned. 'That sounds like quite a sight, Your Royal Highness,' he drawled.

'Please call me Kate if we're going to be friends. And I do hope we are,' she added coquettishly. 'Are our dinner companions not interesting enough for you?'

Grant's grin became a full smile. 'Far from it,' he laughed. 'Present company excepted, we're the oddest bunch of celebrity freaks ever gathered under one roof. What the hell prompted Peter to invite such a bizarre crowd to dinner, sure has me guessing. There's a lifetime's study for a psychiatrist in this room alone.'

It was Kate's turn to laugh. 'Well put – I was thinking the same thing myself. But I'm sure Peter has a good reason for it. He'll probably tell us. That is, when he can tear his eyes off your fiancée... and she is very pretty. It's said he's had more conquests than Hugh Heffner.'

Glen, who had temporarily forgotten Rachel's existence as he indulged in a vision of himself and the Princess on a fireside rug, suddenly found Kate gazing at him amusedly, waiting for a response. 'Oh, er... Rachel is more than capable of looking after herself. It was she, remember, who picked out that dress, knowing... how can I put it... that men would find the bits that are missing more attractive than the bits it's made of. From the way she's eyeing up Peter Flint, it's perhaps he you should be worrying about, and not Rachel. I knew all about her taste for adventure before we became engaged,' he added, with a smile. 'But what would life be like without the occasional escapade?'

Kate raised her glass and tilted it against his. 'I'll drink to that, Mr Grant, indeed I will. I've found that such adventures can begin in some of the strangest of places – and in the strangest company.' She stared into his grey-green eyes through slightly lowered lashes and then gave him a huge, conspiratorial wink.

Glen felt a sudden rush of adrenalin as he realised the Princess was making him an open invitation – and felt a genuine feeling of excitement for the first time in years. He wanted to take her right now, in front of everyone, and marvelled at the potency of this long forgotten urge, and at the formidable sexual attraction of the young woman in front of him.

For him, the evening had suddenly become a whole lot more interesting, and surely, he thought, an opportunity would present itself before the party broke up.

Across the room, June Temple, who was politely listening to an interminable anecdote from the US Ambassador – which had even managed to silence Georgie Brown – had wistfully followed the body language of the beautiful couple in front of the fire, and been momentarily almost overwhelmed by sadness that her own life was so devoid of romance, or the intimate proximity of another caring soul. How pleasant it would have been if a handsome hunk like Glen Grant had come onto her in the way he was clearly doing with Kate.

With a guilty start, she realised Saul Goldman had finished his story, and that she had missed the punchline. Swiftly assessing the faces of the Ambassador's wife and Alison Best, who were both smiling, June forced herself to grin. She was saved from having to make a comment by Georgie Brown, who had missed the point of the story entirely and had simply been waiting for the opportunity to speak again himself.

'There are almost as many of you Jewish blokes in politics in America as we have here running showbusiness,' he said. 'Here, it's for the money. So what's the big attraction for you?'

The sheer rudeness of the question left June and Mrs Goldman open-mouthed, and even Alison, who was almost immune to Georgie's legendary bad taste, flinched at his comment. But the Ambassador, with all the tact of someone who had spent years in the diplomatic service, simply laughed aloud.

'Well, had I chosen another profession, I'd never have had the pleasure of meeting you, would I? And the perks are pretty good, too, although I'm sure they're nothing compared to what you TV guys enjoy. Still, they're quite sufficient for an old country boy like me. Now I do believe Peter is about to lead us all off for dinner, so we'll have to pursue this interesting conversation a little later, Mr Brown.'

After bowing slightly to June and to Alison, he proffered his arm to his wife and walked her across to where Peter Flint was still cheerfully enduring more flattery from Rachel Friedman.

'You didn't comment on my outfit, Peter, I hope it meets with your approval,' she purred, turning slightly to give him a better view of her almost visibly naked body.

'Approval given,' he replied. 'But I must warn you, it gives more pleasure than is probably good for the heart of an old man like me. I've placed you opposite me at dinner so it might even prove fatal though I can't imagine a better view.'

'Oh, you're such a rogue, Peter. But how can any woman resist you?'

He was saved from making a reply by his butler. 'If you're ready, Sir, dinner will be served presently.'

TWENTY

In Downing Street, Bobby Temple sat alone at the vast mahogany table in the Cabinet room, scene of some of the most momentous decisions in British history, his fingers toying with the cut-glass tumbler containing whisky and soda in front of him. His thoughts were on another, imminent and similarly momentous decision which would, he was certain, change the course of British history forever... and, he believed, secure power for the Modern Labour Party for the duration of his lifetime – and beyond.

It was already dark, but the tall windows, looking out onto the private garden at the rear of the building, remained undraped, and the single wall light that was on was insufficient to chase away the deepening shadows from the edges of the room. The highly polished table top was, on this rare occasion, devoid of papers and other Cabinet clutter. Only Bobby's glass and a simple black telephone at his elbow disturbed the warm splendour of its surface.

The Prime Minister glanced slowly around the table, picturing his Cabinet colleagues in their usual places. How many would stay loyal to him after May Day, he wondered. And of those who disapproved, how many would actually have the stomach to oppose him? Just four more days and he would know for certain who was with him... and who would have to be sacrificed.

When the telephone buzzed, Bobby deliberately didn't answer it immediately. He had placed the call with the Downing Street operator himself, only five minutes earlier, and knew who would be on the other end of the line. He could well imagine Ivan Brekov's irritation at being kept waiting, and it amused him to play this little game with his old friend. Ivan had always been an impatient man, even as a university graduate, and Bobby vividly remembered how the big Russian had savagely twisted the locks of his coarse black hair, his eyes burning with frustration, if he was kept waiting for more than a moment.

Finally, after sipping his drink, he picked up the receiver and heard the voice of the operator.

'I have the President of Russia on the line for you, Prime Minister.'

'Thank you,' said Bobby, 'I'll take it.'

There was a slight click as the call was connected, and Bobby waited for a second click to indicate that the operator had disconnected before he spoke. On Bobby's orders, the call would not be routinely recorded and the microphones in the Cabinet room were switched off.

'Have you got any hair left to pull out, Ivan?'

A huge bellow of laughter came down the line from Moscow, 1,500 miles away. 'If it had been any other fucker on the planet but you, I would have given up after ten seconds. Far more importantly, you interrupted a very enjoyable teaching engagement I'm involved in, with a new political agent from the sticks. I was showing her some of our big town ways.'

More booming laughter echoed down the line, producing a grin on Bobby's face in response.

'But even the pleasure I get from her can't match the pleasure it gives me seeing you stick it to the fucking Americans. I saw a video of your performance in the Commons. Fucking brilliant! I hear the Yanks are shitting themselves. Slung out on their arses by their number one allies. They still can't believe it's happened. I'm told some of their fucking generals are advising the President to stay put and refuse to leave... that you will come to your senses.'

'I'm getting the same reports,' said Bobby. 'Though what they'll do in four days' time when we announce that your air force, navy and troops will be taking over all their former bases is anybody's guess. The President will probably shoot his brains out. Your people will be ready to move immediately?'

'Oh yes,' Brekov answered quickly. 'They're ready to move right away. They are very happy now that they're getting paid regularly again – with all their back pay settled as well. 'I've already confiscated enough criminal money to keep the armed forces and the police in pay for another two years – and there's plenty more where that came from. And you can easily imagine how our sailors in Vladivostok are looking forward to being stationed in Faslane and Portsmouth.

'Best of all, my engineers have assured me the oil pipeline from the eastern fields can be up and running in two years. Then we'll have enough oil to keep both of us supplied, without depending on the Yanks or the Arabs. When that day comes, we can play real hard-ball politics in the Middle East. Though the Americans probably can't see that far ahead. They'll still be busy trying to find a new place to park their troops and weapons.'

'That was exactly the news I was hoping for,' said Bobby. 'I'm very much looking forward to our meeting on the 30th. Meanwhile, I'm going to let you get back to that important lesson with your political agent.'

The bear-like laughter boomed in Bobby's ear again. 'I thought you fucking knew me better, Bobby,' roared Brekov. 'She's been paying excellent attention to her teacher all through our conversation.'

When the Prime Minister hung up the telephone, the laughter was still ringing in his ears.

TWENTY-ONE

There were gasps of wonder from Peter Flint's guests as he led them from the circular reception room, ringed by its Greek pillars, through the 10-foot high white ash double doors into the subterranean dining room.

The young pianist, who had provided background music on the Bechstein, continued his recital as they entered the vast, glass-ceilinged chamber. Shimmering patches of liquid light filled the vast space, playing across every surface, as the giant Koi swam lazily through the floodlit waters above. More spotlights positioned behind the waterfall cast twinkling, radiant prisms across the room, and on the faces of the astonished onlookers.

Gold strip lights softly highlighted the stunning works of art, and six four-stemmed, silver candelabra along the table made the glassware and cutlery sparkle in the flickering flames.

Even Kate and June, who had seen it before, found that Flint's underwater dining room had retained its 'wow' factor. The others, none of them exactly strangers to an opulent lifestyle, found it quite awe-inspiring.

Despite his attempt at cool, Wayne Bryan could not restrain a 'Bloody hell, what a blast!' above the general hubbub as the guests all pointed out the different features to one another.

Their initial delight was, though, for some of them, tempered by the inevitable muttered complaints, as several were clearly less than happy about the seating arrangements.

'Between a fucking poofter and a priest!' snarled Georgie Brown quietly to Alison when they discovered they were seated together at one end of the table. Wayne Bryan, two seats away from Brown, was furious to find himself placed at the opposite end to Kate and on the other side of the table. Rachel, next to him, was thrilled with the arrangement. She was seated exactly opposite Peter Flint, who had placed himself midway along the other side, flanked by June Temple on his right and Princess Kate to his left.

Grant, on Rachel's right, was equally content to be facing the Princess, and had the added bonus of having the beautiful black supermodel, Beverly, on his right. Ashley Bodin and Rachel Friedman, occupying the two end seats, were both satisfied with their places, and the American Ambassador found himself the envy of most of his male companions by being seated next to Kate.

The waiters began pouring mineral water and a '97 Puligny Montrachet as soon as everyone was seated. Flint tapped his glass with a knife and stood. He waited for silence and, opening his arms in a gesture of greeting to everyone, he said, 'Thank you for being here tonight. I know you're all incredibly busy people, but tonight I'm hoping to tap your brains, and your very varied talents in respect of a pet project I have in mind for London.

'I want to bequeath a new art gallery and I want it to reflect all that is good and innovative in the past few years. A museum of ultra-modern art and design which I hope will also be a manifestation of that which is avant garde in the theatre, cinema and television today. In fact, a display of all that is best in all of the Arts.

'I would like to hear your thoughts during the evening. So please discuss it among yourselves and, after we've eaten, perhaps we can open it up to a more general exchange of ideas.

'Now, Father Luke, if you will say grace, we'll get dinner under way.'

As the corpulent priest struggled to his feet, Peter noticed some bemused stares that had followed his remarks, especially Georgie Brown, who clearly had as little understanding of why he had been invited to tonight's dinner as Flint himself. He mentally shrugged and, as Father Large concluded his short blessing, nodded to his butler to begin serving the food – seared scallops with shredded spring vegetables, ginger and crème fraîche.

At least he had fulfilled his promise to his friend – and the strange dinner party was finally under way.

TWENTY-TWO

Careb Sinclair's expert 'locksmith' sniffed disdainfully when he saw the electronic keypad controlling the massive 200-year-old wooden gates which secured the northern approaches to Belmont Place. He opened a small briefcase and removed what looked like a handheld computer, which he attached, via a suction device, to the side of the keypad.

'Just as we thought,' he told Sinclair. 'I'll have this open in a jiffy. The other bugger… ' he motioned to the large new deadlock set below the control panel, 'will take a minute or two longer.'

As he finished speaking, the six-digit release code flashed up on the mini computer screen and the black-clad figure tapped them into the entry port keyboard. Careb heard the locking bar, which straddled the two gates on the inside, slide smoothly aside, and he patted the man's shoulder in admiration. Two minutes later, as the man had predicted, the deadlock succumbed to a pair of chopstick-length metal picks, and the doors swung silently open.

'That just leaves the alarm,' murmured the locksmith. 'And we can be on our way.'

The back gates to the Belmont Place estate were located on a poorly-lit, country lane, and just over half a mile from the main house. Once inside the boundary, Sinclair had no difficulty

identifying the house's location. It stood at the summit of a slight
rise and was brilliantly floodlit, as were the gardens and trees in a
100-metre radius around it.

Five minutes after entering the estate, the two big, canvas-
covered military trucks reached the edge of the tree line, and the
engines were cut. Sinclair had brought the main bulk of his team
with him. Two men were with the third truck, by now tucked out
of sight in the barn of a deserted farmhouse a mile away, acting as
back-up if any serious problems arose. Two others were with the
helicopter, which was about to get airborne at Pagward Hill, and
was just ten minutes away.

Careb, Emma and the other nine men were dressed identically
in black tracksuits, black, rubber-soled boots and black balaclavas.
Careb, Davey and one of the other hired hands carried odd-
looking, long-barrelled pistols. The others were armed with an
assortment of state-of-the-art automatic weapons, ranging from
XM-29 SABR laser-sighted assault rifles to Sig Sauer 9226
handguns and Heckler & Koch MP5 submachine-guns.

No signal was needed. As Careb stepped out of the shadows,
the others moved, almost as one. They jogged crouching across
the great gravel courtyard, up the dozen steps to the terrace which
ran the length of the house and gathered at the front door.

By now, they knew they would have been spotted on one of the
dozens of CCTV screens which formed a vast observation panel
in the basement control centre, and that an alarm would have been
sounded at the main gate behind them, over a mile away, at the
end of the winding drive.

The controller there, obeying standard orders, would
immediately contact the local police headquarters in Reigate and
a minimum response unit of two cars and four officers would be
dispatched to investigate within minutes of receiving the call.

Even before knowing the full extent of the emergency, the
station duty officer would not, on this particular night, delay in

sending the minimum response team. The Chief Superintendent had spent almost the whole of this last week reminding everyone exactly who was going to be on their patch tonight. To the local coppers, it was a premium cast list, and a major security risk.

The front door was not locked and, once inside, the raiding party, acting to a well-rehearsed plan, split up. Two remained in the immense entrance hall, while four raced up the great marble staircase to the bedrooms and servants quarters above. Two others had been assigned to check the ground-floor rooms, leading off the wide, carpeted corridors, which ran from the hall in each direction for the entire length of the house. With the possible exception of Flint's secretary, Jennifer, all the rooms on the ground floor were expected to be empty.

Sinclair, Davey and Emma, pausing only to find their bearings in the hall, filed unhesitatingly in that order through a small, arched opening to the left of the front door, which led to a staircase down to the security centre.

The normal house staff were expected to be either off-duty and in their rooms, or downstairs with the butler, attending to Flint and his guests in the dining room. Only the security staff and the protection officers accompanying June Temple and Kate were likely to create a problem in the main house.

Jim Weston, Flint's Chief of Security, was in transit from the dining room to the main house when the bleeper on his wrist vibrated. He glanced down, paused mid-stride, and stared in astonishment at the twin flashing red lights.

The signal had been devised by him so there was no chance of his being mistaken. It told him there were intruders in the house. He turned the bleeper off and continued along the corridor, which ran from the back of the house to where the main corridor gave onto the hallway.

The first to come face to face with the intruders was a member of his security team, who had been on duty in the basement control room and who was now, contrary to Weston's instructions, pounding upstairs to establish the identity of the shadowy black figures spotted crossing the courtyard. It was a job he should have left to the CCTV cameras. According to his express instructions during such an eventuality, at the first sign of danger, he and his colleague should have sealed themselves behind the steel doors of the security centre and concentrated on feeding information to the security guards at the front gate. But surprised at this first ever breach of security – after years of numbingly boring routine – all thoughts of correct procedure had left the security guard's head in an instant, and he was eager to check the situation out in person.

Now he was paying for this lapse in discipline. In his eagerness, he almost charged headlong into Careb, who was leading the swift descent into the basement. Surprise, and then fear, overcame him when Careb, descending in almost total silence, materialised on the stairs above him. He was an intimidating figure, clad all in black, and the security guard's look of fear turned to absolute terror when the Salamander leader raised the pistol he was carrying and pulled the trigger.

The drugged dart took almost instant effect and the guard collapsed on the stairway. On blacking out, clutching his chest, his last conscious thought was a belief that he had been fatally shot.

The three intruders barely paused in their descent, stepping around the fallen man, and rushing into the security centre, just as the remaining guard, belatedly remembering his training, flicked the switch which brought the heavy steel door sliding across the entrance.

'The horse has long since bolted, I'm afraid, old man,' said Careb Sinclair, not unkindly. 'But we'd prefer it if you'd just unlock the stable door for us. There's work to be done.' And he motioned towards the control panel and the door mechanism switch with his pistol. Faced with three armed intruders, the guard had no intention of displaying any foolish heroics and obeyed instantly.

As Sinclair studied the bank of television monitors which ran the length of the room, Davey pressed the transmit button on a small walkie-talkie.

'Bring the trucks up to the front door and start unloading,' he said. 'We'll be there to help you in a few minutes.'

His attention was caught by Careb Sinclair who was stabbing at a few of the hundred or more switches spaced in serried lines across the huge, desktop control panel. Each CCTV camera could be controlled independently from this vantage point – the angles, zoom and lighting simply required the flick of a switch, and the manipulation of a master control joystick.

Right now, Careb chose one particular image, and transferred it to the large central screen for better visibility. It showed the main entrance gates, where four men were seen alongside a Land Rover. Two uniformed policemen, who had presumably been summoned from their patrol car outside the gates, were moving to join them.

Careb turned to his friend. 'Let's try to dissuade them, Davey... But in case they decide to be stupid and be heroes, you'd best have your reception committee ready.'

'Roger,' grinned the Irishman and, bundling the captured guard ahead of him, he led the way back up the stairs. When they reached the first guard still slumped on the stairs, Davey grasped him under one armpit and told his colleague to take him under the other, and they hauled the unconscious man, feet dragging up the steps, as far as the hall.

Careb Sinclair, still standing by the console, picked up the microphone and pressed the 'talk' button.

'Gatehouse.'

A speaker on the wall crackled into life.

'Gatehouse here. What's going on up there? Have you managed to identify the intruders and, if so, how many of them are there?'

'There are too many for you to cope with,' he said conversationally. 'Stay exactly where you are, and do not try to approach the house. We are extremely well-armed and anyone coming within sight of the house will be killed.

'No one has yet been hurt but if any attempt is made to enter the house, or even come near, people are going to start to die. The lives of the people inside are in your hands, so I hope you understand what I'm saying. We will kill without hesitation if my orders are disobeyed. And you can start by telling those people getting into the Land Rover to stay put. This is not an exercise, and it is not a joke. I mean exactly what I say.

'Stay where you are and I will speak to you again shortly. Try to take any other course of action and I promise you the consequences will be dire.'

'Who the hell am I talking to?' came the voice over the speaker, and Sinclair silenced him with a flick of a switch. On the big screen, he could see the men around the Land Rover had been joined by someone from inside the gatehouse. A lot of hand waving was going on and some of the men appeared to be arguing. But the Land Rover stayed put.

'I don't think we'll have any bother from them until the top brass arrive,' said Careb to Emma. 'So let's get back upstairs... And then,' he added, with a grin, 'it will be time to join the party.'

As they left the security centre, Davey's voice sounded on Sinclair's walkie-talkie. 'Everything secure upstairs. They're being rounded up in the hall now.'

When Emma and Careb reached the hall, some 20 members of Peter Flint's staff were sitting on the lower steps of the grand marble staircase, their hands clasped on top of their heads. In the light of the giant chandelier, they looked for the most part pale and frightened, and some of the women, including Margaret Clayton, Kate's maid, were crying.

The cause of their distress was the three, black-clad figures facing them with submachine-guns at the ready, pointing towards them. As intended, they looked horrifyingly menacing.

One man, the Princess's protection officer, Tim Mortimer, lay face down, but still breathing, on the granite-tiled floor, another victim of the intruders' drugged darts. June Temple's Special Branch protection officer sat sheepishly among Flint's servants. He had been surprised on his way downstairs and disarmed before he had had a chance to draw his weapon.

The still-conscious guard from the control room had been placed with the servants and his unconscious colleague had been dumped close to the main double entrance doors, which were wide open.

Five of the Salamander squad were already moving equipment from the trucks into the hall and the Special Branch officer's eyes widened as he recognised rocket launchers, heavy machine-guns, laser guns and other electronic devices he could only guess at among the mass of items accumulating on the polished tiles.

Careb Sinclair went to stand between two of the gunmen guarding the prisoners.

'For you lot, the show is over,' he announced cheerfully. 'I want you to stand up now and make your way out through the front door, and to keep on going down the road until you get to the front gates. Some of you can pick up our two unconscious friends and either drag or carry them out with you.'

'What the hell do you people want?' asked the Special Branch man. 'Who are you?'

Sinclair put his finger to his lips. 'No more talking, there's a good boy,' he cautioned. 'It isn't a quiz and there are no prizes for guessing the answers. Just keep the mouth zipped or one of my friends here will have to use a more permanent method of shutting you up.

'I want all of you to move out now and get as far away from the house as you can because if I can still see anyone out there in five minutes' time, then the only one to benefit will be an undertaker. No second chances, no excuses. Hang around and you will be killed. Now get going, fast.'

There was a concerted scramble towards the front door as everyone tried to obey at once. Several of the men combined to half-carry, half-drag the unconscious captives with them into the chill night air and, within 30 seconds, the hall was cleared of prisoners.

From behind one of the bulky drapes, tied back on either side of the corridor entrance, which led to the dining room below, Jim Weston had listened to the events of the last few minutes with mounting apprehension. It didn't take a genius to realise his boss and guests were in terrible danger, or to recognise that, alone and unarmed, there was little or nothing he could do to prevent this obviously highly disciplined, well-armed bunch of attackers from achieving whatever it was they were there for.

To try and warn Flint now would probably achieve nothing, except to hasten his own capture. He reasoned that, having secured the house, these men would be turning their attention to Peter Flint and his guests. There was no other purpose Weston could think of for their being here. If robbery had been the motive, they would hardly have needed this much manpower, or the sophisticated weaponry still being carted in through the front door.

If a kidnap or hostage scenario was on the cards, then his boss was in no immediate danger. There would be little value in making such a huge effort, only then to kill the person, or persons, they planned to hold here. Better by far, thought Jim, to keep out of sight until he could fathom the raiders' real intention, and until he could get to his own weapon, illegally stashed behind a secret panel in his office.

Decision taken, he crept silently back a dozen paces along the corridor to where a side-door opened onto the back of the house, slipped through it and locked it quietly behind him.

He immediately became aware of a loud clattering noise overhead and, looking up, spotted the dark shape of a huge helicopter angling down towards the flat-roofed central section of the house. As it dropped into the beams of the floodlights, which lit up the house from below, he recognised it as an American military twin-rotor Chinook, and felt a rare moment of real fear. This was no mere transport aircraft but a fully equipped, armed-to-the-gills gunship. The banks of rockets and air-to-ground, air-to-air missiles were clearly visible, as were the heavy machine-guns on rotating stands peeking from the main doors on either side.

It sank to the rooftop and the harsh noise of the engines began, almost immediately, to die away as the ignition was switched off. With the house standing on a slight hill and parked behind the 1 metre parapet façade surrounding the roof, the rotors, Jim realised, would be barely visible from almost anywhere in the grounds. Other than from the air, this particular weapon in the raiders' arsenal might go completely undetected. He found himself speculating on what they could possibly have in store that would require such formidable firepower.

He had left his hiding place behind the corridor drapes with only moments to spare. No sooner had the prisoners been bundled out of the house than Careb Sinclair turned his attention towards the dining room beneath him.

Leaving six men to secure the ground floor, divert communications and monitor screens to the hall, and with orders to open fire on any people or vehicles approaching the house, Careb, Davey and Emma, and two other armed men, strode along the corridor Jim Weston had just vacated towards the dining-room entrance.

Large sash windows on either side looked onto the rear terrace and formal gardens and the intruders passed between a treasure trove of rare and valuable paintings lining the walls. The corridor's end opened into a large, square indoor terrace with two staircases leading down from the right. These descended to a common landing, from the centre of which a single, wide flight of carpeted stairs led down a further 3 metres to the pillared reception room, where the pianist was still playing.

Careb Sinclair recognised a Gershwin classic and began humming the tune as they walked nonchalantly down the stairs to the thick, white carpet covering the vast circular reception area.

'Don't worry, it's just pianist envy... ' murmured Davey to no one in particular.

Smiling broadly at his friend's quip, Careb was alongside the pianist before the man realised he was there and, waving his pistol languidly like a conductor, he leaned forward and whispered loudly, 'Just keep on playing. More Gershwin, if you can manage it... if you want to keep me really happy.'

The man's eyes bulged, but it said a lot for his self-control that his fingers continued to dance their way along the piano keys with barely a break in the rhythm.

Turning from the pianist, Careb led his team through the great double doors, which were wide open, and into the subterranean paradise itself.

The long, lavishly spread table at the room's centre, backed by the shimmering waterfall and lit by candlelight, as well as from the shimmering light above, was like a scene out of the Arabian nights.

'Christ... I'm in a Grimm Brothers fairytale!' breathed Davey. 'Now isn't that just the most beautiful sight you ever saw? Yon Mr Flint has got style with a capital "S", and no mistake.'

So far, no guests had noticed the black-clad new arrivals, and the level of chatter, the waterfall and the piano precluded any other distraction. Careb had other plans, however.

'I think you'll have to make a bit more noise if you want to get their full attention, he muttered to Davey.

The Irishman smiled and nodded, then quickly strode the ten paces to stand between Saul Goldman and his wife, reversed his pistol in his hand and hammered the butt hard on the table.

Everyone in the room fell silent and all eyes turned to the end of the table where Davey, backed by his four companions, faced them.

'And may God bless us… every one!' said Davey.

'Though not if you stand up, he won't,' added Careb quickly, as Glen Grant and Ashley Bodin started to rise. 'I want all of you to stay in your seats.'

He motioned them to sit with the 15-round Sig Sauer 9226 automatic pistol. 'These guns are real and they're loaded, and if we shoot you then you will be killed. And I will not hesitate to shoot any one of you – and I do mean anyone – who doesn't obey, absolutely, what I say.'

'This is outrageous,' said Peter Flint angrily. 'Just who are you damned people and what are you doing in my house?'

'Who we are is very simple, Mr Flint. We are your worst fucking nightmare come true, we are the hell that makes people pray for heaven! We are not simply the bad guys – we are the most evil guys you would ever want *not* to meet.' All this was delivered in an impeccable public school accent, but now Careb allowed his voice to harden. 'As for our reason for being here… *you* are the reason, Mr Flint – you and your 13 guests. I'm surprised that didn't strike you as being unlucky because this is a very unlucky night for you all. You are now prisoners, and it will not be a chore for us to tie you up and make you very uncomfortable, if that's what it takes to convince you. Any attempt to escape is not only useless but will end in your being shot. No one is coming to rescue you. And if any of you believe in miracles, let me assure you that such things do not happen.'

When he paused, several of the guests began speaking at once, and Careb lifted his right hand, palm out, towards them. 'Shut up, all of you! You are to speak only when you are asked a question… otherwise, if you open your mouths, you will be severely punished, and I mean very severely punished indeed.'

Princess Katherine opened her mouth to protest and Sinclair pointed his pistol directly at her.

'I really did mean all of you, Princess. And that includes you. Titles, you will soon discover, mean absolutely nothing to any of us. Neither do fame, nor fortune. So everyone stay just where you are and keep very quiet while we do a little housekeeping. Oh, and you can go on eating. In fact, I advise it, because it is very doubtful if you will be eating again for a very long while.'

The two waiters and Flint's butler, who had been in the room when the raiders entered, had remained frozen, the two younger men trembling visibly and holding their hands raised above their heads.

The two gunmen, who had accompanied the three leaders of Salamander now grabbed the pianist and herded him and the three servants through the opaque glass swing doors which led through to the kitchens. They, the chefs and the other kitchen staff, were then bundled into the service lift, leading up from the walk-in pantry to a much larger storehouse at ground level, which itself was disguised as a summerhouse.

As soon as the servants had left the room, Careb and the others removed their balaclavas.

As Emma shook free her waist-length red hair, there were several audible intakes of breath among the diners.

'Will you look at the effect you're having on them, Emma, dear,' said Davey. 'Bad girl you may be in their eyes, but they've obviously never seen a more beautiful one.'

Careb smiled at the Irishman's observation. But it was true, he thought. Despite some very serious competition from the women captives – four of them particularly, he mused – Emma was still in a class of her own.

As he and Davey removed their balaclavas, they had the full attention of their captives, who were all eager to see the faces of their captors. Despite Careb's suggestion, none had eaten another mouthful since the interruption to their meal.

Glen Grant, his legendary chivalry outraged by the intruders, was already looking for ways to hit back, although a glance around the table at the faces of the other men did little to boost his confidence. Only Ashley Bodin's eyes expressed defiance. Peter

Flint and Saul Goldman didn't lack for courage, he was certain, but their age eliminated them from taking part in any swift, physical retaliation. Wayne Bryan and Georgie Brown looked to be on the verge of pissing their pants, he figured – that is, if they hadn't already done so – and Lynsey St John Beauchamp was quietly sobbing into his napkin.

The only other man at the table was Father Luke, and although the priest showed no outward sign of fear, Glen did not think he could be counted on if it came to a physical assault on the armed mob. He knew that to have any chance of overpowering the strangers at all, any move must be made before the two other gunmen returned from the kitchen.

He managed to catch Ashley's eye and flicked his own eyes towards the threesome, grouped behind and to the right of the black politician, then raised his eyebrows questioningly.

Ashley nodded, almost imperceptibly, and tensed his leg muscles in preparation for a leap from his chair. But the silent dialogue between the two captives had not gone unnoticed.

'Don't be after making a mistake that your loved ones will all regret,' said Davey softly. 'Applause is fine for the living, but accolades fall on deaf ears when their owners are dead, as you both would be the moment your arses leave your seats. You and our actor friend are brave fellows but violence isn't really your game and you're up against experts. Just relax and do as you're told, and that way you might stay alive long enough to tell the story to your grandchildren.'

Ashley looked across at Glen Grant, who nodded grimly. 'Do like he says, Mr Bodin,' he drawled. 'For the time being, at least, these guys hold all the aces.'

'Very sensible,' said Careb, 'and will somebody stick something in that baby's mouth,' he added as Lynsey's sobs grew louder.

June Temple stretched a comforting arm around Lynsey's heaving shoulders and pulled him towards her. 'Don't worry, Lynsey,' she whispered, 'they're not going to hurt any of us unless we do something stupid. Whatever they're up to, they need us alive to achieve it. So try and stop crying as it only upsets the others.'

On Lynsey's other side, Father Luke patted his arm reassuringly. 'We're in God's hands, remember. Nothing will happen if we put our trust in him.'

'Anything can happen if you don't all shut the fuck up like the man told you,' hissed Georgie, glaring malevolently across the table. 'I don't want to die just because you stupid bastards can't keep your traps closed.' He threw an appealing look towards Careb Sinclair, the one he usually reserved for an audience if he wanted their sympathy for a contestant. 'If it's a ransom you're after, let's not waste time. Get on to my agent, Marty, and get the negotiations going. I don't give a shit about the rest. But Marty will raise what it takes to get me out of here. So how about it?'

Emma spoke for the first time, her revulsion clear in her voice. 'You have an awful reputation, Sweet Georgie Brown. But I do believe that in the flesh you're even more disgusting than the reports say. If the time does come to have to kill you, then I'm going to reserve that special pleasure for myself. Meanwhile, take your own advice and shut the fuck up!'

TWENTY-THREE

By the time the first of the freed servants and the two protection officers reached the main gate, Tim Mortimer was completely recovered. The effects of the knock-out dart had worn off quickly in the chill night air and he had been able to support himself, unaided, within a few minutes.

He and Graham Phillips, June Temple's Special Branch detective, had gone into an immediate huddle with local police sergeant Bill Wisley – the senior officer present – and Flint's security team. Wisley had been part of the four-man squad dispatched from Reigate Police headquarters when the alarm was sounded.

'There are ten or a dozen men, at least,' Phillips told the police. 'They appear to be professionals, not fanatics, and they are well-armed. Some of the equipment I saw being carried in was high-tech stuff. They seem to be getting ready to withstand a siege. They also have two army trucks and I saw a helicopter coming in as we were leaving. To me, it looked big enough to carry all of them if they need to make a fast getaway.'

Sergeant Wisley, who was outranked by royal protection officer Tim Mortimer, found himself totally out of his depth. Armed terrorists, sophisticated weaponry and helicopters in the

191

usually peaceful Surrey countryside were too complex for him and he deferred to the senior officer.

'What do you think, Sir?'

'To start with, you'd better talk to whoever's in charge locally and get some armed officers over here sharpish, and I'll talk to the Yard. The Home Secretary will need to know about this... and the Prime Minister,' he added. 'His poor bloody wife is one of the hostages. The Queen will need to be told, too. Princess Katherine may not be the family's favourite at the moment, but they'll need to know.'

As it turned out, the Reigate Chief Superintendent was no keener to take charge than Sergeant Wisley. 'I'll organise armed reinforcements and get down there myself,' he said, 'but this is too big for me to handle. This is one for the Chief Constable.'

As they were speaking, the Chief Constable of Surrey, Sir David Clayton, and his wife, Jane, were toasting a group of friends at a champagne reception in the Grosvenor House, Park Lane, which preceded the annual Soho Ball.

His police driver located him there just as Sir David and his party were about to go through into the banqueting room for dinner. The brief message he whispered in Sir David's ear signalled, the Chief Constable recognised, the immediate end to his evening's fun.

After a brief apology to their guests and a kiss for Lady Jane, who was wearily accustomed to being a last-minute stand-in for her husband, Sir David strode to the lift, which his driver had already summoned and was holding open, and began quizzing the policeman for further details.

The facts were few – Peter Flint's home had been taken over by armed raiders, who had cleared the place of servants and were assumed to be holding Flint and his celebrity guests hostage.

Sir David paled when he heard the guest list. He remained silent until they reached his car. 'I'll speak to the Home Secretary first. He's probably gone home already but his office will patch me through.'

On the car telephone, he was advised that the Home Secretary had already been informed and Sir David should go directly to Downing Street, where an emergency meeting was to take place.

It had been John Potter's unenviable job to break the news to Bobby Temple.

'Hell, he'll go bloody mad,' had been the Home Secretary's immediate reaction when he learned that it was he who would have to speak to the Prime Minister. But his fears proved unfounded. Temple, no stranger to crisis, remained completely calm. He ordered Potter to summon Commander Brian James, head of the Anti-Terrorist Squad, and Defence Minister Peter Westcroft, to the Downing Street conference, but first to have Peter contact 22 SAS at Hereford, and advise their Colonel, George Ulysses Norman Spencer – known to his men as 'Guns' – to stand by for a message from the Prime Minister.

By 8pm, just 45 minutes after the Salamander squad had entered the rear gates of Belmont Place, Bobby called the meeting to order in the Cabinet room.

Present were Sir David, John Potter, Commander Brian James, Sir Duncan Gough, deputy director of MI5, Jack Benson and various Downing Street aides. Also there, rushed over from the House of Commons bar, and seemingly confused about the exact nature of the emergency, was Peter Westcroft, the Minister of Defence.

On his way to the meeting, Sir David had used the car telephone to talk to Chief Superintendent Bill Warden, who was now located in the gatehouse at Belmont Place.

'There's nothing to add to what you've already heard,' he told the Chief Constable. 'Flint and his guests are almost certainly being held hostage by an unknown group of terrorists. So far, no demands have been made but my people have been told to keep their distance or be shot. They also threatened to harm the hostages, should a rescue attempt be tried.'

'I'm very sorry, Prime Minister,' Sir David said, 'as I understand your wife is among the hostages. But until we know a lot more about the people we're up against, I can offer very little reassurance about the ultimate safety of Mrs Temple or any of the others.'

'Do we know anything about them at all?' asked Bobby. 'Which country, or faction, they represent – where they sprang from?'

Sir David shook his head. 'Only that one of their leaders appeared to be English, and that another man sounded Irish.'

'Irish!' Bobby switched his gaze to Sir Duncan. 'What's happening on the Irish front at the moment?' he asked the MI5 deputy director. 'I've heard nothing myself.'

'Nothing at all,' answered Sir Duncan. 'The Real IRA and most of the other offshoots are still busy shooting off one another's kneecaps, but there hasn't been a whisper of any incursions planned on the mainland. It doesn't sound like their type of operation anyway. If we had bombs and mortars going off, I might start to think otherwise, but this isn't their style at all.

'I know it's not much help, Prime Minister, but I haven't heard of any suspect group setting up for business in England at all. It's all been fairly quiet except for a couple of low-level fanatics – and this is far too organised for them.'

Bobby looked around the table. 'Any other suggestions?'

Peter Westcroft shakily raised a finger. 'Not now, Peter,' Bobby told him brusquely. 'I'll come to you later.'

He pointed a finger at John Potter. 'OK, John, what do you propose?'

The Home Secretary swallowed hard and looked desperately from Sir David to Sir Duncan. 'Well,' he spluttered, 'we'd better get some more people down there, and someone will need to make contact with these terrorists and find out what their demands are.'

Bobby rolled his eyes. 'Jack?'

'I suggest we contact Hereford straight away and get a full squadron of the SAS on its way to Dorking immediately. That's what we have them for. They are our top anti-terrorist force and they know best how to handle something like this. I imagine, Commander,' he turned to Brian James, 'we will need a top negotiator, which I'm sure you can provide.'

James nodded.

'And in my opinion, Bobby, Commander James himself should be put in overall charge of the operation. With your permission, of course, Sir David,' he added, aware that, technically, the Yard had no jurisdiction in the county, unless invited in by the Chief Constable.

Sir David Clayton nodded vigorously. 'Of course, Chancellor,' he concurred. 'I'll go there myself to make sure he has everyone's full co-operation. I suggest we pull in a couple of police helicopters, which can put down here on Horseguard's Parade and ferry us straight down to Belmont Place. Shall we report back to the Home Secretary, or to your office, Prime Minister?'

'To me,' said Bobby, decisively. 'I'm putting Jack, here, in charge of the operation from a political aspect. Everything is to go through him. Particularly how this is released to the media. With the names involved, the media are going to go berserk. There appears to be a hostage to match every taste of newspaper – from the *Financial Times* to the *Daily Star*. Almost as though they were hand-picked to have greatest media impact. Jack will handle them here but I think you, Sir David, should deal with them on the spot. And I know that won't be easy. I think that will be best, John, don't you?'

It was clear from the relief which had flooded the Home Secretary's face from the moment Jack Benson began speaking that he would be in total agreement.

'Yes, Bobby. Whatever you say.'

The Prime Minister stood. 'Then let's get on with it. I want all those hostages out of there – and fast. Just do whatever it takes, Commander. I'm counting on you – and they are, too.'

As the others rose, he motioned to Peter Westcroft to remain seated. 'You and I have a job to do, Peter,' he said.

He waited until the others had left the room and picked up the telephone. 'Get me Colonel Spencer at SAS headquarters in Hereford,' he ordered his private secretary. 'Tell him that I and the Minister of Defence wish to speak to him.'

He replaced the receiver and fixed his eyes on Westcroft, who was watching him nervously from across the table.

'I'm going to brief the Colonel on what's going on and then I want you to give him his orders, Peter. You're to tell him to use all the force necessary to clear out this viper's nest. It's a shoot-to-kill operation and you, and the whole country, are expecting fast results.'

'But what about the hostages?' stammered the Defence Minister.

'Just do it like I've told you, Peter, and leave the thinking to me. Now, do you remember what you have to say?'

Westcroft nodded unhappily.

'Good boy,' said Bobby, as the telephone buzzed and he reached for the receiver.

TWENTY-FOUR

Jim Weston, feeling a hundred times more confident after a foray into his office, and with a .38 machine pistol in his hand and a loaded revolver tucked in his belt, crawled, almost on his stomach, through the shrubs and flower beds, and cursed the floodlights which lit up the approaches to all sides of the house.

He eventually reached the big rockery, where water cascaded down into the lake, and crouched, motionless, in the shadows. From there, he could just make out the distorted dining room and its occupants below, through the glass bottom of the lake – and what he saw brought him no comfort.

Peter Flint and his guests were seated around the table under the watchful eyes of three armed raiders. And one of them, he suddenly realised with a start, was a woman, a very beautiful woman, with long red hair streaming down her back. All three, he saw, looked like white Caucasians. *What the hell kind of terrorists are these*, he wondered.

A sudden explosion, less than 30 yards behind him, sent Weston face down into the rocks at the edge of the lake. It also sent his meagre hopes plummeting further when he realised the explosion had come from the mock summerhouse, from where the service lift led down to the kitchen store room below. The terrorists, he correctly concluded, had sealed off the only alternative entrance to the underground dining room. The one remaining access was through the single corridor, which led from the house. A handful of men could easily hold it against an army.

The only solution, he quickly concluded, was somehow to force the terrorists to transfer their captives to the main building, where there were a dozen or more access points. It was the only way to change the odds and make them more favourable for any would-be rescuers.

A glimmer of an idea had taken shape, and Jim felt the first surge of excitement as he desperately tried to gain some sort of upper hand. But it would not be easy on Peter and his unfortunate dinner guests, he mused. His plan to dislodge the raiders from their subterranean hideout would inevitably put his boss and best friend in some danger.

He had seen Flint half rise from the table when the explosion was heard and watched him being firmly pushed back down by the blond-haired assailant. Peter was a captive, but he was certainly not cowed, decided Jim. Flint, he knew, would be racking his brains to come up with a way out of this situation. Whether Jim's idea worked or not, he knew the buccaneer tycoon would approve. For an adventurer like Flint, anything was better than just sitting there waiting to be told what to do.

Weston reached for the radio at his belt, which he had also retrieved from his office, and pressed the call button. 'This is Jim Weston,' he said, softly but clearly. 'Is anyone receiving?'

For all he knew, the enemy could well have taken over the gatehouse by now. But almost immediately, the voice of his senior duty guard, Ron Booth, resounded loudly in his ear. 'Christ, it's good to hear your voice, boss! We're here all right but what's happening up at the house... and where are you? We just heard an explosion.'

'They've blown the lift shaft down to the kitchens. That's where they're holding Mr Flint and the others... in the lake room. At the moment they're safe, but I don't know how long that will last. What back-up have you called for?'

'The whole works,' said Bob excitedly. 'There are several police already here, and an armed police squad is on its way. So are the Chief Constable and a Scotland Yard Commander, who's going to take charge. The Prime Minister himself is involved, and he's organised a squadron of SAS blokes down from Hereford, who will be flying in shortly.

'For now, we're all staying put until someone can work out a way of dealing with these bastards. No one has been hurt so far, but they have said they'll kill anyone who approaches the house.'

'That's fine,' said Jim as loud as he dared. 'Just stay there for now. But listen carefully. Tell the Commander there are at least a dozen men – and one woman – deployed around the house. They are well-armed and have a whole stockpile of weapons as back-up... including a gunship helicopter on the roof. At the moment, I don't think the hostages are in any immediate danger – but that could well change very quickly if any force is used against these people.

'Let me know when the Commander gets there, by clicking on the radio three times. Don't speak in case there's someone near me – I'll speak when I can. But I do have an idea which I think could make it a little easier for us to jump on these guys.'

Jim clicked off the radio and edged further back into the shadows, from where he could still watch the tableau in the room below. For now, all he could do was to remain vigilant, and wait for his chance to act.

TWENTY-FIVE

To Major Peter Stevens, the prospect of imminent action was the nearest thing he could imagine to total bliss. The 32-year-old bachelor had been a professional soldier for nine years – the past six spent in the élite 22 Special Air Service regiment based in Hereford. Yet in all that time, he had seen action only once, and that was merely a brief skirmish with South American bandits during the cocaine wars.

Stocky and blond-haired, Major Stevens was affectionately known to his men as 'the Laughing Orange', because of his crew-cut hairstyle and round, permanently florid face. The odd nickname was in no way intended to question Stevens' toughness. The powerful, bull-necked, ex-public schoolboy had been a boxing blue at Cambridge and had played rugby for the Paratroop Regiment before applying for Selection to the SAS. Selection is the world's toughest military test, and only a handful of those who apply get through Stevens not only survived Selection but was considered the best candidate of his intake.

He and the 68 members of D Squadron were now aboard two giant Chinook helicopters speeding southwards towards Belmont Place in Surrey, and nearing the end of their 40-minute flight.

As all the world now knows, there are four squadrons in 22 SAS, based at Bradbury Lines, Hereford, and four troops in each squadron – Air, Boat, Mountain and Mobility. Their titles are pretty much self-explanatory and members of each troop become experts in their field, whether it be high-altitude/low-opening parachute drops, handling underwater demolitions, freeclimbing a cliff or rock face or operating a specially adapted, long wheelbase Land Rover or motorcycle bristling with weaponry.

Special Service troops are expected to learn all the disciplines so they can operate with a troop that specialises in something other than their own area of expertise. Their unique training means that the SAS are generally considered to be the best soldiers in the world, and Major Stevens considered D Squadron to be the best of the best. He had been their Squadron Commander for just over a year and was itching for an opportunity to lead them into action to show off their, and his own, superiority.

At last, he was being offered the chance to demonstrate what he was made of, he thought. The time had come to flaunt his virtuosity, and show he was the equal of any hero from the regiment's illustrious past. Stevens was tingling with anticipation over what lay ahead – armed terrorists holding some of the biggest names in the world as hostages, and clear orders to shoot to kill if the situation warranted it.

Success here, he conjectured, would make the ending of the Iranian Embassy siege in London look like child's play in comparison. He was in ebullient mood and, unbeknown to his men, a terrifying source of danger to them all because of it.

He had experienced a powerful adrenalin rush after Colonel 'Guns' Spencer summoned him to the Hereford briefing room 90 minutes earlier to give him his orders, and little had happened since to reduce the sheer exhilaration coursing through his body.

'Hopefully, we'll have more information for you by the time you reach the target, Peter. The Minister, and the Prime Minister himself, want to see this thing cleaned up quickly, though it seems to me, from what I've been given so far, that it's something which shouldn't be rushed. It is, though, a priority project. No need to emphasise that. There are some very big names involved and, if things get messy, the repercussions would be catastrophic.

'On one point, our orders are emphatic, too. If necessary, you will shoot to kill. That is an order from the Minister himself. You'll be working under Commander Brian James, who heads up the Anti-Terrorist Squad at the Yard. I've met him, and he's a sound chap. But you and your men, Peter, will eventually be the ones at the sharp end. If you have to then don't hesitate to kill the bastards. OK?

'Thank you, Sir, for giving this one to D Squadron. We won't let you down.'

Nor would they, he thought, as the helicopter dropped through light, low cloud and he caught his first glimpse of the vast, ancient estate less than a mile ahead. As the big helicopter banked towards the floodlit car park beside the gatehouse, Major Stevens could see, out to his left, the massive seventeenth-century mansion lit up like a Hollywood film set.

'Those lights are going to have to go, Buzz,' he commented to his squadron Sergeant Major, Alan 'Buzz' Sawman, seated alongside him behind the pilots and peering over his shoulder.

'Right, Peter. More lights there than at Blackpool bloody illuminations! Bit too bright for our kind of operation, that's for sure.'

He used the officer's first name with easy familiarity, it being a long-held tradition in the Special Services that all ranks, under that of Colonel, refer to one another by their first names.

As usual for officers, he was dressed in identical combat fatigues to his men, and wearing the famous beige SAS beret – though devoid of its coveted winged dagger badge and 'Who Dares Wins' motto. It was customary for the Regiment never to wear identifying insignia in action.

'Tell the men we'll be on the ground in one minute, Buzz. I want them and their gear out of the choppers and under those trees ahead of us ASAP. You and I will go into the gatehouse and make ourselves known.'

Moments later, the undercarriage of the leading Chinook thumped onto the black tarmac surface of the car park and before the twin rotors had even begun to slow, the first D Squadron troop were through the doors and heading with their weaponry towards the tall firs which bordered one side of the area. Less than a minute later, the second helicopter, carrying two Land Rovers, as well as troops, explosives, heavy machine-guns and rockets, touched down 30 yards away.

When Stevens and his Sergeant Major entered the gatehouse control room, it was already crowded with police and civilians. Commander James, who had been examining a plan of the main house on a table running most of the length of the room, was the first to take Stevens' outstretched hand.

'Good to have you here,' he said, nodding to Sergeant Major Sawman. 'Unsnarling this mess isn't going to be any kind of picnic. At present, we have 20 armed police officers and eight others, including the Chief Constable, Sir David Clayton.'

Sir David raised a hand to acknowledge the SAS men.

'What I want done first of all is to clear this room of everyone except essential members of the team. I'm making this our temporary command headquarters. If you will both stay,' he said to the SAS men, 'and you, Sir David, and your Chief Superintendent. And you two men as well.' He indicated the two protection officers. 'I'll try to bring our newcomers up to date.'

He waited until the room had cleared and propped his backside on the edge of the table facing Stevens and the others, who were grouped in front of him. Behind them, a bullet-proof glass screen ran the length of the guard control room and below it, a wide console bearing an intricate array of lights and switches. A 2-foot square sliding glass panel allowed the guards to question drivers and pedestrians before allowing them access.

On the table, where Commander James was perched, were a bank of telephones and a microphone.

'I think that until you fellows have taken a closer look, there isn't much point in making any detailed plans,' he said, nodding towards Major Stevens. 'To decide anything at the moment would, in my opinion, be foolhardy, as well as extremely dangerous to the hostages.

'Our options appear to be very limited at the moment. Since I arrived, we've had only one communication from the terrorists – I'll continue to call them that until we have more information – and it didn't tell us much. They have a list of Basque, Irish and Arab prisoners who are being held in British jails and they are demanding their immediate release.' He held up his hand as Stevens tried to interrupt. 'Let me finish please, Major. I've studied the list and, believe me, it doesn't make sense. There's not even a hint of a connection at all between these groups of prisoners.

'This is hostage-taking on a grand scale and whoever's the brains behind it, he has access to some very good information. To stroll in here and take over as smoothly as they have done involves a great deal of planning – and that means advance knowledge. They must have targeted this place almost from the moment Peter Flint planned this junket for tonight. That could mean nothing, or it could indicate they had help from someone on the inside.'

Sir David looked shocked. 'Surely you're not suggesting anyone on Flint's own staff could be involved in this business. I find that very hard to believe.'

'I'm not accusing anyone at the moment, Sir David. All I'm saying is that they must have had a tip-off from someone who knew about tonight's event, and at a very early stage. They certainly didn't stumble on this get-together by accident. I am saying that it would be very useful to know how they came by the information.

'The more pressing problem at the moment, I admit, is how to get them the hell out of there without putting the hostages at risk. And that's not going to be easy either. Their welfare and best interests must be paramount at all times.

'I'm going to give Major Stevens and his men a chance to deploy, and try to find out what's going on at the house. But first, let's get Jim Weston on the radio so he can bring the Major up to speed on what's happening in the room beneath the lake.'

The big Texan had been lying in the same position for two hours amid the ferns and shrubs on the rockery overlooking the lake. He was stiff and cold, and suffering a recurring spasm of cramp in his right leg. But no amount of discomfort – in fact, no power on earth, he had decided – was going to let his boss out of his sight. Like the Western heroes of old, he was quite prepared to rush in with both guns blazing, if he believed that Peter Flint's life was threatened.

As it was, apparently very little had occurred during Jim's two-hour observation of the room. The guests were still seated around the big dining table and the terrorists were positioned around them, some sitting and others standing. But all of them appeared to be fully alert, and their weapons remained unerringly pointed at the hostages.

At first, when Jim heard the clicking noise, it didn't register as a signal. Then he suddenly realised the noise was coming from his radio and slid it from his shirt pocket. The voice he heard had a crisp, no-nonsense tone: 'Weston… this is Major Peter Stevens. I'll shortly be moving towards the house with a full squadron of SAS troops. I understand you have both the hostages and several of the enemy in sight. Maybe you'd like to fill me in on exactly what's been going on.'

Simply and with no elaboration, Weston recounted exactly what he had heard and seen since the terrorists arrived. The SAS Major acknowledged his obvious professionalism with a curt, 'Thank you.' Then he asked, 'Do you think the hostages are in any immediate danger?'

'No, I don't. Everyone appears to be calm at the moment, but I'd be a lot happier if they were up in the house. It would give us a darned sight better chance of rescuing them than if they're trapped beneath the lake. Since these guys blew the lift shaft there's only one way into the lake room and I imagine they have that well sealed off by now. But there is a possible way to flush them out.'

'Say again.'

'I've worked out a way of forcing them upstairs into the house. It's risky, of course, but it just might work.'

'Keep talking… ' said Stevens, 'but first let me get this on the speaker so everyone can hear.'

After several failed attempts, he found a switch which brought the guardhouse speakers to life and told Jim Weston to explain his plan.

'There's a pumping mechanism which carries water from the pool beneath the waterfall back up to the lake. It pumps at the same rate as the amount of water leaving the lake to form the waterfall. If the pumps were to be switched off, and the waterfall sluice gate left open and running, then the room would gradually flood, and when the water eventually became deep enough, which it would do, then it would force the terrorists upstairs.'

Sir David whistled appreciatively and Stevens' florid face was lit up with a large grin.

'That's quite a plan,' he conceded. 'And I agree with you, it could force them to pull out of the basement, though there has to be a definite risk for the hostages. The bad guys are not going to believe this is happening by accident, and when they work it out, they could well turn nasty. In which case, we may as well go the whole hog and speed up the operation by blasting a hole in that end of the lake bottom, and really start a flood. It would take them by surprise and we might well have a chance to jump them. I have the finest combat team in the world out here, and the bastards haven't been born who can match them.'

'Hang on in there a second,' said Weston, his Texas drawl

becoming more pronounced under the stress. 'I didn't suggest we start World War Three. If you try to combine a flushing-out exercise with a full take-over, people are going to get killed – and they're likely to be *my* people – the hostages. Let's think this through very carefully before we jump in up to our necks... because it's not *our* necks that are on the block.'

Stevens' response was abrupt: 'Stay put and I'll come back to you.'

His eyes fixed on the Commander. 'If we flood the room fast, it won't give them time to think. They'll be so busy trying to get out, they won't have time for us or the hostages.'

'Well, they definitely won't have wetsuits with them,' said the Commander, but there was a note of caution in his voice. 'I really don't think it's a good idea to imagine we can force them out and free the hostages in one action. If we fail to take them out – all of them, that is – in the first few moments, then we know their threat. "Any reprisals," they said, "and hostages will die." And I certainly don't want to be the one to have to tell the Prime Minister I've just caused his wife to be shot.'

This brought a temporary silence as each man in the guard-room considered the possible, terrifying results of a botched rescue attempt.

'First of all,' the Commander continued after a few moments, 'I need to talk with their leader again. He calls himself "Salamander" by the way. I have to tell him there's no possible chance of meeting his demands. No one is going to be released, no matter what happens down here tonight. But, in my opinion, that's not the reason they're here, anyway.

'Meanwhile, if you and your men want to move in towards the house, Major, you can take the armed police with you, and at least we'll get the place surrounded while we decide what happens next. I'd better talk to the Prime Minister and bring him up to date.' His eyes narrowed dangerously. 'But until I give the go-ahead, there'll be no pre-emptive strikes, Major. And that's an order.'

TWENTY-SIX

Princess Kate could sit still no longer. She turned to face the handsome, blond-haired man, who appeared to be the gang leader, and who was seated on the stone wall in front of the waterfall.

'I don't care if you shoot me, but I need to go to the toilet, and I refuse to pee in my pants just to keep you lot happy. Despite your behaviour, you at least talk like a civilised man, and I expect to be treated in a civilised way. I'm going to get up from my chair, and I'm going to walk to the toilet, which is out by the piano, and if you want to kill me, that's what you'll have to do to stop me.'

'And I'm going with her,' said June Temple, rising from her chair. 'I haven't peed my pants since I was a toddler and I don't intend to start again now. So you'd better be ready to shoot two of us.'

Careb Sinclair burst out laughing, and a glance across the room at the grinning faces of Emma and Davey confirmed that they, too, had been amused by the women's show of defiance.

'Well, I'll give you one thing, Your Royal Highness, and you, too, Mrs Prime Minister... you're certainly not lacking in courage. Braver than the men in your party, that's for sure. But I think I knew that from the start.

'All right, you can go in pairs. But one of us goes with you – and whatever is done, is done with the door open. No matter how uncivilized you think we are.'

He nodded towards Davey. 'Perhaps you'll be kind enough to accompany these ladies on their visit.'

'And, sure, it'll be a great honour to do so,' said Davey in his broadest Irish accent. 'Gentleman of the Chamber Pot, that's me.'

As others at the table also began to rise, Careb raised his pistol, the smile gone from his face, and told them harshly, 'Sit down, all of you. You can go in pairs, but only when I say so. Anyone who thinks otherwise, and chooses to remain standing, can expect a bullet through the brain.'

Most of those who had risen from their chairs sat down again quickly, but Glen Grant paused and glared at Careb before reluctantly taking his seat again. The gesture wasn't lost on Careb, who noted, for the second time, that the American actor required special watching.

A gentle buzz in his earpiece radio refocused his attention. 'Yes?'

'Heinrich,' came the voice of one of the two German members of the team. 'The first phase is complete. All charges were laid without opposition.'

The smile returned to Careb's face. 'Thank you, Heinrich. Let me know when phase two is completed.'

In the toilets, Davey had pointed to adjoining cubicles. 'Let's get it over with as quickly as possible, Ladies. And remember, the doors stay open.'

Kate and June exchanged glances and entered the neighbouring cubicles. June lifted her tube dress to thigh level and reached beneath to pull down her pants to her knees before sitting on the toilet, head bowed. Kate, who was wearing no pants, hoisted her tight silk dress almost to waist level and, with no obvious embarrassment, sat gracefully on the toilet, making no attempt to hide her pubic area. She stared directly at Davey, who was still smiling, and who stared straight back into her eyes.

His eyes remained fixed on her face until she had finished and, as she and June went to wash their hands, he gave a slight bow and grinned.

'You're a brave pair and no mistake. I hope you both come out of this with no harm done to you, I surely do.'

'If you were really that worried, you'd let us both go,' said the Princess.

June shook her head. 'Don't waste your breath, Kate. This man is a professional killer – they all are. And if it suited their purpose, they'd kill you and me, and all of us without turning a hair. Isn't that so?' She turned and almost spat the last words at Davey, who finally nodded.

'I'm afraid she's right, Your Royal Highness. But let's hope it won't come to that.'

Davey was surprised to realise he really did hope no harm would befall these two plucky and stunningly beautiful women. He motioned with his pistol for June and Kate to walk ahead, and followed them back to the dining room.

As they returned to their places at the table, Rachel Friedman leapt to her feet, pushing her chair backwards so violently it crashed to the floor.

'I'm not having any damned man getting a cheap thrill out of watching me take a tinkle,' she snarled. 'If I'm to leave the door open, then at least send a woman in with me.'

She stood, hands on hips, head thrown back, teeth bared and glared defiantly at Careb through narrowed eyes. He stared back, a trace of a grin tugging the corner of his mouth, then slowly and deliberately let his eyes rove her body from neck to waist, returning, eventually, to where her clearly visible nipples, prompted by anger and adrenalin, had become swollen and were threatening to burst through the thin mesh covering, which barely restrained them.

'I don't understand a woman who deliberately chose to wear a dress like that, inviting her breasts to be stared at by every man present, suddenly developing such modesty. Request denied. You're an actress, so just imagine you're playing a part. The door stays open, and Davey will be there to see you don't do anything naughty.'

'Bastard,' Rachel hissed.

'And if you harbour any ideas about closing the door, just bear in mind that he won't waste time trying to break it down. He'll simply shoot the lock off, and almost certainly add a few more interesting but painful holes to the butterfly net you're wearing.'

'Dirty bastards,' snarled Rachel again, but her show of defiance had been utterly deflated by Careb's quietly spoken threat, and she began walking, head bowed, towards the foyer, followed by Alison Best and Davey.

No one else among the hostages chose to challenge their captors and, during the next 15 minutes, all of them, in pairs, took the opportunity to relieve themselves.

When Peter Flint, who had waited until last, returned to the table, he paused before retaking his seat and spoke directly to Careb.

'Now look here, son. I don't know what it is you want, but you must know that I'm a wealthy man, and I can tell you now that I'm prepared to pay a damned generous ransom to see my guests don't come to any harm.'

'From what I know about you, I would have expected nothing less, Mr Flint,' said Careb, 'but it isn't money we're after, not yours nor anyone else's. We have other objectives in mind – far less tangible ones. You and your guests are merely pawns. Rather important pawns, it is true, but nevertheless just pawns to be used, as required, to achieve those objectives.

'In the past half-hour, one of my colleagues has been contacting the news desks of all the major newspapers and television stations alerting them to what is happening out here in your home. I imagine by now there's a small army of reporters and photographers racing in this direction. By the morning, the whole world is going to know that some of the biggest names on the planet are in mortal danger. And that means the pressure on the Government to comply with our requests is going to be quite substantial, don't you think?'

Flint had paled visibly while Careb was talking and now sat down heavily in his chair, looking shocked and bewildered. In truth, though, it was not Careb's words that had temporarily overwhelmed him, but the growing recognition that he might have been set up.

But that was unthinkable. His mind refused to accept that his trusted friend could have asked him to arrange tonight's get-together, knowing what was going to happen... to have deliberately hand-picked these people to die. There had to be another reason, he told himself, or this terrorist invasion was just an awful coincidence.

But somehow, Flint knew this was not so. He was certain now that Careb's words were prophetic; he and the others had become pawns. But just whose pawns they were, Flint had yet to work out.

It was Beverly Gladstone who broke the silence. 'Does that mean you're planning to keep us sitting round this fucking table all night?' she asked. 'Where the hell are we supposed to sleep? This whole thing is becoming totally fucking ridiculous, if you ask me.'

'If the worst that happens to you is that you have to spend an uncomfortable night or two as our guests, then I really don't think you have very much to worry about, Miss Gladstone,' said Careb gently. 'I'm sure you've had to spend many an uncomfortable hour in the name of fashion. Think of it as just another difficult shoot.'

'You guys are going to have plenty to worry about when the cops and the Special Forces people get down here,' said Wayne Bryan, his fear of Careb overcome by his hatred of being too long out of the limelight. 'They are experts at dealing with thugs like you. You don't have a ghost of a chance of getting away with this – you'll all end up dead, just like the bunch who held the Iranian Embassy lot hostage. Your best bet is to let us all go and get out while you can.'

'Let me educate you, Mr Bryan,' replied Careb. 'It would take a huge and very well-equipped force to defeat us, and even then they would probably fail to get most of us. But long before that happened, all of you – and I particularly mean you, Mr Bryan – would be dead.

'Just pray to whichever gods you favour that the powers-that-be are not prepared to face the public backlash, should harm befall their favourite stars, and no one is stupid enough to attempt a rescue, and do something that you, personally, will live – or not – to regret.'

The chubby singer's face had turned grey and his lower lip had begun to tremble violently. 'You wouldn't dare,' he stuttered.

At the same moment, several of the other captives began speaking and Careb raised his hand. 'I don't want any more whining from anyone right now. If your public could see you now, I don't think they would be all that impressed. With just a couple of exceptions, you certainly haven't impressed *me* so far.'

TWENTY-SEVEN

At that very moment Major Peter Stevens was putting the finishing touches to exactly the type of stupid plan that Caleb Sinclair had just explained would be much regretted by at least one of the hostages. The Major, in common with most Special Forces personnel around the world, held firmly to the belief that the majority of military problems could be solved using high explosive.

True to this fundamental belief, 22 SAS D Squadron arrived at Belmont Place carrying more than 100 pounds of Cyclonite and Pentaerythrite Tetranitrate mixture – more commonly known as Semtex, the explosive of choice of both international terrorists and the Special Services. When mixed with TNT, this extraordinarily stable explosive, as easily twisted into shape as children's modelling clay, becomes a fearsome charge, known as Cyclotol. Just a half-pound of Cyclotol is sufficient to blast a Jumbo jet out of the sky.

It was Major Stevens' intention to use a small lump of Cyclotol to smash a hole in the glass bottom of the lake and allow 10,000 gallons of water to flood the room beneath. What he also wanted was that he and his men should drop in at the same time, and literally ride the crest of the massive wave he would create to sweep the terrorists before them, killing or capturing them while they were caught by surprise.

'If we can grab the five terrorists in the lake room and free the hostages, then we can simply storm the house afterwards and wipe out the rest of them if necessary. There'll be no hostages there to get in the way,' he told Commander James.

The anti-terrorist squad leader looked unconvinced. 'I would like to give this a lot more careful thought before we rush in with explosives and guns blazing,' he said.

The original team in the guardroom had now been joined by Sir Duncan Gough, the deputy head of MI5, and Sir Peter Goddard, the boss of MI6, whose inability to co-operate – indeed, whose primary aim seemed to be to undermine each other's departments – was well known in Intelligence circles.

'I'd rather like some of my chaps to have a look at these characters before any action is taken at all,' said Sir Duncan. 'Knowing who we're dealing with could make things a whole lot easier.'

'It's much more likely my people have come across them,' chipped in Sir Peter, thrusting his way forward to stand right in front of the Commander. 'A couple of my top terrorist experts are on their way down now. It's essential they get a close look at these targets before anything is decided. I know these SAS fellows would rather blow things up and ask questions later, but in my experience, an intelligent mind can usually achieve a better solution than a bloody bomb.'

Commander James, who was accustomed to the bickering between the two Intelligence chiefs, was relieved that neither one of them was advocating an immediate attack on the terrorists. He turned to face Major Stevens. 'I think, Peter, that we should hold off for a bit longer, at least until we can find out a little more about what we're up against. But flooding the room is the only feasible plan anyone's come up with so far, so if you and your men would like to go ahead and work out a detailed plan, I'll make a decision later.'

He noted the crestfallen look on Stevens' face and thought, *God preserve us from gung-ho heroes! What this situation needs is caution rather than impetuosity.* 'I know the Prime Minister favours your plan, Peter, but we're still working almost blind and no harm is going to come to the hostages if we postpone taking any action for a while.

'That's my decision for now. What would be very useful is if we can get a wireless camera out to Jim Weston so we can all see what's going on down in that room. It would also give our Intelligence experts a chance to look over the opposition. Perhaps some of you could put your heads together on how we can manage that.'

TWENTY-EIGHT

The first newspaper to contact Downing Street was the *Daily Mirror*, at a few minutes after 11pm. Within the next ten minutes, eight other national dailies and six television news programmes were trying to get through.

Jack Benson had left word with the press office that all calls concerning the hostage situation should be diverted to his office. He had been prepared to play down the raid but, within a few moments of his own press spokesman taking the *Mirror*'s call, realised, listening in, that their reporter knew almost as much about the situation as he did himself.

The Chancellor, who was still mentally reeling from the shock of discovering that the man he had hero-worshipped for more than 20 years was, in truth, a complete enigma, had been uncertain how he would deal with the press. With crystal clarity, Bobby's dramatic exposure of his real self had shown Benson which line he should take with the media. He clapped his hands sharply to get his staff's attention and told them all to put their calls on hold while he gave his instructions.

'Confirm everything for them except the names of the prisoners the terrorists wanted released. That just isn't going to happen, so there's no point in going into pointless detail. I want you particularly to stress the danger in which all the hostages find themselves. And tell them that the Prime Minister is making the freeing of the hostages, and their safety, his number one priority. Bobby Temple has emptied his diary and will be personally taking charge of the hostage crisis.

'This means he will probably have to cancel his forthcoming visit to Moscow – but the safety of the hostages takes precedence over everything else. The fact that his wife is one of the hostages is obviously important to him, but he will be endeavouring to find a way of bringing *all* the hostages out of this safely.

'His personal involvement will not, however, alter the British Government's position with regard to dealing with terrorist demands. In common with all Western governments, there's no question of acceding to terrorist threats or demands. On this, he is resolute.

'Bobby has already spoken to the Queen, and she has given her full backing to the Government on the way this should be handled. Her prayers are for Princess Katherine and for all the hostages and their families. That's it, folks.'

He nodded and the room was immediately filled with chatter as the half-dozen men and women who had been called in to assist the duty press officer began passing on his words to news-hungry journalists.

Benson sat on the edge of a desk and listened as they passed on the details, which would form the basis of tomorrow's front pages. *OK, Bobby. Now see if you can rush things along to suit yourself and Brekov. If someone gets hurt, the whole world's going to know who to blame.*

He reached for a telephone and asked to be put through to Chief Constable Sir David Clayton. Better fill him in on the line to take with the press.

The first to interrupt their standard transmission with a newsflash was *Sky News* at 11.15pm. They announced armed terrorists had taken a star-studded group of hostages prisoner and had threatened to kill them if their demands were not met. Captives included the Prime Minister's wife, June, Princess Kate, pop superstar Wayne Bryan, cinema idols Glen Grant and Rachel Friedman, TV legend Georgie Brown, international model Beverly Gladstone and celebrity Catholic priest Father Luke Large.

Pictures of the hostages were flashed on the screen as the announcer added that firebrand black MP Ashley Bodin and the US Ambassador were also among the very unlucky 13 guests invited to dine that night with billionaire Peter Flint in his palatial mansion near Reigate, Surrey.

Viewers were told that armed police and troops had already sealed off Belmont Place and that a squadron of the élite SAS would also be involved in any possible rescue attempt. The siege was likely to be a long one, and there were unlikely to be any further developments until the morning, when the Prime Minister was expected to make a statement on the situation.

TWENTY-NINE

If Major Stevens had his way, plenty would happen before the morning.

'It's bad enough with all the bloody floodlights, but once daylight comes we're not going to be able to get to that rockery without being spotted from the house. Our only chance is to do it now while we have the partial protection of darkness.'

Buzz Sawman nodded vigorously in agreement. 'You're talking suicide mission if we try it in daylight, boss. And I'd much rather we pulled the fucking plug on all these lights before we go in! The main cable has to come in through the gatehouse so it wouldn't be much of a problem.'

'Agreed,' said the SAS officer. 'Except the damned terrorists have already warned our policeman friend they'll shoot somebody if we interfere with the electrics. I personally don't think they would go that far. Not before getting what they want, and if none of their people is hurt. But I don't think the Commander could be persuaded to take the risk.'

The two men were on their stomachs, just within the tree line, and 150 yards from the back of the house. Stevens had already deployed the rest of his men and the armed police in a wide circle around the house, but concealed in the trees, 10 metres apart.

Stevens could clearly see the rockery, where Jim Weston had already endured four tense hours of imminent discovery, and still lay in hiding, watching the events in the lake room.

'What are the chances of taking a four-man squad in there to join him without being spotted?' he asked the sergeant.

'You're the best team leader I've got, and by far the most experienced. If we do go in to blow the lake bottom, I'll want you to be in charge. If you'll accept it, that is.' (The Special Forces have a tradition that no one has to head a mission unless he is willing to accept it.)

But Buzz Sawman didn't hesitate: 'Affirmative, boss.'

Stevens nodded, expecting no less. The Sergeant Major was extremely tough and courageous – an utterly ruthless killer when required, as lethal with a knife as a whole range of weapons. He was an inspiring leader whose men would follow him into any situation.

'Once you've hit the target, all hell's going to break loose out here. If you set the charges, and then pull out before the balloon goes up, you should be OK. There'll be covering fire, of course. But if we follow on down once the place is flooded, then, however briefly, we're going to be exposed to anyone firing from those first-floor windows at the back of the house. If we get the OK to go in, I'll be coming with you, along with another eight-man squad.'

Sawman considered this for a moment. 'Well, we could always mess things up a bit, and make it easier on ourselves,' he said, grinning. 'I could lay a couple of smoke bombs to trigger at the same time as the main charge, then for a couple of minutes all they'll see from the house will be a bloody big black cloud.'

Stevens grinned back: 'That sounds good to me, Buzz.'

The two men wriggled backwards, well into the trees, before standing.

'How long will it take you to prepare the charge?' Stevens asked.

'About 20 minutes. It only needs an ordinary stick detonator timer. Once you give me the go-ahead, I reckon me and the lads could be out there, in place, in half an hour.'

'OK, get to it! I'm going back to talk to the Commander and try to get some action.'

THIRTY

Major Stevens' arrival in the gatehouse coincided with Commander James taking a call from Downing Street. As soon as he heard Bobby Temple's voice, he sat up to attention.

'Yes, Prime Minister,' he said. 'The situation here remains unchanged. We have the house surrounded and there's no sign of any movement inside. The press have arrived and we're keeping them outside the perimeter. Chief Constable Clayton is out there now holding a press conference, but he has no intention of explaining anything except the barest details.'

'Keep it that way!' snapped Bobby. *They already know too much*, he thought to himself. *It's on every TV and radio station.* 'But tell me about the SAS: When are they going in?'

There was a lengthy pause. 'I really think it's much too early to be talking about using force, Prime Minister.' The Commander's tone of voice was placatory. 'No one has been hurt as yet, and so far we haven't even been able to establish a dialogue with the terrorists. To rush into action this quickly could bring very serious reprisals. As you are aware, they have already threatened to start killing the hostages if we try anything.'

Bobby cut him short: 'For Christ's sake, Commander, they've had plenty of opportunity to hurt people if they were so minded.

But their first move was to let a whole lot of people go free, even the professional bodyguards and security people. It seems quite obvious to me that they don't want blood on their hands. They must realise that when we finally take them, as we eventually and inevitably must, then it will go very badly for them if they have shown any brutality towards their prisoners.'

'But, Sir, these men are terrorists! Terror is their business. Hurting and killing people is what they do. One mustn't assume that they're squeamish just because they haven't murdered anyone yet. That would be a tragic mistake, in my opinion.'

'What does Major Stevens think?' asked Bobby brusquely. 'Have you asked him for his professional opinion?'

'Well, it just so happens, the Major is with me now, Prime Minister. Perhaps you'd prefer to talk to him in person?'

'Put him on,' commanded Bobby curtly.

As Commander James handed the telephone to the SAS officer, he briefly covered the mouthpiece. 'Go easy,' he whispered. 'He's trying to rush things, and that's both stupid and dangerous in this situation.'

Major Stevens made no reply, but his eyes were gleaming with excitement as he took the proffered telephone and placed it to his ear.

'Major Stevens, Prime Minister.'

The big, red-faced officer listened for a few moments and smiled. 'The action I have in mind would ensure the hostages are moved from their present location to the main house, which will make their extraction far easier when the time comes. But I would personally favour our going in immediately, right after we flood the underground area. Only a handful of them are guarding the hostages down there and they'll be thrown completely off balance by our attack. My men can go in – in force – and cut them down in seconds.'

He paused as Bobby interrupted with a question.

'Yes, Sir. There's always a risk that during an exchange of fire some of the hostages could be hit, and maybe die. But I can guarantee the losses would be minimal.'

He listened for a few moments longer, his expression becoming gradually less cheerful.

'Yes, Sir… indeed, Sir. I'll pass you back to the Commander.'

He handed the telephone back to Commander James and shook his head at the others.

'No balls,' he mouthed.

A mistake. Bobby Temple certainly had the balls, but was acutely aware of who would be blamed if hostages were killed as a result of direct orders. It was one of the very few circumstances that could lead to his being removed from his position. He bitterly regretted just how high-profile this particular bunch of hostages were, and resented the fact that they now wielded some influence over his career. But he managed to suppress his desire to see this situation ended by brute force and opted instead for a more pragmatic approach.

'I think phase one of Major Stevens' plan to force the terrorists into the house is justified,' he said coldly. 'But I agree with you, Commander, that too strong a show of force at this stage could place the hostages in unnecessary danger. I want to be kept fully informed of the results when the SAS make their play, no matter what the hour.'

He hung up without saying goodbye.

THIRTY-ONE

Using the squadron Range Rover and driving by the light of the moon, Major Stevens took only a few minutes to travel from the entrance lodge to the thinly wooded area to the rear of Flint's mansion. He doubted the terrorists could see beyond the leading tree line but chose, as a precaution, to crawl the last 50 metres to where members of D Squadron and the police had formed an armed ring surrounding the house.

Buzz Sawman was waiting, seated with his back against a tall silver birch, securing the straps on a small canvas knapsack as the Major emerged from the darkness beside him.

'All set, Peter,' he grinned, his face appearing to twist grotesquely under its heavy layers of greasepaint camouflage make-up. 'We just need to get that civilian bloke, Weston, out of there, then I'll go and plant this little beauty where it'll give the fuckers underneath the shock of their lives. According to Weston, the glass is specially toughened, 3.5 centimetres thick. So if I've done my sums right, I reckon this charge will knock a hole in the lake bottom about a metre square. That'll send some 500 gallons a second pouring down on them. The whole bloody lake will be empty in two minutes.'

Stevens found himself grinning in reply. 'That should dampen their spirits down a bit. At that rate, they'll have to abandon the basement area pretty damned sharpish or they'll be up to their necks in water.'

'What about us, boss? Do we follow the water down the plughole?'

''Fraid not, Buzz,' Stevens answered curtly, the smile disappearing. 'The powers-that-be are all terrified we might compromise an innocent target down there by accident.'

'Don't they fucking realise the risk will be the same whenever we go in? At least this gives us the element of surprise.'

'Sorry, Buzz,' said the Major. 'Of course, I know you're right, but this is a direct order from the Prime Minister himself. Who are you taking in with you?'

The Sergeant shook his head. 'If we're not following in, it'll be a lot simpler to do it on my own. It's a five-minute detonator, which I've left sticking out at the top.' He pointed to the knapsack on his knee. 'I just need to twist it, slide this pack down the side of the rockery onto the glass bottom and get the hell out of there.'

Stevens nodded in agreement: 'Let me pull Weston back here and you can go in straight away, Buzz.'

He unhooked the radio from his belt and pressed the transmit button.

'Hello, gatehouse. This is Major Stevens. Patch me in to Jim Weston and tell the Commander we'll be blowing the lake bottom in ten minutes.'

Moments later, he heard the whispered voice of the American security chief.

'Weston, this is Major Stevens. We've decided to adopt your idea of flooding the basement and we're going to blow a small hole in the glass bottom by the rockery. You are right in the danger zone so I want you to pull back to the trees, away from the house. I'll be waiting for you here.'

'I hear you, Major, but I have no intention of letting Peter Flint out of my sight. I don't give a god-damned turkey shit about the rest of them, but my job is to take care of Peter – and that's what I intend to do!'

'I understand, Weston, but five minutes after that charge goes off, your boss will be heading up the stairs and into the main part of the house. We have orders not to follow the water down into the basement, but you can bet your life the explosion will get a lot of attention from the terrorists still in the house – and if the blast doesn't kill you, chances are, they will. If you want to help Peter Flint, get your arse back here, intact! That way, you'll be in one piece when the real action starts.'

There was a 30-second pause. 'I suppose that makes sense. I'll pull out now. Weston out.'

Stevens snapped off the radio. 'Right, Buzz, in you go. Don't hang about after you've set the charge. I want you back here by the time it goes bang. OK? Radio when you're done.'

'Roger.'

Buzz Sawman twisted the knapsack onto his shoulders and snaked off across the grass towards the nearest flowerbed bordering the rockery. The area he was crossing was out of direct range of the floodlights surrounding the house and, with the moon hanging low behind the trees, lay in deep shadow. Major Stevens lost sight of him within seconds, but he continued to stare towards the rockery and, two minutes later, became aware of a larger, dark shape snaking towards him across the grass.

'A friend approaching,' he called to his men on either side. Then, to Jim Weston: 'Keep on coming, Weston. into the trees.' He stood up, shielded by the trunk of a large juniper, and,as the huge Texan rose to his feet inside the tree line, grasped his right hand and shook it.

'Nice to meet you at last. I'm Peter Stevens.'

'Good morning, Major. I passed your guy heading the other way. I hope to Christ you fellas know what you're doing. If you get it wrong, the whole damned floor of the lake might go – and that will kill them all.'

'Don't worry about it,' said Stevens. 'Sergeant Major Sawman is the best explosives man I know. He could blow a pimple off your arse without you feeling a thing. Nothing will go wrong. Five minutes from now, your boss and his guests will be a bit wet, but nothing worse than that. And then they'll be in a place where we can get at them much more easily.'

'I sure as hell hope so,' said Weston staring the Major directly in the eyes. 'Because if anything goes wrong, I'll be holding you personally responsible. I've spent too much of my life taking care of Peter Flint to see him drowned or shot because of one man's crap decision.'

Stevens was saved from making a reply by static on his radio. 'Go ahead.'

'I'm setting the charge now. The balloon will go up in five minutes.'

As the device was armed and placed in position, in the main part of the house the terrorist called Heinrich was calling Careb Sinclair.

'Phase two is now complete, but we have a situation. As you anticipated, the security forces have set up a cordon around the whole building. They are between 150–170 metres back, mainly seeking concealment among the trees. At present, there are some 70 men involved. He glanced briefly at the four 2 metre square, giant TV monitors, each covering a 90-degree segment of the perimeter. Their signals were fed from the latest heat-seeking cameras, which Heinrich and his team had set up earlier around the house. It was the product of a highly classified US military project based at a top-secret army base in Colorado. Several US Defence Committees, who had rubber-stamped an astronomical budget for the development of a prototype, would have screamed for blood had they known where its first practical application would take place. The screens showed the precise location of the SAS and police personnel deployed around the mansion. It also showed one pulsing red marker 50 metres inside the general cordon.

'There is one target figure positioned at the end of the lake right above you,' reported Heinrich. 'He could well be observing you through the glass ceiling. Would you like me to deal with him?'

'Affirmative,' said Sinclair. 'Do it now. And if any of the others move forward from their present positions, take them down, too.'

He noticed that Davey and Emma were watching him expectantly.

'It seems we have an observer in the garden who is rather keen on finding out what we're up to down here.' He paused. 'At least Heinrich thinks it's only an observer.'

He strode quickly to the wall and used the flat of his palm to click off the half-dozen dimmer switches on the panel. 'But it'll do no harm to make quite sure.'

Now the only light, apart from the candles, came from the floodlights on and in the lake above.

'Jacques... Peter... ' he motioned to the two men who had destroyed the lift shaft. 'Watch our guests and if any one of them moves more than an inch, kill him or her immediately.

'Davey, you and Emma help me check the ceiling – just in case some madman up there is thinking of breaking in from above. I expect them to get round to turning off the pumps eventually, but I doubt they'll go any further at this stage.'

Each taking a section, the three began a careful examination of the transparent lake bottom, walking slowly back and forth, their eyes scanning the sheer glass surface above them.

At that precise moment, in a rear first-floor window of the mansion, Heinrich was carefully lining up an extremely complex-looking weapon. This assault rifle – the AT/Heckler-Koch XM-29 SABR/OICW – which combines a 20mm grenade launcher with a 5.6mm rifle, is considered by its American inventors to be 500 times more effective than any current equivalent, but is not officially due to enter service, even in small numbers, for another two years.

The version used by Heinrich would not become available to American infantry even then. Its target acquisition/fire control system, mounted on the top, combined telescopic day and night vision capabilities with laser range-finding and could be coupled to the tactical heat-seeking computer.

Through these sights, Heinrich had a clear view of several clumps of daffodils, and other flowers and dwarf plants at the base of the rockery overhanging the lake. This conventional view alone would not have revealed the man hidden among the vegetation. But the XM-29 was far from conventional. Taking its range and direction from the computer a floor below, to which it was wireless radio-linked, the control system showed a small, pulsing red star right at the centre of a large clump of daffodils which, as Heinrich adjusted his aim, became centred in the telescopic sights.

The assault rifle was now aimed directly at the concealed man's most easily identifiable bodily organ: his heart.

Heinrich took up the slack on the trigger and gently increased the pressure.

Sergeant Major Buzz Sawman depressed his radio transmitter switch for the final time. 'OK, boss, I'm out of here.'

'Make it snappy,' ordered Stevens, the tension briefly showing in his voice.

'Roger to that.'

Buzz reclipped his radio to his vest pocket, glancing, as he did so, through the large clump of blooming daffodils, which he confidently assumed shielded him from any observers who might be watching from the house.

Best to make quite sure the coast is clear, he cautioned himself. He was mindful of the seconds ticking by, but unconcerned about the explosive charge resting on the lake bottom just a few feet below his position. The detonator had a full three minutes left to run and, from long experience, Buzz knew that by snake crawling, on elbows and knees, he could cover 50 metres a minute at least, if necessary.

The main blast would be felt above and below the charge, and he knew the lake bank would protect him from the sideways blast even if he were only ten metres from the water's edge.

His only slight worry, that he may have exposed himself to a much graver and more immediate danger, came while making his final visual check towards the house. But by then, it was already far too late to save himself.

He clearly saw the muzzle flash of the XM-29 in the first-floor window – but never heard the distinctive, crisp crack of the assault rifle as it launched the round that killed him.

When the second shot came, just a second later, Sergeant Major Buzz Sawman was already dead. The first bullet entered through his left eye at a speed of more than 2,500 miles per hour, tore through his tongue, throat and part of one lung and shattered his heart before exiting through his lower abdomen.

His lips pulled back from his teeth in a reflex grimace of agony but when the second round removed the back of his skull and sent a fine mist of grey brain matter spraying across the yellow daffodils, he was already beyond any feeling at all.

At the moment of his death, Buzz had partly supported himself on his left elbow. This now collapsed, and set his body rolling slowly down the rockery slope and into the lake, where it finally came to rest face down at the bottom, his stomach resting completely across the pre-set knapsack.

Intrigued by their captors' sudden preoccupation with the ceiling, the hostages also stared intently at the illuminated glass above them.

It was Princess Kate who was first to see, and recognise, the SAS man's body, and she screamed in horror, pointing towards the waterfall end of the room. The face pressed against the glass above was horrific. Blood snaked in tiny tendrils from the open mouth, its bared teeth, exposed in an agonised snarl, distorted the grease-painted face, and oozed from the ragged hole where the left eye had been.

Two of the other women began to scream and Careb silenced them with an almost scream-like yell of his own. 'Stop that hysterical racket now! If any of you make another sound, I can promise you that you'll live to regret it – most sincerely.'

He turned to the guards: 'If anyone makes a noise of any kind, shoot them where it hurts.'

'I think we could have a problem,' said Emma quietly. 'I spotted something out of place just before he dropped in. Now he's lying on it – it looks like some kind of bag or satchel.'

Careb and Davey stared at the bag, trapped under the dead man's stomach.

'Did he drop it by accident when he was shot or did he place it there beforehand?' mused Davey. 'I don't think it's worth taking chances. We ought at least to pull back from this room to be on the safe side.'

'Agreed,' snapped Careb, turning and striding towards the dining table. 'Get on your feet, all of you, and move out of here now. It's just possible some lunatic has got it into his head to play Dambusters.' He reached the table where most of the hostages were still seated unable to grasp his meaning and jerked Alison, the nearest, to her feet. 'Get out of here!' he shouted, and pushed her towards the end doors leading to the marble foyer. 'The ceiling could come down at any moment, which means – with the exception of any fucking mermaids among you – the situation is going to become somewhat unpleasant.'

As the others began to scramble away from the table, Georgie Brown let out a great wail and sprang towards Careb, reaching for his neck and shoulders.

'I can't swim,' he screamed, terror forcing his voice up an octave, 'you've got to save me!'

'Then get the fuck out of here!' snarled Careb trying to disentangle the panic-stricken celebrity's arms from his neck. But Georgie was far too overcome by fear to listen to reason.

Davey solved the problem by slashing the barrel of his MP5 compact submachine-gun across the TV star's knuckles. Georgie immediately let go his grip and began to howl with pain, sinking to his knees, his damaged knuckles pressed into his armpits. Careb hauled him up by his collar and kicked him hard in the rear, sending him careering towards the door just as the charge in the knapsack exploded.

Brilliant flashes of red, yellow and orange flames lanced downwards at the same moment as a tremendous explosion shook the underground room. The effect of Buzz Sawman's body lying across the charge meant that far more of its force was directed downwards than had been intended, consequently blasting a hole about three times the original size in the reinforced glass sheet.

Immediately, thousands of gallons of water, great shards of glass and dozens of stunned Koi cascaded into the room, producing an instant 5-foot tidal wave, which swept with terrifying speed across the chamber.

Emma, who had been standing nearest to the explosion, was instantly lifted off her feet and carried along, her arms flailing uselessly, by the unstoppable wall of water.

As she was forced under by the sheer power of the curling wave, her head caught a glancing blow on the end of the table, which knocked her unconscious, and her limp body was dragged further down by the swirling water, which slammed her, stomach first, against one of the massive corner legs. Her upper body and arms were to one side of the table leg, her lower torso and legs on the other, wrapped almost double and held there by the immense pressure of water.

The only person to witness her desperate plight was Father Luke Large. Pushed aside by the panic-stricken Georgie Brown, Luke had remained near his place until he was certain that June Temple, next to him, was safely on her way to the exit. He had then rounded the head of the table to try and assist Lynsey St John Beauchamp who had been pushed back into his chair by Wayne Bryan as the singer, with characteristic disregard for everyone else, stampeded past Rachel and Glen Grant and elbowed Beverly Gladstone aside in his determination to reach safety.

When the explosion came, Luke had only an instant to prepare himself as a solid mass of water thundered down through the gaping hole in the glass ceiling and surged towards him. He spun around, bracing himself with both hands his huge stomach against the table as the wave struck, knocking most of the breath out of him.

But even as his legs lost their purchase and he was gradually pulled under, Tuck was aware of Emma's predicament, just a couple of feet to his left. With a massive effort, he retained his grip on the table top with his right hand and reached across and down gripping Emma's limp left arm just above the elbow. Aware that his last breath of air, sucked in moments before the water hit, was being exhausted by his exertions, Tuck knew he would get only one chance at saving his captor. The fact that he was risking his own life to save one of the terrorists, never occurred to the priest, who believed fundamentally that all human life was sacred.

He mentally steadied himself then let loose his grip on the table top and twisted sideways and down to grab hold of Emma's other arm with his right hand. The force of the water against his huge bulk did the rest, pulling Emma free from the table leg and sweeping the pair of them along the marble floor towards the other end of the room.

When Tuck, completely out of air, struggled to the surface – still clinging with both hands to the unconscious Emma – they were carried through the doors and into the foyer. As he sucked in great lungfuls of air, and tried to keep Emma's mouth above water, Tuck registered that the terrific force of the initial wave had diminished. Although he could still hear water crashing into the dining room and the water level was still rising, the enormous pressure had been reduced to that of a strong, but manageable current.

As Tuck, kicking with his legs, neared the staircase, which was more than half-covered, he was spotted by Careb Sinclair, who had already reached the stairs.

Careb didn't hesitate, but immediately dived back into the water and, with two powerful strokes, reached the struggling priest. In seconds, they had pulled Emma to the stairs and dragged her well above the rising water line to the first landing.

Careb turned her onto her stomach, placed her head to one side, and began to apply artificial respiration. Half a dozen powerful thrusts forced almost a litre of water from Emma's pale lips – but there was no sign of life. Careb rose from his position straddling her waist and turned her body over. Tilting back her beautiful face, he pinched closed her nostrils with his fingers and forced a large breath into her open mouth.

Her lips felt cold and lifeless against his and Careb, not a religious man, found himself begging God to spare his friend. He hadn't realised he had spoken the prayer out loud until Tuck, who had fallen to his knees alongside them, spoke.

'A merciful God can answer the prayers of even the worst sinner,' he said. 'Let's hope together we can get His help.'

Careb switched to pressing his full weight, through the palm of one hand, onto Emma's chest, and releasing it. Every three beats, he leaned forward and gave the kiss of life.

He heard a commotion further down the stairs and then a loud cry of anguish, but refused to be distracted. His attention was focused only on Emma. A burst of gunfire from below again caused his head to spin round, but he ignored it, and carried on with what was starting to look like a fruitless task. He would rather, he suddenly realised, sacrifice the whole project than lose Emma Vale. Only now, as she teetered between life and death, had he discovered just how much he loved this remarkable, beautiful woman.

Suddenly, Emma coughed and spluttered, and then took a shuddering breath on her own. Careb believed he had never before felt such utter joy. After about another 30 seconds, her eyes opened. She looked puzzled for a few moments and then recognised Careb, who was seated astride her.

'Any excuse… to play with… my… tits… ' she gasped, and coughed again as more water trickled from the corner of her mouth. She turned her head and saw Luke. Her face filled with revulsion.

'What's this fucking priest doing?' she spat through another bout of coughing.

Careb found himself laughing and almost crying with joy. 'Well, this particular fucking priest just saved your life,' he announced grandly. 'You would have drowned if it hadn't been for him, you ungrateful bitch! He almost drowned getting you out. Now, if you've quite finished scaring the living daylights out of me, I think I may be needed down there.'

He glanced around him. Five of the hostages were sitting or lying on the first landing and none of them looked up to trying to make a run for it. He glanced back at Emma, who, thanks to her excellent physical shape, was already sitting up, and came to a fast decision. He drew his pistol from its holster and handed it to her.

'Keep an eye on this lot while I see what's going on,' he said.

On the steps, where the water level continued to rise, he found Jacques, the younger of the two guards, laying face up in the water, his shirt front leaking blood from half a dozen or so bullet wounds.

On the steps above, Davey was leaning over the motionless body of the black MP and junior minister for the Arts, Ashley Bodin, who was lying face down and either unconscious or dead. A thin trickle of blood seeping onto his dress shirt collar seemed to originate from a wound on the side of his head. As Davey rose,

Careb saw that his friend had been handcuffing the hostage's hands behind his back... which meant he was still alive.

Bodin had been one of the fastest to react when Careb gave his warning, and was through the doors and protected from both the initial blast and the main force of the wave when it came. He had waited until the water level rose and then let the continuing surge carry him to the steps, and was ready to spring when Jacques, who had lost his footing and swallowed a good deal of water, was washed hard against the marble steps, disorientated and confused.

Bodin had initially managed to wrestle Jacques' Heckler and Koch MP5 from him, but had dropped it on the steps when the former French paratrooper had kicked out and caught him on the wrist with the metal-capped end of his boot. Ashley Bodin screamed in pain and then, cursing loudly, and finally able to release all the suppressed anger and frustration which had built up over the past few hours, stepped forward and repaid his assailant in kind, kicking him as hard as he could. He had aimed for Jacques's chin but struck his shoulder and, instead of knocking him senseless, simply hurled him back against the opposite wall, forcing the air from his lungs.

Despite the punishment, and being badly winded, Jacques kept his wits about him and quickly drew his knife from its sheath, which he kept strapped to the outside of his right leg. Holding the blade low, and well out in front, he gathered his strength and breath with the intention of finishing off the hostage.

Ashley's left hand and arm were completely numb and he was barely capable of moving them. But as the knife came into view, he had no doubts at all about the seriousness of the danger he was in.

Keeping his eyes fixed on his assailant, he bent and scrabbled around on the steps for the submachine-gun. His fingers came into contact with metal just as the terrorist launched himself from the opposite wall and lunged with his knife outstretched towards Bodin's gut. Using the weapon as a simple shield, the MP managed to block the knife thrust and force Jacques onto a lower step.

But the terrorist was now almost fully recovered from his near-drowning and able to return almost instantly to the attack, again thrusting forwards and upwards towards Bodin's lower torso.

But this time, Ashley managed to spin the submachine-gun around and he squeezed the trigger as the blade flashed towards his stomach. The raucous clatter of the gun, as the 15-round magazine emptied in a little over a second – took them both by surprise. The bullets stitched a haphazard line across Jacques' chest and sent blood spraying from half a dozen jagged holes, first stopping him in mid-lunge, then sending him staggering backwards down the stairs to collapse in the water. The remaining spray of bullets had struck the wall, gouging large chips of marble before ricocheting harmlessly away.

Ashley crouched, his finger still pressing hard on the trigger of the now empty machine-gun, his eyes widened in horror as he stared at the bloody corpse of the man he had just killed. He was still transfixed in this pose when Davey launched himself from the water, momentum carrying him up the next two steps, and slammed the barrel of his Sig Sauer 9226 handgun hard against the side of Ashley's head.

The MP crumpled immediately. He had landed on his side, but Davey roughly turned him over until he was face down, and then produced a pair of handcuffs from the belt at his waist. He was just snapping them onto the fallen man's wrists when Careb came down the stairs.

'As you can see, Jacques is dead and Peter is rounding up the last of them down below. I haven't done a full count but I don't think anyone is missing.' He grinned. 'For a while, I half expected to see the SBS in wetsuits coming at us with guns blazing.'

'They might still,' said Careb, glancing down the stairs, where the water appeared to have reached its maximum height, a couple of feet from the foyer ceiling.

Sam Goldman, the American Ambassador, was being helped onto the dry steps by Glen Grant, who, apart from a bloody nose, appeared to have survived the trauma unscathed. Not so Rachel Friedman, who sat one step above the waterline, her feet still submerged. Her eyes, saucer-like, were fixed on the bloody corpse floating just a few feet away, and she seemed too shocked to move. Careb took her upper arm, pulled her to her feet and began leading her up the steps. She followed him, seemingly oblivious to those around her.

Grant and Sam Goldman were next up the stairs and, as they passed, Davey caught sight of Princess Kate, looking fresh and in her element, swimming on her side while tugging Lynsey along by the shoulder. His alabaster face was tilted up towards Davey, who could just make out faint pink froth issuing from the man's half-open mouth. His hands seemed to be holding onto something at chest height just under the water.

As Lynsey reached the steps, he seemed to make a great effort and managed to stagger one pace upwards out of the water. Davey briefly closed his eyes in involuntary abhorrence, and heard Kate gasp, 'Oh shit!' as she tried to help him up.

They had both seen what it was that the young man was gripping – a large, icicle-shaped sliver of glass protruded nearly a foot from the front of Lynsey's chest. It appeared to have been rammed through from the back. Little blood was coming from the actual wound but the glass and Lynsey's hands were dripping red, and Davey realised he had sliced his fingers to shreds trying to dislodge the projectile from his chest.

The Irishman stepped down and gently took Lynsey by the shoulders, turned him and sat him down on the stairs. Kate began ripping strips from her blue silk dress. Davey gripped the young man's wrists and told him, 'You've got to let go if we're going to be able to help you, lad. Just open your hands and then I can try to sort you out.'

Sobbing loudly now and still spewing pink froth from his mouth, Lynsey finally opened his deeply sliced and bleeding fingers. Davey moved them away from his chest towards Kate.

'Wrap them up,' he told her. 'That's all we can do for now.' Kate wrung out the excess water from the silk strips and carefully bandaged Lynsey's mutilated hands.

'What are we going to do now?' she asked.

'I'm going to have to pull this glass out,' Davey told her. 'From the look of the blood coming out of his mouth, it has gone through a lung… and that's not good. But with this thing sticking through him we can't lie him down, and it's going to be hard to move him without knocking it, and possibly causing more damage internally. I know you're down to a mini-skirt already, girl, but if you can give me another strip of material to protect my hands, I'll pull it out.'

'But won't that kill him?' asked Kate, as she tore free more of her skirt, leaving her thighs almost completely bare.

'Maybe,' said Davey. 'But I'll have to do it. Otherwise, we can't move him and he'll die where he is.'

He positioned himself, legs apart and back against the wall, behind Lynsey, and with his hands wrapped in the remnants of Kate's skirt, took a firm grip on the 18-inch long shard which protruded from the injured man's back.

'I think it tapers all the way to that point we can see sticking out at the front,' said Davey. 'So it should come out easily… unless it's trapped between his ribs, of course.'

Kate sucked in her breath and momentarily turned her head away from the gruesome sight.

'I need you to hold onto his shoulders and steady him while I pull,' said Davey. 'Be brave for just a couple more minutes and it will be over.'

She managed a weak grin. 'That's what all the boys say,' she managed, and grasped Lynsey firmly by his shoulders. His eyes were less than 2 feet away, stretched wide with pain and fear.

'You're going to be fine,' Kate told him, and pulled him gently forward as Davey nodded and pulled on the angled base of the glass spear.

As the missile's end withdrew into Lynsey's chest, a great spurt of blood gushed from the open wound and he screamed in agony. Then he collapsed, unconscious, against Kate's blood-soaked breast.

Throwing the glass shard into the water below him, Davey thrust his hands under the limp man's armpits and began dragging him, backwards, up the stairs. Seconds later, he was helped by Glen Grant, who had witnessed the last few moments from the landing above, and rushed down to assist.

He took Lynsey's legs and, together, the two men carried his limp body to the top of the second flight of stairs at the end of the corridor, which led directly to the ground floor of the house.

But when Tuck and Flint went down to help Ashley Bodin, Careb ordered them back upstairs. 'Mr Bodin MP is the least of my worries… and should be yours, too,' he told them. 'He just killed one of my men and, for that, there will be an inevitable punishment. Your would-be saviours outside were warned of the consequences of making any rash rescue attempts and have chosen to ignore it. You, as I promised earlier, will be the ones to suffer.'

Careb took Ashley by his manacled hands and dragged him down to the water where he immersed the unconscious man's head completely for several seconds. Then he hauled him clear and kicked him brutally in the side.

He repeated the operation, and this time Ashley coughed and choked. He suddenly opened his eyes to find himself staring straight into the bleakly cold, pale-blue eyes of his captor.

'On your feet and upstairs,' he said quietly. 'It's immaterial to me whether I kill you now or later. But if you make the slightest wrong move, it'll mean your death sentence. I'll kill you where you stand.'

He prodded the still groggy MP in the shoulder with his pistol. 'Now get moving before I give myself a treat and kill you now.'

When they reached the top landing, they found most of the hostages corralled in the corner and guarded by Peter and Emma, who appeared to have fully recovered.

'We're all ready to move out,' she told him. 'But that one is going to have to be carried... if he lasts that long.' She nodded to where Lynsey lay on the corridor floor surrounded by Kate, June Temple and a tearful Wayne Bryan. 'I think the tears are more for the Princess's benefit than for his boyfriend,' she added. 'I don't think that arsehole has ever experienced a decent feeling in his life.'

His tears appeared to be having absolutely the desired effect, for Princess Kate was comforting the sobbing star, a reassuring arm around his shoulders. She and June had torn strips from June's dress to pad the appalling wounds in Lynsey's back and chest, and had bound them in place with his dinner jacket, knotting the two arms across the front. A trickle of blood was still coming from Lynsey's mouth, and his face and lips were almost white. His eyes were closed.

Wayne Bryan clung to one of his shirt-sleeved arms, keeping his hand well away from the blood-soaked makeshift bandages wrapped around his lacerated fingers. 'Oh, Lynsey, my darling, what have they done to you? Please don't die... I can't bear it.'

'Nobody did it, Wayne,' said Kate. 'It was just bad luck. When the glass ceiling came down, a spear of it must have been carried along by the force of the water and hit him. It was just bloody awful luck, that's all.'

'They say it's down to you that he's alive at all,' sobbed Wayne, clutching Kate around the waist with his free hand. 'I'll never forget that. Never! I should have been there to save him myself, I know. But I was nearly drowned as well. I was lucky that the wave pushed me onto the stairs... more dead than alive.'

He looked at Kate, appealing for sympathy. But whatever she was about to reply was drowned out by Georgie Brown. 'That's complete bollocks,' he yelled shrilly, his eyes blazing with hatred. 'You knocked everybody out of the way to get out first! You tripped Rachel and pushed me flat on my fucking face, you bastard! Nearly drowned? You were charging up the stairs when the water hit me.'

'That's a fucking lie,' screamed the singer, 'I nearly drowned like the rest of you!'

Georgie laughed again, his face twisted in loathing. 'If that's right, you twisted fuckwit, then why is it that only your trouser bottoms are wet, and you're not dripping like the rest of us?'

There was a sudden silence as everyone, including the captors, stared at Wayne. Kate looked at her arm, which was around the singer's shoulders, and slowly released it. His burgundy silk dinner jacket was completely dry, and now, as she looked more carefully, she saw that only his trousers, up to the knees, were wet.

Wayne cringed away from the look of sheer disgust on her face, his own turning bright crimson. Then he leapt to his feet and charged towards Georgie Brown. 'I'll fucking kill you, you miserable, sleazy old shit!' he screamed, raising his clenched fists high, with the obvious intention of battering Georgie's head. The TV star raised his arms and cowered back in sudden terror as the incensed singer rushed towards him.

But Careb Sinclair was faster still and, leaping forward, kicked Wayne Bryan's legs from under him, sending him crashing hard to the floor, where he lay badly winded and gasping for air.

'Well, what do you know... ' said Davey. 'And it's us who are supposed to be the bad guys.'

'We could certainly learn a thing or two from them... especially him,' Emma said, shooting a glance at Wayne. 'And I've always hated his singing.'

Careb grinned: 'Now that we've had a bit of excitement, let's get this lot into the main building. Then we need to teach our friends outside a little lesson in appropriate behaviour.'

THIRTY-TWO

Major Peter Stevens saw the muzzle flash from the sniper's rifle at the first-floor window and shouted an order to the SAS men within earshot. 'Incoming hostile fire... first floor... third window from left. Take him out.'

Yet as the SAS troops on either side opened fire with their M4 rifles, Stevens knew it would already be too late. Even before he brought his night-vision binoculars to bear on the sniper's window, he was certain the terrorist would no longer be there and, as he had anticipated, the window was empty.

'Hold your fire,' he yelled, then ducked for cover as the Cyclotol charge exploded 50 metres away, causing the ground under him to tremble.

'Where the fuck is Buzz?' he called out. 'He should be back here by now.' Then he closed his eyes and took a deep breath as the sniper's shot suddenly made perfect sense.

'Fuck...' he breathed, scrabbling for his radio. 'Delta Zero One, come in. Base to Delta Zero One... are you receiving, Buzz? If you are, talk to me.'

But the only sound from his radio was static. He depressed the transmit button again, but before he could speak, a large hand grabbed his shoulder and spun him round.

'If you want my opinion, your Sergeant Major is dead and your whole fucking plan has gone pear-shaped. You can see from here that most of the damned lake has already vanished underground, so that fucking charge must have been one hell of a sight more powerful than you guys planned.

'The room below will have filled up with water in a matter of seconds and that means some of those innocent people down there probably drowned. And you'd better start praying to whichever favourite god you have that one of those people doesn't turn out to be Peter Flint.' Jim Weston grabbed Stevens' khaki jacket in his right fist and shook the Major violently. 'If it is, then you, mister, are a dead man.'

When the big Texan finally stopped shaking him, Stevens almost collapsed. It took a huge effort to remain standing, and he felt his legs trembling uncontrollably. 'Let's hope it's not as bad as that,' he finally managed to gasp. 'I suggest we get over to the gatehouse and try to talk to the terrorists, and find out what's actually happened before we jump to conclusions.'

'That's the first sensible thing you've said so far tonight,' said Jim, reluctantly letting go of Stevens. 'But remember, soldier boy, I'm still holding you responsible for anything that's happened.'

The Major switched frequency on his radio and alerted the gatehouse that they were coming in. Commander Brian James fired off half a dozen questions but Stevens refused to answer.

'There's been a hiccup – I'll explain everything when I get there.'

Ten minutes later, he had finished briefing the command group on events up at the house.

'If that's what you call a hiccup, Major,' said Brian James caustically, 'I'd hate to be involved in one of your real cock-ups.'

Not one member of the group smiled. There were now seven of them gathered in the gatehouse – the Commander, Sir David Clayton, the two Intelligence chiefs Gough and Goddard, protection officers Graham Phillips and Tim

Mortimer, and Chief Superintendent Bill Warden from Reigate Police Station.

'It sounds an absolute mess,' the commander went on. 'And it genuinely frightens me what these men might do by way of retaliation. Their warnings were very specific – and so were their threats. I fear that if this thing has gone badly wrong down there, then the repercussions are going to be extremely unpleasant for the hostages.'

'Do you want me to have my men standing by to go in?' asked Major Stevens, suddenly looking brighter.

'No, I damn well do not!' replied James. 'We'll wait and see what your first action has cost us before making another bloody stupid move. I'll try and get through to their spokesman to find out, if I can, exactly what your heavy-handed tactics have cost us.'

But as he reached out for the main security telephone, which connected to the house system, it began to ring. Commander James hesitated a moment. 'It seems someone at their end wants to talk to us as badly as I want to talk to them,' he said, and picked up the receiver.

'I want to talk to the person in charge.'

James recognised the voice of the ringleader who had spoken earlier and switched on the speaker, so that those around him could all hear.

'You're speaking to him,' he said, 'Commander Brian James of Scotland Yard.'

'Good. This is Salamander. You were warned earlier about doing something heroic or stupid, and I told you what the results of that would be. Now it is time for you to pay the price of your folly.

'As a result of your actions, one of my men has been killed and one of the hostages seriously injured. As punishment for the killing of my companion, I have decided to kill six of your men, Commander. Plus one of the hostages.'

'But you can't just... ' the Commander began, but Careb cut him off.

'I can do what the fuck I want, Commander! And you'd have been better off if you'd accepted that sooner than later. For I can assure you, it will only get worse... for you and the hostages, that is.

'I assure you, this is not a callous action, but a simple act of retribution. To show you how compassionate we can be, I am going to hand over the injured man – Mr St John Beauchamp. You can send in a two-man stretcher crew, on foot, and collect him from outside the front door. But I warn you, in advance, that if there is any trickery at all, then the punishment I have already specified will be doubled.

'Mr St John Beauchamp has a serious chest wound and requires immediate surgery. He was speared through the chest by a jagged section of glass from the shattered lake bottom. An own goal, I think you call it. Pick him up in ten minutes or the offer is withdrawn.' With that, the line went dead.

Major Stevens could contain himself no longer. 'Bullshit!' he cried. 'Our men are back in the tree line, well screened from the house. There's no way he can take out six of them, just like that. And this time we'll be watching. If any of his men appear at the house windows, we'll get them.'

Commander James waved him down. 'Let's save the heroics for later, Major. Or didn't you hear what the man just said? You do understand English, don't you? Our priority right now is to get that injured man to hospital. I've got a fleet of ambulances out in the road standing by, just in case.

'Chief Superintendent, tell one of the crews to drive to within 100 metres of the house. Then to go forward on foot with a stretcher and pick up Mr St John Beauchamp from outside the front door. They can take him straight to the nearest main hospital.'

As Bill Warden hurried outside, he turned to the Chief Constable. 'Sir David, perhaps you wouldn't mind alerting the hospital and explaining that a badly injured man, with serious chest wounds, will be with them in under half an hour.'

Sir David nodded and reached for an outside phone.

'And I suppose I'd better telephone the Prime Minister and let him know what's happening. I'm sure he'll be concerned to know the identity of the terrorists' first hostage victim. After all, he does have a personal interest.'

Jim Weston glared at Major Stevens. 'You'd better start praying they don't pick on my boss,' he said curtly. 'And I agree with this guy. We've had enough of your heroics, Major. You're bravery has led to other people dying – doesn't really inspire confidence, does it?'

THIRTY-THREE

The scene in the guest drawing room was far removed from that of just a few hours earlier when the guests had gathered in pleasant anticipation of a memorable evening to be spent in extremely interesting, if slightly bizarre, company.

Now, with the notable exception of Wayne Bryan, whose clothes were comparatively dry, and who was being ignored by the others, they had herded together by the fireplace and looked a miserable and bedraggled bunch – dazed, soaked and cold, and stripped of their glamour by fear and the shocking events of the past few hours.

Their captors in the room now numbered six – Careb, Davey, Emma, Peter and two others, Peruvians Luis and Rudolfo, whom the hostages hadn't seen before, and whose names had not been mentioned.

Lynsey St John Beauchamp, who had mercifully lapsed into unconsciousness, had been left on the floor in the main hall. He had been carried there by Glen Grant and Father Luke Large. Princess Kate and June Temple had begged to be allowed to stay with him, but Careb had refused.

Jacques' body was also in the hall, carried there at gunpoint by the still-handcuffed Ashley Bodin and the disgraced rock singer Wayne Bryan. These two men were now the subject of a quiet but heated discussion, involving Careb, Davey and Emma, who were huddled out of earshot of the hostages.

It was Ashley, Careb declared, who had killed their colleague and was therefore the one who deserved to die. Davey favoured dispatching Wayne Bryan. The podgy singer was a coward and a liar, he argued. At least the black MP had shown courage in taking on one of his armed captors. Emma, who had taken an instant and total dislike to Wayne Bryan, sided with the Irishman.

'He's everything we detest in a person,' she said passionately. 'He is weak, deceitful, a braggart and disloyal, as well as being a coward and a liar, as Davey already said.'

'But his value to us will come later,' reasoned Careb. 'Ashley Bodin is, with the exception of St John Beauchamp, the lowest ranked male hostage on the celebrity ladder. And I don't think any of us want to shoot Beauchamp.' He looked quizzically at the others and they nodded. 'We are dealing with men out there who are just as ruthless as ourselves and a great deal more stupid. They're not going to get the message this time... or probably next time, or even the time after that.

'And each time, when we need to choose a candidate, we need to escalate their importance. We need public and media opinion to get to work to achieve what we want, and that means upping the stakes all the time.

'Father Large is also a lesser-known figure, I know, but we owe him big time for saving Emma, and if that means keeping him alive at the moment, so be it.'

'I don't have any problem with that,' said Davey instantly.

They turned to Emma, who finally nodded agreement. Feeling charitable towards a man of God was so alien to her, and in such contrast to some of her strongest-held and most basic beliefs that she was unable to express herself verbally.

'I suppose you're right about Bryan,' she conceded, changing the subject. 'He's a far bigger fish than Bodin… and stinks a hell of a lot more, too,' she added emphatically.

Davey smiled briefly: 'Well put, Emma. So I suppose the miserable sod gets a reprieve, at least for now.

'On a different subject entirely, what are we going to do about dry clothes for our guests? Mrs Temple and the Princess will have stuff upstairs, and so will Flint. And the old boy can probably supply enough other gear for the rest of them.

'I suggest Emma goes upstairs first and sorts out the women's clothes and then I'll find something for the men. We have plenty of dry outfits among our own stores for ourselves.'

'Agreed,' said Careb. 'But before all that, you and I, Davey, need to deal with the more unpleasant events on our agenda. Emma, if you and the others will shepherd our friends over to the two windows, where they'll get a good view of the show, Davey and I will set the stage.'

He walked to the long bar, where Ashley Bodin had been handcuffed to one of the stout metal supports, and released him, momentarily, before securing the opened handcuff to the MP's free wrist.

'You're needed for stretcher duty,' he told him, and motioned him towards the door with his pistol.

Beverly Gladstone, who had watched the release of her boyfriend from the other end of the room, now sprang forward. 'Where are you taking him?' she cried, her large, jet-black eyes huge with fear, her trademark bee-stung lips trembling. 'I want to go with him.'

Davey, who had exchanged his Sig Sauer handgun for an XM-29 assault rifle, swung the weapon lazily in her direction. 'Hold it, girl!' he warned gently. 'Your man's got things to do which you really don't want to get involved with. And getting yourself hurt isn't going to help him at all now, is it?'

Beverly stared at the assault rifle and bit hard on her lower lip. 'I want to know what you're going to do with him,' she said defiantly.

'Dear God, but the women here are a hell of a sight braver than the men,' exclaimed Davey softly.

'Don't worry, Bev,' said Bodin, breaking in. 'Nothing's going to happen to me. They daren't harm a member of the Government. They'd stand no chance of getting out of this alive if they did. I'm too important, and they know it,' he sneered. 'They just need me to do their dirty work for them and move poor Lynsey. That's what they want you to watch through the window.'

Beverly remained unconvinced, but faced with the menacing twin barrels of Davey's rifle, she stayed where she was, as Careb pushed Bodin ahead of him through the door. Davey followed, closing the drawing-room door behind him and trailed them along the corridor to the main entrance lobby, where Careb halted the MP next to Lynsey's unconscious form.

'You take his arms and walk out of the front door backwards,' Careb ordered. 'I'll be carrying him by the feet so don't do anything stupid.' He took the mobile security phone from his pocket and buzzed the gatehouse. 'I hope your men are ready, Commander. We're about to deliver Mr St John Beauchamp outside. We've also connected a video camera to the house security network so you'll be able to see what happens for yourselves.'

He hung up and exchanged the phone for one of his own group's radios. 'Heinrich and Thomas... on my signal, I want you to each take out three of the opposition forces in front of the house. Grenades should provide our viewers with the necessary visual impact, I think. Jonathan, it's time for you to start turning the cameras. The moment has come for action.' He said the last word loudly and winked at Davey. 'It's just the showman in me,' he said. 'I can't help myself sometimes.'

'So you're taking your revenge,' intervened Ashley Bodin, smiling slightly. 'Nothing wrong with that... if they're just cannon fodder. But I know you don't want to hurt me – I'm too valuable.'

Careb and Davey exchanged looks, faces expressionless.

'And valuable to you, too. That's my real insurance. I've made millions out of cocaine.... and I'm prepared to cut you in, big time.'

The terrorists' eyes widened slightly. 'Well now, Mr Member of Parliament... you're full of surprises, aren't you,' said Davey, whose loathing of drugs was only slightly eclipsed by his hatred of the British Army.

Misunderstanding his captor's irony, Ashley's smile widened. 'Yes, and I can pay any ransom you want to name... within reason. Much more than anyone else you're holding.'

'You're right, Davey,' said Careb, 'I think we had Mr Bodin figured all wrong during our little talk back there. I feel much better about things now... don't you?'

'Absolutely,' agreed Davey. 'I think he's just confirmed that he'll be out of here before anyone.'

Careb stepped between Lynsey's motionless legs, bent down and took a firm grip just below the knees. 'Now if you'll just do the same at that end... ' he told Bodin. 'Hold him just above the elbows and go out backwards... we'll get this sorted, then. And when I tell you to stop, stay right there until I tell you to move, even when the medics appear. OK, Davey, perhaps you'll do the honours?'

The Irishman was already standing by the massive front doors and now turned one of the door knobs and slowly swung it inwards, wide enough for the MP and Careb to carry the limp body outside.

Through the zoom lens of the video camera directed from a first-floor window in the west wing, the men in the gatehouse saw the pair shuffle out from the entrance, past the imposing portico columns and on to the marble flagged terrace. From there, a dozen steps led down to the driveway and the great circular fountain, where several brightly illuminated plumes of water shot high into the night air.

They carefully lowered Lynsey to the ground. The camera now zoomed in on the MP. Commander James was the first to recognise him.

'That's Ashley Bodin, the Arts minister,' he said, and reached for the external telephone. He quickly dialled the Prime Minister's hotline and it was picked up on the second ring.

'Temple,' said the familiar voice.

'There has been a further development,' said the Commander. 'They have brought out the injured man, and one of the people carrying him is Ashley Bodin.'

'What about their threat to kill our people?' asked Bobby Temple.

'Nothing yet. But I thought you would want to know what's happening. These people have thought of everything. This is all being filmed on a video camera and we are watching it live in our emergency headquarters in the gatehouse. Our ambulance team has just reached the house and they're going forward now to retrieve the injured man.'

As he spoke, the camera slowly pulled out until the viewers could see the whole scene on the terrace. They noted that the other man, who had helped carry out Lynsey, appeared to have already withdrawn into the house.

'Perhaps they are sending the minister out with a special message,' suggested the Yard Commander, with little conviction. 'Surely they can't be meaning to shoot him? Not an MP... that's inconceivable.'

This, in almost the same words, was what Princess Kate was telling a tearful Beverly Gladstone, as they watched the drama unfold from behind one of the 2-metre wide windows in the guest drawing room. She reached her arm further around the other woman's heaving shoulders and hugged her tightly.

'They surely won't do anything that horrible,' she whispered.

The arrival of the ambulance team carrying a stretcher should have reduced the tension a little, but all the onlookers remained strained and anxious, barely daring to breathe – they were all terrified their worst fears might be realised.

'The ambulance men have put Beauchamp on a stretcher and lifted it,' Brian James recounted to the Prime Minister, 'but Mr Bodin is not moving. They are starting to move away... it could be that they are being given their instructions from someone in the house... we can't see. Just a second, the camera's zooming in again... all we can see now is Ashley Bodin's face in profile. He looks fairly relaxed.'

What none of the transfixed spectators could see was Careb Sinclair, standing in the deep shadow of one of the giant columns of the portico, just 10 feet away from the waiting MP.

'You're a very bad judge of people, Ashley,' he called softly. 'In fact, you're very bad in so many ways. I promised you'd be out of here before anyone else. Well, I'm going to keep that promise. Goodbye.'

Careb raised his Sig Sauer handgun and shot Ashley Bodin straight between the eyes. Commander James guessed what was about to happen from the unmistakable look of terror which transformed the MP's handsome face still framed in close-up on the TV screen.

'Oh Christ... no!' he shouted, and then gasped in revulsion as the nightmare vision was played out live in front of him. There were shouts of disbelief and anger from the other members of the security team, and then silence.

In the guest drawing room, several of the woman screamed, the loudest being from Beverly Gladstone, who slowly sank to her knees.

The bullet which struck Ashley Bodin in the centre of his forehead removed half his skull and what appeared to be a large portion of his brain. The black MP was thrown off his feet by the force of the bullet and landed, sprawled on his back across the top two stairs. The TV camera had obligingly pulled back to show the full impact on the MP's body as it fell.

Immediately after the execution, Careb stepped back quickly inside the front door, which was slammed shut by the Irishman.

His voice was perfectly calm as he produced his radio and ordered, 'Heinrich and Thomas... go,' and then to Davey, 'He made it almost a pleasure.'

In the deep shadows of the trees around the house, SAS troops and police, who had watched the killing of Ashley Bodin through telescopic sights or binoculars, pressed themselves further into the ground, suddenly feeling more vulnerable themselves. An irrational fear, perhaps, because they knew themselves to be invisible to the terrorists holed up in the big house.

They were unaware, though, that the two gunmen, Heinrich and Thomas, had already selected their unsuspecting victims, having fixed them in their sights as clearly as if they had been lying out in bright sunshine. Using the heat-seeking device again, they were easily able to identify the troops and policemen hidden within the bank of trees some 10 metres apart.

Both men were again using the high-tech AT/Heckler-Koch XM-29 SABR/OICW, but this time selecting the upper barrel which launched 20mm high-explosive grenades. Unlike traditional grenades, which explode on impact, the XM-29 high-explosive warhead detonates above the target, using a blast and fragmentation effect. Used against a human target, it is devastating and invariably lethal.

With the target acquisition/fire control system on top of their weapons coupled to the tactical heat-seeking computer system, the terrorists were able to fix their victims' positions with a laser beam which pinpointed the source of body heat and automatically set the detonation fuses on the grenades at the moment of launching. From a six-round clip, and with their targets only some 150 metres away, the gunmen could each fire their three grenades in under five seconds.

Barely had the stunned Commander time to pass on the news of Ashley Bodin's murder to the Prime Minister before the grenade attack was launched.

'Another development, Sir. The camera has now focused on the trees in front of the fountain and there are a number of explosions. It looks very much like an attack on our troops who are surrounding the building. It could be a random attack but I suspect these bastards are far better organised than we thought. They promised to execute six members of our strength here, and I fear that is what we have just witnessed.

'I'm afraid to tell you, Prime Minister, that the decision to flood the underground dining area has now cost eight lives. And if Mr St John Beauchamp doesn't survive, then that could soon be nine. It's not going to sound too good on the morning news.'

'No, it isn't,' snapped Bobby Temple. 'But I suggest you leave the problem of dealing with the public to us, Commander, and you concentrate on how you're going to prevent any more of our people dying.'

Inside the main entrance of the house, Careb was working on their next move. 'It's going to take everyone a while to digest what's happened,' he said to Davey, 'but I can't see them making any more rash decisions for a few hours. Time, perhaps, to clean up and get into some fresh clothes. And get our guests into some dry things as well.'

'OK, boss,' said Davey. 'A clean-up it is, it'll make us all feel better. It's not quite how we envisioned it, but things could be a hell of a lot worse. One thing we can say… the game, as young Will Shakespeare once put it, is very certainly afoot. Let's make the most of it.'

'We will,' agreed Careb. 'But talking of games… ' He pulled out his transmitter. 'Jonathan, did you get those links to the TV newsrooms?'

'I did,' the voice replied. 'And the dish transmitter is on the roof and set to go. That footage I shot will be with them all during the next 30 minutes. It's going to slip down a treat with their cornflakes!'

THIRTY-FOUR

Bobby Temple faced Jack Benson across the large Georgian desk in the Prime Minister's Downing Street office, the national morning newspapers spread out between them. It was still early and neither man had snatched more than a few hours' sleep since the news of Ashley Bodin's murder. That, and the hostage siege in general, dominated the world's television and radio networks and more than half the pages of the newspapers.

Predictably, most editors had used Princess Kate on the front pages, with June Temple and the executed minister. But the lives and careers of the other hostages were fully covered inside, and passionate, strident, self-righteous editorials demanded that Bobby and the Government move quickly to free them, while, at the same time, blaming the Prime Minister for responding over-aggressively and precipitating the murder of Bodin.

'Damned if I do, damned if I don't,' said Bobby. 'As always, the bloody vultures are short on common sense and anxious to find someone's bones they can pick over. Hypocritical bastards, the lot of them. And how did they get all the information, Jack? I thought you were going to take care of the press personally. They seem to have been told everything there is to know, almost down to the colour of June's knickers. How the fuck did that happen?'

'Well, Bobby,' began the Chancellor, 'I took the view last night that, with so many people involved, there are bound to be leaks. I also believe that it would rebound badly on you if the press found out we hadn't been straight with them from the start.

'Peter Westcroft has been accused of sending in the SAS prematurely, so you're not being blamed for that. But we're going to have to be bloody careful from now on not do anything equally stupid, and possibly incur the same dire results. It's time to back off and let things calm down.'

'CALM DOWN?' Bobby leapt to his feet, demonstrating to his trusted lieutenant the full force of his frustration. 'If we don't do anything positive, then this kind of siege could last for days... even weeks. And time is a luxury I can't afford right now. I'm not going to let a bunch of criminals dictate my agenda to me. I intend to be in Moscow on Monday – and with June at my side – so don't talk to me about taking things easy!

'I want those bastards out of there, and in hours, not weeks. I want suggestions for action, not appeasement. Think positively, Jack! Why the hell do we have intelligence organisations and terrorist units if they can't come up with the right information or the right solution? Time for you to kick arse, Jack.'

He ceased his pacing of the office and turned to face the Chancellor. 'Don't let me down on this one, Jack. Get it right, and do it quickly. Understand?'

Benson returned the Prime Minister's stare with an equally stony look. 'Are you threatening me, Bobby? I'm not Peter Westcroft or one of your other lapdogs. Not only do I know where all the bodies are buried, I helped you bury a lot of them... from the galloping Major down.'

For a moment, raw hatred blazed in Bobby's eyes, then he shook his head slowly and forced a smile to his lips. 'There's no threat, Jack... don't be silly. I just want you to realise how important this is for me… for all of us. We are on the brink of leading our country into a whole new and glorious period in its history and nothing should be allowed to delay it. When history beckons, then other things, however desperate the circumstances, must not be allowed to interfere.'

Bobby's eyes began to blaze again with the now almost familiar religious fervour and Jack Benson shuddered inwardly. *However could I have not seen the flaw in him before now?* he asked himself. *He's become completely irrational. This kind of blind obsession can only end in disaster for everyone and everything — the country included.*

THIRTY-FIVE

In the guest drawing room at Belmont Place, tension was also running high. There had been fierce objections from several of the female hostages to stripping off their wet clothes and towelling dry in front of one another, but these had been curtly over-ruled by Davey, who had repeated his observation that few of them had left much to the imagination in their choice of outfits that evening.

With the exception of Princess Kate, June Temple and Peter Flint, who had changed into their own clothes, the others were wearing a mismatched selection of items gathered haphazardly from the wardrobes of maids and other servants. As the hours ticked by, some managed a little broken sleep in chairs, or on the two large sofas, and in the case of Beverly Gladstone and Alison Best, on the thick pile carpet, with a cushion under their heads.

Since waking, Beverly had succumbed to several long bouts of sobbing, unable to rid her mind of the abrupt and brutal manner of her boyfriend's execution. Several of the women had tried to comfort her, but she was now sitting with her back to the wall, knees hunched under her chin, silently grieving with tears streaming down her beautiful face.

Davey and Peter, another of the Salamander team, had guarded the hostages for the remainder of the night while Careb and Emma

Vale slept in two of the many guest bedrooms on the first floor. They had only just returned to the drawing room and were chatting quietly to Davey, out of earshot of the hostages, before he went off to catch up on sleep himself.

When Beverly finally focused on Careb, her face contorted in hatred. 'Murderer,' she screamed. 'You're nothing but a cheap hoodlum… a common killer. You're not man enough to have tied Ashley's shoelaces.'

Careb stared hard at her for a moment. 'Your boyfriend's execution was a matter of simple justice,' he said calmly. 'He had killed one of my men, which was a good enough reason to dispose of him. But there is also the little matter of the thousands of people who have died or had their lives made utterly miserable by all the drugs he smuggled into this country. It was justice for them, too.'

Judging from the reaction among the hostages, this was news to most, if not all of them. But to one of them, at least, it changed nothing.

'How can someone like you use words like "justice"? You have no honour, no morals. It sickens me to hear you talk about justice.' Glen Grant's characteristic drawl gathered momentum. 'You're just a bunch of savages… gangsters on the make.'

Careb's features turned to thunder, and his eyes narrowed: 'Some of you will probably thank God for my justice and honour before this business is ended, Mr Grant… and my mercy and charity, too, no doubt.'

'I'm talking about action, not just words,' snarled the star. 'If you really were a man possessed of any kind of honour or decency, you would accept a personal challenge to settle this thing.'

Careb smiled, but looked puzzled. 'I can't quite see where the conversation is going, Mr Grant. Perhaps you can enlighten me.'

Grant had risen from his chair near the fireplace and now pointed dramatically to the spot above the white marble mantelpiece where a pair of long, tapering cavalry sabres were hanging unsheathed on the wall. They were a famous pair of blades, made in Toledo for General George Custer, flamboyant commander of the US Seventh Cavalry and hero of the battle against the Sioux Indians on the Little Big Horn River in Dakota in 1873, when he and all his men were slain. One had actually been retrieved from the battlefield, heavily stained with enemy blood. Peter Flint, who had a passionate interest in reminders of his country's turbulent history, had bought the prized pair of sabres at auction in New York for a record sum.

'I'm talking about a challenge – man to man, me and you – until only one of us is left standing. If I win, we all go free. If you win... ' he shrugged. 'I don't suppose I would be around to care what you did to me or anyone else.'

'Yeah, right on,' whooped Beverly, springing to her feet and wiping her tears away on her sleeve. 'Cut the bastard down to size, Glen – literally!'

Everyone, including his own people, now looked expectantly at Careb, who glanced over to Emma and exchanged a conspiratorial grin. One of the regular disciplines in their daily workout was a punishing series of hard-fought duels with rapier and sabre. Each was an outstanding exponent of both weapons.

Rachel Friedman spotted the brief exchange of looks between Careb and Emma and it set alarm bells clanging in her head. 'Be careful, Glen – they're not fools. Please don't get into something you can't handle.'

'But I take it Mr Grant considers himself to be a useful man with a sabre,' said Careb. 'Isn't that so, Mr Grant?'

'Good enough to take care of a piece of shit like you,' snarled the movie star. 'If you've got the guts to face me, that is.'

He stood, hands splayed on hips, head back, in typical Glen Grant hero stance, reminiscent of at least a dozen swashbuckling Hollywood blockbusters.

'Well, you don't lack for courage, Mr Grant, that's quite certain. Though as for foolhardiness, I wouldn't be quite so sure. It could be amusing, though, to see how far that bravery will take you. Remember, though, you won't be play-acting here. There is no one around to shout "Cut", or order a stuntman to take over when things get difficult. And the points on these sabres are, I imagine, very sharp and very real.'

Grant continued to glare at him from under his shaggy blond fringe and Careb nodded. 'If you want to prove that the age of chivalry is still with us, then so be it. Let us accept for the moment that I agree. But, to take one of Georgie Brown's sayings, "What's in it for me?" What do I get out of it if I win? You all stand to win your freedom. What could possibly be worth the risk of losing my life? Apart, that is,' and he made a deep and dramatic bow to them all, 'from defending my honour.'

His eyes flicked around the circle of captives and he smiled again. 'Perhaps one of you ladies is prepared to make the ultimate sacrifice in pursuit of your freedom. A lady's honour thrown into the ring might make the contest a little more appealing to me.'

'Christ almighty, just how low can a guy like you sink?' said the US Ambassador in disgust. 'You want one of these ladies to commit her body to you as a prize for killing Mr Grant?'

'I don't want anything,' said Careb sharply. 'Can I remind you that this is all Mr Grant's idea, and he wants to fight for big stakes. Freedom for all of you, with my life as the price. If I'm to accept the challenge, there has to be something in it for me.' He spread his arms wide in appeal.

Princess Kate, who had risen to her feet during the last exchange, walked forward and stopped a couple of feet in front of him.

'You could have me,' she said, simply. 'Always providing, of course, that you turn out to be man enough to cope with that. And with me.'

There was a snort of laughter from Georgie Brown – swiftly smothered by a withering look from Alison.

June Temple leapt to her feet. 'Your Royal Highness… Kate,' she pleaded, 'you can't do it… give yourself to this man? It's unthinkable.'

The Ambassador backed her up. 'You really can't do it, my dear,' he said. 'It's very brave, but out of the question.'

'He's right, Kate. We couldn't let you do that,' said Peter Flint gently.

'Why not?' The whining voice of Wayne Bryan cut in. 'If it means getting the rest of us out of here, then why the hell not?'

'Right,' interjected Georgie Brown. 'Let's face it, it's not as though this is the first time.' He glared round at the shocked faces. 'If her adding another bloke to her tally can get us out of here, I'm all for it.'

Kate laughed out loud. 'Did somebody just mention the age of chivalry? Though I can think of worse prospects… my husband for one.' She raised her chin and smiled fondly towards Glen Grant. 'But I have every confidence in Mr Grant. I recognised his special qualities when I first met him, and I have every confidence he will prove a fitting champion for a princess's honour. I also remember him in *Robin Hood* and *Captain Courageous*, and his swordplay in those roles was just about the most thrilling thing I've ever seen. So how about it, Mr Gangster? I don't think you stand a chance against our superhero, but will I do as a prize?'

Careb glanced again towards Emma, who was grinning broadly. As was Davey, with a look on his face that was part admiration, part envy for his friend's once-in-a-lifetime opportunity.

'The best possible prize,' agreed Careb. 'Now let's get on with it, shall we? I can see young Davey here needs his beauty sleep and we just can't keep him up any longer.'

Before striding over to the fireplace, he paused by Davey and whispered, 'If he wins, kill him and carry on as planned.' He winked broadly. 'I think you should take the Princess as a consolation prize anyway.'

At the fireplace he reached up with both hands and grasped the twin sabres by their ornate, silver-and-gold hilts. He carefully lifted the exquisite swords from their fixings and turned to face the room. Glen Grant was standing in the centre by one of the small, antique coffee tables that dotted the drawing room. The others were all on their feet now, hovering around the edges of the room in differing states of anticipation, fear and hope.

Careb held one of the sabres halfway along its blade and offered it hilt-first to Grant, who took it with confident familiarity in his right hand and slashed several times at the air, testing the weapon's balance and feel.

Some of the hostages spontaneously broke into applause. 'Make sure you slit his fucking throat,' yelled Beverly, clapping louder than the rest.

Finally, Glen turned to face Careb, eyes bright and unwavering, sabre raised.

Careb raised his own blade and let them touch lightly, the fine Toledan steel emitting a light ringing sound. Slowly they circled each other, suddenly tense, each watching the other intently. Grant was the first to strike with a sudden slash at Careb's neck, which he parried effortlessly – the two glittering blades sliding together. Then his defensive parry became a lighting thrust, which Grant was barely able to push aside, the silver blade passing just beyond his rib cage.

He stepped backwards, suddenly looking more wary and noticeably less confident. Then he lunged for Careb's stomach, changing the blow for a backhanded slash at his head. Careb blocked the other's blade and, for a few moments, they were locked together, hilt to hilt, eye to eye.

Careb smiled a wicked, knowing grin. 'Different like this, isn't it?' he said, as their sabres disengaged. His words goaded Grant to a flurry of action. He launched a series of attacks, cutting and thrusting, the two blades dancing and producing flashes of reflected light, ringing with the metallic crash and rasp of steel on steel.

They circled again, Grant pressing forward, keeping Careb on the back foot. It was a relentless onslaught but Careb remained completely controlled, blocking the cuts and turning the thrusts aside with apparently effortless grace.

After several minutes of non-stop action, Grant was beginning to slow, the sheer ferocity of his attack taking its toll on his stamina and nerve. Although both were just in shirt sleeves, the two men had started to perspire, with tiny beads of sweat running down their foreheads and faces.

The onlookers were utterly still, mesmerised by the deadly duel taking place only feet in front of them, and knowing that each of the protagonists was only a split-second away from a hideous death. Only when the razor edge of Grant's blade slit the arm of Careb's shirt, and passed perilously close to his flesh, was there a loud gasp from some of them, including Emma.

On it went, cut and thrust, back and forth, around and around… block, retreat, thrust, parry, all to the jarring, grating sound of steel on steel.

Gradually, the force of Grant's attacks began to weaken. His breathing became heavier and his arm was tiring. Even his great reservoir of hate-driven energy was beginning to empty.

Not so Careb, who appeared unaffected by the ferocious duel. Then – in an instant, it seemed, to those who were watching – he switched from effortless defence to blistering attack. The shaft of his sabre became a blurred patch of silver light which Grant was scarcely able to follow or deflect. Defending desperately, he gave ground rapidly, a look of fear and panic on his face.

The end, when it came, was shocking. Careb suddenly executed a series of moves that were almost too fast to follow with the human eye, and used his blade to pluck Grant's sabre from his grasp.

The onlookers scarcely dared to watch. 'In your films, the hero would now stoop down and return his opponent's weapon to him,' said Careb. 'But, as I warned you, this is not make-believe. Welcome to the real world, my friend.'

And he thrust the point of his sabre clean through Grant's chest, just below the left shoulder.

Several of the women screamed, shocked by the casual indifference of the strike, and Wayne began to retch as Careb withdrew the blade and a gush of scarlet blood spurted from the wound.

Grant staggered and then sank to his knees when he realised what had happened. 'Christ, I think you've killed me,' he croaked and raised his right hand to try to stem the flow of blood. June, Kate and Alison had all rushed forward, frantically tearing at their skirts for material to staunch the blood. Kate glared at Careb, who was retrieving the fallen sabre.

'You were playing with him,' she snarled, her blue eyes filled with anger. 'He didn't stand a chance, did he? He was being brave and you were just having fun. I despise you… you sick fuck!'

Careb wiped the blood from his blade, and carefully replaced the sabres on their stand above the mantelpiece before turning. 'Take it as a further warning as to who is the master here. You must obey the rules and do as you are told,' he said calmly. 'Your movie hero will survive… at least, he'll survive that wound. There are no vital organs where I hit him. I could just as easily have killed him.' He grinned. 'A sore shoulder is little punishment for so stupidly believing he could affect the outcome here. You are prisoners and you will only be released when I say so. If you are disobedient, you will be killed.'

He paused and stared directly at Princess Kate, the smile spreading from his lips all the way to his eyes. 'And that brings me to you, Your Royal Highness. There's also the small question of a favour. I'm sure you haven't forgotten your generous offer. You'll excuse me if I don't collect my champion's prize immediately – I have a few things still to arrange.'

Kate stared at him open-mouthed.

'Let's enjoy it at a more convenient time, perhaps?' and he bowed low and turned away.

THIRTY-SIX

Bobby Temple was seething with anger and it was the latest bulletin from Belmont Place which had caused it. There had been a total lack of communication from the terrorists since last night's killings. No further demands and no obvious activity up at the house. But far worse, in Bobby's mind, was his own team's lack of a strategic plan.

The SAS and police survivors of the grenade assault had spent the remainder of the hours of darkness digging trenches on their perimeter and erecting corrugated iron covers to protect against further attacks. Major Stevens had paid a dawn visit to the scene and, after debriefing his junior officers, had returned to the gatehouse and was conferring with Commander James and the Chief Constable when the Prime Minister's call was put through.

At this stage, his trio of experts told Bobby Temple, the safety of the hostages must be their paramount concern. Even Major Stevens accepted that retaliation must play a secondary role. The terrorists had shown just how ready they were to carry out swingeing reprisals if attempts were made to free the hostages. It would be downright irresponsible to try anything that would jeopardise their continued safety. 'First, because we owe it to the hostages themselves not to do anything rash,' Commander James told the Prime Minister, 'and second, because the public would accuse us of being killers if we forced another execution like that of Ashley Bodin. The press would crucify both us and you. And rightly so, in my opinion.'

'Other than defeatism, have you got any plan of action at all?' asked Bobby bitterly. 'Perhaps I should be looking for other experts to assist you.'

'Whoever you put in charge,' Commander James replied, 'they would have to be very certain indeed of success through a forceful intervention before committing themselves. Right now, it's true, we don't have any suggestions on the table that look very promising. So, for the moment, Prime Minister, I think we are going to have to sit it out.'

It was exactly the answer Bobby did not want to hear, and it took all of his self-control not to let loose a tirade of abuse at the Scotland Yard Commander.

'Keep me informed,' he said tersely, and he hung up. *If these spineless bastards are not prepared to have a go, then I know someone who will... and who won't give a shit about the public's reaction,* thought Bobby, and ordered his secretary at Number 10 to connect him on a scrambled line to Ivan Brekov.

'I'm surrounded by incompetent fucking idiots,' he ranted to the Russian President a few moments later, finally able to give full vent to his anger. 'I want these bastards out or dead and I want it fucking fast! What have you got for me, Ivan? It had better be good or I may not be coming to see you after all!'

The Russian President chuckled. 'It's good to know you can still get so angry, Bobby. But much better, as you Westerners always say, to get even.

'I have a small detachment of Spetsnaz, our own special forces, ready to leave right now. Their orders are to get these bastards out at any cost. Say the word, and by tonight I expect your problems to be over, my friend.

They will be travelling as a diplomatic group and my people in London will pick them up and take care of the rest. As soon as you can give me the name of an airport and arrange diplomatic immunity, they'll be on their way. Oh, and by the way… it wouldn't be advisable for Customs to see what they will be carrying.'

Five hours later, a small, twin-engined jet with no external markings touched down on the runway of RAF Northolt, the famous ex-fighter base to the north of London's Heathrow airport, which, while remaining an operational military base, had lately become a favourite transit point for VIPs, heads of state and royalty.

The pilot of the 50-seater Antonov AN-300 aircraft was advised by ground control to taxi to an isolated standing area, well clear of the main buildings. The station commander had already been advised by the Ministry of Defence of the Russians' arrival and their diplomatic status. He had seen nothing unusual in the instructions; such arrivals had become commonplace of late. Had he known the details of the plane's cargo, however, it is certain he would not have been quite so disinterested in his latest arrivals.

As the jet came to a standstill, an RAF Land Rover led a large, luxury coach onto the tarmac and across to where the automatic steps were being lowered. The driver of the Land Rover had been told not to hang about. The Russian passengers began to disembark and then with a wave to the coach driver, the driver turned back to the main buildings.

Once disembarked, the Russians waited until a hatch covering a large section of the plane's underbelly was hydraulically lowered to almost ground level. It was piled high with cargo, which the men began transferring to the coach's huge luggage compartments. Some of the smaller packages were carefully carried aboard the coach as the men silently completed the transfer.

Minutes later, the coach was heading for the exit to RAF Northolt and the M4 motorway, en route to the M25 orbital motorway.

Less than an hour later, as dusk approached, the coach arrived at an enormous mansion, in a private road off Wimbledon Common, in south-west London. It was guarded by an 8-foot wall and uniformed police. Concealed behind large wooden gates, it served as the main residency of the Russian Ambassador.

Under instructions from one of the staff, the passengers, with their cargo, were directed to a large summerhouse in the residency's two-acre grounds. Despite his orders having come from the Kremlin itself, the Ambassador preferred to distance himself from this particular group of visitors. These he knew to be a nine-strong team of crack Spetsnaz troops. The Ambassador knew the inevitable result of their presence was violence and mayhem, death and destruction and, just as inevitably, serious problems for those who had had any contact with them.

The Russian Special Forces personnel were completely unconcerned by the apparent lack of formal welcome from their host or his household. They were entirely occupied on arrival with the inspection of their cargo, and changed immediately into black combat suits, ankle-high black boots and chin-strapped helmets.

Chest bandoliers, which they strapped across their shoulders, carried flash-bang and fragmentation grenades and, in a special hip pocket, each man carried a large combat knife. The only insignia on their uniforms was a small shoulder badge featuring a black bat, the emblem of the Spetsnaz.

At 10.30pm, the Captain gave a quiet order and he and his men began strapping on their backpacks containing highly manoeuvrable, black silk parachutes. Their faces and hands were already blackened with greasepaint and they looked a formidable force. It was what Nikolai Boretsin expected of the men under his command.

He had been hand-picked for this important mission by his Colonel and commanding officer, Alexander Sopov, who considered him the finest officer of his section. Nikolai was a veteran of numerous successful anti-terrorist operations in the former Russian satellite countries and a highly-decorated hero of the Republic.

He, in turn, had been allowed to select the two sergeants and six other men who, with him, would form the classic Osnaz or nine-man operational unit of the Spetsnaz. These were all experienced, hardened combat troops – among the best in the world, he believed – and he knew they would cheerfully volunteer to join him in his worst nightmares, if he required them to do so.

Apart from their skills with guns and knives, each man was also an expert in Systema, the unique Russian art of hand-to-hand combat, which, unlike Asian styles, has no predetermined fighting stances, but equips a man to defend himself against attack from any position. It had been developed by the early Cossacks, more than 1,000 years ago, and was considered so dangerous that it was prohibited to all except the élite Russian fighting forces, from the time of the October Revolution in 1917 until the end of the Communist era in 1991, when the outside world became aware of its existence. Systema devotees develop exceptional courage in the face of all sorts of adversity and learn to relax physically and facially – to smile, literally, in combat – rather than announce their murderous intentions with screams or snarls.

Casting a last, approving eye over his men, Nikolai gave the order to collect their weapons and move out. On a special landing deck in the centre of the huge lawn sat their transport, a Russian-built Mi-8 MTV 5 twin-engined helicopter with sophisticated night vision capability, originally designed as a troop carrier.

Without a word, the men, each carrying either a modified Nikonov AN-94, a silenced AS VAL, or the latest KBP snub-nosed, compact assault rifle, filed aboard the big, black helicopter. As they took their seats, Nikolai Boretsin told them to take a last look at the photographs they had been studying throughout their journey from Russia. They were photos of the 12 remaining hostages, and each man had committed their features to memory. The hostages' lives would depend on it, because their orders were simple:

'Anyone you do not recognise, you kill.'

THIRTY-SEVEN

The pilot of the Mi-8 Russian helicopter made the 15-minute flight to Belmont Place without need to resort to night vision. Sixteen miles due south of Wimbledon, they crossed the M25 and, from there, could clearly see Peter Flint's sprawling country mansion, which was starkly floodlit from every angle and, from the sky, resembled a giant, illuminated movie set.

A further three miles over open countryside brought them to a point half a mile east of their target, just north of the A25 and the village of Buckland, where the pilot stationed the huge craft at 3,000 feet.

A quiet command brought the Osnaz detachment to their feet and, without further orders, they attached their parachute ripcords to a steel static line on the main cabin ceiling and stood, silently in line, each man with his left hand on the shoulder of the man in front. In addition to their standard combat gear, four of the men were carrying thick coils of stout rope around their necks.

With the slight easterly wind, Nikolai Boretsin had estimated a parachute descent time of just under three minutes to transfer his unit from the helicopter to the flat roof of Belmont Place. Through his binoculars, he could see the various, spectacular groups of chimneys, positioned mainly to the back of the roof with their bases partially obscured by shadows. One unforeseen obstacle, though, was a large helicopter, parked in the centre, towards the north parapet.

'We want the south side anyway,' Nikolai told his men. 'And it still leaves us 1,000 square metres to land in. You should be able to do that blindfolded.'

Several of the men grinned, and all returned his thumbs-up sign. Seconds later, he flicked the warning light above the open door to green and, without any hesitation, the first of his men leapt into the dark void.

They left the helicopter at intervals of ten seconds, with Captain Boretsin bringing up the rear and, by the time it came for him to jump, the first of his men was halfway to the target, approaching at an angle of 45 degrees. He landed, running, at least 10 metres clear of the rooftop helicopter. After ten paces, he stopped, spun around, and began hauling in his parachute, just as the second member of the team touched down.

Staring skywards, he had great difficulty spotting the others, even knowing where to look. The black silk canopies, dark camouflage uniforms and greasepaint-blackened faces made them near-invisible against the night sky.

By the time Nikolai landed, his men – with the exception of one, whose parachute had caught on a trio of chimneys leaving the young Russian dangling 2 metres above the rooftop – were safely down. In the time it took the officer to gather in his 'chute, his trapped compatriot had freed himself, slashing through the tangled lines above his head and dropping, cat-like, to the roof below.

The four men with the ropes were already attaching them with purpose-built clamps to four of the nearest chimneys and, when satisfied they were secure, tossed the eight free ends over the south parapet, along a 10 metres stretch to the west of the main entrance portico below, and outside the ground-floor room where Intelligence had reported the hostages being held.

They wasted no time before launching themselves into an attack, and Nikolai's teeth flashed white in a rare grin. Though had he, at that moment, witnessed the scene taking place four floors below him, his confidence would have been severely undermined.

George, the terrorist technician in charge of the electronic observation and alarm equipment in the hall, was speaking to Careb Sinclair on the radio handset.

'Intruders on the roof,' he said. 'Nine of them... and they're gathering right now above the drawing room where you are.'

Careb snapped his fingers loudly to alert Davey and Emma. 'We've got visitors on the roof,' he warned. 'I imagine they'll be coming in through these windows at any moment, so let's get our little flock of sheep into another room.' He added urgency to his order by grabbing the two nearest hostages, Father Luke and Beverly, by their shoulders and hauling them from their seats.

'Move it... to the door... now,' he commanded and thrust them ahead of him. The rest, of whom a few had guessed that a rescue attempt was underway, were made to follow them – some reluctantly, others still a little dazed, having just been woken. Within two minutes of the warning being received, the drawing room was empty.

Under a minute later, they had been herded into the library 20 yards further along the corridor, and were able to look out on the now empty lake at the back of the building.

'Sit down on the floor... keep still and silent,' ordered Careb. 'If any one of you moves or makes a noise, Peter here will shoot you dead.'

His light-blue eyes, now hard as crystal and dark with menace, spoke more eloquently than any words, and the hostages had no doubt that he meant precisely what he had said. Careb turned instantly to his radio: 'Everyone assemble in the hall now... ' and with Emma and Davey close behind, he ran from the library and along the corridor.

Within seconds of them reaching the hall, where George was based, and where most of their equipment was piled, the other seven members of the team had joined them.

On the roof, Nikolai was ready for the next stage of their assault. He and seven of his men had already clamped themselves onto the ropes and were now balanced on the edge of the parapet, their backs almost parallel with the ground four floors below. It would take them only 10 seconds to drop the 20 metres and position themselves, a pair to either side of each of the two big drawing-room windows.

In the hall, Davey was already anticipating the attack. 'They'll abseil down the front and probably use flash-bangs and gas,' he said, matter-of-factly. 'We can either take them out at the front, or wait until they're inside.'

'Too late for the front,' George interrupted, equally matter-of-factly. 'They're on their way down now, except for one man left on the roof.'

'Right... gas masks, grenades and assault rifles. Thomas and Luis... you take the front. Wait until they've gone in and then cut them down if they try to retreat.'

With the exception of George, the technician, monitoring the screens and other devices, who simply strapped on a gas mask, and Thomas and Luis, the other members of the Salamander team quickly located the equipment they needed and regrouped in the corridor outside the drawing room, where the large door, as Careb had deliberately left it, was still wide open.

'They'll enter through the windows as soon as the flash-bangs go off,' said Careb. 'We'll give them a few seconds, then lob in a few grenades of our own. I'll then go in with Simon, Heinrich and Jonathan. Davey and Jim take care of the guy on the roof and Emma and Rudolfo stay out here and mop up any of those who get past us.'

Careb and the three men who would lead the main assault on the enemy were still pulling grenades from their pouches when the first of the flash-bangs exploded.

Even through the padding of their gas masks, the blasts of the stun grenades, which had been hurled through the windows, were almost deafening. They were followed, within seconds, by the sound of smashing glass and woodwork as the abseiling attackers launched themselves, feet first, through the windows.

Nikolai certainly had not expected a counter-attack. But what he did expect to see were bodies, either unconscious or severely stunned.

It took him and his men just moments to realise that their Intelligence had been inaccurate. His instinct immediately took over and, rightly fearing a trap, he pointed to the open door and swept his arm forward to order his men out of the drawing room. Simultaneously, four grenades were launched through the door and went off almost at once, exploding with devastating effect among the unprepared Russian troops.

Four of his men were killed instantly, two being disembowelled and one decapitated. In moments, the room had been transformed from a sophisticated and beautifully decorated reception room to a bombed-out slaughterhouse.

Two of the Russians, displaying lightning reactions, had dived head-first back through the shattered windows, tucking into a forward roll and ending in a knee crouch with weapons ready.

It was a brilliantly executed manoeuvre but, unfortunately for the Spetsnaz pair, Thomas and Luis were well armed and already waiting for them just 20 feet away. Such was the power of their automatic assault rifles that two short bursts each, fired before the Russians had barely stopped moving, didn't simply cut them down in their tracks, but literally tore their bodies apart. Large chunks of flesh and limbs were blasted away, and what remained was unrecognisable.

Pleased with their brief but satisfying victory, Thomas and Luis momentarily – and for one of them, fatally – allowed their guard to slip. They stayed in position and on alert should more of the enemy decided to use the same exit. But they made the costly mistake of concentrating their attention only in that direction. They were subsequently attacked from an unexpected – albeit totally predictable – quarter.

SAS troops, alerted by the grenades and rifle fire, and still outraged at the cold-blooded reprisal killing of their colleagues the previous night, were eager to exact their revenge and, without waiting for official orders, opened fire on the two terrorist gunmen.

The chattering of submachine-guns, and the swarm of incoming rifle rounds zapping around them, sent Luis leaping for cover behind one of the massive portico columns. Thomas, just as fast to react, was, however, caught further in the open, and didn't stand a chance. As he dived towards safety, two rounds smashed into the centre of his chest and he was dead before his body had hit the marble.

Meanwhile, in the drawing room, Nikolai and his remaining comrade – who had taken a deep shrapnel wound to his shoulder, and was still stunned – were preparing to fight for their lives.

The first man into the room was Simon Wojak, who found himself almost face to face with the Russian officer. Instead of trying to shoot him, Simon reacted instinctively and used his own weapon to smash the other man's assault rifle from his hands. But he did not allow for Nikolai's lightning reaction. In a split-second, he had grabbed Simon's rifle and, twisting it free, hurled it, almost contemptuously, to one side.

In almost the same movement, he swept his arm downwards and backwards and plucked his large combat knife from its scabbard, squaring up to his enemy in crouched readiness.

During this brief skirmish, Jonathan and Heinrich had, almost simultaneously, targeted the wounded Russian, each letting rip with a burst of automatic fire and killing him instantly. Now they paused to watch the conflict.

Simon had also drawn his knife and was eyeing the Russian officer warily. Nikolai smiled back pleasantly and, with absolutely no warning, launched a low-level attack at Simon's stomach, which he only managed to avoid by a fraction of a centimetre.

'Systema... ' muttered Careb, as he raised his weapon and shot Nikolai Beretsin between the eyes. 'In other circumstances, I would like to have seen more... but not at your expense, Simon.'

The German rounded on Careb, his eyes betraying the dent to his pride. 'I would have taken him easily,' he snarled.

'Unlikely,' said Careb pleasantly. 'I'm sorry, old man... no reflection on you, but these are some of the greatest hand-to-hand fighters in the world, and I would hate to see you used as a pincushion. Look at the insignia... these guys are Spetsnaz... and that puts them a long way from home. Some genius obviously believes an away team could achieve better results than the local lads.'

Simon Wojack continued to glare at his leader, still smarting from the insult.

'It's over, Simon,' snapped Careb. 'Get along the corridor and reinforce Peter with the hostages.'

He strode to the door, removing his gas mask, and waved the all-clear to Emma. 'Everything's fine in here. What about Davey and the boys out front?'

They walked into the hall where George had been watching the action on the roof.

'All accounted for,' he told them. 'But I'm afraid we lost Thomas. He wasn't killed by the latest group, though, but by the troops over in the trees.'

Careb's eyes darkened with fury. 'They just won't learn, will they? It's definitely time to give them another lesson in obedience.

But this time, if you agree, I think we should make the lesson a salutary one.'

He glanced around the circle of grim faces and received a nod of assent from each in turn.

THIRTY-EIGHT

When the first cluster of grenades exploded, shortly after midnight, even though a mile away and half-asleep, at least two of the men occupying the dimly-lit gatehouse recognised the sounds and became instantly alert.

Commander Brian James sprang to his feet and glared accusingly at Major Peter Stevens, who had become rigidly upright in his chair as the unmistakable detonations forced him to become fully alert.

'What the hell are your boys up to, Peter?' demanded the anti-terrorist squad chief fiercely. 'We all agreed to hold off until we got some kind of dialogue going with those people.'

'It's fuck all to do with me,' snapped the indignant SAS officer. 'And don't go imagining either that any of my men would have taken pot shots without consulting me first. In fact, I'd stake my life on that.'

'Not yours, perhaps, but maybe somebody else's,' said the stony-faced Commander. 'I'm certain of one thing, though… somebody is taking a bloody big risk with the hostages' lives, and those of our men, too.'

He grabbed his overcoat from a wall peg and headed towards the door. 'We'd better get over there and find out what's going on.'

He was interrupted by the thump of several more grenades followed by sporadic, automatic rifle fire.

'Whatever it is, it's something major,' he added, as they ran from the gatehouse towards the SAS Land Rover standing outside. The driver, who had seen them coming, gunned the motor as the pair jumped into the back seats.

As they sped towards the house, Major Stevens finally raised one of his lieutenants on the radio. 'What the hell's going on?' he yelled.

'A group of men in combat uniform have just abseiled down from the roof and gone in through the windows, where we believe the hostages were being held. There's been a lot of grenade action on the inside and some rifle fire. Two of the raiders re-emerged through the same windows and were killed by terrorists, who appeared at the front of the building. Some of our guys saw an opportunity and opened fire... they've hit one of the terrorists. Confirmed fatality.'

'Oh, Christ,' wailed Stevens, urgently pressing the transmit button. 'Tell them to cease fire immediately. Repeat... immediately. I want no further hostile action from our chaps.' He peered ahead. 'I'll be with you in 30 seconds. But get them to stop fucking shooting now!'

He turned to Commander James. 'You heard that?'

The Commander nodded.

'You don't suppose my people have got the right idea... that we should get moving now and launch a full attack while everyone is off-balance?'

Commander James held up his hand, an incredulous expression on his face. 'Off-balance, Peter?' he queried. 'Off-balance? The shooting inside has ceased and two of the mystery raiders are dead on the ground outside. I don't think the terrorists are "off-balance". In fact, I suspect they have almost certainly won a very decisive victory. At the very least, I wouldn't bet on our have-a-go heroes, whoever they are, still posing any threat at all. What's important from our point of view, is that no matter who organised this fiasco, the terrorists are going to assume that we were in the know – and that means further reprisals.

'If we try to go in now, unprepared and with zero intelligence, then the body count on our side will be appalling, and the chances of maiming or killing the hostages – wherever they are now – is far too great to consider taking such a risk. Am I making myself clear enough for you?'

Stevens nodded grimly as the Land Rover skidded to a halt, still 50 feet within the tree line. The two men stepped down from the four-wheel-drive vehicle and raised binoculars to their eyes as an SAS lieutenant materialised alongside them and saluted Major Stevens.

'Good to see you, boss. I'm sorry some of the lads opened fire, but it seemed too good an opportunity to miss – catching the terrorists in the open like that. The two unknown raiders are on the ground in front of the broken windows and the dead terrorist is at the top of the marble steps near the front door.

'Since we ceased fire, there hasn't been a sound from inside or the slightest sign of movement.'

Stevens, peering through his powerful binoculars, could clearly see the bodies, including that of Ashley Bodin, which still remained where it had fallen.

'I've no idea who the pair are outside the windows,' he told Commander James. 'They're obviously military, but I can't identify a regiment from this range.'

He turned to face the Scotland Yard Commander and his lieutenant. 'If they came from the roof, then we have to assume they got up there by using either microlights or parachutes, and I favor 'chutes. That's how I'd have done it, which means they could be paras.

'The Defence Department must know, because they're the only ones who could have authorised such an attack, though I'm amazed they didn't inform us in advance.'

'I agree,' said the Commander. 'At least I pray to God they did. Because if it wasn't them who sent these blokes, then we've got a bigger problem than we figured. I think it's time to go and get Bobby Temple out of his bed. He, or someone close to him, would seem to have a lot of bloody explaining to do.'

Bobby was sitting alone in his office in Downing Street when the call from Commander James came in. For half an hour, he had been expecting news from Belmont Place that the terrorists had been massacred by Russian Special Forces, and he had been mentally applauding himself for bringing in Brekov and his élite troops.

'Our new allies,' he purred to himself.

A slight smile of anticipation was on his boyish face as he instructed the switchboard to patch the call through, but the volley of words which issued from the other end of the line were not those which Bobby had expected. Commander James's voice was unusually harsh and he wasted no time on the usual pleasantries.

'Prime Minister, we have a disaster on our hands.'

A wave of nausea swept through Bobby and threatened to overwhelm him.

'What we have to assume is that an attempt to rescue the hostages has been made by an unidentified military force. It was almost certainly a complete failure and we must assume they did not survive the operation.'

Bobby couldn't believe what he was hearing. He was consumed by an intense panic and he had to force himself to grip tightly onto the telephone receiver to prevent himself from dropping it. *But Ivan assured me... the best of the best... there would be no mistakes... the perfect prelude to a new era of co-operation...* Bobby's head was swimming. Commander James's voice seemed to be coming from the end of a long tunnel.

'At this stage, we have no information on the status of the hostages, some of whom may have been killed or seriously injured during the heavy grenade attack and shooting which took place inside.'

It took Bobby several moments to register that the Commander had finished speaking. He literally shook himself and wiped his glistening forehead with the back of his free hand.

When he finally managed to speak, his voice sounded strange even to himself. 'Have you any idea who these rescuers might have been?' he asked.

'No, Sir,' said the anti-terrorist squad Commander coldly. 'We assumed that you would know that... that the attack was authorised by yourself or by the Defence Department... despite our advice not to take action.' Commander James could not help himself from adding this last rebuke.

Bobby squared his shoulders, took an even firmer grip on the telephone receiver, and tried to inject as much confidence and sincerity into his voice as he could muster. He had always prided himself on his ability to lie convincingly.

'It was certainly not authorised from this office,' he told Commander James flatly. Then, with more emotion, 'It would have been playing games with the hostages' lives.' Bobby began to relax. The worst, he told himself, was now over. The big lie out of the way, so the rest should be easy. He began to feel more like his real self. 'I will contact Defence personally and start an immediate inquiry,' he said firmly. 'Although I can only imagine that someone's lines must have become crossed somewhere. This can't have been intended.'

He slipped a handkerchief from his pocket with his free hand and mopped his forehead free of sweat. 'I'll let you have my results as they come in. And I want you, Commander, to keep me fully up to date with developments down there, particularly on the status of the hostages. I want the information as and when it becomes available – no matter what the hour. Meanwhile, let's try to get to the bottom of this fiasco as quickly as possible.'

He replaced the receiver and stared at it. *What a complete and utter fuck-up. Ivan, you're going to have to answer for this... but not yet. First, damage limitation...* Bobby picked up the receiver again, and punched in a number hurriedly. *Peter Westcroft, you're about to learn the meaning of the words 'ministerial responsibility'.* In a calm, steady voice, he asked to be connected to the Minister for Defence. 'I want to talk to him, no matter where he is,' said Bobby. 'I don't care how you do it, but find him.'

In Peter Flint's study in Belmont Place, Careb Sinclair, Emma and Davey were just concluding their own crisis meeting. They had all agreed that, in order to achieve the maximum effect, their reprisals against the captives and troops should not take place until later that same Saturday morning after full daybreak.

As self-appointed stage manager, Careb would arrange for the nine Russian corpses to be seated outside with their backs to the wall between the two shattered windows of the drawing room. This window dressing would be carried out during darkness with the spotlights outside temporarily switched off and the watching troops warned to hold their fire or face further reprisals. An artistic addition, he decided, would be to have the officer at the centre holding a cut-out of a black bat against his chest.

The dead Russians would form a macabre, though fitting backcloth to the drama which would later unfold for millions of television viewers.

'I think we're approaching the end game,' said Careb. 'Today should see the final arrangements put in place, and I don't believe any of us will be sorry to see it over with.'

'Amen to that,' said Davey. 'Apart from meeting a few brave souls, there hasn't been much about it to savour, that's for sure.'

Emma nodded agreement. 'It's not exactly the swan song I would have chosen for Salamander,' she conceded, then grinned infectiously. 'But let's not be too glum. There's always the future... and remember, my dear friends, tomorrow is another day.'

The two men both began to laugh and the three of them reached out and outstretched their right hands, each grasping his or her companion's wrist, to form a triangle. 'To the future,' they chorused.

In the library at Belmont Place everyone was still wide awake, whispers circulating as they tried to make sense of the earlier explosions and rifle fire.

'Whoever they were, they must have been killed,' Peter Flint commented to the Ambassador for the umpteenth time. 'If not, then we would have been freed by now.'

'I fear that's the truth of it,' replied Saul, also for the umpteenth time. 'But if it was a failed attempt to free us, then I'm also afraid it could cost us dearly. I hate to say this, old friend, but our captors are utterly ruthless and they've given us enough warnings of what will happen if there's any attempt at rescue or escape. We may not be responsible for the attack, but I believe that some of us, at least, are going to be made to pay, possibly the ultimate price.'

Flint shuddered and then sighed. 'I think we may have an even more immediate problem than that... ' With a casual glance sideways, he indicated Simon, the German guard who had been assigned to watch them. 'There's something about the way he's been staring at Kate... he's almost undressing her with his eyes. You can see exactly how his mind is working, and I don't think it'll be long before he actually makes a move. Then what do we do?'

The terrorist had, as Flint rightly observed, been eyeing up the Princess ever since he had come in to back up Peter. He was in a foul mood and convinced that Careb had deliberately humiliated him in front of the others. This made him both dangerous and unpredictable. He had rejected Peter's attempts at conversation, except to snarl obscenities and curse Careb in his native German.

'I'll show that bastard,' he told his fellow guard. 'I'm just as capable... and I'll prove it.'

Since then, he had stood by himself, glowering at the hostages, and staring directly at the Princess, who was making every effort to avoid eye contact with him.

Slowly, he had moved to stand almost directly over where she was sitting on the carpet, with her back to some of the bookshelves, and carrying on a whispered conversation with June Temple. He was staring down fixedly at her breasts.

The other guard, Peter, who had become unnerved by the German's sudden obsession with Kate, tried hard to distract him. 'There's a decanter of port on the table over here, Simon. Let's toast our success.'

'What success?' he growled, without taking his eyes off Kate. 'I was made to look a fool by Sinclair – I could have taken that bastard one-handed but I was never given the chance.'

'I know that, Simon,' agreed Peter. 'You'd have chopped him to pieces. I'll drink to that... so come and join me.'

The German shook his head. 'I think I'd rather celebrate with a piece of this,' he laughed menacingly, and prodded Kate in her thigh with his boot.

She glared up at him. 'I'm not here for your entertainment, you filthy bastard, and I'm certainly not here to be kicked either. So crawl back under whatever stone you came from and leave me alone!'

Simon swung his assault rifle, which was in his left hand, so it pointed directly at her stomach and, at the same time, grabbed her hair in his right hand and pulled her away from June. Kate screamed and tried to kick out, but the man dropped her and slapped her hard across her face with the back of his open right hand.

She lay half-stunned on the floor as he knelt beside her, took hold of her right breast and squeezed it hard... while pointing his rifle towards the other hostages.

'I'll show you what entertainment you're here for,' he snarled, squeezing her breast even harder. Then he yelled in pain as the clenched knuckles of a fist smashed into the side of his head just in front of his ear.

Unseen by Simon, Davey and Emma had entered the room just as he had begun his assault. After motioning Peter to keep back, the Irishman had crossed the room in half a dozen silent paces and, without a pause, landed a savage punch to the side of Simon's head. Then, as he collapsed on his side, Davey stooped and twisted the assault rifle from his left hand and, turning, tossed it to Emma, who neatly caught it in mid-air.

As the big German staggered groggily to his feet, Davey stepped back a pace. 'Is it only the girls you like to beat up, Simon, or would you like to take your chances with a man? I hear you were disappointed Careb wouldn't let you have a go at the Russian. Well, I'm sure I'm nowhere near his class, so I should be easy for you.'

He smiled as Simon removed his combat knife from its cover.

'That's it, lad. Now you can show us what a real man you are.'

'I could have taken the Russian and I'll take you,' snarled Simon. 'You're already as good as dead. And after I've dealt with you, I'll see to this bitch.'

Davey backed off further, drawing his own knife, and looked beyond the German to where Princess Kate was still sprawled on the carpet. 'You don't look very scared, Your Highness. But I think it's best if you close your eyes now. Simple Simon is about to be taught a lesson in manners, and it won't be very pretty.'

He leapt backwards and to one side as Simon suddenly lunged for his throat with the long, double-bladed Bowie knife and, with a lightning strike of his own, slashed his razor-sharp blade across the other's upper arm, slicing deep into the flesh through the sleeve of the combat uniform.

It brought a howl of pain and rage from Simon, and a rush of blood from beneath his sleeve and onto his hand. He switched the big knife to his other hand and launched a wild, stabbing attack at Davey's stomach, which the Irishman managed to avoid easily.

For a full minute, they circled one another, each thrusting or slashing, while avoiding the other's attack. As they paused, crouched in the centre of the room, apparently taking stock of one another, Davey suddenly let out a loud, wolf-like howl and, at the same moment, punched his left fist high into the air.

Simon's eyes instinctively followed it and, in that instant, Davey lashed out with his right boot and kicked him hard just below the left kneecap.

There was a scream from Simon and a sharp crack as his kneecap was smashed, and he collapsed on his side. In a flash, Davey lunged forward and sank his knife deep into the gasping German's neck, puncturing his jugular and almost severing the vertebrae and the upper cervical spinal cord. He was dead before Davey withdrew his blade.

'Yes!' yelled Kate instinctively, then she quickly covered her face in confusion as she reminded herself that the victor was also one of those responsible for the torment they were all enduring. Peter Flint clapped slowly and bowed slightly towards Davey.

'Thank you,' Davey grinned, acknowledging the compliment. 'But don't let it be worrying you, Ma'am,' grinned Davey, 'it's all part of the service, so it is.' He motioned to Peter. 'Find someone else and get this bag of shite out of here.' Then he turned to Emma. 'We'd better let Careb know that another one of the bad guys has bitten the dust, and I wonder if he'll be surprised when he hears it's one of ours.'

THIRTY-NINE

When the Downing Street flunky opened the door to Bobby's office and announced the Defence Minister, Peter Westcroft came into the room nervously and stood to attention in front of the Prime Minister's desk, for all the world like a cowed and terrified schoolboy called before the headmaster.

'Sit down, Peter,' said Bobby, impatiently. 'I'm not going to bite you.'

Peter smiled uncertainly, as though not totally convinced, but sat gingerly on the edge of the chair which faced the Prime Minister.

'It's about those Russians you arranged to permit entry through Northolt, Peter. They appear to have caused a bit of mayhem.'

'But it was you who told me to call Northolt, Bobby. I was only following your... '

'Well, I don't remember it quite like that,' said Bobby, his voice cold. 'It was a military decision... Russian Special Forces... that's your department.'

A heavy flush spread up Peter Westcroft's neck and his eyes searched the room for help of any sort. He found none, and eventually met Bobby's acid stare.

'Special Forces?' he whispered. 'You said nothing about Special Forces. In fact, I'm sure you said they were on a diplomatic mission.

I wondered at the time why you needed me to intervene... apart from it being RAF Northolt... ' His voice petered out.

Bobby made no attempt to hide the contempt in his voice. 'Don't pretend to be even more stupid than you are, Peter. You really have disappointed me, you know.'

'I'm sorry, Bobby, but I'm not going to hold my hand up to something I haven't done. I don't know anything about this. What's happened?'

'A complete, fucking, cast-iron disaster... that's what's happened, and if you didn't authorise it yourself, then it must have been one of your tin-pot generals acting without authority. Whoever it was, people are going to assume you were responsible.

'These Russians went in with grenades and guns to try and free the hostages, and seem to have got themselves killed in the process.' He glared at the Defence Minister. 'That's what happened, Peter.'

The silence that followed was almost unbearable for Westcroft. He appeared to be having trouble with his breathing, but eventually managed to force in enough air to gasp, 'I swear I knew nothing about this, Bobby. I would never have sanctioned something like that. It's crazy to think it was me... What do you want me to do?'

'Do nothing and say nothing,' said Bobby abruptly. 'If this is mishandled now, then it could bring the whole Government down.'

'But, Bobby, it's not my fault... ' Westcroft was almost in tears. 'You know I'd never let you down.'

'I know that, Peter,' said the Prime Minister a little more warmly. 'But we need to use delaying tactics. Until we get this siege situation under control, I don't want anything else destabilising the party. What I want you to do is to go straight home and go to bed. Don't talk to anyone... and I mean anyone at all. It's essential no one gets confirmation of this Russian involvement until later today. If it comes out prematurely, it could ruin the next big attempt to flush these bastards out and release the hostages.

'Don't accept any calls until you know it is me, personally, on the line. Then, when I tell you officially about this business, you will announce that there is to be an immediate Inquiry. After that, just stall everyone – the press, other politicians... everybody. Ignore all questions, just sit tight. I'll protect you, if you want us to survive, that is.'

'Of course I do, Bobby. I'll do anything to help – you know you can count on me.'

Bobby walked around the desk and clasped Westcroft by the shoulder. 'I know I can,' he said, earnestly. 'You'll be a key player in my Cabinet for many years to come. Get off to your bed now. Then make your announcement in the morning just as I've told you, and sit tight. Leave everything else to me.'

Westcroft rose and clasped Bobby's right hand in both of his. 'Thank you, Bobby. I won't let you down.'

As his Defence Minister left the office, the Prime Minister shook his head in amazement. *To think I might actually have had to count on somebody like that in time of war,* he mused. *You are just about to perform your only important role in my Government, Peter. What a pity you won't live long enough to learn something from it.*

His next action was to place an urgent call to Brekov. It was already 3am in Moscow but the Russian leader sounded wide awake.

'Only bad news travels this late, Bobby. What is it?'

'Thanks to you, we have a serious problem... but there is also a solution. It involves our old friend Peter Westcroft. He's under an almost impossible strain at the moment...'

FORTY

As the early dawn mist cleared, the grotesque line-up of Russian corpses, seated like a row of broken puppets against the front wall of Belmont Place, became clearly visible to the onlookers. Even for the hardened troops of 22 SAS Regiment, the spectacle was a revolting one. Some of the dead were hideously mutilated, several with limbs blasted away and one of them headless. It was like a scene out of a particularly offensive Hollywood horror movie.

'Not a very pretty sight before breakfast,' murmured Major Peter Stevens to the SAS lieutenant alongside him.

'But not the main show either, I fear,' said Commander James, who was standing with them, among a copse of beech trees, 100 metres from the front of the house, and staring through binoculars at the carefully arranged bodies. He pulled a face. 'What do you make of that board propped against the middle chap's chest? It looks to me like something out of *Batman*. Is it some kind of a gag, do you think?'

'No, I don't think it's a gag,' said the young SAS lieutenant slowly. 'In fact, I think the bastards are telling us the identity of the assault group. It reminds me of the insignia of the Spetsnaz – the Russian Special Forces...' The truth began to emerge through the

haze. 'That's why we didn't recognise them as some of ours…
they're all bloody Russians.'

'Are you absolutely certain?' said the Scotland Yard
Commander, his throat suddenly feeling very dry.

'Yes. He's right… ' said Stevens interrupting. 'That's obviously
why no one knew anything about the raid in advance. Well
spotted, John.' He turned to the young lieutenant. 'That badge
definitely identifies them as Spetsnaz,' he told the Scotland Yard
anti-terrorist chief. 'Though how the hell they came to be
actively deployed over here is another matter altogether. It goes
against every possible Government agreement and protocol in
existence. Which is not to say, of course, that this kind of thing
hasn't happened before,' he added, with a wry grin. 'My outfit's
been involved in a few foreign adventures without the host
Government knowing anything about it. So have the American
Navy Seals. But this was far too overt to be classed as a secret
mission,' he went on hurriedly. 'These blokes made no attempt to
hide themselves or act in any way clandestinely. They just
steamed straight in, with all guns blazing, so to speak. Someone
had to have known about them in advance. And given the go-
ahead,' he added quietly.

Commander James stared hard at the two officers. 'What you're
saying is that our own Government has to be secretly in cahoots
with the Russians… that they deliberately acted against all our
advice, and regardless of the consequences for the hostages.
Which also means,' he added ominously, 'that there's going to be
hell to pay when it comes out. I wouldn't be at all surprised if some
very senior heads didn't roll because of this.

'Damned right, too, in my opinion because we definitely haven't
heard the last of this from the terrorists. I'd better get straight back
and talk to the Chief Constable and the Home Secretary. It could
be that this goes all the way to the top – and God only knows
what will happen if that turns out to be true.'

It was a very nervous Home Secretary who telephoned Downing Street at 8am later that morning, and asked to speak directly to the Prime Minister on a matter of great urgency. Bobby Temple was already in the Cabinet room seated opposite Jack Benson with the morning's newspapers spread out between them.

All the papers had reported the explosions and gunfire at Belmont Place on their front pages and some had speculated on an Iranian Embassy-style midnight raid by the SAS to free the hostages. But Bobby's imposed blackout on any information at all being given to the press had worked, and there were very few factual details in the reports.

Bobby had been giving Jack Benson a heavily censored briefing on events when the call came in. He told the secretary to put it through and listened to the almost hysterical voice of John Potter, the Home Secretary, for almost a full minute before interrupting.

'Russians? Special Forces? What fucking nonsense is this, John? Are you out of your mind?'

Benson could clearly hear his Cabinet colleague's stammering voice from across the table.

Bobby interrupted again. 'You'd better get all your facts straight and get round here as quickly as possible. I want the whole Cabinet to hear it, and I don't want a word of it leaking out before they've been given all the details and until we've got some proper answers. Meanwhile, I'll speak with Peter Westcroft and see if he knows anything about this.'

He replaced the receiver and looked up, to find himself meeting the challenging gaze of his Chancellor.

'What's going on, Bobby?'

'Something very odd,' said Bobby gravely, leaning casually back in his chair and, he hoped, successfully masking the waves of panic coursing through his body. 'It's about the bizarre events of last night which we were just discussing.

'John Potter has heard from our people down there, this morning, that it was a full-scale attack on the building and they claim it involved a nine-man team of Russian Special Forces. He suggests they may even have been brought in to assist by someone from our own military. The whole thing sounds bizarre to me, but I intend to call Peter right now and demand to know what the hell's been going on. I don't have to tell you, Jack, what the potential repercussions might be. The press is going to crucify whoever is responsible.'

'Not to mention the risk to the hostages,' said the Chancellor bleakly. He stared across the table at his former best friend and political hero of 20 years and felt as though he was staring into the face of a complete stranger. Just ten days ago, he would have trusted this man with his life, his soul even. He was shocked to discover that nothing at all remained of that trust. Somewhere along the way, unnoticed by him, power had replaced policy, and obsession had ousted political integrity. The Bobby Temple he believed he had known no longer existed. Of that, he was increasingly certain.

'Please tell me that you weren't involved in this dreadful business, Bobby,' he said softly. 'That this wasn't something you cooked up with Brekov for a quick fix?'

Bobby's gaze was resolute. 'With my own wife in the firing line?' he said, with what appeared to be genuine horror in his voice. 'How can you, of all people, suggest such a thing? I'm as angry and puzzled as you are, Jack, and I'm determined to get to the bottom of it right now if I can.

'I'm going to call Peter and find out exactly what he knows. I'm as much in the dark on this one as anyone. I can only pray that nothing dreadful happens to the hostages because of it.'

Benson continued to stare at him unwaveringly, searching for the truth behind the Prime Minister's words. 'I hope to God you're telling the truth, Bobby, because if not, then this will destroy you and everything we've ever dreamed of achieving.'

FORTY-ONE

An almost tangible air of despair hung heavily over the library at Belmont Place where even those hostages who were awake were lost, silently, in their own thoughts, for the most part brooding anxiously on the awful events of the previous night. With few real facts to go on, they had quickly exhausted all the possibilities as to what might have taken place in the drawing room after their evacuation. Then, even more rapidly, because of the inevitably morbid conclusions, they had guessed at the possible repercussions and had managed to agree generally on only two things: the rescue attempt – if that's what it had been – had turned out to be an absolute failure; and the inevitable repercussions were certain to be drastic. They remained helpless prisoners, and were wholly at the mercy of their captors.

Even the fight they had all witnessed in front of them, which had led to the killing of one of the terrorists, was no longer a topic for conversation. June Temple marvelled at how quickly they had all adjusted to the bloody and almost unspeakable acts of casual violence they had witnessed in the preceding 36 hours. Was that due to the natural human ability to anaesthetise the senses against unacceptable horrors, or was it proof that, in reality, they were all still savages operating under a very thin veneer of civilised behaviour? She was no longer certain.

Two new guards, armed with assault rifles, were stationed at the far end of the room from where the hostages lay and sat around the fireplace and they refused to answer even the few questions directed at them.

Of the hostages who were awake, only Georgie Brown and Rachel Friedman had helped themselves to breakfast from the very limited selection of food piled on an oval Queen Anne table between the two large picture windows. Basic supplies, including cold meats, cheeses and bread, had been delivered to the house in a police truck the previous afternoon in response to a demand from the terrorists.

The dead guard, whose killing they had unanimously agreed had been an execution rather than murder, had been dragged outside, and only a large, dark stain on the library carpet provided evidence of the killing ever having taken place. Soon after that, the terrorist named Peter had gone off to sleep and the two new men had taken over his custodial duties.

At a little after 8am, Careb and Davey entered the library together, and those who were already awake sat up and began exchanging anxious glances, and rousing those who were still asleep. Only Glen Grant remained lying on the carpet, asleep or unconscious, a heavily bloodstained, makeshift dressing draped across the right side of his chest, where Careb had run him through with the sabre. The others quickly sat upright, some rising shakily to their feet.

'Good morning, one and all,' said Davey brightly, as he and Careb, both armed with Sig Sauer handguns, walked towards the hostages, who were all clustered around the fireplace end of the room. 'I need two of you to take part in a little tableau we're putting on for our friends outside.' He pointed his pistol first in the direction of Georgie Brown, and then at Wayne Bryan. 'You two lads will fit the bill handsomely. So I'll invite you both to take a stroll outside with us.' The two men remained frozen in their places. 'NOW,' he barked loudly.

Sweet Georgie Brown, for the very first time in his life, found he did not have an expression to call on which would adequately convey his feelings to those around him. Abject terror was not something he had experienced a great deal during his television career. As he got slowly to his feet, he found it increasingly difficult to breathe and his chubby face became drained of all colour.

Wayne Bryan, in complete contrast, had a wide smirk on his face. The distraught rock singer had been shunned by everyone, guards as well as fellow prisoners, for much of his time in captivity, which, to him, had seemed an eternity. He was overjoyed to be back in the limelight once more, and he was absolutely certain why he had been selected – he was, simply, the most important person in the room. Even the psychotic fuckwits with the guns had finally seen sense – they needed Wayne Bryan.

He stood, posing, hands on chubby hips, glorying in the moment. Then he seemed to become aware that someone else might be upstaging him. He glared scornfully at Georgie Brown, a few feet away, who appeared ready to burst into tears.

'What the fuck are you shitting your pants for?' he snarled viciously at the violently trembling television star, his contempt almost palpable. 'Do you really think these guys are stupid, or what? We're their meal tickets out of here. At least I am,' he announced grandly in a supreme display of arrogance. 'Can you imagine they'd ever be allowed out of here alive if they did anything to me? I'm global. The last thing they want is anything happening to me. Isn't that right?' he demanded of Davey.

The Irishman found himself momentarily speechless. The temptation to cut him down to size with a prolonged burst of gunfire was almost too much to bear. *Your time will come*, he reassured himself.

'I have to admit that you have a great following, the both of you,' he finally answered, the earlier slight smile returning to his lips. 'Though I must say I have never understood it myself. Mr Bryan is right about one thing, though. The both of you are certainly going to help convince the powers that be that we mean business, to be sure… ' The irony of his exaggerated Irish brogue and warm smile was lost on Wayne.

'You see,' the rock star whined, 'You've all been treating me like dog shit! Now I'm going to save your arses. They know how much influence I have.' He turned to Georgie. 'And I suppose you'll attract a bit of interest, in your own little way,' he nodded condescendingly to the TV personality, who had started to look slightly less terrified.

Being faced with submachine-guns and imminent death was one thing, but Georgie was not going to stand for a foul-mouthed rock singer belittling his career or reputation. All thoughts of being executed evaporated as he yelled, 'I'm bigger than you in the UK, where it really counts… How many millions watched your last TV appearance then?

'I pull 20 million viewers every week,' Georgie spat, 'the highest ratings in history. You can only manage a third of that… if you're lucky.'

Davey threw up his hands in mock horror. 'Please, ladies, put your handbags down. I think I can safely say that your next television appearance will pull the biggest world viewing figures of all time.'

Wayne Bryan drew in his stomach, stuck out his chest and regarded the others with a mixture of condescension and loathing. He hadn't forgotten how they'd regarded him as a coward throughout this ordeal. 'You'll all be thanking me before long,' he told them. 'Once I tell the public how much I've suffered, they'll give these people whatever they want to arrange our release. They won't let me... and the Princess, of course... stay cooped up as prisoners in these conditions. Or even the rest of you for that matter. Trust me.' He turned back to Davey. 'OK, mate. Point me towards the cameras and I'll fix everything for you. Though I'd like to do my hair and clean up a bit first. It wouldn't be fair to let my fans see me like this.'

Careb, who had remained silent until now, exchanged glances with Davey. 'I do apologise, Mr Bryan... we neglected to bring a hairdresser with us on this particular engagement,' he said. 'But I'm sure you'll look just perfect when it's time to go on.'

He waved his Sig Sauer handgun towards the door but, as he and Davey went to shepherd the two hostages out of the library ahead of them, Alison Best sprang forward. 'Be brave, Georgie,' she wailed. 'I'll be praying for you.'

By the look on his face, it was the last thing the game-show star had expected to hear. Then, equally unexpectedly, he grinned. 'That'll give you a new reason to get down on your knees,' he leered, with a sudden flash of his old cruelty. He then shot her a weak smile, the kind he usually reserved for contestants who were doing their best but didn't stand a chance of winning. 'But I'll be glad all the same,' he said softly.

As Alison began to sob, Careb paused and looked back. 'Don't worry, you're not going to miss anything,' he told the hostages. 'I'll make quite sure you get to see the whole of their performance on television later.'

It was 8.30am exactly when the screen of the big security monitor in the gatehouse flickered into life. Seconds later, the sound of Careb's voice filled the large room. Everyone present, which included all those who had been called in on the first night of the siege, ceased what they were doing and turned towards the screen.

'I want you all to pay very close attention. Everything you are about to see, and everything I say, is being beamed directly to all the main news channels, and I have no doubt will be broadcast worldwide within a very short while.

'Last night, a team of nine Russian Spetsnaz troops – that's a Special Forces team, to the uninitiated among you – made a foolish attempt to overpower my colleagues and I, and free the hostages. That was despite all our warnings to the British Government of the consequences of them trying such a futile assault. It was a very lamentable performance for which the perpetrators of this folly paid with their lives.'

On screen appeared a wide-angle view of the Russian corpses propped against the front wall of the house. The camera slowly zoomed in on the body of the first soldier and panned along the line. When it reached the centre figure, it paused. The black bat emblem propped against Nicolai Boretsin's chest was plain to see. Then the camera resumed its journey along the line-up, stopping at the last, headless, body.

'Christ, they were hacked to bits… ' said Sir David Clayton, the Surrey Chief Constable, who was seeing them for the first time. 'Enough to make most people throw up. They'll never be able to show this on prime-time television.'

'Don't be too certain,' murmured Brian James. 'People are used to seeing far worse in the average action movie. They're probably immune to the real thing.'

As he spoke, the view on the screen returned to the wide-angle view of the front of the house, which showed the corpses seated against the wall, and the shattered drawing-room windows, their heavy silk curtains drawn on the inside.

'You can all see what became of the foreign assault team your Government sent in against us,' resumed Careb evenly. 'Sent in, even though they had been repeatedly warned what would happen to the hostages if anything like this were to happen.'

'Where the hell is that camera operating from?' asked Major Stevens, 'Can't we knock it out?'

'It's almost certainly a remote camera they set up by the fountain during the night when the lights were out,' said Commander James. 'It's bound to be well protected by the fountain itself and I'd bet on it being operated remotely by someone in the house.'

'Oh fuck,' exclaimed Stevens loudly, 'I think they're actually going to do it... '

Almost as Commander James had finished speaking, the curtains had been suddenly drawn aside to reveal a figure, spread-eagled in each window frame, arms and legs identically stretched wide, so they each resembled a large diagonal cross. The ropes attached to their wrists, which kept their arms widely angled above their heads, were clearly visible.

'Because of the serious nature of your Government's deceit, I have chosen to impose a much more severe punishment than the last time. They were fully aware of the consequences should they choose to oppose us, but they chose to ignore them. This is the result of that failure on their part. I sincerely hope this is a lesson they will find more compelling than the last.'

The camera suddenly zoomed in on the face of Wayne Bryan, a face stripped of all pretence and dignity, which even his most ardent fans might have failed to recognise. Tears streamed down the singer's fat-jowled cheeks, his piggy eyes bulged hugely in their sockets and he was unmistakably terror-stricken. The usually slack mouth was open in a silent scream, his usually simpering lips grotesquely pulled tightly back over cosmetically perfect teeth.

Perhaps sensing that the camera was on him, he began to shout, but the sound was not picked up on the microphone Careb was using. It was hardly necessary, however, to hear the words for they were impossible to misinterpret. Over and over again, Wayne Bryan screamed, 'I don't want to die!'

The picture of Sweet Georgie Brown, which suddenly replaced that of Bryan, was almost more shocking for its stillness. His face seemed to have shut down, blocked off from all emotion. His eyes were closed and his body hung limply on its rope supports as though he were already unconscious.

'Perhaps he's fainted,' said the Chief Constable. 'At least I hope so, because he won't have to suffer what I fear is coming next.'

'Do you really think they're going to kill them?' asked the MI6 chief in amazement.

No one bothered to answer him.

The scene on screen widened again to show both hostages.

'Mr Bryan and Mr Brown both hoped their last live appearance on television would be a memorable one, and I assured them it would,' Careb continued calmly. 'Unsurprisingly, they were both eager not to share the fate of their fellow hostages. They both believed they were more worthy of life than the rest, and tried to buy their way out. Like most cowards, when it came down to it, they were only concerned with saving their own skins. It made their selection so much more simple,' he said, allowing some emotion to enter his voice.

The silence which followed was abruptly shattered by the loud chatter of automatic rifle fire from within the house. The bodies of both men kicked and danced violently against the restraining ropes as great gouts of blood and flesh erupted from their torsos. Wayne Bryan gave one, last agonised scream as he died.

Sweet Georgie Brown died silently and, whether by accident or design, his usually expressive face remained impassive.

In the gatehouse, no one uttered a word, each man trying to come to terms with the savage double murder they had just witnessed. Yet even this vicious act of barbarism was not to be the climax of the morning spectacle. There was more to come.

As the bodies of Bryan and Brown ceased their last spasms, four hand-launched missiles burst from the first-floor windows of the house and zoned in unerringly on the surrounding trees, where they exploded, almost simultaneously, in front of four of the freshly excavated dug-outs, instantly killing eight of Major Stevens' men and two police officers.

The horrified silence which followed was again broken by the voice of Careb. 'Here endeth the morning lesson,' he said. 'Take heed.'

FORTY-TWO

Sky News was, as usual, first to break into its normal transmission with a special bulletin on a breaking story. Newsreader Richard Mayland interrupted a live report from the Belmont Place siege to announce that the Press Association had released the news that the body of Defence Minister, Peter Westcroft, had been found earlier that day at his home in Pimlico. He was understood to have been found hanging from an internal first-floor balcony rail.

'At the moment, police are not treating the death as suspicious,' he said. 'Shortly before he died, the 47-year-old Cabinet Minister was said to have launched a full-scale investigation into last night's alleged attempt to storm Belmont Place, the details of which are still not fully known. A Downing Street spokesman said that the Prime Minister is deeply shocked by the news and says that Mr Westcroft's death is a tragic loss to both the country and to himself.

'Mr Temple said that Peter Westcroft was a close personal friend and had been expected to play a leading role in Modern Labour's first term in office. He will be sorely missed.'

Reports on the Defence Minister's apparent suicide dominated the television news channels for the next half hour, but were then, with the ruthless objectivity of all professional news media, swiftly axed from the top slot by an even more sensational breaking story.

Again, Sky News was the first to carry this world exclusive featuring 'the most sensational video footage ever shown on television'. After a brief but grim warning that the report they were about to show contained scenes of explicit violence, which those viewers of a nervous disposition may find disturbing, they ran the unedited video of the double execution exactly as it had been viewed live by the onlookers in the gatehouse earlier that morning. They ran it, as Commander James had rightly predicted, in its entirety, accompanied only by Careb Sinclair's original commentary.

Other news organisations were quick to follow suit and, among the press, the London *Evening Standard* was first on the streets with a special edition containing eight pages of graphic pictures taken from the video.

It was later calculated that within one hour of Sky News breaking the story, it had been seen by over 40 million people in Britain and, within 12 hours, the worldwide audience had reached one billion. Careb Sinclair's promise had indeed been fulfilled – Wayne Bryan and Sweet Georgie Brown had achieved the highest world ratings for a single event in the history of television.

One of the earliest viewers to see it was Sergeant Bob Brooks at RAF Northolt, who was helping clear up the fall-out from a particularly boisterous Friday night session in the Sergeants' Mess.

The television set in the main bar was normally tuned to sport, but this morning had been left on a news channel and, by chance, no one had yet shown sufficient interest, or disinterest, to alter it.

'Jesus wept!' he exclaimed loudly when the close-up of the Russian corpses filled the giant screen in the main bar of the Mess. 'I know those blokes... they were supposed to be fucking diplomats,' he spluttered to a Flight Sergeant, who had paused to stare, open-mouthed, at the extraordinary events unfolding in front of them.

'It sounds like you've got a useful bit of info there,' replied his fellow sergeant, not taking his eyes from the television. 'Should be worth a good few quid to the television lot, and the papers, I'd imagine,' he added enviously.

It took Sergeant Brooks only few seconds to come to the same conclusion and he was already mentally spending the money as he dialled the number for directory enquiries and asked for the Sky News telephone number. A minute later and, after a brief explanation of his purpose, he was through to a senior assistant on the news desk, who quickly passed him on to the News Editor himself.

'The funny thing is,' the Sergeant told him, 'that although the instructions – to pass these Ruskies through – came from the Defence Department, the bloke who rang through to Northolt said he was actually arranging it at the request of Downing Street. I was there in the office when the Wing Commander took the call, and that's exactly what he told the Flight Lieutenant. He said it came "straight from the Prime Minister's office"... Yeah, that's what I said – the Prime Minister's office.

'I drove ahead of their transport to guide them out to the plane and saw the Ruskies from less than 20 feet. I'll swear on my mother's grave they were the same blokes as the ones you're showing on the news... except they were still alive then.'

When he finally replaced the receiver, Sergeant Brooks stared wide-eyed at his fellow sergeant. 'You were absolutely fucking right, mate,' he said, 'but I'd never have thought it would have been worth that much. It was your idea, so if you want to help me, call the rest of the TV stations and the papers, then I'll happily split whatever else we get.'

Probably among the last people in the country to see the news report were the hostages themselves, for it was almost midday when Careb returned to the library and switched on the television, which he flicked over to a news channel.

At this stage, few, if any, of the remaining hostages believed they would ever again see their former fellow prisoners alive. They had already concluded as much from the earlier bursts of automatic rifle fire inside the house. It seemed as clear a signal as they were likely to get that the men would not be coming back. Nevertheless, they were totally unprepared for the sheer horror and callous brutality of the killings, and most cried out with repugnance as the video unfolded.

When it came to the part where Georgie Brown's spread-eagled body was shown strung up in the window being torn apart by gunfire, Alison Best covered her eyes with her hands and began to wail, 'Oh, Georgie, you were such a rotten bastard in so many ways, but I would never have wanted this to happen to you... '

Father Large clasped his podgy hands together and closed his eyes in silent prayer. None of the others tried to comfort Alison; they all seemed to have been stunned into temporary paralysis by the sheer enormity and horror of what they had witnessed.

Only after the sound of the missiles exploding outside the bunkers had faded, did they appear to become again aware of their fellow prisoners, and nearly everyone started to talk at once. Suddenly, June Temple's voice rose above the others.

'Let's just hear what's being said,' she yelled. 'It's our first chance to find out what people are saying about all this. It would be foolish to miss it.'

The others quickly fell silent, recognising the common sense in what she had said and, except for Alison, who continued to sob, turned their attention back to the television screen.

The presenter was saying, 'It is now known that the Russian troops entered the country only yesterday, on a direct flight from Moscow, and it has been definitely confirmed by a spokesman at RAF Northolt that they disembarked there.

'Police believe their arrival may also be linked in some way to the probable suicide, earlier this morning, of Defence Minister

Peter Westcroft, who was found by an aide hanging at his home in Pimlico.'

June was quite unable to contain a loud groan.

'Before he died,' said the presenter, 'Mr Westcroft had ordered a full internal Inquiry into how the Russian Special Forces became involved in what was believed to be a totally domestic terrorist incident. This seemed to indicate some kind of British military collusion with the Russians. But the latest information reaching us is that the orders to admit the Russian assault squad came directly from the Prime Minister's office.'

June allowed another, low groan to escape her.

'So far, there has been no word on this from Downing Street, who are refusing to comment on any aspect of the Belmont Place siege. Our Chief Political Correspondent, Anson Black, who is currently at Downing Street, tells us that if the orders for the abortive Russian attack – which led directly to the killing of Wayne Bryan and Georgie Brown and an unknown number of British troops and police – proves to have come from Number 10, then the resulting political scandal could engulf the whole Government and might even threaten the position of the Prime Minister himself.'

'And serve the bastard right,' wailed Alison Best, whose eyes were dark-rimmed and heavy with tears, and who had been listening intently. 'He may be your husband,' she pointed towards June, with a trembling, outstretched finger, 'but if he caused all those deaths, he's a prize fucking idiot and we'd all be better off without him!'

June nodded. 'I hear you,' she said softly. Then, with an intense feeling of nausea flooding her stomach, she pulled back her shoulders, raised her chin high, and turned to face Careb, who had been observing their reactions as they watched the news reports.

'I don't know what it is you really want… ' She spoke clearly and without emotion. 'But if you want to get out of here in one piece, then you'd better let me speak to my husband.

'I think I know of the only certain way out of this, for everyone.'

FORTY-THREE

For the first time since taking office, Bobby Temple found his position as leader under threat from his colleagues in government. The Cabinet members had turned openly against him and, led by Jack Benson, were now demanding explanations that he either would not, or dare not provide.

While aware that he would have been as big a fool as most of his Cabinet not to have recognised the gravity of his position, Bobby still found room, amidst his churning emotions, to feel secretly amused that the usually meek and subservient ministers should at last dare to show their public defiance of him. The tame dogs hadn't yet learned to bark or bite, but were beginning to show their teeth. He couldn't prevent the inward smile from straying to his lips.

Jack Benson, the only man in the room whom Bobby recognised as a real threat to his survival, could scarcely contain his anger. 'This isn't a laughing matter,' he snapped at his leader. 'There isn't anything even faintly amusing about the situation. As a Government, we are as much under siege at this moment as the hostages in Belmont Place. And to have a chance of survival, we will have to come up with some damned convincing explanations as to what has gone wrong. The public want to know who to blame for this awful mess – and so do we.'

The circle of ministers nodded energetically in agreement, like lemmings, thought Bobby, happy to let the Chancellor lead the attack. Most were still scared of him.

Bobby shrugged his shoulders. 'If you want somebody to blame then you're looking at the wrong man,' he said coolly. 'I hate to talk ill of the dead – and I want us to acknowledge all the good work he achieved during his short time in office – but the man you should be pointing the finger at is Peter Westcroft.'

It was Benson's turn to laugh, although it was unmistakably contemptuous. 'That buffoon couldn't even tell someone the time of day without asking you first, and we all know it. No one's going to believe that he dragged in a bunch of Russian killers off his own bat to storm into such a delicate situation without being told to do so.'

Again, the others vigorously nodded their support.

'Normally, I might even go along with you on that, Jack,' said Bobby reasonably, spreading his hands, palm upwards, above the table. 'But Peter wasn't being his normal self. He confessed to me yesterday that he felt personally to blame for the SAS's failure to free the hostages. He felt riddled with guilt and quite desperate to make amends. Who knows what strange ideas might have surfaced when he was in that state. What's more, Ivan Brekov himself is of the same opinion. He's just as furious as we are about the Russians getting involved and has already managed to unearth a few salient facts.' He paused dramatically to lend his next words more weight. 'He told me they now know that Peter was in contact, early yesterday, with one of their top generals in the FSB, who has a regiment of Spetsnaz under him. Brekov assures me he'll have a full account of their collaboration by the end of today.'

Benson's disbelief could not have been plainer.

'Hear me out, Jack, if you please,' said Bobby, making a cautionary gesture with his right hand, and leaning forward confidently towards his Chancellor. 'Ask yourselves… why else would Peter have killed himself?'

The Cabinet members began to look even less certain of themselves and, Bobby noticed with further amusement, those on either side of Benson began discreetly to lean a little further away from him, as though anxious to disassociate themselves with his challenge to the authority of their leader. Suddenly, it all seemed so much less clear-cut. At last they seemed more willing to hear Bobby's account of events, and he felt the knife-edge tension recede to be replaced with that old, familiar confidence. Bobby looked around the table and expanded on his theme: 'He must have felt very guilty about something vitally important to take his own life like that.'

'It's not yet certain he did commit suicide,' Jack interrupted.

'Really, Jack. What do you think happened, then? That the Russians and Downing Street got together to organise his murder as well? We have been busy!' His eyes met those of the Chancellor. *I wonder what they would all say if they knew that's exactly what did happen,* he thought with a vague feeling of satisfaction. 'He might easily have told his aides he had the backing of Downing Street to let the Russians through Northolt just to make sure there were no complications. We'll probably never know the truth. But I do know that I had nothing at all to gain by dragging in the Russians… and a hell of a lot to lose, personally, with June being one of the hostages, if anything went wrong. Can you believe I would ever risk harming her?'

He glanced around the table and, as he had expected, found returning support flooding the faces of his ministers. It was a moment of triumph shattered by the shrill ringing of the telephone at Bobby's elbow.

He snatched it up and snarled into the receiver, 'Don't you understand the simplest instructions? I told you I didn't want any calls coming through until I said so. Why on earth would you disobey a direct order?'

'But… Prime Minister… ' stammered the secretary, 'I have Mrs Temple on the line… she's calling from Belmont Place and she wants to speak to you.'

The sudden concern on all their faces must have reflected Bobby's genuine shock.

'It's June,' he mouthed to them, by way of explanation. Then to his secretary, 'Put her through straight away.' Bobby wiped a hand across his forehead and cleared his throat.

'Bobby?' June's uncertain voice was heard on the line.

'Darling, how wonderful to hear your voice. Have they let you go? How are you?' The words tumbled out quickly in a single breath.

'Please, Bobby, just listen to what I have to say,' said June evenly. 'I'm all right so far but I'm still a prisoner. So are the rest of us, and I believe there's only one way we're going to get out of here alive. It's up to you… otherwise they will go on killing us until we are all dead.'

'But, June, sweetheart,' said Bobby hesitantly, 'you know I can't give in to their demands, no matter what they are, even though you're involved. It's an international agreement. We can never give in to terrorist threats.'

'There are no demands any more. You don't have to agree to give them anything,' June told him. 'Though, Bobby, I do believe you may well need them as much as they need you. I know you'll have come up with a hundred reasons why you were not responsible for this morning's killings. But the public are never going to believe you're not to blame. These madmen are killing their idols. What do you matter compared with them?'

'It wasn't me at all,' Bobby snapped, his voice rising. 'I never ordered that attack, believe me.'

'Oh, Bobby,' said June, her voice raw and husky with emotion, 'it's too late for simple excuses. In the eyes of the world, you are the guilty one… you caused Wayne's and Georgie's deaths as surely as if you had signed their death warrants. There is now only one way I can think of for you to redeem yourself with the public. To make yourself the true people's hero again… a leader they can be proud of. You must offer to exchange yourself for the hostages. Put your life on the line, in place of ours.

'These people have received all the publicity they need for their cause, whatever it might be, and by putting yourself in their hands, you will get them ten times the kudos. Their leader likes the idea. He says if you arrange a jet to be standing by at Gatwick, fully fuelled, they will make the exchange there, and fly you, with them, to North Africa, where they will release you. They guarantee it.

'No matter what has happened so far, it will all be forgotten. When you return to London, tonight, you will be greeted as a world hero. And you will still be able to go to Moscow.'

'Can you trust these people, June?' said the Prime Minister. 'It's a massive risk.'

'It's the same risk all of us have been under all along,' cried June. 'But think of it… you'll be the man who offered his own life to save his wife and her friends. It will wipe the slate clean, Bobby. They won't be able to deny you anything after this. Their leader says that I can call you again in five minutes to get your answer. If you agree to this, he'll spell out the details of what they want.

'I'm not asking you to do this for my sake, darling, but you must do it for yourself and your future.'

As Bobby Temple slowly replaced the receiver, watched intently and expectantly by all his Cabinet ministers, his eyes burned with an evangelical zeal. He pushed back his chair and stood up. 'I am about to take the boldest action that any political leader has ever taken,' he said, addressing his audience like a latter-day revivalist preacher. 'I am about to step willingly into the valley of the shadow of death. Yet again, gentlemen, I am about to risk everything to save us all.'

FORTY-FOUR

Once the decision had been taken, events happened swiftly and, by mid-afternoon, all the essential arrangements had been agreed and a Boeing 727 airliner was reported to be already standing by on the concrete apron at Gatwick airport, seven miles south of Flint's estate.

Commander Brian James, the Chief Constable and the two security chiefs were, by then, well on their way to the airport in a convoy of limousines flanked by police motorcycle outriders, leaving behind Major Stevens to observe the terrorist withdrawal, which was also well under way.

Careb and the other nine surviving terrorists had abandoned the bulk of their equipment in the hall, along with Glen Grant, who, because of his condition and lack of mobility, was considered an unnecessary impediment to a smooth and rapid transfer. His wound was still raw and he was suffering severe and constant pain, against which the few aspirin his fellow hostages had managed to come up with were proving almost totally ineffective. He had been left stretched out on a make shift bed, which was nothing more than a dozen cushions piled on top of some wooden ammunition cases.

'With your courage, you deserve to be the first one freed,'

Princess Kate had whispered to him urgently, before she and the other hostages were herded upstairs. 'I'm looking forward to later when I can thank you properly and give you my special reward for what you did,' she added, with a sudden impish grin. 'If you're up to it, that is…' she smiled wickedly.

He made a giant effort and reached up to clasp her arm. 'I'll fight my way through a stampeding herd of Hollywood producers, if I have to,' he rasped, fighting against the pain, 'and I'll have you know, there's nothing more dangerous than them.'

Kate was still smiling when she reached the roof, where she found herself, almost immediately, being ushered up a short flight of metal steps into the belly of a massive helicopter. Behind her, with some trepidation, she heard Peter Flint say to the American Ambassador, 'Whoever brought this down, in the dark, must have been one hell of a pilot. It has to be at least 50 feet long and those rotors must be more than that across. I don't much fancy the ride that's coming up…'

The Princess shuddered, although she felt a little more encouraged when she heard Saul Goldman reply, 'I was thinking the same thing… the rotors are well above the height of your chimneys, though, which is one small mercy. It'll make lifting off a lot easier than coming in.'

Careb had already settled himself behind the right-hand set of controls, but it was George Travis who took the senior pilot's customary seat on the left-hand side of the flight deck and who, with a sure and experienced touch, began bringing the dozens of instruments on the complex control panel to life.

There were no seats on this version of Boeing's American military aircraft. In fact, there were no comforts of any kind, and everyone, including the terrorists, had to sit on the hard floor of the main cabin.

'I guess we're not going to be offered cocktails,' said Rachel flippantly. 'Christ, I'd give anything right now for a large Martini.'

'Or a gin and tonic on ice,' sighed Alison seated next to her.

Any further conversation was drowned out as George started the two powerful engines of the CH-47 Chinook, which he then slowly revved up until the rotors overhead brought the rhythmic throb to a deafening crescendo. Then, by raising the angle pitch lever with his right hand, he caused them to lift gently off from the roof.

In under 30 seconds they had left the grounds of Belmont Place behind them and, flying at just under 100 feet above the ground, skimmed quickly across the A24 main road and out over the lush, green Surrey countryside.

Despite the constant racket from the engines, the two pilots were easily able to communicate through the radio headphones which linked them on the flight deck and, almost immediately, on a signal from Careb, George adjusted the rotor angle again and the helicopter lost forward speed until it was hovering, stationary, above a huge, square, stone-paved farmyard, some 200 feet across, which was edged by a large, ramshackle house, stables, garages and sheds, and a long and ancient barn which had been allowed to fall badly into disrepair. Its thatched roof sagged badly along the ridge and one end wall had become a crumbling ruin.

Into the centre of this rural idyll, George deftly set the big helicopter down.

'Nicely done,' complimented Careb, as he unbuckled his seatbelt and clambered free. The faces of those in the cabin turned expectantly towards him as he stepped through the cockpit door.

'You'll be sad to hear that it's time for some of us to say goodbye,' he shouted, above the decreasing noise of the engines, but with no hint of apology in his voice. 'From now on you'll just have to make do with my colleagues here, who will see you safely through the next leg on your journey to freedom.

'I don't imagine you're really going to miss us, but that is only to be expected, I suppose.'

He looked around and spotted Kate, and a broad smile came to his face.

'My only real regret in all this, Your Royal Highness, is that I never got to collect my trophy,' he told her, bowing deeply. 'It would have been a very great pleasure indeed, I'm sure.'

Kate tossed back her blonde hair and gave him a baleful glare, her eyes flashing with hatred. 'I would rather have died than have you touch me,' she said simply.

Davey Carey, who, with Emma, had joined Careb by the door, chuckled gleefully. 'Now you, girl, even for British royalty, are what I call a really bad loser. Though I must say, I like your style.' He turned to Careb. 'Probably the biggest put-down you'll ever get, my lad. You know, I think even I would stand a better chance with this lass than you.'

'Then you're as big a dreamer as he is,' snarled Kate scornfully. 'You may have saved me from that brute back there, but that doesn't make you any better than him. In my opinion, you're all just as bad as one another. And that goes for her, too.' She pointed her chin imperiously in Emma's direction.

Davey sighed theatrically and swung open the exit door. 'No future for any of us with this one. Perhaps Oscar Wilde was right... "To fall in love with oneself is the sure beginning of a lifelong romance." Come on, Emma, and you, too, Careb. I don't think any of us are wanted here.'

The three of them were smiling as they disembarked the helicopter, where they were greeted by two reserve members of their team whom Careb had based off-site should they have required external assistance. They had been staying at the farm since Thursday and were disappointed to have missed the action. After a few brisk words of greeting, the men climbed aboard the aircraft, slamming the door behind them. With the exchange successfully completed, George revved the engines back to full throttle and, less than two minutes after touching down, the big Chinook was again airborne and heading south for Gatwick.

On the ground, and wasting not a moment of time, Careb and his two companions were already heading for one of the large garages, where they pulled back the two heavy, wooden doors. Inside, exactly where they had left it four days earlier, was a plain, black Mercedes saloon car.

'Let's all take a moment to clean up and grab a change of clothes, and then we'll be on our way,' said Careb.

It was a still bright day, with a cloudless, pale-blue sky, a faint breeze picking up as the helicopter flew over the Gatwick airport perimeter.

George Travis, following instructions from the control tower, set down about 50 metres from a Boeing 727, in British Airways colours, and parked a good half-mile from the nearest other aircraft, which were clustered around the airport's North Terminal. He pressed the radio switch linking him to the cabin and ordered, 'Everyone except Peter and Jonathan stay put. I want you two to go aboard the Boeing and check it out thoroughly. Make sure there's no one else on board, and don't forget to go below and inspect the galley area and the holds. When you've done that, and have checked the fuel gauges, and you're happy with everything, then come back and report.'

He flicked the radio switch over to outward transmit and hailed the control tower. 'Where's the Prime Minister?'

'A little above you and to your right,' came the clipped reply. 'He's in that Koala, with RAF markings, which is just about to set down next to you.'

George peered out to his right, through the flight deck side window, and saw a small helicopter settling on the concrete apron about 20 metres away.

'Tell the pilot to offload his passenger and get the hell out of here, pronto!' George instructed the controller. 'Nothing is going to happen until he's on his own.'

'Roger,' said the controller. 'I'll pass on your instructions to the RAF pilot.'

The message must have been received and understood because, moments later, the small cockpit door in the Koala opened outwards and Bobby Temple, hair blowing wildly in the rotor downdraught, stepped into view.

He looked calm and relaxed, as though about to enter just another routine political meeting. But from close up, one could determine the tension around his eyes and mouth, and his usual arrogance seemed less evident. No one would have guessed, though, that he was about to stake everything on a wild throw of the dice, and that his political career and his very life were now in jeopardy.

Half a mile away, on the North Terminal observation balcony, hundreds of camera shutters, most of them attached to giant, long-range lenses, generated a non-stop chatter as representatives of the world's press – alerted by Downing Street – recorded the moment. Television cameras from a dozen or more news organisations were also there to record the unfolding drama for posterity, and for the millions of viewers watching live across the nation, all mesmerised by the drama of this ultimate reality show.

With everyone's attention focused on Bobby Temple, few spared more than a brief, casual glance at the tiny, executive Lear jet, which was, at that moment, climbing gracefully away from the airport's main runway.

At the controls, the pilot, a stunning redhead, gently eased the central steering column to the right as they climbed through 1,000 feet, and banked the aircraft towards the south-east. To her right, in the second pilot's seat, Careb Sinclair was accepting two glasses of Krug champagne, passed forward by Davey Carey, who was seated behind them. He handed one to Emma.

'As that great Anglo-American writer and drunk, Daniel Farson, famously once remarked, "There is always time between a crisis and a catastrophe for a glass of champagne". To our future.'

Emma smiled and raised her glass, excitement and satisfaction dancing in her striking, violet eyes. 'A strange thing has happened in the past two days since that fat priest saved my life,' she said. 'I think that I've actually begun to experience a sort of warmth, deep down ... you know... ' and she giggled mischievously. 'So, yes... here's to the future,' and she added with a wicked grin towards Careb, 'and here's to fun as well.'

Behind them, Davey started to laugh. 'Well, isn't that grand... ' he said. 'But you'd better be looking out, Careb, lad. I think the lady may well have designs on you. If you're not careful, you may end up on a one-stop flight to paradise.'

On the Chinook, it was a full half-hour before the two men returned from the Boeing to give the all clear. For all of that time, since alighting from the helicopter, Bobby Temple had been left standing alone, buffeted by the wind and cut off from contact with anyone. The RAF pilot, obeying instructions, had departed immediately once the Prime Minster had been dropped off.

After giving the order to unload the hostages, George Travis removed a Sig Sauer handgun from his pocket and walked directly across to the Prime Minister, who was standing with one hand thrust casually into his trouser pocket, somehow managing to look unconcerned.

'I want to speak with my wife,' he said immediately.

'That wasn't part of the agreement,' George told him flatly. 'We must go directly on board.'

Bobby didn't move, but faced the terrorist and looked him squarely in the eyes. 'You're going to take me hostage anyway,' he said. 'What earthly difference can it make whether or not I speak to my wife before we leave? This business can still be conducted civilly, can't it? It's not much I'm asking for... and you do hold all the aces.'

George considered this silently for a few moments and then said abruptly, 'You can have one minute. Come with me.'

On the observation balcony, the cameras continued to whirr

noisily as Bobby was led over to the hostages, who were corralled in a tight group by a circle of guards, all armed with assault rifles.

Commander James and his companions watched, with silent fascination, through binoculars from their own observation post on the elevated loading platform of a hydraulic catering truck. On the concrete apron, the gunmen parted to let George and the Prime Minister through. He rushed towards June and took her in his arms, holding her tightly and facing the other hostages over her shoulder.

'I must apologise to all of you for taking so long to arrange your release,' he told them, with a deprecating grin. 'But now, and mainly thanks to my wife, whose idea this was, you are about to be set free. I'm merely the instrument, but it was she who was responsible for it happening.'

'You really don't have to do this, Sir,' said the American Ambassador, once again showing his courage. 'I'm very happy to let these bastards hang on to me for as long as they want.'

'Me, too,' said Peter Flint, stepping forward. 'None of us wanted it to come to this, Prime Minister.'

'Well, it has. And I, for one, think you're a bloody hero for saving us,' said Beverly Gladstone. 'I thank you from the bottom of my heart for getting me out of this.' She leaned forward on her toes and kissed him hard on the cheek.

'Me, too,' said Rachel Friedman. 'It's the bravest thing I've ever heard of. You truly are a hero, Mr Temple.'

June, pale with emotion, disengaged herself from her husband's arms. 'You see, darling, everybody thinks you're a hero,' she said calmly, with a weak smile. 'And when you come home to us, you'll get a welcome they're never going to stop talking about. You'll be forever remembered as the people's own hero.'

George Travis intervened and grasped Bobby by the arm, tugging him towards the plane. 'That's enough,' he said brusquely, 'we're leaving right now.'

'As soon as the engines are up to speed, we'll call you to join us,' he told the two men he had detailed to stay and guard the hostages, in case the authorities should attempt a last-ditch rescue. Then, after ordering the six remaining terrorists to accompany himself and the Prime Minister, he mounted the jet's rear staircase and vanished into the main body of the aircraft.

Commander James, watching from the distant platform, breathed a deep sigh. 'Even with 50 expert marksmen, we couldn't have taken them all out without risking hitting the PM,' he told the Chief Constable. 'And, of course, the other bastards would probably have opened fire and slaughtered the hostages. It could have been a massacre. This way... '

Sir David nodded in agreement. 'Absolutely nothing to be done at all. But I do hope he comes out of this safely... the Prime Minister, I mean. He has a lot more guts than I ever gave him credit for. A proper bulldog breed, in fact.'

To the onlookers, powerless to speed things along, the next few minutes seemed to last an eternity. But, eventually, just when they felt their nerves were stretched to breaking point, the three giant engines, one by one, roared into life, and a little later a figure appeared on the steps, waving the last two terrorists aboard.

After that, events moved quickly. The rear steps were automatically retracted into the fuselage and, at the same time, the huge six wheels of the undercarriage began to roll.

No one had thought to provide outer clothing for the prisoners, who were now shivering in the chill, afternoon breeze, and even though they were free, and now able to go where they wished, they stayed huddled together in a group for warmth and comfort. They seemed also reluctant to cut the invisible cords of mutual dependency which had helped sustain them through the recent horror.

'Let's go,' yelled Commander James, racing down from the

elevated platform and across to where his car, engine running and driver ready, was waiting. 'Those people need help.'

Twenty other personnel, including two doctors, joined him in a convoy of cars and vans which sped towards the small cluster of surviving hostages.

One of them was a 6' 2" tall, black American air force colonel, Bill Armstrong, who was a special attaché to the American Embassy in London. Ignoring the other hostages, he marched straight from his car to the American Ambassador, snapped off a casual salute and grinned widely. 'It's sure good to see you safe and well, Mr Ambassador,' he drawled in an accent from the Deep South. 'You've had us all pretty worried about you these last few days. The President has been calling non-stop.'

Saul Goldman shrugged. 'Well, you can see we haven't personally come to any harm... but a lot of other decent folk have,' he said sombrely.

Sir David was also saluting the Princess and June Temple. 'It probably doesn't feel that good to be free while your husband is still in danger, but it's very good to see you anyway, Ma'am,' he said. 'And to you, Your Royal Highness, I have a special message from Her Majesty. She asked me to convey to you her heartfelt pleasure at your release, and she greatly looks forward to greeting you, in person, when you return to London.'

'Well, the Queen will probably have to wait,' said Kate matter of factly. 'I intend to stay with June and the others until we hear that the Prime Minister is safe. And then I may find myself a little tied up... ' she added, with a knowing smile at June, who understood implicitly the rendezvous she would probably keep with a certain American actor. June's gaze, though, returned swiftly to the airliner which had just reached the runway, from which her husband would soon be carried to God knew where.

The other freed hostages, swathed in blankets, were all talking at once, only just capable of surrendering to the blessed relief of knowing they were out of danger at last. Commander James then drew their attention to the distant runway, where the Boeing 727 was about to take off, and they fell silent, all eyes following his pointing finger.

As it reached take-off velocity, the Boeing's nose-wheel lifted slightly and, moments later, the huge jet rose smoothly from the concrete and roared into the pale-blue sky.

Within seconds, the undercarriage had been raised and, rapidly gaining both speed and height, it flew over the airport perimeter and soared towards the late afternoon sun.

Beneath it, in a nondescript grey van parked close to the perimeter fence, the man in the driving seat waited until the airliner had passed overhead. Then, delicately, he pressed his right index finger on the glowing red button of a radio transmitter on the seat beside him.

The explosion, when it came, sounded flat and dull to those on the ground and might, in isolation, have been ignored. But the great gouts of red, yellow and deep orange flames that burst 30 metres in all directions from the disintegrating fuselage were conclusive evidence of the fatal and cataclysmic explosion which had suddenly, in a split-second, overwhelmed the Prime Minister's aircraft.

The first blast seemed to stop the plane's forward movement and then it simply disappeared in an almost blinding flash as the 8,000 gallons of aviation fuel ignited with a thunderous roar and a force that shook the ground.

In an instant, the 76-ton airliner was reduced to thousands of tiny fragments, which plummeted, like a blazing meteor storm, onto the fields below.

By the time the sound of the second explosion reached them all that the group on the ground could still see was a billowing cloud of grey-white smoke, spreading wider as they watched, 300 metres above the ground. It was the only airborne reminder that the Boeing airliner had ever existed.

Almost as one, those around her turned to stare at June Temple, who stood, still gazing into the sky, with large tears pouring down her cheeks. The first to approach her was a stranger, the American air force colonel, who was proffering a mobile telephone.

'Excuse me, Ma'am, but it's urgent… I have the President of the United States, Mr Gordon Wilson, for you. He says that you would want to take his call.'

June nodded, and reached for the telephone, making no effort to wipe the streaming tears from her face. 'Mr President,' she said, 'as you must know, it's over.' She turned from the others, who now seemed embarrassed to catch her eye, and walked away across the expanse of concrete to be out of earshot. 'I don't feel particularly proud of myself or in a mood to rejoice, and I doubt if you do, either, but despite the awful cost in innocent, and not so innocent lives, I believe we handled the problem in the only way that was open to us.

'My thanks for your help and I'm sure, if the real story were ever to be told, that the whole of England would want to thank you, too. As it is, we both know they all came a lot closer to losing their freedom than they will ever probably realise.

'And we both know, too, that without us, that is exactly what would have happened.'